M000228865

RAPTURE'S FIRE

There wasn't a glimmer of light so Dani felt her way along the outside wall, searching for the door like a blind person, trying to find the keyhole. At last they were inside where flickering gaslight barely illuminated their way across the kitchen and through the hallway to her bedroom.

Roman closed the door and turned the key.

"At last we're alone," he murmured, his lips close to her ear. "I've been longing for this moment since the first time I saw you. I knew it would happen—willed it to happen." His fingers worked expertly at the buttons on the front of her dress.

Her heart throbbed violently at his touch. He lifted her face to his with one hand and put his cool lips against hers.

Dani knew from her long-ago days in Poland what happened between a man and a woman. She had whispered and giggled with her schoolmates about it. But now, every inch of her flesh afire from Roman's searching caresses, she felt what she had never felt before, overwhelming sensations she could not have imagined.

This was how it was to love someone completely, Dani thought. This was how it was to be loved in return. . . .

HISTORICAL ROMANCE AT ITS BEST!

WILD RAPTURE   (1534, $3.75)
by Kay McMahon
Beautiful Amber had been blackmailed into marrying Nicholas
Chandler, but she'd be damned if she'd share his bed. But even as
she longed to slap the arrogant smile from his handsome face, she
found herself succumbing to his wicked, wanton loving, trapped
in his embrace.

ECSTASY'S CONQUEST   (1438, $3.75)
by Kay McMahon
Looking into the steel-blue eyes of her captor, lovely Victoria
knew her life as a pampered belle was over. Won in a card game
by this devilish rogue of a pirate, she was now his to do with as he
wanted, and as he caressed her silken curves she knew he wished
to make her ECSTASY'S CONQUEST.

PASSION'S SLAVE   (1297, $3.50)
by Kay McMahon
Beau Remington was the kind of man to stalk his prey until he
got what he wanted—and he wanted lovely Alanna. But determined and defiant young Alanna would never surrender . . . until
she tasted Beau's fierce demanding kisses and melted into his embrace, until she learned she was forever PASSION'S SLAVE.

ECSTASY'S EMBERS   (1538, $3.50)
by Victoria London
Determined to put the notorious rake Lucien Fraser in his place,
Virginia belle Samantha Thornton taunted him with her saucy
green eyes, teased him with her supple curves, and relished the
thought of being the first to deny him. But when the insolent man
trapped her in his arms and plundered her sweet lips, she forgot
her schemes and surrendered to the burning pleasures of . . . EC-
STASY'S EMBERS.

*Available wherever paperbacks are sold, or order direct from the
Publisher. Send cover price plus 50¢ per copy for mailing and
handling to Zebra Books, Dept. 1628, 475 Park Avenue South,
New York, N.Y. 10016. DO NOT SEND CASH.*

Passion's Triumph

PATRICIA TITO

ZEBRA BOOKS
KENSINGTON PUBLISHING CORP.

ZEBRA BOOKS

are published by

Kensington Publishing Corp.
475 Park Avenue South
New York, NY 10016

Copyright © 1985 by Patricia Tito

All rights reserved. No part of this book may be reproduced in any form or by any means without the prior written consent of the Publisher, excepting brief quotes used in reviews.

First printing: July 1985

Printed in the United States of America

To
Theresa who is nothing less than perfection
and to
Al who loved us both

Although there is, in fact, a community called Bridge-port in Chicago and the city was honored to have a legendary mayor named Richard Daley, the rest of this story is entirely fictional.

War is fought for power and hate . . .
Still I often wonder why.
Death, no matter, sets a date,
Why fight wars to make us die?

—Frank Tito
1922-1982

Chapter One

February sleet tapped a sharp staccato upon the roof and against the lone window of the gray weatherbeaten house, while a howling north wind diligently sought entry though mismatched planks of timeworn wood. For every crack painstakingly plugged by day, two seemed to sprout in the unguarded night to mock and frustrate the numbed occupants. And so it had been every desolate winter since this dreary village in Poland had first come into existence generations ago.

Casimir Mrazek huddled close to the pitifully small fire in the grate, warming his chilled scraped hands that washing never completely cleaned anymore, not after the twelve-hour days he put in working deep in the coal mines where he'd toiled since he was fourteen. As he held his outstretched hands closer to the fire, tears streamed down his hollow cheeks. Should he wake the two children sleeping across the room? He could have shared his news with them during or after supper, but he'd been too bewildered and confused to talk coherently then. Instead, he had eaten silently, trying to assemble his scrambled thoughts. Both children had looked up at him questioningly several times, wondering why their father's face held a vacant, faraway look.

Usually Casimir's deep, pleasant voice filled the room, asking questions, telling stories of the past or just spouting nonsense that brought a smile to the children's faces. But that night, as soon as they had eaten their meager meal of potato soup and brown bread, he had sent his son and daughter off to bed where at least they would be warm under their *piezynas*, the soft down comforters that warded off the streams of icy air which swept through the old house during the bitterly cold winter months. Body heat, trapped beneath these covers, held the cold at bay, at least for a few hours, while they slept and dreamt warm dreams. The comforters had been painstakingly sewn by his wife in the early days of their marriage. The young pair had laughingly searched and bartered for precious duck and goose feathers whenever they'd had a bit of free time. If it contained nothing else, a home was rich if it had a loving partner, soft covers to ward off cold nights, and enough food to keep one's stomach from rumbling with hunger. Now Casimir's beautiful wife was gone, but he still felt wealthy because of the children, her precious legacy which sustained him. They couldn't take her place, but they could instill in him a feeling of pride and continuity.

Casimir decided to save his news till morning as he poured himself a tiny measure of the precious vodka put aside for special occasions and had an imaginary conversation with his beloved Maria who had died in her prime. Even after six long years he missed her wisdom and the companionship they had shared in the late evenings after long grueling days of work. Without her presence his world was a lonely, empty place. But he had to go on, for he had promised her solemnly during those last days when she clamped her lips shut against the pain and agony of dying that he would raise the children as best he could and do his utmost to give them a better life. It was his dream to get their son out of the mines where he now toiled long hard hours at his father's side, and Casimir wanted to see his daughter married to someone far better than a common laborer. Maria's strength had bound them together, and if it hadn't been for the children who had her blood coursing through their veins, he would have given up after her death. It would have been far easier to retreat into a fantasy world of bygone days and sweet tender nights until he was reunited with Maria in death.

Maria had married far beneath her station when she had run off from Warsaw with Casimir and settled down in the bleak Polish mining village of Ruda. Countless times he wondered what had possessed him to steal her away from a life of luxury. Only love, he thought. Just love.

When, in his early twenties, he had once had the good fortune and unexpected pocket money to visit fabulous Warsaw, the tantalizing sights of the huge city had left him so dazed and impressed that he'd stopped at an inviting little park to rest and attempt to fully digest the kaleidoscope of spectacles the renowned Polish capital offered a sightseeing villager. Maria had been sitting alongside a pond, laughing at a knot of small boys who were floating their sailboats carefully along the shore. As soon as he spotted her he was entranced by her pristine beauty, her laughter floating on the spring air, and her vitality. Making a pretense of helping a young lad retrieve his collapsed boat, he accidentally bumped into her and apologized profusely while they both smiled at the crestfallen look on the boy's face as he noticed the broken sail on his tiny craft. Casimir quickly mended the boat, then he and the lovely vision he had met sat side by side near the water, quietly talking for the rest of the afternoon. They found a myriad of topics to discuss and were keenly interested in comparing their lives. It was as if a magic wand had been passed over them, so engrossed were they. Casimir saw a fairytale princess come to life, one with long flaxen hair, deep blue eyes, and lean petite limbs, and Maria saw a man who was strong, gentle, protective, and noticeably different from the young men of her acquaintance. She found those she socialized with as boring as their corpulent fathers, totally involved with pseudo-politics and moneymaking. In the prime of their manhood they were nonetheless pompous jaded fools. The young husbands in her circle treated their wives as chatelaines or adornments for their homes. Maria supposed this had come about because these men could afford to indulge their every whim, be it rich food, wine, or mistresses. She had never met a man who toiled long and hard to earn a living. It was a new and educational experience which fascinated her and made her desire to learn more about him.

As the sun set slowly on that memorable day, she promised to meet Casimir the following afternoon, and in the ensuing three weeks he courted her furiously without thought of the future. She daydreamed of him when she was alone, fell asleep with the image of his handsome face dominating her thoughts, visualized his lean, hard body dressed in the coarse but clean clothes he wore. They met during the afternoons, sometimes exploring the city which she knew so well, sometimes staying in the park and talking earnestly. Shyly she would let him hold her hand as they walked and talked, and she could feel strength emanating from his clasp, the power in his hands sending shivers down her spine. One afternoon as she took him through a portion of Warsaw University, noted professors smiled and nodded as they passed, some stopping to chat for a moment. Casimir was obviously impressed by her range of acquaintances and friends so Maria explained that her uncle was a professor there and that she had visited him at the university since she had first been allowed to walk through the streets unchaperoned. Besides, she explained, her home wasn't very far from this noted center of learning. When Casimir met her uncle, Anton, he liked the kindly man with the thick mane of white hair and the twinkling blue eyes that instantly put one at ease. However, as they were bidding Anton goodbye, Casimir heard him admonish Maria. The words were whispered but he heard enough to feel a fleeting pang of guilt.

Anton asked softly, "Do your parents know you're seeing this young man or are you being defiant again, young lady?"

Maria only laughed and took Casimir's arm. "I'll tell them soon," she promised with a saucy air as they walked away.

Anton shook his head, the twinkle in his eyes dimming as he watched his beautiful niece and her companion walk down the corridor. Your mother has higher standards for a young man, he thought to himself. He'll never do for you, my dear. Your parents will make sure of that even if they have to send you away until you regain your senses. Marriages aren't made in heaven. They are carefully arranged and planned, down to the last detail, by well-meaning but calculating parents.

That night at dinner Maria told her mother and father about Casimir. When she asked if she could bring him to dine with them the next evening, her parents were aghast at the mere suggestion. Maria's mother threatened to lock her in her room, and her brothers laughed at her unsophisticated pleas. These young men considered their sister lacking in common sense. Since her earliest years she had been unconven-

13

tional: siding with the underdog, giving away her small cache of coins to poor beggars, bringing any stray dog or cat into the house for shelter. She drove her mother to distraction with odd requests, yet she never pleaded, as did other girls her age, for pretty new dresses or trinkets. Instead she begged for permission to keep the misfit animals she toted home or to invite derelicts to eat in their well-stocked kitchen. Once, when she was eight, she even begged to keep a baby that had been abandoned on the church steps. To quiet her tears her mother had promised to see to it that the infant was placed in a good home, a home that needed and wanted a child. Maria, in turn, despised her elder brothers. All three were certain to be stocky replicas of their peers, living useless lives but imagining themselves scions of the financial world.

Dinner came to an explosive halt when her father took her into the library and attempted to talk sense to his only daughter.

"Maria," he began impatiently, "you'll be eighteen in another month and your mother and I have great plans for you. We won't force you into an arranged marriage, but you must have higher aspirations. As a banker's daughter you can have your pick of the finest men in Warsaw. Surely among our large circle of friends there is one man that appeals to you, one you can love? I know a poor boy from the mining region, no matter how handsome, cannot support you properly." He noted the stubborn look settling in his daughter's eyes and attempted to placate her in a gentler manner. "I'm partly to blame for allowing you to roam the city day after day. I should have listened to your mother and had you chaperoned properly. Maria, believe me when I say it's not love you're experiencing now, it's only a

14

sexual attraction that will diminish in time. You've been thrust into an unusual situation by meeting someone who has lived a vastly different life and the difference fascinates you. Poverty, my dear child, is not exciting—nor would you get used to it, not after having all this." He waved his hand around to encompass the beauty of their home.

Maria lowered her eyes, hiding her anger. Although she loved her father, who almost always took her side, she hated his bigotry. The important gods in his world were prosperity, position, and prestige. She couldn't imagine spending the rest of her life being concerned primarily with jewels, clothes, and parties. Someday, if she were fortunate enough to have sons, she would refuse to raise them as replicas of her brothers. That would be a total waste. As for daughters, she would allow them freedom of choice, encourage them to develop open minds, and inspire them to confide their innermost feelings. Above all, she would be understanding.

Her father rambled on.

"Now my dear, you'll have to give me your promise not to meet this Casimir again or I'll have no other alternative than to agree with your mother to keep you under careful watch until this fellow runs out of money and leaves Warsaw. When he does run out of money, which I imagine will be soon, remember one thing: I have the influence to have him arrested for vagrancy. If that doesn't make him see the light and he gets stubborn, I'll personally see to it that he doesn't find work here. Has it ever occurred to you he might be looking for an easy life and that you might be his entry into prosperity? He's a fortune hunter, Maria. If he weren't he would know his place and stay far away from his betters. Do I make myself clear? Now look

15

your papa in the eyes and promise. In return, I'll promise your freedom will not be curtailed in any way."

Maria crossed her fingers, mumbled a hurried promise, and ran from the library to her room. "Oh, Papa," she cried to herself in bed, "the promise doesn't count you know, not if I crossed my fingers."

Maria's mother was placated when her husband informed her there would be no further transgressions on their daughter's part. "I've given her firm warnings," he said, "and Maria knows when I mean business."

Deliberately breaking her word, the next day she stayed with Casimir in the park until the sun set and in the end she gave in to his demands, promising to throw away a comfortable life to elope with this impetuous man with the charming tongue who wanted to take her from her educated, wealthy family and spirit her off to a mining area where he knew jobs were always plentiful.

That evening, during her last dinner at home, she acted as her parents had expected she would after being denied her way. In response to their questions as to why she was late she told them she had visited Anton and had paid no attention to the time. As she bowed her head over the soup her father winked at her mother. They felt confident that they had won this latest battle of wills. With Anton, Maria had been in good hands and if by chance she had confided in him, he would have given her sound advice. Fortunately, Maria had always respected Anton's wisdom.

During the night Maria took with her the clothes on her back and whatever she could fit into a small carry-all, and crept out of the darkened house on silent feet, excitement making her heart beat wildly as she stole away after leaving a note to inform her family of her decision. Casimir was waiting for her in the darkened bushes at the end of the deserted street and they clung to each other tightly, laughing as they made their way to the railway station that would spirit them away to a priest and the consummation of their passion.

In the early months of her marriage Maria tried to keep their house and clothing clean despite the black dust that permeated the air and seemed to settle everywhere. She developed a cough, but slowly she accustomed herself to their harsh life and never once complained. She loved Casimir dearly and she seemed content. At least he hoped and prayed she had been. Many times he cursed himself for his rash youthful act and longed to kiss the hem of her skirt for standing by him when eking out their living was cruel and demanding. Some days their meals were meager indeed— potatoes, a few soggy carrots, and a scrap of meat—but Maria concocted tasty fare from the poorest staples. Painstakingly, she learned to sew and gathered up whatever scraps of material she could find in order to make the children look presentable. They, husband and wife, laughed at her first attempts at sewing, but she never lacked determination, and as time passed, she mastered that task and countless others she had never performed before. In an age when men did not share household chores, Casimir was the exception, he willingly helped whenever he could. There wasn't much class distinction in Ruda; everyone was poor. Yet, through their many hardships, Maria wove her thread of laughter, and life seemed sunnier in her presence. The couple's only period of unhappiness came when their firstborn died hours after birth. Maria was despondent for several weeks, but when spring arrived her vigor and love of life were renewed.

As expected, her parents disowned her when she eloped, and in the following years, even though she wrote them regularly, her letters were never acknowledged. The only news from home came from dear Uncle Anton. He at least found time to write once or twice a year, keeping her abreast of family happenings and attempting to soften the blow of her parent's irrevocable decision. Now her father and mother were dead. They had died without mentioning their only daughter's name. The considerable estate they left went to Maria's three brothers who, in their greed, refused to send her one zloty. She had made her bed, they declared, and now she must lie in it. To their way of thinking they had no sister. Disowning her was a just punishment for the scandal she had created by running off with a poor, uneducated man. Casimir was outraged when he heard, outraged at himself for causing the rift between his wife and her parents, but Maria remained detached.

"It's over," she said calmly. "What's done is done and there's nothing we can do to change it so we'll just put it out of our minds." That was typical of her attitude toward life. No regrets. But Maria was gone. Pain had wrung the last breath of life from her. In the end, Casimir was thankful that she died, thankful to see an end to her suffering for there was nothing he or the children could do to ease those final days. How powerless he felt, watching the shining light ebb out of her pain-racked body that had grown so thin and skeletal in such a short time. Frustrated, he hacked angrily at the coal with his ax, sending up clouds of black dust to mask the tears streaming from his eyes. He worked longer hours to earn enough to buy nourishing ingredients for the soups that Maria could manage to swallow and to obtain the precious bottle of opiate that would give her a few hours respite. Now he considered it his solemn duty to see that their son and daughter had better lives as he had promised.

One day as Casimir headed home after another long day at the mine, the village solicitor—he called himself that and no one questioned it—hailed him and told him the news. Anton, who had died months ago, had left a sizable amount of money to his nephew through marriage and to his great-niece and -nephew. Maria's brothers had hired lawyers to contest the will, but Anton had anticipated this move and had made certain his will was ironclad. His solicitor and his friends had testified to the soundness of Anton's mind and the magistrate had declared the document valid. Maria's greedy brothers had had to admit defeat. Upon hearing Ruda's solicitor explain this, Casimir was stunned. He wasn't usually a lucky man but today fortune had finally smiled on him.

"Maria," he opined aloud, "if only you could have lived to see this day. What a difference it would have made in our lives. I could have sent you to the hospital in the city where medication would have eased your pain. An operation might have made you whole again, but the money came too late," he cried forlornly.

It wasn't a great fortune that Anton had left them, for he had also made several bequests to poor students, but it was enough to take them out of the village, enough for Casimir to move to a warmer climate and to buy a farm, where his son would still have to work long hours but where he would be breathing healthy fresh air instead of the killing dust of the mine. Casimir would buy a few acres where they could grow their own nourishing vegetables and grain. They would have a cow, a pig, some chickens and ducks; that would put some meat on the children's skinny frames.

Suddenly another thought entered Casimir's mind. There must be a better plan for his Danuta who looked so much like her mother. She had flaxen spun-gold hair and wide, blue, trusting eyes. At thirteen years of age, she was bright and intelligent. Besides the old priest in the rundown church and the village solicitor, she was the only person in the village who had any education. Although she was only seven when Maria died, already Maria had taught her the fundamentals of reading, writing, and mathematics. Dani had picked up these subjects quickly and as the years passed she continued to learn. She was always seeking books from the rectory or begging the solicitor for his cast-off papers. Villagers asked her to read the mail they received from relatives or to give them the news from the old papers and journals that managed to find their way to Ruda. Casimir's little *aniol*, his angel, seemed to soak up knowledge like a sponge. Her beauty and her intelligence were outstanding; she deserved better than Ruda had to offer.

On the other hand, much as Casimir loved his son, he knew the lad was a plodder, destined to work hard all his days just as his father had. Janek could only read and write simple words. He had never paid much attention while their mother was trying to impart knowledge to them but had spent his time daydreaming, his head in the clouds, until it was time for him to join his father in the mines. When Casimir had attempted to coax him into learning from Dani after Maria's death, he had shrugged and logically explained that the small pittance he earned in the mines was more essential than an education so, after countless hours of argument, Casimir had given up. He was too weary to spend the short evenings arguing after laboring all day with pickax and shovel. Jan was fifteen and claimed he was a man, not a schoolchild.

Now Casimir savored the last drop of vodka, then walked into the only other room in the house, and went to bed. The solicitor was holding the inheritance for them. In the morning he and his son would quit their jobs and begin to make plans. As he drifted off to sleep an idea crept into his mind. It was vitally important that he set aside a sum for Danuta. Special plans must be made for her since she was his special offspring. Though his son would carry on the Mrazek name, his daughter would carry the line much further in America. Yes. He sighed happily. She will go to my sister in America and make us all proud. There she will live a life suited to her beauty and talents. Casimir slept, content. The future belonged to his very own Danuta.

Chapter Two

Throwing caution to the winds in the morning, Casimir piled a heaping supply of wood and coal on the fire. While warmth built up, he stole out the door, although it was still dark, and purchased eggs, sausages, milk, and fresh baked bread from the mine-owned store situated down the dirt street in the center of the village. As he returned home, he noticed with pleasure that Jan and Dani had partially thrown off their covers in the unaccustomed comfort of a warm room. During the frugal winter months, they had always kept the covers drawn over their heads.

Dani woke first, her eyes huge at the sight of a roaring fire, her ears and nose unaccustomed to the sizzle of hot sausages frying in a pan. Her eyes opened even wider when she spotted the pitcher of milk on the table. The aroma of fresh baked bread made her mouth water.

"Papa, what's happening? Am I still asleep, dreaming? You're wasting all the coal and wood I've gathered, and wherever did you get the food?" Wonder of wonders, here were all the things they could afford only on holidays or very special occasions.

Casimir laughed as he removed the cooked sausages

from the pan and began to prepare the eggs. The gaunt hollows etched deeply in his face seemed to disappear as he smiled, and Dani stared at him. He hadn't been this happy for such a long time, not since before her mother died. It was good to see him standing there tall and strong, laughing at her bewilderment.

"Dani my angel, wake your lazy brother. I have a feast prepared just for the three of us. Hurry, get dressed," he ordered, placing breakfast on the table.

"Papa, first you have to tell me what's happening," Dani began, but Casimir cut her off.

"I'll explain later. Come before breakfast gets cold."

Dani saw the first glimmer of dawn creeping through the window. "You're late for work. The foreman will be angry. He'll take away half a day's wages if you don't hurry."

"So be it," Casimir responded gaily. "Now do as I say. Push lazy Jan out of his bed and come to the table."

Still in a daze, Dani stepped across the room to shake her brother and then ran behind the screen to don her washed-out gray flannel dress, one of her two winter garments. The material was worn thin in quite a few spots and her elbows almost poked through the frayed material. The dress was far too short and was tight in the bosom, Dani noted as she pulled up her thick, knit stockings. It would never see her through another winter. Later she would try to figure out a way to get material to sew another. It was almost time for Casimir's sister, her aunt who lived in America, to send another package. These yearly packages contained many surprises, but always several yards of material were included, enough to make a dress for her and shirts for Jan and Papa. But now was not the time for daydreaming, not with this sumptuous feast waiting.

Sitting at the laden table, the three dug in with relish.

24

Jan was wide awake now, torn between asking questions first or getting a good meal down. The desire for appetizing food won out, and not until every last morsel had been eaten did he look expectantly at Casimir, awaiting an explanation.

"Jan, Dani, I know your mother told you stories about her family in Warsaw. You remember that when we married, her parents and brothers washed their hands of her and had nothing more to do with us. All of them disowned us, except for your mother's uncle, Anton. Well, a few months before the Christmas holiday he passed away, and being sympathetic to your mother because of her unfair treatment, he remembered us in his will. Anton wasn't a very wealthy man, not nearly as wealthy as your grandparents, but he did have more than I could ever earn working in the mines all my life."

Dani's eyes registered enlightenment. "No wonder he didn't send his usual Christmas package this year. He never answered my last letters, but no one wrote to tell us he died." She remembered the parcel of gifts Anton had sent each year. Most were impractical, but what they couldn't use they often traded for essentials. Every year there had been a doll for her, and perhaps a child's tea set or some miniature furniture for a dollhouse. The presents had delighted her when she was younger but Anton had never realized that she had grown too old for dolls and toys; so Dani had traded them in for meat and, once, a pair of boots for Jan. Jan always received books and gladly surrendered them to Dani. He kept only the gloves, warm knit socks, and bulky hats. But the packages also included tins of hard candy and bags of oranges; these were savored for weeks. Each year Anton sent her father a long scarf. Casimir now had a dozen of them stacked on a shelf. There certainly was no shortage of scarves in the

Mrazek family. Dani's mother, when she was still living, had received lacy handkerchiefs, a satin robe, and a silk parasol . . . and one year, a marvelously warm fur hat. Dani wore that hat now; the handkerchiefs, robe, and parasol were stored away in an old trunk. Anton was a remarkably intelligent man when it came to historical data but very unimaginative when it came to selecting gifts. Still they adored the kind old teacher who thought of them so generously each year. He was a link to their past and therefore family.

Whenever one of Anton's gifts had to be bartered away, Casimir was morose for days. He wanted his children to keep those luxurious playthings although he realized deep in his heart there were too many necessities he couldn't afford. Even his sister never knew how insignificant his salary was. She knew miners earned very little for excruciating, backbreaking labor, but the years in America had dulled her awareness of Poland's wage scale. Dani had learned not to mention the trading she did to her father. They had an unspoken agreement that neither would say a word about what had to be done. If no one actually spoke about the traded items, Casimir could, at times, push the humiliation to the back of his mind. Dani begged him to let her write Anton and ask for more practical gifts, but her father flatly refused, not wanting to hurt Anton's feelings or to put another chink in his own pride.

"Let him continue to think you're still babies," he always advised. "No harm done. He always meant to visit us but was constantly immersed in the latest book he was writing and time slipped by too quickly. He never realized both of you grew up. During the school year he was busy teaching and writing, and when the summer came he loved to meet with other noted historians in the cool air of the mountains where they

26

spent days and nights discussing our country's struggles for freedom."

Now Dani managed to bring her thoughts back to the present as Casimir continued talking.

"Over the years Anton managed to save money even though he spent a good deal helping some of his poorer students. What he left us seems like an enormous amount, but I must handle our inheritance carefully to make sure it will be put to good use as Anton wished. If we squander it away, his generosity will be wasted. Last night I sat thinking for a long time and I came to the conclusion that there are certain steps we must take as soon as possible to get away from this barren land. First, as soon as the roads are clear, we will buy a farm. Life will be much easier then. Our priest has relatives near Gdansk who will help us locate a parcel of fertile land. Jan, you and I will farm this, and when I'm gone you'll have property to fall back on. You can marry when the time is right, and there will be room enough to raise a family or expand. I'm sure Father Czerny's brother will help us learn all we need to know about raising crops."

Jan finally found his voice. "I don't know if it's wise to take a chance on starting over. We could stay here and live like kings for the rest of our lives."

"And what do we do when the money runs out?" Casimir thundered. "Do you think it will last forever? What would we do for work except go to the mines? There is nothing else for the likes of us. Do you enjoy the thought of becoming old before your time, to have your back bent from stooping your days away, being dirty, breathing foul air?" Casimir looked sadly at his only son.

"Maybe we could open up another store. There's only the one owned by the mining company. We could open a second and sell for less. That way we would still have an income and not work as hard."

Casimir pulled his hair in exasperation.

"Have I raised a complete idiot? Do you think for one moment that the owners of the mine would allow us to compete? Be sensible. They wouldn't hesitate to drive us away. The mine owner is a powerful man who owns everything and everyone in the area. He'd find a way to run us to the ground with our tails between our legs. No! You and I will become successful tillers of the soil. It was your mother's dream to live on a farm so she could feed you rich cream, eggs, and meat. Thank God, you'll at least be out of the mine. Your lungs will be filled with pure fresh air instead of coal dust. What's more important, we'll be eating our own produce, not the garbage the company store sells us." He banged his hand on the table, rattling the now-empty plates. "My mind is made up. We'll be leaving in another month or so and you'll be with me. That's my decision."

Dani looked at her father, a puzzled frown on her thin elfin face. "Papa, you've made all these wonderful plans, but so far you haven't even mentioned me. Surely I'm going along with you?" She bubbled on. "It will be wonderful working outdoors for a change. Even though I dust and wash every day, the dirt keeps piling up endlessly in this house. I'll keep our new home spotless and take care of the chickens, plant a garden, and—"

"One moment, young miss," Casimir interrupted. "You didn't hear your name mentioned because I have another plan for you. You're going to America to my sister, Tekla, and you're going to prove to all of us what fortune can be found there." He saw her look of denial. "Don't get upset, Dani. I'm not asking you to work and send money back to us. No. I want you to get a proper education, to meet and marry a young man who will take good care of you for the rest of your days. Anything can happen in America for it's a land of a thousand opportunities. Why, my sister owns a fine home in Chicago. She's a prosperous woman even though she never married. Look at the things she sends us. Tekla will see to it that you have all the advantages and meet the right people. You must write to her today and tell her you'll be coming to her soon."

Dani burst into tears. "Please, Papa. I want to stay with you and Jan. Don't send me away. When we move to the new farm I'll meet many fine young men. I can marry one and still be near you and Jan. It won't be like living here and being a miner's wife. Please change your mind and say I can go with you. Please."

Jan piped in. "If you don't mind, I'll go to America instead. Then later when I've found a good job, I can send for Dani."

"And how will you find a job?" Casimir asked. "People in America all know how to read, write, and do figures but you never bothered to learn. There's no opportunity there for uneducated people. They just remain common laborers. No, my son, you'll stay here with me and together we'll learn how to raise plentiful crops." It almost broke Casimir's heart to see the desolate look on Dani's face, but he had to remain firm. If rumors were correct, a great war was in the making, and this being the case, he had to get her safely away. Poland had been torn apart many times, but a strange premonition that this war would be much worse than any in the past nagged at him repeatedly. He stood up and walked over to his daughter, gently wiping away her tears. "Dani, if the farm doesn't work out for us, I'll sell it and Jan and I will join you in two years time. Just give us two summers to prove ourselves. All right, little one?"

A tiny smile crept across Dani's face. "Promise? Papa, I can't imagine you being a farmer so you'll have to come to America after me, won't you?"

"Yes, I imagine so. Now while Jan and I talk to the foreman to say we'll be leaving the mine, you write that letter. Then I want you to spend as much time as possible with Father Czerny, learning all the English he can teach you. He speaks the language a little, and you must learn some of it before it's time to leave."

"Yes, Papa. As soon as I wash the dishes I'll begin."

Casimir patted her shoulder. "You're a good child, Dani. Study as hard as you can with the priest. It won't be easy in a strange country if you don't understand what is being said. Every little word you learn will make it that much easier for you."

A worry line creased Dani's face as she sat down to write her aunt. There was enough time, she decided, to try to coax her father into a change of heart. In the month she had left, she would use all her wiles to get him to reverse his decision. Actually he wasn't a stern parent but was rather soft-hearted. She would work on him whenever they were together.

Dear Aunt Tekla,

A most surprising thing happened and it's left me very happy but desolate too. Mama's uncle left us some money. That means we can leave this forlorn village and move near another city where Papa plans to buy a farm. I don't know exactly where we're going yet, only that it's somewhere near Gdansk where the village priest's brother lives. Father Czerny told Papa that the climate is milder and crops are plentiful. As soon as I know where we're going, I'll send you the address so we won't lose touch. Papa is acting very strange since this windfall came about. He wants me to come to Chicago to live with you. Dearest Aunt, I'd love to come, but you must understand it's important that I stay with my father. He only has Jan and me, and Jan will not take care of him: cook, clean, sew, or do any of the things to make a good home. Please write to Papa as soon as you get this letter and do your best to convince him that my place is here in Poland. Perhaps, when I'm older, I'll visit you but not now. Now I'm too anxious to see what our new home will look like and how different life will be. Try to do your best to help me.

Love,
Your niece, Dani

She put on her hat and coat and took the letter to the general store for mailing. Next she walked to the rectory which was connected to a small crumbling church. She found Father Czerny huddled next to a fire, dozing. He woke with a start.

"Danuta, what a welcome sight on a bitter gray day. What brings you here, my child?"

"Father, I suppose by now you have heard the news of our good fortune?"

"Yes. News, good or bad, travels fast in this small community. You must remember to give thanks to God for this material blessing bestowed on you."

"Yes, Father. But first I have a favor to ask. Papa tells me you speak some English. Could you find time to teach me what you know? Papa wants to send me to his sister but I won't be able to make my way in America without knowing any of the words. Perhaps he will change his mind and let me stay with him, but until I can persuade him that I belong here, I'll have to begin to learn the English language." Dani's hurried words came to an abrupt halt.

The old Father's face brightened. Outside of saying mass, praying, and visiting the sick, time lay heavily on his hands in the long winter months. He couldn't go out much because the bitter chill permeated his arthritic bones and the pain was excruciating. Imparting some of his knowledge to this bright young girl would help to while away the hours.

"Danuta, I'll be happy to teach you what I know, which isn't much I'm afraid. I only had a year's study of the English language at the seminary and that was so many years ago, I've probably forgotten the correct pronunciation. But now and then, words pass through my mind and some of them stick. Before we begin, however, I want to caution you that obedience is a great virtue. Your father knows what's best for you, and if he has decided that you're to live with his sister, it's not for you to question his motives but to obey. Do you understand?"

"Yes, Father."

"Good. I know that the thought of leaving your family seems unbearable, but in time you'll be happy your dear father made this choice for you. Poland is a harsh country for the poor, and here you will always remain poor. But given a chance in a new country, who knows what awaits you? I've heard even the poor in America live better lives than we. God has granted you a wonderful oportunity and you must take advantage of it."

That afternoon Dani learned how to say "thank you," "hello," "goodbye," "please," and a few other words in English. As dinner time drew near, the priest called a halt to the day's lesson, promising to give Dani another the next afternoon. Dani took home a precious sheet of paper on which she'd written all the words she'd learned.

Having hurried home because she expected to start

dinner, she was surprised to find the meal almost ready. A pot of stew bubbled over the fire, and her father stood stirring the contents of the pot while Jan set the table, a scowl on his face.

"What took you so long?" Jan asked. "This is woman's work."

Casimir waved the spoon in the air. "Jan, no more. Dani has much to learn in the coming days and the three of us will take turns with the chores. Be glad that you didn't spend the day in the mine." He turned to his daughter. "There was a minor cave-in today. A man was crushed to death."

Not again, Dani thought. So many lives were lost in the mines because the owner wouldn't spend the money to ensure safety.

"Who was it?" she asked quietly.

"Mr. Kapinski. The rest of the men in the crew and their wives are with his widow now, trying to comfort her. Life won't be easy for her with two small children to raise."

"I'll go there after dinner and bring them something to eat," Dani said sadly.

When they had all sat down at the table, Casimir held up his hand. "I have something to say before we begin. Since the news of our good fortune traveled swiftly, I am besieged by friends and neighbors asking for a small loan or an outright gift of money. I don't like to refuse them, but if I give to one, there'll be no end to the requests. I must act the miser. I'll leave a donation to the church as a special thank-you to God, and of course, I'll give Mrs. Kapinski a small sum but nothing more. I know that my old friends will shun me because I do this, but it's for the best. We'll have to leave quickly even though the weather is bad, before greed and jealousy make life miserable for us. We leave in three weeks. The solicitor is arranging to purchase a horse and wagon for us."

"So soon?" Dani asked.

"Yes. You must spend the next days studying as much as possible. You'll take the morning chores. Jan and I will cook the evening meal and pack while you spend every afternoon with the priest."

After the dishes were done, Dani ran over to Mrs. Kapinski's house. She took with her a half pot of stew and a loaf of bread. The house was crowded with mourners, but Dani managed to speak to the widow in a quiet corner.

"Mrs. Kapinski, I'm truly sorry about your loss. I know there's nothing I can say to ease your sorrow, but if there's anything I can do to help, I'll be happy to do it. I know you have a thousand worries on your mind, wondering about the future and how you'll support your family, but everyone will help, they always do. Just wait and see. The other miners will share their food, and their wives will help watch over your children while you try to find work. Maybe Mr. Jedla who owns the mines will find work for you at his house." She patted the widow on the shoulder. "I can bring the children breakfast in the mornings until it's time for us to leave or take them over to our house and keep them occupied."

The distraught woman stopped sobbing long enough to answer Dani. "You're a good child, but the children will be fine here with me. You can bring the food though. God knows we'll have need of it now that my husband's gone. Every little crumb will help stave off starvation. You're so lucky to be quitting this miserable village. How I envy you. If your father would allow it, I would be more than happy to leave with you and act as housekeeper for you, Jan, and my fatherless children, but I'm afraid Casimir said that was impossible. Can't you try to make him change his mind?"

34

Dani didn't know what to say. Why was this woman asking to go along with them? Her husband hadn't even been laid to rest yet. Before Dani could think of the right words, Anna Kapinski spoke up again after hastily wiping her eyes. "You might leave me a remembrance, Danuta. Maybe one of your mother's lace handkerchiefs or her satin robe. You'll not need those with your new wealth."

Dani was shocked at the avarice in the woman's voice. Papa was right. Poor Mr. Kapinski was laid out on a table in this very room where his greedy widow was asking for finery. The last thing Anna Kapinski could use here in this dust-choked village was a lace-trimmed handkerchief or a satin robe.

"I'll leave you a handkerchief before I go," Dani answered.

That is a small price to pay for learning a valuable lesson, she thought. Until the time they climbed into the wagon she would keep to the rectory, or she was afraid she would find herself without the few belongings her mother had left her.

In the ensuing weeks Dani learned quickly. She now knew that American money consisted of dollars and that a hundred pennies made up a dollar, as did twenty nickels, ten dimes, or four quarters. That was the most important lesson, the old priest cautioned. He didn't want her taken for a fool and overcharged because she couldn't understand the monetary system, so he spent a whole week on that alone until she knew her nickels and dimes as well as she knew the Polish coins, and until she could count with ease in English.

"I'm sorry," Father Czerny said toward the end of the third week. "I can't teach you more for that's all I know. It's a difficult tongue to master because so many words that are spelled the same way have different meanings. The rest you'll have to pick up as you go

35

along and gain experience." Dani took home the papers she'd filled with finely written words so she might study them. Carefully folding them, she placed them in a knit purse for future reference.

The morning of their departure dawned cold and crisp. Casimir stood outside the door scanning the sky. Good, he thought. So far no sight of rain or snow. It would be cold, at least for the beginning of the long trek. The thaw hadn't begun yet, but March was a treacherous month. By the time they had traveled fifty miles it might be a completely different story.

A few people remained inside the house saying their goodbyes to Dani and Jan. Certain that Dani was giving some of her belongings to the grasping women, Casimir shrugged. He didn't begrudge them the few possessions Dani had stored away. Many of their neighbors hadn't even come to say farewell. Those had expressed ill will toward Casimir in the weeks since he had inherited his wealth. Strange, he thought, how a little money can alter friendship. When all were poor, the villagers worked together although they spent long hours bemoaning their poverty and hardships. But when one villager advanced himself, the others resented his good fortune. Last night Casimir had visited the priest and had left some money for his personal use and some for the church. He had also given the priest a sum to be used in case catastrophe hit the village, but he had cautioned the good father not to mention this money until the time came when it was needed. He had then gone to Mrs. Kapinski's house and left enough to see her through the year. By that time, he guessed, she would be remarried. There were more men than women in Ruda and she would make one of them a dutiful wife. With two small children to support marriage was her only choice.

"Jan, Dani," Casimir called, "it's time. Let's be on our way." Dani hugged her few friends, and then they looked on with envy as she clambered into the back of the wagon and settled herself snugly atop the piled quilts. She was glad it was not raining. She looked at the roll of canvas attached to one side of the wagon. It was bound to rain sooner or later. Then she would be forced to pack the quilts in the trunk to protect them and she would have to sit on the rough floorboards huddled under the canvas. All but one of her mother's handkerchiefs were gone, as was the parasol. All she had left from her mother were the fur hat, the satin robe, and a pair of tiny gold earrings her mother had worn on the night she had run off with Casimir. Dani looked back only once to wave goodbye, and she didn't shed a tear. Why cry? Her family was still together and a better life lay ahead.

As they passed the church, Father Czerny came out to bless them. He spoke to Dani in halting English.

"God be with you, Danuta."

She answered in the same tongue.

"Goodbye, Father. Thank you."

As she spoke tears found their way down her cheeks. She would certainly miss this man of God who was full of kindness.

When the wagon was passing the general store, the storekeeper, who also acted as postmaster, came running out, waving a letter in one hand.

"Casimir wait! Here's a letter. I believe it's from your sister. Thank heaven I was able to catch you before you left or who knows how long it would have taken for the letter to reach you?" He handed the envelope to Casimir. "Goodbye and peace and luck be with you."

37

The two men shook hands solemnly, and then, Casimir tossed the missive back to Dani.

"Read it aloud. My hands are full handling this crazy animal."

The horse was rather spirited and Casimir wasn't very proficient at the reins. He was more accustomed to the tools he used in the mine than to the vagaries of a frisky horse.

Dani opened the envelope slowly. It was much too soon for this to be a reply to her letter. Their letters must have crossed en route.

My dearest family,

I'm writing this letter with great fear in my heart. Rumors fly about daily that war will soon be coming to Poland, and this news hangs heavy here in our Polish community. I beg you, Casimir, leave Poland now while there is still time. Please listen to me for once in your life. Lay down your stupid pride and accept passage money from me. If you are not concerned for yourself, at least think of the children. They are all that is left of our family and they must not be subjected to the horrors of war. Knowing how obstinate you can be, I have taken matters into my own hands and have sent passage money with a neighbor's cousin who will be arriving near the end of April at the port city of Gdansk. He works on a freighter. The captain, who is also Polish, has promised berths for you and the children. He will get you safely to New York and from there you will take the train to Chicago. I have enclosed a map of the United States so you can realize the great distance that has to be covered. As soon as you receive this letter, travel quickly to Gdansk so you can be there by the time the freighter docks. Its name is the *Destiny* and you must ask for Captain Murow (he changed his name from Murowski) or Raymond Patek, my neighbor's cousin who will direct you to the captain. Captain Murow is holding the passage money and train fare as well as some money for food. The *Destiny* is far from being a luxury ship but it will take you to America. Casimir, I beg you not to delay. The time has come to leave the old country and to ally yourself with the United States. Raymond Patek will see that you get on the right train from New York, and he will send me a telegram stating when you will arrive in Chicago. The rest is simple. I'll be waiting at the train station to take you to my home. You remember I wrote that it has two apartments; one I rent out. But with my six rooms, we'll have enough space to be comfortable. My friends will find good jobs for you and Janek. Danuta can continue her schooling. There's a fine parochial school a short distance from me. She can walk there in five minutes. Many of the children are learning English so she'll not feel out of place. The parish is a large one run by Polish priests and nuns. You'll be pleasantly surprised to see how many Poles have settled in Chicago. They call it little Warsaw. It's predicted that one day there will be more Polish people here than in Warsaw. At times I find this hard to believe but then again, who knows? Please make haste as soon as this letter arrives. With the ports being taken over by the Germans, I'm afraid there will be no time to wait for papers to be processed so you could sail a passenger ship. Captain

Murow will ignore the rules in your case. At least Raymond assures me he will. He said it might take months to get a proper visa, and he should know for he sails around the world and makes several trips a year to Poland. Don't disappoint me again. Every year I expect to hear that you've changed your mind, but you live in a fool's paradise. If I could I wouldn't hesitate to come and get you myself, but that's not possible, especially now with political affairs so uncertain in Poland. Give in my dearest brother.

Love,
Tekla.

Dani folded the letter with trembling hands. Her own letter had been a waste. How could war possibly be in the offing? Certainly there were rumors and constant threats from larger, more powerful countries, but those were commonplace. They had even heard of trouble in Silesia, although no one in Ruda could verify the fact.

Casimir remained silent. It seemed his fears were being substantiated sooner than he'd thought. The sooner he got his daughter safely away the lighter his heart would be.

"Hurrah," Jan roared. "Now we can all leave together. Of course you agree, don't you, Papa? Are we heading in the right direction for Gdansk?"

"Yes, son, we are. It's about one hundred miles from the farm we're buying. We'll stop and put our money down on the land. A few acres right next to Father Czerny's brother. A four-room house stands on the property. Louis Czerny will take you into town to buy seed and implements. You'll stay and start the tilling while I take Dani to meet the ship. As soon as I see her safely off, I'll return for the planting and the purchase of the animals."

Dani moaned through clenched teeth. "Papa, Aunt Tekla wants all three of us. Haven't you listened to a word I was reading? We must all leave together."

"No." Casimir was adamant. "If war comes Jan and I will see it through. I will fight for my country if need be. It's my duty not to run like a coward. Poland will need all the food it can raise too. I told you before, Dani, I must stay for two years to prove myself. If there is no war, I'll join you but not until I've had the two years." Casimir's face set in a stubborn scowl that brooked no further argument.

Dani sat, stunned, knowing there was no shaking her father's determination. For once she was unable to cajole him into her way of thinking. She resigned herself to making the long trip alone. At least Papa and Jan will be joining me soon, she comforted herself.

The weather stayed fair, though a trifle cool, on the road that first week and they made excellent progress. They stopped each night at a farm. Casimir paid a small sum and they were provided with food and a place to sleep, usually in the hayloft. For a few extra zloty the farmer's wife packed them a light lunch to see them through until it was time for another stop. At noon they rested the horse, usually in a field, where they sat and devoured a meal of kielbasa—plump Polish sausage—and bread or pierogi—hefty dumplings filled with cheese, meat, or potatoes. The youngsters thrived in the open air, especially Dani who glowed with excitement at the change in scenery from black mining town to green rolling hills.

"Jan," she confided one day. "Remember the stories

41

Mama used to tell us about Gypsies? We're living just like the Romanies, traveling from village to village, sleeping wherever we lay down our heads for the night. The only thing we're missing is the wild dancing, the fortune telling, and the camaraderie of a large caravan. I wish we could just go on like this for a long, long time until we see all of Europe. Wouldn't that be a marvelous adventure?"

"It would," Jan answered. "But I'd much rather be going with you. I don't think I was destined to be a farmer. Actually I hate mining too. I think I'd like to be a sailor. If only Papa weren't so stubborn I could sail the sea across with you. I hope the crops we plant are all ruined. That would change his mind!"

"Don't talk like that Jan!" Dani said, shocked. "It's a terrible sin to wish bad luck on anyone, especially on your own father. I'll keep writing letters to Papa, saying how lonely I am and how sick without him, and you must keep saying how much you miss me. Between the two of us, we'll turn him around eventually."

"Well, if he doesn't change his mind in two years, I'm leaving without him. I'll stow away, and if they find me, I'll work my way across the ocean!"

Dani was silent. She had never heard Jan utter more than one or two complete sentences at a time. If he wasn't daydreaming or working, he was always going for long walks alone. There was a time when she used to think him dim-witted because of his reluctance to speak. Today, as his words poured out, she realized that beneath his calm surface lay intelligence and passionate feeling. Poor Jan, she thought before drifting off to sleep. I wish he could take my place. Why was her father so blind when it came to seeing what was good for his children?

Loud blasts of thunder woke them just before dawn,

and a downpour began. Several raindrops fell through cracks in the barn roof and plunked down on Dani as she lay enfolded in her quilt in yet another strange hayloft. Casimir and Jan woke with a start, packed away the pillows and quilts, and fastened the canvas cover over the wagon. Although the farmer generously offered his barn as a refuge for as long as they liked, Casimir insisted they be on their way in the afternoon even though the sky was dark and overcast. From that day on misfortune after misfortune plagued them all the way to their destination. The rain seemed to follow them as they crept along the muddy roads. Countless times the wheels became mired in thick mud, an axle broke and it took days to repair it, the horse became lame and had to be rested and reshod.

The trip took three times as long as it should have, but tired, soaked and bedraggled they finally came to Oblonz. Dani was coughing and flushed with fever when they arrived at Louis Czerny's comfortable farm. Lottie, his wife, descended on the trio like an angel of mercy, feeding them hot steaming czarnina, the strengthening duck's blood soup. She waved Jan and Casimir off for a hot bath and stripped away Dani's sodden clothes. In a daze, Dani was put into a hot tub of water, plunked in like a baby, and when the chill left her bones, her chest was coated with an evil-smelling salve and she was wrapped in hot flannel compresses. Awakening three days later, she found she didn't remember the whole of the last week, only the horror of trudging through an endless morass of mud or huddling under the dripping canvas. It had been worse for Casimir and Jan who had had to sit out in the open and handle the nervous horse. If it wasn't the rain or the chills coursing through their bodies, it was the damp penetrating mist. The only time they dried out was

43

when a kind farmer took pity on the trio and made them sit in front of a warm kitchen fire until they steamed dry. Not that it did much good, for the next day only held more of the same. Even the food they managed to buy tasted damp and moldy.

On the third day after she awakened, Dani felt like herself again, and blessedly the sun shone. She was able to get into the wagon with her father and Jan and go to inspect the new farm. Even though the house needed repair, Dani loved it. It boasted four rooms: a parlor, a kitchen, and two bedrooms. Each room had a window, and there were two fireplaces. The well was outside the kitchen door so fresh water could be handily brought up. The water tasted sweet and pure. With a little whitewash and some carpentry work the house would make a real home. It reminded Dani of a fairy-tale cottage and she pictured it finished, fresh curtains covering the windows and furnishings in place. It was a sound house with no chinks of light shining through, easy to keep warm in winter. The wood floors only needed a good scrubbing and they would be white as snow. The previous owner had left a table and four chairs, several kettles, and some hooked rugs. Naturally the rugs were soiled, but a little soap and water would bring out their bright colors again.

Casimir saw the wistful look in Dani's eyes as he took her back to the Czerny farm. Perhaps it had been a mistake to take her to see the house in which he and Jan would be living.

"Rest and eat well," he advised her. "We'll be leaving tomorrow for Gdansk, this time with a faster horse and a wagon I've borrowed from Louis. The *Destiny* should be in port by the time we arrive."

Dani tried one last maneuver.

"It's so lovely here, so different from Ruda. People

hereabout look happy and cheerful. Lottie Czerny tells me there are festivals all summer with singing and polka dancing. Everyone has more than enough to eat all year long. Papa, it would be very good for me to stay. The air smells so clean and healthy. Won't you say you've changed your mind?"

"Do as I say."

Casimir strode away from her to finish consulting with Louis on what was needed to make his land productive again. It was getting harder and harder for him to stand firm when challenged by Dani's pleading eyes.

Dani wanted to cry out her refusal to go along with her father's plans. All through the night she sobbed pitifully but no one heard except Jan who came in and sat on the edge of the bed holding her hand in his rough clumsy ones. His choked voice told her he was also on the verge of tears.

"Dani, please stop. Calm yourself. You'll only get ill again if you keep on this way. Listen to me. I have a better plan. Hear me out. I watched Papa hide the rest of the money just before dark. After he left I opened the steel box and counted what was left. I'll help him get the planting done and the first harvest in. In the autumn I'll go to the strongbox and take only enough to start my journey to meet you. Before the winter's over, I'll be with you and Tekla. Dani, are you listening? In seven or eight months I'll join you."

"But that's stealing," Dani sobbed. "You can't steal from Papa."

"It's not stealing. I'm not taking all of the money; just enough to get to America. Look, didn't Aunt Tekla send enough to get all three of us out? Isn't the captain holding that money?"

"Yes."

"Well, that's extra money Papa wasn't counting on,

45

isn't it?"

"Yes, I guess so."

"When Uncle Anton died he left his money to all three of us. Before I leave I'll write a note to Papa explaining that I've only taken my share. Surely then he'll realize that with the two of us gone he'll have to follow. He'll be so worried about us he'll have no other choice. Remember, he promised Mama he would always take care of us. When he sees I'm gone too, he'll remember that promise. Now that isn't a bad plan, is it? Just think of it as the three of us going but on different ships at different times."

Dani managed a wan smile. "If only what you're telling me could come true, I wouldn't feel so miserable."

"I promise you that's the way it will happen. Now try to get a little sleep. It will be dawn in another two hours and you need your rest. Good night little one."

"Good night Jan."

Exhausted, Dani soon drifted off into a dreamless sleep.

In the time they had spent at the Czerny farm, Lottie had managed to sew a dress and a petticoat for Dani to take with her. Casimir bought her a pair of fine leather boots, a hat, and a coat. She wore the new dress and the boots. The rest of her belongings, along with her mother's mementos, were packed into the small trunk she was taking. Lottie packed a hamper of food that would last several days: cheeses, smoked sausages, fresh bread, apples, and a tin of cookies and candies. Now it was already an hour past dawn and Casimir was fidgeting with the horses.

"Dani, it's getting late."

"I'm coming."

Hurriedly Dani kissed the Czernys and then she turned to Jan who was standing shyly in the doorway.

"Good-bye, dear Jan. Remember your promise."

He winked, then whispered in her ear.

"I've slipped a calendar in your trunk. You can start marking off the days as soon as you're aboard ship. Before you know it, I'll be with you. Take good care of yourself and listen to all the instructions the captain gives you. Once you're on the train nothing can happen. Good-bye, little sister. I love you." He gave her a great bear hug. "Now go."

Dani jumped on the front seat of the wagon next to her father and waved until her brother was only a tiny speck on the horizon. She forced herself not to cry. It won't be long, she told herself over and over.

The roads were in excellent condition, the borrowed horse fast, and they arrived in Gdansk shortly after midnight, having traveled two and a half days. Casimir was directed to an inn near the waterfront where they could spend the night. He had Dani go up to her room while he went to make inquiries about the *Destiny*.

As the owner of the inn sat in the taproom having a late supper, Casimir approached him and apologized for interrupting.

"No bother," the huge man said. "How can I be of help?"

"I wonder if you've heard anything about a ship called the *Destiny*. It should be putting into port soon. My daughter's due to sail on her."

"The *Destiny* you say? That freighter docked a week ago. It's due to sail in a few hours. What's your name?"

"Casimir Mrazek."

"Don't look so frightened. I'm not in league with the German officials stationed here." The innkeeper spat

47

on the floor. "Some of the captain's men made inquiries here this past week. Mr. Mrazek if you're sailing on that ship you'd better get on it immediately."

"Which one is the *Destiny?*" Casimir asked.

"Come with me."

Casimir followed the man over to a window facing the sea.

"There she is, over to the left. Look you can just make out her name in the fog."

Casimir peered to where the burly man was pointing.

"I see it. Thank you. I'd better get Dani over there right now."

"Need any help?"

"No. Thank you, but I can manage. I'll be staying the night. My daughter won't need her room though."

"But the seamen said three of you were expected to sail."

"No, only my daughter. I have to be back in Oblonz quickly."

The owner shook his head.

"I must have misunderstood, but make haste. They'll be pulling up anchor soon."

Casimir climbed the stairs and knocked sharply on Dani's door. She opened it cautiously, first making sure it was her papa. The bustling city made her feel a trifle uneasy. It was huge and confusing compared to their small village. Casimir noted that the sandwiches and the tea he'd had sent up were gone.

"Good. You've finished eating. Put your coat back on. It seems we've just made it in time. The *Destiny* arrived a little early. If we had dawdled another day we would have missed it. It's leaving soon."

Everything is going against me, Dani thought miserably. It seemed that God intended her to leave Poland. If only she'd pretended to be ill a day longer, she would have missed the boat, then she could have stayed with her family. By the time other arrangements could be made, Papa would have been used to having her around, but that just wasn't meant to be.

Casimir hefted the trunk to his shoulder. "Come, let's look for the captain."

The fog was a little thicker now but Casimir could make out the ship's name a short distance ahead. Their steps rang loudly in the muffled air. A man stood on the dock next to the ship smoking a pipe, and he glanced up as Casimir and Dani loomed out of the fog.

"Can I help you?"

"Yes. Is Captain Murow here, or Raymond Patek? My daughter's due to sail with you."

The sailor tapped out his pipe. "You must be the Mrazeks. Captain had us looking all over for you. You've just made it in time. Follow me, I'll take you to his quarters." They followed the sailor up the gangplank and then he led them to a small but compact cabin. Captain Murow sat at an old chipped desk studying several opened charts.

"Captain, look who just arrived, the Mrazeks."

"Thank you, Jablonski." He waved Casimir and Dani over to two chairs across from him. "You had me quite worried. I promised Raymond Patek that we would get you out safe and sound, but I had almost given up hope of seeing you here on time. We should have left yesterday, but against my better judgment I was persuaded to delay for one extra day. Raymond was about ready to jump ship if you didn't come, and I would hate to lose a steady dependable man. My guess is he would have tried to make it to Ruda, for he did make a promise to a friend to help you out. I believe he's below right now, just back from making several more inquiries at some of the inns. He'll certainly be

49

glad to see you. Jablonski," the captain yelled.

The seaman must have been right outside the door for he opened it quickly.

"Yes, Captain?"

"Get below and tell Raymond we've got the Mrazeks safe on board."

"Yes, sir." He closed the door softly.

Captain Murow turned to the two seated across from him. "But there are only two of you. Where's the other?"

Casimir looked sheepish. "I'm sorry for the trouble we've put you through but there will only be one passenger. Only Dani will be sailing with you, no one else."

"But three of you are supposed to go, not just one."

"My older sister makes grand plans. She loves to manage people's lives; Dani will explain the whole story once you're under way. It's not possible at this time for Jan and me to join you. Will you take good care of my daughter until she's on the train to Chicago?"

"Yes, of course I will. But are you positive you won't change your mind?"

"I'm quite sure."

"Well, in that case there's nothing else I can do except to give you my word that Raymond will put Dani on the train as soon as we dock. While she's on my ship I'll treat her as I would my own daughter." He pulled out a ring of keys and opened a locked drawer in his desk. Pulling out a thick envelope, he handed it to Casimir. "Here's the money your sister sent for the passage."

"Please take out the amount of Dani's fare," Casimir instructed.

Captain Murow took out several bills and handed the envelope back to Casimir and Casimir handed it to

Dani. "You've learned about money, little one. Whatever is left will give you a good start. There won't be any dowry for you so take care how you spend this."

Dani just sat, frozen and mute.

Captain Murow sensed her fright.

"Come, both of you. I'll show you to Dani's quarters. There's nothing grand about this ship. It's rather an old tub, but your daughter will be comfortable." He led them down a stairwell, opened the first door on the port side, and lit a hanging lantern. They stood in a tiny cabin which contained a bunk and a night stand, both battered from years of usage, but the sheet and blanket were clean and crisp. Casimir set the trunk down next to the bunk. It would do. A grimy porthole was slightly open, letting in the night breeze.

"It's fine," Casimir said closing the porthole against the chill. "Far better than I expected after some of the stories I've heard about stinking pestholes in the holds of some ships."

"Yes," the captain agreed. "I've seen some of those. Half the passengers never make it to their destination on those hellish vessels."

Dani's eyes opened wider then, and Captain Murow sent a warning look over to Casimir. "Don't be frightened, Danuta. That is your full name isn't it?"

She nodded her head.

"You'll have dinner with me every night and we'll talk about your new homeland, weather permitting that is. If the sea gets a little rough I have my duties to perform, but it won't get too bad. I think you're going to like sailing the ocean. Now if you'll excuse me. I'll leave you two alone for a few minutes. Then, Mr. Mrazek, you'll have to leave. We have a thousand details to attend to and we're going to weigh anchor soon." He shook hands with Casimir. "Your sister will keep in touch through Raymond, about when we're coming back. Perhaps you'll join us on the next voyage."

"Thank you for all you've done, Captain. I feel much better knowing Dani has someone to depend on."

Casimir sat Dani down on the bunk next to him and he tilted up her face, looking deep into her blue eyes, his love shining through like a beacon. She could only stare back. She felt abandoned and unwanted. "Dani, my angel, you know if I didn't love you above all else I wouldn't be doing this to you. I would lay down my life without hesitation to keep you safe from harm. A long time ago I promised your mother that you would have every opportunity it was possible for me to give you. Until now I was unable to keep that promise. You don't belong in Poland, little love. I'm afraid for you here. I'm certain there will be war, and if there is, countless atrocities will be committed. War isn't just winning and losing; it's bloody gruesome death, starvation, rape, theft. Brother will fight brother in an attempt to stay alive. I won't have you subjected to that. You're thinking at this minute that I don't love you but you're so wrong. I'd give my right arm to have you stay and marry a local man so I could watch over you for as long as I live. It takes a greater love to send you away." He clasped her to his chest and she could feel his tears trickle down her cheek. She had to be brave now in this upside-down situation.

Speaking softly into her father's ear she whispered comfortingly. "Everything will work out fine, Papa. I know it will. All of a sudden I have this joyous feeling that you and Jan will be joining me soon. Captain Murow seems an honorable man, and in no time I'll be on the train; then I'll be with your only sister who loves all of us. You can tell she does just by the way she

rites. Why did she leave Poland?"

Casimir wiped away the trace of wetness on his cheeks. "Many years ago," he began, "she sailed away just as you're doing now, but she was a little older, twenty. Her fiancé had sent her money so she could join him in Chicago where they were going to be married. He'd left Poland two years earlier to find a proper home and open up a small business. She was so happy the day she left she couldn't wait for the wagon to come and take her to the port. We held a party for her the night before, and she danced the whole night away, saying she couldn't sleep a wink anyway because of the excitement of joining her love. All the townspeople waved her off. We didn't live in Ruda then, but in another larger mining town where everyone was so happy for her. She had waited patiently all those months for her fiancé to notify her that everything was arranged to his satisfaction. A few months after Tekla left we received a letter. She and Józef had had two glorious days together before tragedy struck. Then after they had seen the priest to arrange the marriage, Józef never realized what was happening until a second before he was struck down and trampled. Mercifully, it was a quick death, over within minutes. Tekla was hysterical for months before she pulled out of her melancholy. Her friends and I wrote repeatedly asking her to come back home, but she insisted she would stay to take care of the business Józef had started and by staying she could always remain near him. As time passed she became used to life without him. But all this happened a long time ago and now she is content. She never once regretted her move to Chicago, but she did regret losing the only man she ever loved. She wrote me letters over the years, telling me how many offers of marriage she had, but she refused them all. Instead she

53

devoted her life to her business and the church. Ever
morning she goes to church where she finds peac
knowing she'll be joining Józef sooner or later. N
doubt she'll tell you the whole story one day."

Dani saw that talking about the past made her fathe
more relaxed and less anxious about her imminen
departure.

"Is Aunt Tekla pretty, Papa?"

"When I last set eyes on her she was the most beauti
ful, gay young woman in our town. Young men cam
calling from miles around, courting her, but she woul
have no one but Józef. He only wanted the best for he
That's why he went to America. He saw no future fo
them in this country, but he told her in America the
would lead fine lives in a few year's time. That neve
came to pass for he died an untimely death."

A sharp rap on the door announced that it was tim
for Casimir to leave.

"Take the money, Dani, and put it into your petti
coat so no one will rob you."

Dani took some pins from her purse, and she soo
had the envelope of American dollars safely tucke
beneath her full skirts.

Casimir kissed her one last time. "Be brave, m
angel. Even though I'm not with you, I'll be watchin
over you in my thoughts. I'm placing all my hopes o
you. I love you and Jan dearly, but I feel you are th
one who will go further. Make me proud, daughter
We'll not be apart for too long. As soon as you get t
Chicago write long letters and tell me all that's happen
ing, all your impressions." Quickly, he left the smal
cabin before tears flowed again.

Dani scrambled off the bunk and unlocked the trunk
Taking out the calendar Jan had given her, she crossed
out the day. One less day to wait. She turned off th
lantern and looked out the porthole, rubbing away

ome of the dirt with her hand. The fog was beginning o lift, but she saw no one on the deserted dock. Fully lothed she lay back on the bunk and drew the rough lanket over her shoulders. Exhausted from the lack of est over the past few days and the excitement that hurned in her stomach, she turned over and then fell nto a troubled sleep, tossing fitfully from nightmares n which she was lost in a sea of strange unfriendly aces.

Chapter Three

Neither the rumbling of the engines nor the motion of the ship aroused Dani from her long deep sleep, but twelve hours after boarding, a sharp tapping at her door startled her to wakefulness. Although somewhat bewildered by the unfamiliar surroundings, she quickly rose from the bunk, patted down her braided hair, and smoothed her wrinkled dress as best she could. Carefully she opened the door a crack. Before her stood a small wiry man with brown curly hair and laughing eyes. Dressed in typical sailor's garb, he held a tray in one hand and was raising the other to knock again.

"Ah," the sailor said happily. "I finally get to meet one of the elusive Mrazeks. You must be Danuta. While I was in Chicago visiting my cousin I met your aunt. I was off duty for a few months because of an injury so I had time to relax and to meet many people in the Bridgeport section of Chicago before I reported back to New York and the *Destiny*. Your aunt was one of my favorite new friends." He continued talking as he set the tray down on the small stand. "When Tekla learned I was sailing through the Baltic to Poland, she asked what I could do to get her family out of the country. Normally we don't take on passengers, but once in a while the captain makes an exception because we usually have a spare cabin or two. I give you fair warning though; your aunt will be mightily disappointed when she sees you traveling alone. She expects all three of you. Start eating your lunch while I keep you company."

Dani pulled the cloth off the tray to reveal a bowl of chicken soup and a chicken sandwich made with thick slices of rye bread. A cup of strong black coffee completed the meal. She looked down at the man sitting on the edge of the bunk.

"You must be Raymond Patek," she said.

He had the grace to blush slightly.

"Sorry, I should have mentioned that as soon as I came in but my tongue gets carried away. You missed breakfast you know. I knocked several times but you didn't answer so I thought you needed your sleep. I suppose the trip to Gdansk was a long one, and I imagine leaving your family wasn't easy on you either." Dani finished the soup while Raymond rambled on. "You must explain why your father and brother aren't with you. Captain Murow told me your father was here last night but that he said it was impossible for him to make the trip. Why?"

"My father always dreamed of owning a farm and when we came into some money he felt he had to try farming for at least two years. My brother and I told him he could just as easily own a farm in America but he wouldn't hear of it. Papa feels there's going to be a war soon and he won't desert his country, but he did promise me he would only stay two years to try his hand at farming. If there is no war, he'll keep his promise." Dani took a bite of the thick sandwich and tried to sip the coffee, but it was so strong she almost choked.

Raymond laughed merrily. "It takes a long time to

58

get used to the coffee served on this ship. The men like it strong, thick, and black. I would have liked to bring you milk, but you'll not find a drop on board. Your father is right you know. There is definitely going to be war. Germany, Austria, Russia—they all want their portion of Poland. The great powers are always land hungry, and Poland lacks arms and properly trained soldiers to defend itself. Poland would have a slight chance of winning against only one country but not when everyone surrounding us wants to throw a shroud over the land. Now our country is beginning to organize itself after almost a hundred unproductive years, but I think it's too late. The effort to organize should never have slackened off. There is one great man, Józef Pilsudski who's attempting to implement a stronger military strategy, but is that enough? I think not. What a blessing it would be if they all left our homeland in peace. Well"—Raymond stood up—"I have work to do and I've bent your ear long enough for one day. The captain says you're to have dinner with him tonight. Someone will call when it's ready. By the way, there are two other passengers on board. I don't think you'll be seeing much of them though. They're an elderly couple and already they're quite seasick. I imagine they'll be staying close to their cabin all the way across. You're allowed on deck whenever weather permits. I'll take you up tomorrow and show you where you can walk so you won't be in the way."

"Thank you. You've been very kind to me, Raymond."

"It's nothing. Anything for a relative of a friend."

When Raymond left, Dani went over to the porthole. There wasn't a speck of land in sight, but so far she wasn't feeling at all queasy. She hoped she wouldn't be overtaken by the seasickness she'd heard about. It sounded so embarrassing. Sitting back on her bunk, she took out the list of English words she must practice. "My name is Danuta Mrazek," she said to herself over and over. "I go to Chicago. I am fourteen years old."

And so she was. For her birthday last week, her father had bought her the fine leather boots, the dress, and the coat. Only he'd forgotten to give her his felicitations in all the rush and excitement. He'd remembered when she'd thanked him for the new finery and he'd slapped his head in frustration. "My mind is filled with too many plans," he'd said apologetically, and to make up for his forgetfulness he had taken her to a real café in Oblonz where he had told her to order anything on the menu even though she'd protested that the clothes were more than enough. When he'd insisted she'd ordered crisp roast duckling, but the portion was so generous, and was accompanied by so many side dishes, that she couldn't finish her dinner. However, the cook had been kind enough to wrap the meat in a clean white cloth, and she had shared the treat with Jan after they'd returned to the Czerny farm.

Time passed quickly as she concentrated on learning words, and she was surprised when a knock sounded again on her door. Captain Murow himself had come to escort her to his cabin for dinner.

"My quarters are not large," he apologized as they walked together, "but I seldom have guests for dinner. I can squeeze in four people, however, tonight there will just be the two of us since the other passengers aren't up to eating. Both of them are feeling the rigors of sea travel. They only requested tea."

"Perhaps I can be of some help to them tomorrow," Dani offered politely.

"I would appreciate that, Dani. I can't regularly spare one of the crew to act as steward. This ship wasn't made for pampering passengers, only for carrying cargo. I would consider it a big favor if you would look in on them a few times a day. Maybe you could sponge off their faces, get them to drink a little water or tea and eat some crackers or bread. They'll only feel worse if they eat nothing at all. By the time we get to New York, they could be quite ill if they take no nourishment. You don't have to do anything until tomorrow. Tonight one of my crew is seeing to them. Now, are you ready for dinner?"

"Yes, Captain. I ate lunch, but suddenly I find I'm very hungry again."

"It's the sea air that gives one an appetite," he responded.

Dinner consisted of roast beef and a tangy salad of greens. When the captain apologized for such plain fare, Dani looked at him in surprise.

"In Ruda we only had beef once or twice a year," she explained. "To me this dinner is a feast!"

After dinner Captain Murow suggested she go on deck for some fresh air. "It's a beautiful night and you can see hundreds of stars. I can't stay with you because I have to check our course, but I'll show you the way. Just be careful and walk only where the way is clear." He guided her to a section piled high with tarpaulins and sat her down on a smaller bundle. "You'll be quite safe here and you can go down whenever you're tired. Good night, Danuta. Sleep well."

"Good night, sir," she answered in English.

He laughed then. "Ah, I see you know a little of my adopted language. We'll have to practice whenever we get a chance. Raymond can teach you too. Most of the crew aren't familiar with Polish. Only Raymond and Walter Jablonski speak it fluently. We have a wide variety of men on board: Italians, Chinese, Swedes, and, of course, Americans. They're a mixed lot. Some-are good men, some are not." Having said this the

61

captain left her.

Alone, Dani gazed up at the night sky, then down at the waves lit by the moon's light. No one disturbed her while she leaned back to stargaze. It's almost time for me to cross off another day, she thought. By the time the *Destiny* reaches New York, many days will be crossed off. The time will practically fly by because each day will be filled with new experiences. After an hour, a huge yawn shook her from her reverie so she pushed herself off the stiff unyielding bundle of canvas and headed for her cabin. She was amazed to find herself sleepy so early in the evening when she hadn't done any work that day. She wondered briefly if the rich became sleepy early in the evening although they did no hard labor. What is it like to be truly wealthy? she wondered. Mama had once described her early life in a huge home with servants, and she had said she hadn't liked it very much because her family was very snobbish and inclined to look down on the poor. Mama had been friendly to everyone, even the poorest of beggars, and her family had disapproved of her charitable nature.

The next morning, Raymond knocked lightly, hoping Dani was an early riser. In their one short meeting, he had found her an irresistibly appealing young woman who looked more mature than her fourteen years. At first sight he had taken her to be at least seventeen. Her spun-gold hair shone with highlights, her blue eyes twinkled with merriment when she spoke and her figure was nicely rounded. Her eyes held one spellbound while she talked. At least he would have interesting company during his free time on the voyage. Although he enjoyed sailing the seas, visiting various ports around the world and seeing new and exotic sights, this particular trip, to Poland and back, was one he had made many times, and talking with the crew became monotonous. No doubt the men would contrive to catch a glimpse of Dani while she was on deck, and there would be lewd talk when they settled in for the night. Some of the old sea captains were right, he thought. A woman shouldn't be allowed aboard any ship except a luxury liner, certainly not on one with a lusty crew who were without women during the weeks it took to get from port to port. He decided to make it his official duty to watch over Dani so that she wasn't bothered by any of the bolder men who spent their free time in port visiting the local whorehouses.

After a few seconds Dani opened the door and saw her friend carrying a tray.

"I'm so glad to see you!" She smiled. "I've been up for an hour waiting for you to show me the ship. I didn't want to risk going about alone. I didn't want to cause the captain any displeasure."

"I'm glad you waited for me. You just sit on your bunk and eat your breakfast. I'll be back in fifteen minutes to escort you topside. Did you sleep well?"

She nodded her head affirmatively. "Dinner with the captain was delicious, and sitting on the deck got me accustomed to life at sea. I think I'm going to enjoy the whole trip."

She drank her tea and ate the boiled egg and bread quickly, eager to begin exploring with Raymond. Her cabin was cramped—it only took four or five steps to get from the door to the porthole—and she wasn't used to being idle. Raymond could show her where the ailing couple's cabin was located. Helping them would pass the time, and she looked forward to walking the deck in the space allowed her. Maybe the cook in the galley could use some help too. Her energy and vitality had returned and she needed outlets for them.

Raymond returned in exactly fifteen minutes. He picked up her tray and led her first to the galley. The cook was a fierce-looking Oriental who didn't seem to understand her offer of help.

Raymond laughed at her attempt to communicate. "No, you mustn't get in cook's way. He'll only rebel and wave his butcher knife around, threatening to chop off someone's head. This is his domain, and no one enters it except to pick up or drop off a tray."

"But I can't just sit or sleep all the way across the ocean," Dani protested. "There must be something I can do to keep busy. Will you take me to the sick couple? Captain Murow said I could help them so one of his men wouldn't be tied up with nursing duties."

"Yes, they're next door to your cabin. I believe I heard groans when I passed their door earlier, but when I asked if they needed any help, I was told to leave them alone. After I show you around the ship, you're free to help the Smenteks."

Raymond began his tour below, in the hold. It was a dark cavernous space filled with huge crates. Dani found the creaking noises most unnerving for it seemed to her that at any moment the rivets holding the ship together might break and that the sea would rush in and claim them all. She was afraid of the hold and of the engine room where the noise was deafening, the men grimy, and the heat oppressive. The leers the men gave her as she passed made her uncomfortable.

"There's no need to worry that I'll ever go down there again," Dani gasped, filling her lungs with fresh air as she came up on deck.

Raymond stood with her for a few minutes before taking her back to the cabin. When they reached it he pointed to the section that contained the crew's sleeping quarters and warned her to stay away from the heavily barred iron door that separated the two areas.

"Most of them are a tough wild lot, Dani. I caution you about striking up any conversations. The men

64

become quite lonely for female company and you are a beautiful young woman. You understand don't you?"

Dani nodded. "I'm hardly what you would call beautiful but I'll heed your advice. Now show me where I may go."

She'll find out soon enough how attractive she is, Raymond thought. He only hoped she'd be cautious and guarded when she talked to strangers. She had looks, spirit, and elegance enough to wed a prosperous man. She did not look at all like a peasant. He pointed to one of the closed doors in her section. "That is the cabin occupied by the Smenteks. The other doors lead to the first mate's cabin and to a small storage area for our gear." He pointed to another door. "That is a wash-up area for your use. While you're below, you're to stay in this section."

Leading her back to the stairs, he took her to the same spot where the captain had left her on the previous evening. "This is where you may walk about. If the weather gets a little choppy, you must hang on to these ropes while walking. If the weather gets really rough, stay below. The decks get very slippery then, and we don't want you sliding under the rail to become food for the sharks."

Dani shivered at his words. It was so strange to think that a heavy steel ship could float on this vast expanse of water. She couldn't comprehend the engineering required to keep this massive thing afloat. A piece of steel immediately sank to the bottom so what was keeping them atop the waves? She came to the conclusion that God and brilliant men were responsible for the steady stream of progress and the innovations that made life more comfortable and interesting.

Raymond interrupted her thoughts. "If you think I'm trying to frighten you, I am. I've seen careless people go overboard a few times. If you're not familiar with seamanship it's best to take proper precautions. You will pay attention to all I've said, won't you?"

"Yes, Raymond, but up to now it's been so nice. It hardly feels as though we're moving. I love the sea."

"We're only two days out. Don't get overconfident. The weather can change in a very short time, and if it does, I won't have time to keep you under my wing. There's work waiting for me, so you run along and see what the Smenteks need. Try to get them to eat a little lunch while the sea is relatively steady. You can find your way to Kim, the cook. He'll understand the word lunch and you just hold up two fingers. He'll know its for the couple down the hall. I'll see you later this evening if I can."

Dani walked to the door Raymond had pointed out and knocked timidly. There was no response at first, but then she heard a weak "Enter." Opening the door, she saw a couple in their sixties. They looked very ill indeed. Both were squeezed into a single bunk, and a strong foul odor permeated the air. Looking down at the chamber pot near the bunk she noticed that the Smenteks had lost all the food they'd managed to get down. The smell of vomit was overpowering; she knew her first task was to clean out the pot. Throwing a towel over it, she gingerly picked it up and took it to the washing area, trying to breathe through her mouth. That unpleasant task done, she returned to the cabin and managed to pry open the porthole to let in fresh salty air. Within a few minutes, there was a noticeable difference in the room; the stench was receding. The couple hadn't spoken yet. They had merely looked at her with pleading sick eyes.

"I'll be back in a minute. I'm going to get a basin of water and see that you're clean and fresh again."

Going back to the washroom she took a basin from the shelf, poured water into it, and found a clean towel

66

and a bar of rough soap in the cabinet. Thoroughly prepared now, she made her way back to the inert pair who were lying just as she'd left them.

"Won't you please try to sit up for a minute, both of you? I know you'll feel much more comfortable after you've bathed. Just take deep breaths of the fresh air coming in from the porthole."

Mrs. Smentek was the first to groan and make an attempt to rise. Dani deftly maneuvered her into an upright position. In only two days, the woman's appearance had become unkempt. Her hair hung in clumps, and a fetid odor emanated from her soiled body and clothes. Dani opened the woman's dress and pulled it down around her shoulders. Dipping the cloth into the soapy water she began to wash her as thoroughly as possible under the confining circumstances. Then she pulled a clean dress from an open trunk that sat nearby and helped her change into it. By this time Mr. Smentek was sitting up, but he wouldn't permit Dani to minister to his needs. Instead, she helped him to the washroom, where he said he would clean himself even though he was unsteady on his feet. Promising to return in ten minutes, Dani hurried back to their cabin with clean sheets and changed the bed. "I'll wash out your underthings and dress," she told Mrs. Smentek. "They'll be dry by tomorrow. At least if your clothes are fresh you'll feel better."

Mrs. Smentek now managed to speak, although her voice was weak and shaky. "Thank you, my dear. I'm usually a strong, capable woman, and I can't understand this feeling that's come over us just from riding the waves. I never expected to feel this horrid. My husband and I had heard of seasickness, but we never thought it would happen to us. We thought it only struck weak people and that the trip would be so easy. The man who comes in once in a while tells us the sea is calm. God knows I'll throw myself overboard if a storm comes up."

"Don't carry on so, Mrs. Smentek. The captain tells me you'll feel ever so much better if you can manage to walk around and eat some food, even a little. We'll try some lunch as soon as I help your husband back. Then, if you can manage to sit on deck for a while, I'm sure you'll feel even better. The ship doesn't seem to roll so much when you're above, and you and your husband can sit on a stack of canvas and relax for an hour or so."

"We'll see," Mrs. Smentek answered through clenched lips.

Dani helped Samuel Smentek back into the room and warned the pair not to lie down again.

"I'll be back with something light for lunch, and you must promise me you'll try to get a few spoonfuls down," she said as she left them.

Upon entering the galley, Dani raised two fingers and said the word "lunch" to Kim. He smiled wickedly and put some food on a tray. When he had handed her the food he waved her away from his domain.

Back in the cabin Dani uncovered the tray. She noted broth, tea, and crackers. Sitting on their bunk, the Smenteks eyed the food suspiciously. If only I can coax them into eating a little, Dani thought. Placing the tray on the stand by the bunk, she poured the tea and, stirring a little sugar into it, handed them each a cup.

"Try to take a sip or two. We'll see if it stays down."

With shaky hands, both brought their cups to their lips. They managed to take tiny sips while Dani urged them on until each had drunk a half cup. All three then waited expectantly although Dani tried to keep their minds occupied by talking about the ship, describing the areas she had seen. After ten minutes, when there was no recurrence of their agony, she handed each a cracker. "Chew on this and then we'll try the soup." Each nibbled on a cracker and then managed a few spoonfuls of the clear broth.

"Good." Dani said proudly. "Now let's see if you both can walk down the corridor and then come back to your room."

They looked horrified at the mere suggestion, but they gave it a try, walking slowly and holding on to each other for support. By the time they returned to the cabin, both were exhausted and perspiring. Dani was elated. It was a major accomplishment. They had finally eaten real food even though it was only a little. She praised them handsomely and then urged them to lie down again. Thank goodness they were thin people, she thought, or they wouldn't be comfortable in such a cramped space. At least there was a space of a few inches between their bodies. If they stayed perfectly still, the bunk would be bearable.

"I'll check on you later," Dani announced. "At dinner time I know you can eat something if you try. Rest now. I think the worst is over and you're beginning to get used to the roll of the ship."

Happily she left the cabin. Now she had something to do and someone to occupy her mind on the long voyage. If they felt better later, she would take them on deck and after dinner they could pass some time talking.

Captain Murow was busy that evening, but he cordially invited her and the Smenteks to use his cabin for the evening meal. She escorted them up to his quarters and they squeezed around his table while Raymond brought the meal on a large tray.

The Smenteks' faces blanched when they saw the strange concoction heaped on the platter. Whatever it is, Dani thought, it smells so good. It was a welcome change from her usual drab meals back in Ruda where

69

the nightly fare was monotonously the same—stew or soup . . . if you were fortunate enough to have the money to buy a tough piece of beef or a good bone with a few strips of meat on it. When you didn't have the means to do so, supper consisted of whatever you could throw together: Kapusta, cabbage with a few mushrooms and a potato mixed in, or nelesniki, pancakes rolled with jelly. There was always enough jelly because every summer Dani and the other women hired a rickety wagon to take them on a three-day excursion to a place where they picked berries to preserve. Almost all the women and children participated in this annual event and it was a welcome diversion. While picking, they ate their fill of berries, stuffing themselves with the seldom seen fruit. When they returned to the village the fruit they brought was shared with those who couldn't make the trip so that every family had at least a few jars of tangy jelly or preserves for the winter months when food was more costly. On a slab of bread it made a good breakfast, and many a time a slab of bread and a dollop of jelly was all they had for breakfast, lunch, and supper.

Raymond explained that the dish he'd set before the trio was Chinese. It was made up of pieces of pork, shrimp with pea pods, and slivered almonds, all in a thick sauce. Clara and Samuel took one look at each other and shook their heads negatively. They rose from their seats, their mouths clamped shut.

"Wait," Dani pleaded. "Here's a bowl of plain rice too. Surely you can have some of that with a cup of tea?"

Reluctantly, they sat down again and agreed to try small portions of rice which they nibbled while Dani heaped her plate with the tempting foreign dish. It was one of the best meals she had ever tasted. The Smenteks looked at her enviously. Oh, to be young and hearty enough to face all the trials and tribulations of life.

Samuel's stomach rumbled in loud protest of the deprivation it had suffered the last few days.

"Enough is enough," he roared. "Clara, we'll conquer this sickness if it's the last thing we do. We must be strong when we get to the new country, not weak babies to be carried off the ship. This young girl puts us to shame. We must make every attempt to overcome this debilitating agony. Danuta, please serve us each a small portion."

Dani quickly did as she was told.

"Clara, use all your will power and concentrate only on chewing. Don't think of where we are. Think only of bright new places, the country we're going to, seeing your children and grandchildren for the first time. Now chew."

Clara did as her husband ordered, being used to obeying him all their married life. As they slowly ate what was on their plates, Samuel began talking in an attempt to keep his wife's mind occupied with thoughts other than the movement of the *Destiny*. He tried to tell Dani a little of what their lives had been like in Poland.

"My wife and I come from the outskirts of Warsaw. I was a caretaker in a large cemetery there. We have three sons; five other children died at birth or in infancy. We saved for many years to accumulate enough money to emigrate to New York. Years ago we had enough to send our children, and after they left we kept on saving to join them. We never realized it would take so many years to get enough to go ourselves. Originally we'd planned to join our sons in five years but with the economic situation in Poland, it became more difficult to put aside the extra zloty. We wrote, telling our sons to go on with their lives without us, and then unexpectedly, a few months ago, they sent us the extra money necessary for passage. Although all three

71

are married and have families to support, they somehow managed to put together the additional sum we needed. At first we wanted to decline this generosity, but it became clear that if we didn't leave Poland now, perhaps we would never see our children again. It would be stupid to let our pride keep us from seeing the new generation.

"When we arrived in Gdansk there were no ships leaving for the United States, but someone said the *Destiny* should be in soon and occasionally she took on passengers. You see, Danuta, we found out our papers were practically useless; the government isn't allowing ordinary departures." Samuel swallowed another mouthful of shrimp. "Well, we slept outside for a week because we couldn't afford a hotel, and finally we saw the *Destiny* dock. Captain Murow was sorry, but he had no room for us. You see, your father and brother were supposed to have our cabin. We begged the captain to allow us just enough space to lie down anywhere; we promised we wouldn't get in the way. After much pleading, he put us in the cabin but he said we could stay only if your family didn't make the sailing date. When you were the only one to sail, we were fortunate because we were allowed to keep the room. Not that I want you to be separated from your family, my dear, but that's how it worked out. I have a feeling, though, that once we were on board the captain wouldn't have asked us to leave. He would have found some other space for us had your father and brother decided to sail. The captain is a sympathetic man who realizes how difficult it has become to leave the country, and he'll help anyone he can but only one or two at a time. He could lose his job if the authorities discovered that he was bringing Poles out of the country. If the Germans had any suspicion they would be sure to protest to the American government, but in the last two years he's managed to bring fifteen people across to New York."

"I guess it was meant to be that I travel alone," Dani said, shrugging her shoulders. "If we had arrived a day later we would have missed the ship as I was hoping we would. . . . Well, I'm glad both of you were finally able to eat something. Would you like to go on deck now? I'll show you where we may sit, and you can rest there awhile before going to bed."

Clara was reluctant to explore, but Samuel firmly took her by the arm.

"Show us the way, Danuta. I'd like to smoke my pipe for a spell."

She led them on deck, where they settled themselves amid the tarpaulins and enjoyed the night breezes.

Samuel tamped the tobacco firmly down into his pipe. When he lit it the pleasant aroma mingled with the salty air. They enjoyed a companionable silence for a few moments and then he softly continued his story.

"When we arrive in New York, there should be quite a celebration. Our three sons will be waiting with their wives and, between them, ten grandchildren: five boys and five girls. It will take hours just to keep everyone's names straight in our heads."

Clara finally lost some of her temerity and sighed happily.

"I can't wait to see our sons. Will we recognize them I wonder? It's been almost twenty years. They were young men when we last saw them and now one is forty, another thirty-eight and the youngest thirty-four. How did the time pass so swiftly?"

"We'll recognize them Clara," Samuel assured her. "Don't worry so."

"Raymond was telling me we have to register with immigration as soon as we dock." Dani put in. "Captain Murow will wire ahead and try to get us through in a hurry. Some people have to wait a long time, and some are detained if it's suspected they are ill or have some other problem, but the captain has a friend who is an inspector at immigration and he'll use his influence to get us passed through as quickly as possible."

"Immigration? No one told us of them. I wonder if the children know of this."

"I'm sure they do, Mr. Smentek. If not, you can give the captain their address and he can wire them too. Isn't it fascinating how messages can fly through wires in minutes? Someday the scientists will find a way to make people travel almost as fast."

The Smenteks smiled at one another in the dim light. It was wonderful to be young and to have your head filled with foolish dreams. Wasn't this ship with its engines fast enough? They would be in America in a few weeks instead of the months it once took. And then there were trains, miracles of speed. Nothing faster could be invented. We have reached the height of speed, Samuel thought.

Dani continued happily. "Maybe someday we'll be traveling to the stars. Wouldn't that be a marvelous trip?"

Now Samuel and Clara laughed out loud. "Keep your dreams, little one. All too soon you grow old and there aren't many dreams left. Right now I only dream of seeing my family, working hard, and getting to know my new country. My eldest son has found work for me in a cemetery in New York. Basically it will be the same type of work I've done all my life, being a caretaker. My son said I didn't have to work, that it was time for me to retire and rest, but I disagree. I'll work and earn our keep until the day I die. My eldest has a three-room apartment for us in the attic of his home. He says it's small but there is room for Clara and me to be comfortable. How easily he forgets that we raised three children in three rooms in Warsaw. Now the children talk of apartments with six and even seven rooms. I fear it will take us a long time to get used to our new life and to the prosperity that seems to flourish in America if you're willing to work hard." Samuel's pipe died out while he was talking, then he rose slowly, helping Clara to her feet. "It's time to retire for the night. Come. Thank you, Danuta, for all you've done for us. I'm sure the rest of the voyage will be more bearable because of you."

"Good night," Clara added. "We'll see you in the morning, yes?"

Dani saw them to the stairs and then returned to her spot on deck to dream awhile longer.

The next week went well. The weather was calm, and the ship had no difficulty plowing through the sea. All three of the passengers were content to eat light breakfasts and lunches in the cramped cabins where they joined each other for company. Once in a while either Clara or Samuel vomited up the food, but generally they retained what they ate. Every few days Captain Murow joined them for a simple dinner in his cabin. On these occasions, he spent his time teaching all three a smattering of English. To his delight he discovered Dani knew a few phrases and he could hold a short conversation with her in the English tongue. The Smenteks looked on in amazement and even managed to speak a few simple words themselves. Raymond had a little time to spend with them too, and he enjoyed telling them stories about their soon-to-be homeland. They marveled as he described the eastern states, the Midwest, the desert region, and the green forests of the Northwest. Such a vast country they thought, hearing him talk. It must be immense to have such diverse climates and scenery, and to be host to so many nationalities.

As the days passed Raymond was getting more apprehensive about Dani relaxing on the deck late in the evening. He knew harm might come to her, not in the daylight hours for one never knew where the captain would pop up next but the black nights could be treacherous. He had heard the remarks some of the men made as they lay in their bunks, and he hadn't liked what he'd heard. Repeatedly, he warned Dani to keep away from everyone except the captain and himself, even though she laughed when he became overprotective. Dani did obey him except for one starlit night when she wandered to another section of the deck. In the dim light she made her way aft although it was a prohibited area. She was tired of sitting amongst the tarps and walking along her curtailed path. Seeing not a soul about and hearing no sounds except those made by the waves dashing against the hull, she was positive she wouldn't be disturbed. She thought most of the men would be below or at their stations so late at night. It felt wonderfully free to be able to walk the length of the ship, watch the wake made by the great propellers, and feel the sea wind blow through her hair. After standing at the rail a few minutes, she felt a rough hand clamp down across her mouth before she had any inkling anyone was behind her. Kicking and scratching, she was thrown down amidst coils of rope, and a large brutish man threw himself atop her as he muttered words in a guttural language she couldn't understand. Suddenly, he relinquished the suffocating grip over her mouth and nose to tear away the bodice of her dress with one mighty swoop while his other hand forced her wrists behind her. Dani let out one loud cry for help before he swore and covered her mouth again, this time with his own. His breath reeked of sour whiskey and decaying food particles. Why wasn't anyone coming? Hoisting her dress above her waist, he began tearing her underpants away, the material biting into her tender skin. She cried silently. Oh, Raymond, why didn't I listen to you? Why did I think nothing could happen? Now he was forcing her legs apart, and she was powerless to stop him for he must have been three times her size. Her futile attempts at kicking were useless. As he threw the remains of her underpants to the side, she felt something hard and terrifying forcing itself between her legs and she knew she was going to be raped. Rough fingers were being forced into her although she had tensed her muscles to resist the probing filth about to penetrate her body. She gasped for enough air to give her strength but she knew she was losing the battle. Her unknown assailant was smothering her with his tremendous weight.

Suddenly a great beam of light encircled her and chaos followed as several sailors dragged their mate, screaming obscenities, off her. Shamed, Dani clutched her torn clothes around her and gathered up her torn pants from on the deck. She wished she had the courage to throw herself overboard, but just then Raymond came running up to clear away the amused spectators. Throwing his shirt around her he led her back to her cabin where she huddled on her bunk, miserable, afraid to look him in the eye.

"He didn't hurt you did he, Dani?"

"No," she mumbled.

Raymond was embarrassed. "I mean he didn't complete his evil act did he? He didn't, well you must know what I'm trying to ask?"

"No, Raymond, but it was dreadful." Her mouth, breasts, and wrists were bruised from the assault, and her arms felt as though they had been wrenched from their sockets. Her inner thigh, which the attacker had violently pinched, hurt, and her head throbbed unbearably as tears of shock streamed down her cheeks.

Raymond comforted her. "Yes, I know it was awful, but as long as there was no harm done, I think we had best forget the incident. Eric is an excellent worker and this is the first time he's had too much to drink in months. He won't even remember what happened in the morning. When he's told what happened, he'll totally ashamed of himself. I wouldn't like to see the captain get rid of a good man over this. The men will keep quiet if you do. Please, Dani, it wasn't all his fault. What were you doing there anyway?"

"I just wanted to walk the whole length of the ship, just one time, instead of staying in one little corner. Raymond, I thought no one was about. I was positive. I didn't see a soul, so I waited and then walked for a few minutes. I was going to go right back when that horrible man came up behind me. I know I was wrong, but he should be punished. What if he tries again?"

"He won't, I promise you. You won't set eyes on him the rest of the journey. Dani, listen to me. It would be disastrous for Eric's family if he lost his job. He drinks a bit and he'd have a hard time getting another. What triggered his attack on you was too much drink and the stories the men were telling each other about what they'd like to do to you. I told you earlier you are a beautiful woman, and the men were aware of that as soon as you came on board. They've spent the last few evenings fantasizing about your body, and tonight when Gordon brought out a bottle of whiskey, Eric took too much."

Dani was outraged. "They talk about my body? What kind of pigs are they?"

Raymond answered her quietly. "Dani, some of them are normal lusty men, but others are crude and ignorant. They spend all of their shore time in houses of ill repute and they drink a lot, aboard and ashore, but Eric will be afraid now. The captain, if he finds out, will fire him and he will order you to stay in your cabin. He runs a tight ship. Please, for me, won't you keep quiet?"

Dani hesitated, then reluctantly agreed. She did not want to spend the voyage in her cabin.

"All right. You're sure I won't come across him again?"

"You won't. That's a promise. Thank you. Now remember to stay where you belong from now on. I won't be responsible if you traipse around the ship after dark. Here you're close to the captain's quarters so no one will dare to bother you. Now get some sleep."

Raymond left the cabin quietly, his conscience nagging him. Naturally he was outraged at the aborted attempt at rape, but on the other hand, he wanted to taste the sweetness of Dani's body himself. Each day he was more attracted to this girl although he knew she was too young for him. She was practically a babe, yet she had the sensuality of a grown woman. Obviously she was not aware of the potent effect she had on men. With Dani, Raymond thought, I would be gentle. I would slowly awaken her blossoming body to the pleasures of love. Then he cursed himself for his evil thoughts and went to his locker to swig a large gulp of bourbon. But the liquor did not quench his inner fire. He only wanted her all the more. He damned Eric for almost getting what he wanted more.

Dani turned the lamp high and began to mend her torn clothes. She worked diligently till long past midnight. Raymond needn't worry about her roaming around again. How could she possibly face any of the men now after some of them had witnessed her near rape? The story certainly would be well circulated by morning. Blushing, she imagined the leers and coarse comments it would evoke. But she worried about facing the grinning crew in vain, for during the night a powerful storm hit without warning. A clap of thunder, loud enough to drown out the noise of the engines, woke Dani just as dawn was breaking. She looked out the porthole and in the dim light saw streaks of forked lightning piercing black rolling clouds. The waves grew higher as she gazed at the sea and she could feel the ship list. With amazement she realized she had to sway from side to side with the movement or lose her balance completely. Stumbling to the bunk she fell against it as a great wave hit the ship. Pushing aside her feeling of alarm, she thought of Samuel and Clara, and decided to dress. She found it easier to sit on the bunk and pull her clothes over her head. Trying to stand only made her bounce around crazily. She didn't waste time trying to get her boots out from under the bunk. Barefoot, she made her way to the Smenteks' door, calling out to them loudly as she knocked. The wind was rising steadily, and its power could be felt even below decks as Dani pushed open the door.

Unable to speak, Samuel and Clara sat on the bunk, hanging on to each other, their faces a pasty gray. She could tell by the odor in the stuffy air that they had heaved up last night's dinner, and looking down she saw the chamber pot sliding along the deck with each roll of the ship and spilling out its nauseating contents. Clara was whimpering. "We're going to die aren't we? We'll never make it to New York. I knew it was too good to be true."

"Clara, don't carry on so. Both of you must get up and make your way to my cabin. With the ship rolling so crazily I'll never be able to clean up in here. Come along. We can all sit on my bunk and pray. Please get up. Hurry, I'll help you."

Samuel made the effort first, managing to put his feet down. He helped Dani raise Clara to a sitting position; then they all stumbled along, clinging to the walls of the cabin. In the passageway Dani noted water seeping down the stairwell and the small puddle at the foot of the stairs was growing at an alarming rate. When they reached Dani's cabin, they sat down hard on the bunk, Clara in the middle, and they held each other as the minutes ticked slowly by. After a while they noticed a trickle of water seeping under the cabin door. They leaned as far back as they could, tucking their legs beneath them, and for what seemed like hours they stayed in that same position, hypnotized as they watched sea water slowly enter the room. Soon the water was sloshing from side to side and getting higher and higher.

"Isn't anyone going to come down to tell us what's happening?" Dani shouted above the din. "Are they just going to leave us here to drown?"

Summoning up all the courage she could muster, she decided to try to find someone—anyone—who could take them to a safer place to wait out the storm.

"I'll be back as soon as I can," she explained to the petrified couple. "I'll check the other cabins and see if anyone's about, and if not, I'll try to make my way through the steel door to the crew's quarters. Someone has to be around."

"Don't go on deck," warned Samuel. "You'll surely be washed overboard."

"Don't leave," Clara begged. "You'll be hurt. Maybe it's worse on the other side of the door and you'll only let in more water."

"It can't be worse," Dani reasoned. "I promise I'll be back in a little while. I'll only go to the other side of the door." Grabbing onto the doorknob she pulled herself into an upright position, holding her skirts up high. The salt water swirled about her as she carefully made her way down the hall to the door Raymond had told her led to forbidden territory. She saw it was bolted from her side and she struggled, finally pulling the bolt free. Tugging at the handle, she tried to turn it but it was stuck fast. Frustrated, she turned away and headed for the other doors, checking to see if any of the rooms were occupied although that seemed unlikely. Occasionally she had seen the first mate going to his room late in the evening, but he had only smiled in passing and said a quiet good night. He didn't speak her language. The cabins were empty, but in the storage room she saw a steel bar hanging on a wall.

Grasping the bar firmly, she waded back to the door leading to the crew's quarters and began pounding frantically on the handle. Nothing happened. Disgusted with her weakness, Dani slammed the bar against the door, hoping someone would hear the resounding noise. The sound of metal hitting metal made an earsplitting crash in the corridor. Suddenly the handle began turning and the door opened. A huge man, who stood well over six feet and had skin as black as coal, stood there, a scowl on his face. For a few seconds they stood staring at each other. Dani was sure the devil was coming to claim her. She shuddered violently and fainted, dropping with a splash into the water at her feet.

"Oh, Lordy," the man cried in dismay. "What have we here?" He picked up the soaking wet slip of a girl, carried her through the door, and placed her on the nearest bunk. He had gone below to get more rope when he'd heard the noise and wondered who was making such a racket. His first thought was that a beam had split in the maelstrom. Puzzled as to what to do with the unconscious girl he hurried back on deck to find Raymond.

Five minutes later, Amos, the black stoker, and Raymond stared down at Dani. Water dripped from her clothes as she lay sprawled across the bunk.

"Honest, Mr. Raymond, I didn't do nothing. I just heard this great clanging on the door, and when I opened it she took one look at me and fainted dead away. I didn't touch a hair on her head except to lift her and put her on the bunk. Couldn't leave her wallowing in the water, could I? She might have drowned."

Raymond laughed and patted Amos on the back. "Take it easy. I believe you, Amos. I think she's never seen a Negro and you frightened the wits out of her. You are a scary creature, you old reprobate. You're like one of those voodoo priests we saw in Haiti, you with your evil grin."

Dani's eyes fluttered open. When she saw her nemesis still looming in her line of vision, she opened her mouth to scream, but Raymond's face came into view. She was safe then. But why was he laughing at her?

"Dani, Dani, it's nothing. Surely you've heard of black men. Well, you've just met your first. This is Amos, one of our engine-room crew, not a figure out of a nightmare. Amos is a gentle man, not a monster. He only opened the door to see who was making all the noise."

By now Dani was totally ashamed of herself. Her face flushed crimson as she looked up at Amos. "I'm sorry, it's just that we were all so frightened. We thought the ship was sinking and I went looking for help."

Amos didn't understand a word she was saying so Raymond quickly translated for the black man who now smiled broadly, which only made Dani feel worse. God, how stupid she felt.

Raymond lurched as another wave hit the ship. "Amos, carry her back to her bunk and see if the Smenteks can help her out of her wet clothes. I'm needed on deck and you'd better hightail it back to the engine room. We'll need every hand we have for the next few hours."

The powerful man lifted Dani easily as if she were a baby, and he toted her, Raymond following, back to the cabin. The Smenteks screamed in alarm upon seeing the soaked girl, but she quickly told them she was all right.

Then Raymond spoke from the doorway.

"Help her get into dry clothes and just sit tight. There'll be no meals for a while, but we should be out of the storm soon, hopefully by nightfall."

"Are we going to sink?" Samuel asked, fear in his heart as the ship careened madly.

Amos and Raymond appeared unconcerned. "Just stay put. We've been through worse storms than this and come out fine. Don't be alarmed by the water coming in. It won't get much higher, and as soon as things are back to normal it will be pumped out. The steel door is watertight so the water's only in this section. I'll be back in a few hours. Remember, Dani, no more venturing outside this room." Amos grinned and waved at them as they left while Raymond wished with all his heart that he could stay and comfort Dani by putting his arms around her and kissing away her fright.

Shivering, Dani stood in the water while Clara rummaged through her trunk and found dry clothing. Samuel turned his face to the wall as Clara briskly removed Dani's dress and undergarments and toweled her dry. Seeing the tiny girl wet and dripping brought out all Clara's motherly instincts and her own personal fright was pushed aside for the moment. She slipped a dry dress over Dani's head, being careful not to let the hem slip into the water. Then they both sat on the bunk again and dried their feet before curling them up beneath themselves for warmth. Dani's new boots floated out from the underside of the bunk and she snatched them out of the water. They are ruined, she thought ruefully, and they are the only ones I have.

The water didn't rise any higher, but the ship rose and fell sickeningly until it seemed about to plunge to the bottom of the ocean. The bunk was thoroughly soaked as were its occupants who, teeth chattering, held damp blankets around their shoulders. Two hours later, the storm abated slightly and they were finally able to sit without being bounced against one another. Slowly the light outside became brighter; the water receded somewhat; and Samuel, Clara, and Dani relaxed. The worst was over. They voiced their thankfulness, rummaged around for drier clothing, and welcomed the hot soup and tea Raymond brought when darkness fell. Fortunately the mattress was waterproof, and a change of sheets and blankets in both cabins helped them regain their natural body warmth.

The days that followed the storm were calm. The sea was smooth and even the Smenteks were soon back to eating normally. For Dani the storm proved a blessing in disguise. Her encounter with Eric seemed to have been forgotten because everyone talked only of the storm and of the damage done to the ship.

Captain Murow had been very busy assessing repairs

but he invited them to a relatively lavish dinner of roasted chicken and potatoes on what he said was to be their last night on the open water.

Over dessert, an apple cobbler Kim had baked, the captain made his announcement. "Tomorrow we'll sight New York. By evening we should be docked. All three of you will have to check in with immigration, but there's no need to worry. I have a friend in a high position there. He'll pass you through with no problems. Dani, Mr. and Mrs. Smentek, for a token fee of five dollars each you won't have to go through the medical inspection which can be most degrading and embarrassing. I'll write a note and have Raymond take you through the processing. If I had enough time, I'd take you through myself. All you need do is state your name, birth date, country of origin, and your final destination. You'll then be given the necessary papers and will be free to leave. Dani, Raymond will see you to the train station. Mr. and Mrs. Smentek, if no one is around to meet you, Raymond will see that someone takes you to your son's home although I did send a wire to the address you gave me and there should be no problem."

Dani did quick calculations in her head. Five dollars was a great deal of money. She explained the amount in zloty to Samuel.

"It's an exorbitant amount," he protested.

"But well worth it I assure you," the captain answered. "Not everyone at immigration is kind and understanding. Some foreigners are detained, you know. They don't pass the medical test, if the inspector takes an unexplainable dislike. They're quarantined for several days or weeks to be sure they're carrying no disease into the country. I know what I'm suggesting is dishonest, but that's the way it goes. Money always talks. By paying you're assured of speedy processing."

Reluctantly, they agreed with him and then said their good-nights slowly, each thinking of tomorrow when they would be on firm land again. Would it be a welcoming land or would they be greeted with hostility?

Clara and Samuel were exhausted and went immediately to their bunk, but Dani was charged with nervous anticipation. She decided to spend a few hours on the safe section of the deck, marking time, aware that each minute brought her closer to a new life. She settled her back against the smallest tarp and gazed up at the dark sky that was filled with thousands of stars, bright and dim. She started counting them, a futile pastime. The stars were countless. A footstep broke her reverie and she jumped up, fear threading its way through her body as she expected another drunken encounter with Eric, but it was only Raymond. He stood before her, his slight build and curly hair framed by the moonlight.

"I didn't mean to frighten you, Dani," he apologized as he pulled her down gently to sit beside him. "It's our last night together and I thought you'd be feeling the excitement of the end of the voyage. I love the sea, but I always get the greatest feeling when we near land."

His hand trembled slightly as he touched her silken cheek. "If I'm thrilled, the feeling you're experiencing must be magnified a hundredfold."

Dani nodded. "I feel frightened, yet it's a pleasant fright. That sounds nonsensical, doesn't it? It's impossible to feel both at the same time."

"Not at all, my dear. I understand what you're saying."

"Oh, Raymond, do you really? I'm too nervous to sleep. I'd like to just spend the rest of the night sitting out here. I'm going to miss being on this ship even though I'm in a hurry to see my aunt."

87

Raymond clasped her hand in his.

"Then tonight you shall have your wish. I'm off duty till morning and I'll sit with you. We'll keep each other company until we see dawn breaking over the horizon. It's a wondrous sight."

Dani snuggled against his shoulder and he put his arm protectively around her.

"Lean back, Dani, and be comfortable. I won't hurt you."

They sat in companionable silence for a long while, and Dani wondered at his reticence. His words usually flowed nonstop whenever they were together, but they were friends and good friends could share peaceful moments without the need for chatter.

Raymond could no longer hold back the passion throbbing in his body. He turned Dani's face toward him, tentatively kissing the sweet full lips that always smiled enticingly at him. His soft kiss became more demanding and suddenly his tongue was exploring the inside of her mouth. Then, in a rush of hot desire, his lips slid down to her neck. He murmured endearments as a loud pounding erased the outside world.

Shocked at first, Dani wanted to push him away, but instead she relaxed and joined him in another kiss. Hesitant at first, she soon matched his ardor. She could feel the first innocent stirrings of womanhood and they felt good. When his hand caressed her covered breast, she didn't flinch away from this new experience but kissed him deeply, this time letting her tongue dart around his. Her pulse quickened and then they were no longer sitting but were half sprawled along the deck.

By this time Raymond had lost all control. His vow to keep his distance forgotten, he slid his hand up her leg to the ultimate area of satisfaction.

As his fingers touched what he desired most, Dani

pushed him away, guilt flushing through her body. Angry at her compliant folly, she lashed out at Raymond, negating her participation, her exploration of unfamiliar territory.

"You're no better than Eric," she said accusingly. "You tell me to stay away from the other men only because you think you'll be the one to get what they want. I suppose you'll have a jolly time telling the rest of them how you won out."

Raymond stood up and silently walked to the rail until the proof of his desire settled back into normalcy.

"Bastard," he said to himself. "You no-good bastard, she's right."

The full realization of his perfidy left him limp and as he turned to make his apologies he dreaded to meet the accusation in her eyes.

"Forgive me . . . I had no right. But, you see, I love you. In the short while we've been together, I've found myself wanting to spend the rest of my life with you—wanting to teach you how wonderful love can be, to take care of you, to be with you every night. But that's impossible. You're far too young to tie yourself down before you've experienced what life has to offer. You've many men to meet and choose from. You weren't meant for a lonely sailor who'd leave you for weeks at a time. You see, I can't have it both ways. I can't leave the sea—it's in my blood—and I can't consider asking for your hand if I must leave you alone so much until I decide to settle down." Raymond sat again, but he kept a respectable distance between them. "Say you'll forgive me."

His voice broke on the last words of his plea, and Dani felt sorry for this man who had become her friend in these few weeks at sea.

"It wasn't your fault." She knew she had been a will-

89

ing participant in this new game. "Raymond, don't apologize. It was as much my fault as yours. I enjoyed your kisses. I wanted you to do what you did. It's never happened before and I was curious."

"Can we call a truce then? If I come to Chicago in a few years, would you be willing to see me again? Could we at least meet as two old friends and perhaps see what develops?"

"Of course we can." Dani laughed. "We'll have a great time and I'll welcome you with open arms and we'll celebrate."

Raymond breathed a sigh of relief. The gods had smiled upon him tonight. All was not lost. In a few years, if she still remembered him, he would try again to capture her heart. He certainly wouldn't forget her, and if he started saving, by that time he would have enough money to give her the kind of life she deserved. Time would tell. If they were meant to be together, a few years wouldn't make a difference.

"You'd better get some sleep, Dani. We've a lot to do tomorrow." He kissed her chastely on the cheek. "Good night, sweet one. Have happy dreams. I shall."

"Good night, Raymond. You are a truly wonderful person, the best man in the whole world." Her laughter trilled through the quiet night as he led her to the stairs.

Raymond went to his bunk frustrated. The women he'd met had always been willing to share his bed and his ardor. But Dani was different. She deserved his respect, and even though he regretted not having her, he was glad she'd stopped him. She was special.

By early morning Dani, Clara, and Samuel were on deck, straining to see the first signs of land. Dani was the first to spot specks of green on the horizon. A minute later Clara and Samuel were also able to make out the faint traces of their new homeland. Too excited to leave the rail, they brought their lunch on deck and continued to watch America loom larger and larger. By evening they were awed by the sight of the tall buildings and of the famous statue of liberty holding her torch on high. The good captain had brought them safely to the fabled land of plenty. How sweet the air smelled, how they were blessed.

Chapter Four

The apprehensive trio passed through immigration smoothly, bypassing any unnecessary delay as the good captain had promised. Earlier in the morning they had agreed that five dollars each was well worth the price of comfortable entry into a country that had an aura of the unknown and unexpected. The Smenteks, for all of their sixty-odd years, thought of authorities in terms of terror and interrogation. Dani, having come from a small village, had never had any traffic with police or investigators, but Samuel, who had lived in Warsaw, keenly desired as little contact with inspectors as possible. Before they had left the ship, Dani had argued that five dollars was a fortune and should be reported to the inspector's superior, but seeing the fright on Samuel's face, she had changed her mind and had agreed to keep silent and to slip the money unobtrusively into the right hand.

The fortresslike immigration building was fairly quiet, although you could hear faint mutterings behind closed doors. Their steps sounded loudly as they walked down a long hall, Captain Murow leading the way, until they were ensconced in a small dingy office in which dull gray paint was flaking off the walls. The unfamiliar odor of antiseptic mingled with the smells of sweat and fear. Despite a show of bravado, they were full of trepidation as they awaited the attention of the officer who would or would not allow them entry into the country. Captain Murow spoke for a few minutes to the stern-looking man who silently filled out papers and then stamped the documents after asking several easy-to-answer questions. Not once did a smile break across the man's face, and Clara began to tremble from fear that they would be detained or, worse, put back on another ship headed for Poland. Within an hour they were out of the building, breathing a collective sigh of relief because the ordeal was over. Noting that Raymond was waiting for them, the captain headed back to his ship after being hugged and thanked so profusely he was totally embarrassed by the parting.

Samuel and Clara's sons suddenly appeared with their families, a huge welcoming committee. They cried with happiness over the long-due reunion. In the joyful melee, Dani and Raymond stood back, forgotten amid the excitement. At last Samuel regained his manners and turned to encircle Dani's shoulders proudly.

"You must meet our benefactress and ministering angel. Without this young lady I fear your mother and I would have arrived in a very poor state of health. This tiny little slip of a girl shamed us with her bravery and forced us to follow her lead. If it weren't for Danuta we would have made a long voyage without a bite of food passing through our mouths, but she coaxed us into forgetting our misery. Meet my family, Danuta and Raymond, meet them all."

Rounds of introductions were made until names and faces became a blur. There were just too many to remember: sons, daughters-in-law, children, friends. Dani was thoroughly confused. Samuel insisted she come home with them and spend a few nights resting

94

before she continued her long journey, but Raymond politely interrupted and refused the generous invitation.

"I'm afraid tonight's train is leaving soon and I must get Dani on it. Tomorrow we'll be too busy unloading cargo; then we have to prepare for another voyage, an exciting one this time. We'll be making several stops in the Caribbean and in South America. It's been a long while since I've had the pleasure of visiting those exotic lands. Generally it's a smooth trip, and I can't wait to revisit so many of the places I haven't seen for three years so it's best if I get Dani off as quickly as possible. I promised her aunt, you know. She's been waiting for too long already."

Dani, Samuel, and Clara cried over the separation and promised to write often to keep each other abreast of their new lives. After prolonged tears, Raymond managed to pull Dani into a waiting taxi and to hustle her off to the station from which the train was due to depart in fifteen minutes. In a trance, she marveled at being inside a real automobile, and although the taxi stalled several times and frightened several horses, it did get them to the station in plenty of time. Dani was awed by the size of the lofty brick building they entered, and she was impressed by the train, a sleek-looking monster. The engine belched out puffs of black smoke and cinders. To Dani it was far more frightening than the ship that had brought her to America. Raymond led her to a seat and tried to calm her for he noticed Dani's eyes darting to and fro as if she did not know what to expect next. The crowds made her dizzy, and although she had studied English long and hard, everyone spoke too fast for her to understand a word. So much for her pride. She had thought she could walk right into a new country and become a part of it instantly, but she now felt more of an alien than ever for not once did she hear a single familiar Polish word.

"These trains are really quite safe, Dani. Before you know it, you'll be at the station in Chicago, your travels over. Look, here's a hamper of food Kim made up for you to eat on the way. Sometimes it's difficult to buy anything at the stops and I'd rather you didn't go into the dining car. It's quite expensive and the hustle and bustle will frighten you. You're not traveling first class so you won't get preferred privileges. Stay on the train even when it stops to pick up passengers and everything will be fine. Goodbye, Dani. I'll get to Chicago one of these days when you're all grown up. I love you, you know, but I want you to have time to learn what love is. When all your boyfriends begin to ask for your hand, keep a tiny bit of fondness for this old man. But if you find a man you feel you can't live without, someone you love with all your heart, then do the right thing and be happy."

More tears threatened to overflow. "Oh, Raymond, you're my friend and you're not old. Thirty is young. How can I ever repay your kindness? Without you I wouldn't have known what to do. I'd never have found my way to the train or managed to secure a taxi. You've been so helpful and good to me. I know the captain helped, but not as conscientiously as you. Please come to Chicago the first chance you get. It will be good to see you again. Promise me you'll come soon."

"I will, my little beauty. Now get yourself settled and try to sleep tonight if you can. It's going to be a few days before you get to Chicago and you want to be rested."

Just then a woman stopped in the aisle, waiting for the seat next to Dani. She seemed to understand a little of what was being said and broke in gently, speaking a halting English. "Don't worry. I'm going to Chicago and no one will bother her. She'll be perfectly fine with me."

"Thank you," Raymond answered. He kissed Dani with care. "Be happy in your new life."

The train let out a bellowing whistle, and Raymond hurried to leap off before it moved. Dani pressed her nose against the dirty window to watch until Raymond was out of sight. Her very own friend was leaving and she was going to miss him terribly. He wasn't what you would call handsome, but he was very strong and manly for his size. Years of hard work had toughened him to the point where his muscular frame could stand up to any man's and yet he was gentle too. One could talk to him as though he were a longstanding family friend. His closeness these past weeks hadn't stirred any passionate feelings in her but instead had enveloped her with comfort. Now she was truly on her own, with no one to rely on but herself. As her heart slowed its furious beating she could make out other voices in the car. People were settling down to relax for the night and slowly she realized she could understand some of the words being spoken. Pulling her handkerchief out, she sniffled into it quietly and then turned to the window, dreading to go into the unknown again.

Although the woman who introduced herself as Carmella Valenti spoke Italian and some English, Dani knew very little English, so they made themselves understood by using basic words and a lot of sign language. Carmella pulled out a thin quilt from a bag near her feet. It was large enough to cover both of them as they settled down to try to sleep on the first leg of the trip to the Midwest. Even though Dani felt she wouldn't sleep a wink on the rumbling train, after a half hour passed, her eyes closed against her will and she didn't wake until morning light flooded the streaked window. Surprised that she had slept at all, Dani turned to Carmella who was already awake.

With a gesture, the woman bade Dani to follow her

and then led her traveling companion to a line before a small compartment. Although they had to wait and could only take a few moments, they washed before breakfast. Returning to their seats, they took out some food from their hampers and enjoyed a breakfast of an egg fritatta that Carmella carefully unwrapped along with a slice of bread each and two oranges that Dani contributed. The eggs, to which spices, peppers, and onions had been added, were delicious.

"See." Carmella pointed. "Between us we have enough to last the whole journey." Her basket was filled with strange-looking sausages, two loaves of bread, a bottle of wine, and assorted fruits. Dani's hamper held more fruit, boiled eggs, tempting pieces of cold chicken and beef, crisp carrots, and celery and nuts to munch on. There certainly was enough to keep them from going hungry while they traveled. Dani silently thanked Captain Murow for his thoughtfulness and generosity, and Kim who most likely wasn't as ferocious as he looked. Although he never did let her into his galley she'd always found some sort of treat on her tray, like a glass of lemonade, something she never tasted before, or a cookie or piece of hard candy. She had never eaten as well in her fourteen years except at holiday times or when special packages were sent by Anton or Tekla.

So far, with the exception of the threatening sailor on the ship, everyone had been kind. What she had thought would be terrifying was turning out very well indeed. Finishing breakfast, Dani sat looking out the window at the ever-changing scenery. Every once in a while Carmella pointed out something of interest: a beautiful river, a small town, or a field of plowed earth already springing into life with new crops. Papa would have loved to farm here, she thought. These were such large farms, not at all like the few acres he had bought in Poland. Even the farm houses and outbuildings looked neat and prosperous with their fresh coats of spring paint. Healthy, fat, sleek animals grazed in the fields, and once in a while, she spotted a farmer who waved in friendliness as the train sped by.

Dani brought out her precious map, and she and Carmella pored over it, Carmella pointing out where they were at the moment and tracing a faint line as they went along. A conductor came by from time to time to call out a town or city, and Dani laughed at the strange-sounding names. When the train stopped she and Carmella only stretched their legs by walking in the aisle. At one stop when they were sitting in their seats gazing out the window, a swarthy man looked up at them and leered wickedly motioning for them to come out and join him. Dani turned away and Carmella cautioned her never to pay attention to strange men. Dani had no intention of doing so, not after her disgusting experience with the brutish Eric. Never again would she be so foolish as to find herself alone with someone she didn't know.

For lunch they sampled some of Carmella's salami, which was spicy, and had some of the bread and fruit. For dinner, they dug into the chicken Dani offered. Little by little Dani learned that Carmella was a young childless widow going to live with her sister's family. Once in Chicago she would find factory work in one of the industries that were springing up throughout the city. There seemed to be much industry there, Carmella explained. Steel, railroads, mills, even automobiles. Dani had noticed a lot of these vehicles during her fast glimpse of New York, but they only seemed to frighten the horses and pedestrians as they lumbered along making the most dreadful noise. She thought privately that motor cars were frivolity that would never replace the comfort of a sturdy horse and wagon. You only had to feed and groom horses. These monstrous motorized cars had to be cranked up and filled with a vile-smelling oily substance. Often they wouldn't work and men were left cursing in the streets from exasperation, and sometimes they caused massive traffic jams and frightened the horses out of their wits. Choosing a lush red apple from her hamper she wondered if Aunt Tekla had a horse and carriage, or perhaps even a motor car. They surely must be difficult to manage. At least a horse had a brain of sorts and could be trained. How did one go about training an automobile? It was all too complex and best left to the people who understood such intricacies.

They were halfway to Chicago now, and time passed swiftly as they made their way through Pennsylvania and Ohio. Finally they traced the line into Indiana on the last leg of their journey west. Dani insisted that she would see Carmella when they settled into their respective homes but Carmella shook her head negatively. She tried to explain in simple English that it wasn't easy to have friends of different nationalities in the teeming city. Poles frowned on mixing with Italians.

"It's best you stay with your own people," Carmella said sadly. "At least until you get to know your way around the city. Then one day we may be able to meet in the downtown section, perhaps for lunch on a Sunday. Your family would be horrified if you brought an Italian home to dinner. Most of the people think we Italians are all gangsters or killers. Each national group in the city calls the other groups vile names. We Italians are known as wops or dagos—or worse. But when you're with your own kind, life will be wonderful. My sister lives in an Italian section of the city. I'm sure your aunt is in the Polish community. Everyone from the old country stays with their own. Chicago is a lot of countries mixed into one city: Italy, Ireland,

Greece, Poland, even China. But downtown you can mingle freely and no one looks at you with suspicion or calls you names or chases you back home where they feel you belong."

Dani couldn't understand everything that Carmella was saying but she understood the gist of the conversation. She was shocked to think that perhaps people wouldn't like her. She had never been disliked before. Everyone in Ruda was close to one another. Even if you didn't get along with someone at least you were civil, never insulting, as Carmella said the Americans were. Perhaps America wasn't the paradise she had thought.

As they passed through Indiana, they ate the last of the sausage and fruit. By morning the train would be arriving at the station in Chicago, her home for the rest of her life, Dani thought. It was unlikely that she would ever go back to Poland. First of all, Papa wouldn't allow it, and secondly, Jan and he would be here soon anyway. She had no other family in the old country to visit, therefore no reason to go back. Munching on a slice of bread and hard sausage, Dani wondered if her aunt would be loving and friendly. From her letters over the years it would seem that life with her would be pleasant. She had sounded very sincere when she had repeatedly asked them to join her. Dani dozed off. The monotonous clicks of the wheels on the tracks had lulled her to sleep.

As she woke the conductor was cautioning passengers to gather up their belongings. Dani and Carmella checked to make sure all their miscellaneous items were packed in the proper hampers. Changing her wrinkled dress, Dani took one last look at herself in the washroom mirror and brushed her hair until it shone. The train was slowing noticeably and she hurried back to the window to catch a glimpse of the tall buildings streaming by. She noticed more of the infernal automobiles here, mixed with horses, wagons, and carriages. Dani wondered if she could ever learn to handle one of those complicated machines. She tried to imagine the excitement of zipping along a street at the wheel. But so far she'd only seen men navigating them, so perhaps they were men's toys.

The train came to a full stop and Dani's hands started shaking. What if Aunt Tekla hadn't received the telegram Raymond had sent and no one had come to meet her? Could she find her way on her own? She had the address but would they understand her when she said it? Why had Papa put her in this horrid predicament? More strangeness and trepidation had been packed into these past few weeks than into the whole of her previous life. How she longed to be settled, certain of where she would wake up in the morning. At this very minute she wished she were back in Ruda in the crowded, cramped two-room shack that had been her home. There she had felt secure, had been mistress of her surroundings. Here she felt inadequate and stupid. If only she'd had more time to study the language. Doubts ran through her mind and her palms became clammy.

Carmella noticed Dani's uncertainty and patted her on the shoulder.

"Don't worry, you'll manage," she said. "Come, let's make our way down the aisle to the door. I think I see my sister waiting."

They followed the passengers making their way off the train, and Dani stepped down nervously, glancing left and right. Good Lord, she'd forgotten to ask Papa what Aunt Tekla looked like in the haste of departure. She had no idea who she was looking for. Her aunt would be near forty now, and Papa had said she'd been the most beautiful girl in town . . . but that was ages ago. How much had she changed? He'd never mentioned the color of his sister's hair, or of her eyes. He hadn't said whether she was tall or short. Realizing she could not recognize her aunt made Dani very nervous. Carmella noticed that she was upset and hovered close by with her sister, not intending to leave the station until she saw Dani safely on her way.

A rather short plump woman with dark brown hair and merry blue eyes suddenly rushed up to them. "Danuta Mrazek, is that you? Is it really you I'm seeing for the first time?"

Dani nodded, a great smile spreading across her face. This was her aunt then. This kind-looking, happy woman who pounced on Dani like a mother hen. A great sigh of relief escaped the girl. It was going to be all right; everything would work out fine. Papa's sister seemed just as kind as Papa himself, thank God. They threw their arms around each other, crying with happiness.

"Oh, finally," Tekla sobbed. "Finally your father has seen the light. Where is that stubborn man? I feel like choking him." She glanced toward the railway car eagerly expecting Casimir and Jan to be alighting at any moment. Raymond's telegram had been cryptic and brief.

TRAIN DUE 9:10 A.M. THURSDAY. DE-LIGHTFUL SURPRISE AWAITING YOU. RAYMOND

"Aunt," Dani began. "I'm afraid I have some disappointing news. Papa and Jan aren't with me. Papa insisted on farming for two years, unless a war breaks out. In that case he wants to stay and defend his country, but he promised me if there is no war, he and Jan will join us. He doesn't know it, but Jan will be here by late fall or early winter. Jan doesn't think he'll take to farming, although he really hasn't given it a try yet. He thinks he wants to be a sailor, and he's going to leave Poland as soon as the first crop is in."

Tekla stamped her foot in exasperation.

"Oh, that foolish belligerent man. Of course there's going to be a war. It's in the newspapers daily and any simpleton can see disaster approaching Europe. Why wouldn't he listen to me for once in his life?" Tekla's merry blue eyes saddened at the thought of her two relatives trapped in Poland at the mercy of the great powers of Europe, but her dark look vanished as she again wrapped Dani in her ample arms. "Well, I guess one is better than none. I should thank God that Casimir had the good sense to send you. We'll both have to write him to come sooner. Perhaps between the two of us we can convince him, for I am certain that war is imminent. He won't have two years. But that's enough of gloom. This is supposed to be a happy day for you. Let's get your bags and we'll have a marvelous ride on a trolley car. I don't think you've ever been on one. We'll take one right outside the station, transfer once, and we'll be home in no time."

Dani turned around to say goodbye to Carmella, and then she introduced her to her aunt. Tekla held out her hand gingerly, her eyes suspicious as she looked over the dark woman who had traveled halfway across the country with her niece. She was distrustful of anyone from a different background and her feeling showed plainly on her face as she cut the introduction short.

Carmella winked at Dani slyly. "Goodbye, Danuta. Take care. Perhaps we'll meet again soon."

On the train the night before, Dani had written down her aunt's address and Carmella had written her sister's. They would write and eventually make arrangements to meet somewhere away from their relatives if that was how it had to be.

Tekla thanked Carmella politely and hefted up the small strapped case lying alongside Dani's feet while Dani lifted the hamper.

"Is this all you've brought with you, child?"

"Yes. The small case you're carrying has my clothes and some mementos of Mama's. I have some other things from Ruda in the hamper. The case isn't heavy, Aunt, but let me carry it too."

"No, no, that won't be necessary. It's only a short walk up the stairs."

"Aunt, your friend Raymond was so helpful. I don't know how I could have managed without him. He helped me with my English—with everything. By the way, do you speak English?"

"Of course I do, you silly child. It's a necessity and I've been here a long time. It's only right that I know the language so I don't get cheated in my business. There are people everywhere who want to cheat you out of your hard-earned money. You always have to be on the lookout for those sly foxes. Of course, a lot of Polish is spoken throughout our community too, so you needn't feel out of place."

"Then can we speak in English when we're together? I still have so much to learn and I'll need all the practice possible."

Tekla laughed her boisterous laugh.

"Then we'll speak English and if you don't understand as I go along I'll put in the correct Polish words and before you know it, you'll understand the whole complicated language."

"Papa told me you were in business. I can help you in your work now that I'm here, can't I? Do you own a store?"

"I don't think you'll be helping me too often for I

105

own a tavern, my dear, and it's a rough lot that comes in after work for a pail of beer or a shot of hard liquor. Maybe you can lend a hand on Saturday evenings, though, when it's family night. A good many of the men bring their wives and children in for an early home-cooked dinner, and later in the evening, we have polka dancing. I'm not sure if you should be exposed to that yet. We'll see. It's not too bad on Saturdays, until late when some of the men get quite drunk. I don't want you around any of that kind. For you I plan a better life. You're as beautiful as your father always said you were, and he often wrote of how intelligent you are. Do you realize your mother was related to Prince Adam Czartoryski? I believe they were distant cousins. That alone means you deserve the best in life. I know you can marry much better than a common laborer. For you it will be a doctor, an attorney, or a banker, someone of substance."

"Mama was related to an aristocrat? She never told us."

"Well, when she gave up her rich life she thought it best forgotten. It didn't seem right for her to lord it over your father who was poor. She loved him so and wouldn't do anything to belittle him or make him feel inferior. When her parents disowned her for marrying your father, she put aside the past trappings and settled into her new life without any qualms. We wrote often and became quite close. She promised she would try to talk Casimir into coming to America when they saved enough money, but they never did; and she forbade me to even mention the fact that I was willing to send the fare over. She said it would make your father feel inadequate. I have some of her letters yet, and I could tell she was truly a fine lady by reading them. She wrote with such elegance it was like reading a poem. Casimir said you look like her, so now I have a picture in my mind to go along with the beautiful words she wrote. Now, let's get you home. I can see that first thing in the morning we'll have to get you some better clothes."

"Papa bought me these before I left," Dani protested, pointing to the new dress and coat. Her boots had been ruined by the sea water and they squeaked loudly as she walked. "They were a combination going-away and birthday present."

"Yes, that was good of him, but they're hopelessly out of style. You can wear them when you're out working in the garden or helping me around the house, but you'll have to be outfitted properly."

"Aunt Tekla, are you a rich woman?"

"No, child. I'm not rich, just comfortable. I live well with what I make at the tavern and I'm thankful. Men will always drink. In good times or bad they seem to lay their hands on enough money for alcohol. That's why I'm satisfied with the business my fiancé started. Over the years I've never had many financial problems. Careful now, move back. Here comes our trolley."

They stepped in and found a double seat at the front of the car. Dani stared out the window, awed by the sights they passed. She noticed that the trolley went through some poor neighborhoods but none seemed as wretched as the mining town of Ruda. Alighting at the Thirty-first Street intersection they crossed the street, took another trolley, and soon arrived at Fox Street, their stop. As they walked one block south to Tekla's house, they were stopped numerous times by neighbors and friends who wanted to meet the niece Tekla had spoken of so often. Although Tekla owned a tavern, which was almost considered scandalous, she was well liked for her fairness in dealing with drinking men. If a man was careless and left part of his pay on the bar, Tekla saw to it that the money was put in an envelope and returned the next day, for which the women were grateful. That money represented rent, groceries, and clothing. In their cups, the men often forgot they had families to support, but Tekla saw to it that they didn't spend too much of their hard-earned wages. On occasion she even had her burly helper take a man home if he'd had one drink too many. The wives realized that if their husbands had to stop for a few drinks, at least they were in good hands. Tekla's place was not like the other taverns in the neighborhood, where a man could walk in with a week's pay and leave without a penny in his pocket. What the unscrupulous bartenders or owners didn't steal, the coarse women who lurked in the back rooms did. Tekla ran no such place. She dealt only in food and drink. Suppers were served between five and seven on week nights for the men who had no wives or mothers to cook for them; family dinners were served on Saturdays, and that menu remained the same year after year by popular demand. The Saturday meal consisted of roast chicken, mashed potatoes and gravy, dumplings, roast beef, peas, and for dessert, home-made coffeecakes. Heaping platters and bowls of food were laid out, and all Tekla's customers helped themselves to as much as they could eat—and for a fair price. On weekdays only one meat and two vegetables were served but the portions were ample for the hard-working men. Later, on Saturdays, when the polka music started, the children were sent home, their stomachs full, and the men and women danced until the floor boards shook from their thumping, stamping exuberance. Barrels of beer were downed, along with whiskey, vodka, or gin. Tekla's real profit came from the drinks, not the food, but serving the meals was good business. It got her a steady and dependable clientele. Her large tavern was always half filled on weekdays and was crowded on weekends. Other taverns were empty at times but Tekla had no such problem.

The contributions she made to St. Mary's church also gave her standing in the community. She explained to Dani that she made generous donations throughout the year, and if help was needed for any committee, she always volunteered her time or money. When she did work for the church or when constantly being on her feet at the tavern wearied her, Bolie took over and kept perfect order. He was a giant of a man, in his early thirties, married to a petite woman who was about the same age as he. Bolie and his wife had no children, to their dismay, so the disappointed couple spent the majority of their time working for Tekla. She paid them well, and they had even rented a three-room flat next door to the tavern. Bolie, Tekla explained, had been with her since he was fifteen and Martha for the last ten years, since she had wed Bolie whose proper name was Bolislas. The couple were Tekla's best and most trusted friends. "Yes, Danuta, you'll certainly come to love Bolie and Martha Lipinski as much as I do."

By the time Tekla had imparted this information to Dani they were standing before her two-story red brick house. The front lawn was neat, a small square of healthy green grass with a border of spring flowers just beginning to bloom. The picket fence and front door were freshly painted, and crisp white curtains covered the windows on the first floor where Tekla lived. Upstairs, she explained, lived a priest's parents and two of their grown sons who worked nights. Wiping her brow and placing Dani's case on the porch, Tekla brought out a large ring of keys from her voluminous pocket and opened the door. Dani found herself in a spotless living room furnished with a brown leather couch covered with crocheted antimacassars, two large overstuffed red chairs, and several tables filled with bric-a-brac and religious pictures in frames. Imitation Oriental rugs covered the floors of the living and dining rooms. In the latter a large round oak table and six carved chairs left little space. The kitchen contained a huge coal-fed range; an indoor sink; cabinets to hold various dishes, pots, and pans; and another table and chairs. There were three bedrooms, but Tekla led Dani to the one off the dining room. It boasted a pair of sparkling white curtains, and a flowered bedspread covered the shiny brass bed. In a corner stood a small washstand on which there was a pitcher of water, and towels hung on the bar. A tiny closet opened off the bedroom and a large bouquet of lilacs filled the room with their scent.

Dani gazed about her in wonder. "Is this your room, Aunt? It's beautiful."

Tekla moved to the dresser set against a wall and began opening empty drawers. "No, this is yours. Mine is off the kitchen, and your father's and Jan's would have been the larger bedroom off the living room but since they're not coming, you can have that if you like."

"No. If you don't mind, I'll keep this one. It's so bright and sunny. I've never had a whole room to myself. All this space just for me, it's like a miracle." She looked into the closet. "And a closet too. I'll never have enough to fill it. Thank you."

She threw her arms around the ample woman and hugged her tightly. Tears of joy streamed down Tekla's face as she returned the hug. What a good feeling to have someone from one's own family around. Far too many years had passed since she had spoken to a blood relative. She had many friends, but that wasn't the same. Family was blood and, therefore, more important. At that moment she felt as if Dani were her own child, although a grown one, and the feeling was grati-

110

fying. If Jan and Casimir had come too, her heart would have burst with joy.

"Dani, leave your things just as they are. Come with me into the kitchen. We'll have a bite to eat, talk, and relax for a while. I've taken the whole day off. Bolie and Martha will take care of the customers. I confess the excitement of meeting you at the station has worn me out, but I prepared a cold lunch before I left this morning. Let's eat."

Tekla walked into the pantry and brought out a covered plate of sliced beef tongue and a loaf of fresh bread. She instructed Dani to slice a tomato while she went and opened a magical white box that held cold milk and butter and other things. Dani walked over to look at this strange apparatus, puzzled as to where the cold air came from.

"It's an icebox, Dani. Every morning the ice man delivers a block of ice to put inside and the ice keeps perishable food from spoiling."

"Amazing," Dani exclaimed. "Everything in this country is amazing so far. Does everyone own one of these?" She touched the ice with her fingers to make sure it was really cold, and it stung her finger.

"Not everyone, but everyone will soon. The price is going down and they're becoming more affordable. You have to remember to leave a card in the window every morning to show how much ice you want to purchase. The iceman sells four sizes and you have to empty the pan underneath before it overflows. I bought one of these as soon as they came out. It's so convenient and it pays for itself because food stays fresh and untainted."

Tekla took out milk and some butter, and they sat down to share their first meal together. She spread butter generously on Dani's bread, added thick slices of tongue and tomato, and poured out a full glass of cool fresh buttermilk.

"You must eat, Danuta. I can just imagine your trip over. You probably starved. I know I did on my crossing. Of course, it took a little longer then. I was so sick and miserable all the way over that the whole trip was a nightmare I'd rather forget. The only thing that kept me going was thinking of Józef waiting for me. You see, he met me in New York so I wouldn't have to travel alone on the train, and when he first saw me after almost two years apart, he couldn't believe it was me. I was so thin after not eating for weeks, there were dark circles under my eyes, and I almost fainted as I walked toward him. He had to hold me upright until we found a hotel. Instead of taking the train immediately I rested for a few days, but as soon as I put my feet on firm land again my lost appetite returned and I was ready to see my new home. Józef had already put a down payment on this house and he'd had the tavern established for over a year, but we had only two days in Chicago before he was taken from me. The house and the tavern were mortgaged heavily so it took a long time to turn a tidy profit." Tekla looked Dani over thoroughly. "You're too skinny, like a beanpole. We'll have to change all that and put some meat on your bones."

"Actually I ate quite well. The Smenteks, the couple in the other cabin, had a terrible time keeping even the plainest food down, but I ate every meal except for one day when we were in a terrible storm. The galley closed then, and we had to wait for hours till the storm subsided. It was so scary that day, with water pouring down the stairs into our cabin."

Dani described the rest of the voyage to her aunt. She told of her fright at seeing the huge Amos, but she made no mention of Eric, who had torn off her clothes during his attempt at rape. That would be her shameful secret. Dani had an amusing way of presenting a story and Tekla laughed again and again, interrupting Dani

112

with questions now and then. They sat for over two hours, exchanging information about their lives, and then they straightened up the kitchen.

"Let's go walking," Tekla said after their long lunch. "Or would you rather rest for a few hours?"

"I'm not tired. Where are we going?"

"I thought I'd show you St. Mary's church. We can light a candle of thankfulness for your safe arrival at the statue of the Blessed Mother. Then I'll show you the school you'll be attending in the fall. You'll be quite surprised at how large it is, over three hundred students and the tuition is reasonable. Every class is taught by a wise kindly nun. You'll be placed in an upper grade, just to learn more of the language, history, spelling, and naturally, religion." As they approached the church, Dani gazed up at the huge green dome. This wasn't a simple church, it was a mighty cathedral standing tall and majestic. They climbed the steps to the main door and entered the cool vast church sparkling with the multicolored light that streamed through the beautiful stained glass windows. For an hour Dani stared, mesmerized, at the saints portrayed in the myriad patterns of glass, at the ornate carved pulpit, at the multitude of statues, the noble altar, and the choir loft. Then Tekla inserted two coins and they lit their thanksgiving candles in front of the statue of the most Blessed Lady with her lifelike face and her sky-blue and pristine white robes. A priest came out from the sanctuary as they were preparing to leave. He welcomed Tekla warmly.

"This is Father Stefan," Tekla explained. "He plays an important role in the parish by working hard to make everything run smooth for the pastor."

The middle-aged priest blessed Dani and brought her up to the altar steps to view the whole church from a priest's vantage point. It was a privilege not many people enjoyed except the priests, the altar boys, and the nuns who kept the altars clothed in clean crispy linens and arranged the masses of fresh flowers. Throughout the past hour Dani had remained silent, awed by her surroundings. Why one could sit here for hours at a time, she thought, drinking in the sights of the detailed work the church offered. Even the pews made of carved, smooth wood seemed to invite one to stay and meditate.

Outside in the sunshine again, Dani finally found her lost voice. "Never could I have imagined a place as beautiful as this. No wonder you never wanted to go back to Poland. I, too, would loathe to leave. Oh, Aunt, this surely is the beginning of a grand life. Thank you for asking me to come. I'll have to write Papa and Jan tonight. There's so much to tell them. My letter will go on for pages and pages. I must remember to write Clara and Samuel too. They must be seeing much the same in New York."

"You had better tell your father a little at a time. I don't know if we can send pages and pages all at once. Write a little each week and maybe your news will prod them into leaving sooner. I hope our letters get through. It might be that you'll have more influence than I in persuading your father to quit the old country. My life here has been good with the exception of losing Józef and worrying about the three of you. Now I only have to worry about two so you might say some of the heavy load has been lifted from my heart."

Dani went to bed early, just after the sun set, too exhausted to finish her intended letters. A kaleidoscope of pictures filled her mind as she drifted off to sleep. It was all too much for her young mind to comprehend in such a short time.

The next day she and her aunt went to a dry goods store. Tekla purchased soft kid slippers for Dani, another pair of everyday shoes, a rainbow of ribbons, and many other personal articles the girl had never owned before. She now had a hairbrush decorated with pastel enameled flowers, a matching comb, a new purse, and some underthings. Next, Tekla dropped Dani off at the home of a seamstress who lived only a block away from Tekla's place. Entrusting Dani with a key to her house, Tekla instructed her niece to walk home after the measurements were taken because she had to work at the tavern for a few hours.

"I'm sure you'll find something to keep you busy at home while I work for a spell. Feed the chickens and ducks in the coops in the back yard. You'll find feed in the shed and be sure to put fresh water in the trough. I'll be home by dinner time. I used to eat my evening meals at the tavern but now that I have a family I'll be keeping more regular hours. I'll cook, and we'll spend some time together. I'll only go back to the tavern later for an hour or so to take in the day's receipts. I've decided to raise Bolie's and Martha's pay and let them fill in for me till closing time. They'll appreciate the raise. Bolie desperately wants to buy a house and the extra money will bring him that much closer to his dream. Now I'll leave you in Mrs. Melski's capable hands. She's an excellent seamstress and will know just what style is right for you. I trust her taste and judgment completely."

They entered Mrs. Melski's house and went to the back where the middle-aged woman did her sewing. The room was strewn with colorful bolts of cloth and various dress patterns. Tekla decided Dani was to have one good dress for Sundays and four everyday ones, along with two petticoats and two fine lawn nightgowns.

"But that's far too much," Dani protested, aghast at what all this would cost.

"Nonsense, child. The two dresses you have are much too warm for the summer. You'd swelter in the hot sun. Besides, they're far too small even though you're so tiny. You're bursting out at the seams. We'll come back to Mrs. Melski in the fall and she'll make you some winter clothes. Then we'll find you a warm coat."

"But you're spending all your hard-earned money on me. It's not right. I should be working for my keep."

"And who else do I have to spend it on, may I ask? Don't worry, I'm not going to spoil you. This won't be happening every day. You'll have your chores at the house and much studying to do when school starts. You'll be quite busy, I assure you. Now put yourself in Mrs. Melski's hands and then go straight home. I'll be there at six." She kissed Dani lightly on the forehead and left with a sprightly step.

After measurements were taken and patterns shown, it was decided Dani's everyday dresses should be light-weight and cool for the coming summer. One would be a soft yellow cotton with tiny blue cornflowers and blue trim, another would be lavender with purple buttons, the third a sturdy cotton in a neutral tan for everyday use, and the fourth various shades of pink that seemed to shimmer when you moved. Her Sunday dress was to be a beautiful creation of white linen banded on the bottom with green, blue, and yellow strips. Such wild abundance made Dani quite dizzy. She felt like a princess amidst the bolts of material, the ribbons, the multi-colored trim. Well, she decided after the fitting was over, no sense dawdling. Aunt Tekla had better be repaid in some way, she might as well go and do the chores. A light rain started as she walked the block home, meeting no one on the way. Pulling an apron over her dress, she went into the back yard and began feeding the chickens and ducks. One would probably

116

ave to be killed for dinner, but Dani had never learned
ow to do that. Once, in Ruda, she had become
iolently ill when asked to chop a chicken's head off; it
ad seemed a ghastly thing to do. Then, when she had
ried to wring its neck, her nausea had worsened and
an had to finish the job. She hoped Tekla wouldn't
hink her lazy or squeamish. Putting that thought from
er mind, she busied herself scrubbing the kitchen
loor, dusted, and then began to peel potatoes and
repare snap beans for dinner. Good, they wouldn't
ave to kill a chicken after all for she found some
moked sausage instead and prepared it with sauer-
raut. By the time the church bells rang six, the meal
vas complete and the house was filled with tempting
romas. Tekla was surprised to see dinner ready and
waiting on the table for she had planned to cook the
neal herself. She lavishly praised her niece's culinary
kill.

"You'll make an excellent wife one day," she teased.
But not for a few years yet. There's too much to do
efore you settle down in marriage."

"Tell me about my new city," Dani begged. "I want
o know everything."

Tekla laughed at her imaginative mind. "Well I can't
ell you about the whole city in one evening but I'll start
nd every day I'll tell you more.

"Dani, Chicago is a very tough city and the people
who live in it are tough too. It's survived a great fire,
typhoid epidemics, financial crashes—but it's a good
city, a great city. One day, you'll come to love it as I do.
It's exciting too. I came here during the unbelievable
Columbian Exposition, the Chicago Fair we called it.
A huge magical wheel had been erected. It was over
two hundred and fifty feet tall and it went round and
round like a giant toy, carrying people way up to the
top and then bringing them down again. Bolie and

Martha made me go on George Ferris' wheel, and was so frightened I couldn't think straight. It was so windy that day I thought we'd be blown down and smashed to our deaths. That's the day I forgot some of my sorrow over losing Józef and knew I wanted to live. Later we saw the scandalous Little Egypt perform but she wasn't as bad as the newspapers said. I rather liked her style. I liked the entire Egyptian section. About six years ago another spectacular thing occurred. Engineers reversed the flow of the Chicago River, turned it completely around so the river God intended to flow into Lake Michigan just went completely haywire. You wouldn't believe how filthy that river was. Why the papers said it was an infested cesspool, so foul it would sometimes catch fire all by itself from the dirty gases and the slime covering it, but it's cleared up now. And I wish you had been here for the dedication of Holy Name Cathedral. I must take you to see it, Dani. It's far grander than our St. Mary's. We'll go there one day when I have time, and you'll agree it is the most beautiful church you've ever seen."

"It can't be better than St. Mary's. Our church is the grandest in the world."

"You have so much to see, child. Just wait. There are dozens and dozens of churches here, many of them so beautiful it takes your breath away. When I came here there were over a million people already settled so you can see why there was a need for many churches. Why fourteen million animals a year are slaughtered in the stockyards not far from here, just to feed the people in Chicago and the surrounding area."

"Aunt, that's hard to believe. I can't imagine that many animals. The largest herd I ever saw had thirty or forty."

"Would I lie, Dani?"

"No, you wouldn't. It's just so startling it hurts my

118

ead to think of it. What else? Please tell me more."

"Well, you have to see the elevated train down-
own."

"What is an elevated train? I know what a train is."

"It rides up above your head on tracks built up above
he traffic. I've never been on it, but Bolie and Martha
ave. They'll tell you all about their adventure."

"It sounds like a magic city. Nothing bad can ever
happen here."

"But it does, Dani. It is a magical city, but there are
many tragedies too. There was a fire at the Iroquois
heatre in 1903. Almost six hundred people died
ecause some fool didn't have the emergency exits
ixed so they could open easily. The whole city
mourned. That's why I don't like to be in crowded dark
places. They scare me. We've had violent strikes, street
ighting, hunger, cold, icy weather when families
huddle together for warmth because they haven't
nough money for heat. Not everything is good, Dani.
There's a lot of cruelty in the world, but not for you.
You're young and life is just beginning to show you a
glimpse of its greatness. But come. I want you to meet
he tenants upstairs."

Dani and Tekla did not stay long upstairs. Tekla
explained that her tenants kept to themselves. They felt
uperior to their neighbors because they had a son who
was a man of God. This, they felt, gave them immeasur-
ble prestige, and they also felt they had to live their
ives in such a way that they set a perfect example for
he community. Even their sons who worked long
hours in the nearby soap factory didn't mingle much
with the other young men in the neighborhood because
hey had been told by their parents to remain aloof and
o be well behaved.

Before they retired, Tekla gave Dani permission to
explore the neighborhood as long as she stayed within

a safe radius. So on the following day Dani walked eas
four blocks to Morgan Street and then down anothe
four-block stretch of the busy thoroughfare, window
shopping at the glorious stores lined up next to one
another. What a difference from Ruda's one genera
store. There were dry goods stores, bakeries, and
grocery stores with more food stacked on the shelves
than she had ever seen. There was a furniture store with
beautiful modern pieces in the display window and
before a small but sturdy-looking bank a line of people
waited to conduct their business. Fascinated by the
hustle and bustle of the street, Dani stopped at a candy
store that was selling a marvelous treat called ice cream
as fast as it was being made. She had enough pennies in
her pocket to purchase a taste of this delectable
creamy concoction, and she marveled at its cool vanilla
taste. It was so utterly different from anything she had
ever tasted.

She promised herself to write to Jan that very
evening, to explain all these vastly exciting moments.
She couldn't begin to imagine the whole of Chicago it
Morgan Street was this exciting. On the way home she
stopped at the church and knelt for a half hour, not
praying, but taking in the details she hadn't noticed yet.
Every time she entered this holy place she found
something different to concentrate on. One afternoon
the choir was filled with children practicing, and she
stayed for over an hour listening to their harmonizing
as the organist blasted out a hymn and the choir sang.
She would have liked nothing better than to join the
singers, but she was too shy to climb the stairs and
intrude. The songs they sang in Polish she knew well.
Those songs were haunting. The English ones were
unfamiliar but just as beautiful, and she hummed one
to herself on the walk home.

As the days went by the people on her block became

used to seeing her leave Tekla's house every afternoon for her strolls and they began talking to her, saying a polite hello or remarking on the weather. They all agreed Tekla's niece was an attractive young lady who would mature into a beautiful woman. Several of the neighbors with eligible sons looked upon her with approving eyes. Such a beautiful girl who knew the ways of the old country would make a welcome addition to any family, and knowing Tekla's generous nature, they were aware that there would be a nice fat dowry as an added bonus—although with her niece's looks and gracious quiet ways, one wasn't necessary.

Finally at the end of the second week, Tekla brought Dani to the tavern two blocks away, where she helped cook the Saturday meal in the large, organized kitchen. Martha and Bolie were very friendly and Dani liked them immediately. While they worked to get the meal ready, they joked with each other, and so the tasks became fun. Martha told Dani to peel potatoes and shell peas while she baked coffee cakes. Tekla was readying an enormous pile of cut chickens for the roasting pans. As soon as the cakes were out of the oven, everyone stopped working and had a cup of freshly made coffee. Tekla put a large dollop of cream and a spoon of sugar into Dani's cup. They each took a slice of walnut cake still warm from the oven, the melting brown sugar oozing out over their fingers. This coffee tasted entirely different from the cup she'd had on board the *Destiny*, and Dani quickly changed her opinion of this brew. She decided it was a drink she would like. Bolie entertained them with hilarious stories about some of the patrons until Tekla threatened to hit him with her broomstick. Martha and Dani were still in stitches over his last story about a man who'd lost his false teeth when bending down to ask a woman to dance. As he had eagerly awaited the woman's affirmative answer, his teeth had plopped out right onto the horrified woman's lap. Evidently the man was too embarrassed to return to the tavern for over a month but he was back now, this time with his teeth tightly in place. Bolie told Dani to look out for a short plump man called Ziggy. He was the tooth loser. Tekla banished Bolie from the kitchen at that point so they could finish their work in peace, but he stuck his head back in one last time to put a finishing touch on his tale.

"He wears a toupee too, Dani, and it doesn't match the rest of his hair for his natural hair is red and the toupee is brown."

This sent Dani into more peals of laughter, and even Tekla laughed as she recalled Ziggy's round pinkish baby face topped by mismatched shades of hair.

By six the tavern was full of hungry families, and Tekla and Martha were toting tray after tray of food to the buffet table. Since the crowd was unusually large that evening, Dani was allowed to help replenish the rapidly dwindling supply of wholesome food. By the time the three-piece band arrived there was just enough chicken left for the four of them. They ate quickly and then Martha started washing a mountain of dishes. Dani began to dry them and stack them away, but as the music began she slowed her pace and listened intently to the rousing cheers which greeted the song that opened up the festivities. When the kitchen was set to rights, Martha joined her husband at the bar to serve drinks, and Dani sat just outside the kitchen doorway, watching the merry throng go round and round in a fast polka. Oh, how exciting it was. Both men and women were flushed from the exertion of spinning around the floor, and as soon as a song ended, the bar was filled with men seeking to quench their thirst. After each particularly fast dance, the band switched to a slow waltz so the dancers could catch their breath for the next wild fling. Dani's feet were tapping the floor in time with the rhythm of the music, and during a slow waltz she was surprised when a handsome man pulled her to her feet to dance. Not wanting to create a scene, for she didn't know whether or not she was allowed to participate, she followed the stranger's steps as he held her close and guided her around the floor. Her feet followed his perfectly, and she was glad to be feeling gay and swaying in time to the music. The man she was dancing with smelled clean, as though he had just bathed and the exertion of dancing wouldn't make him perspire one drop. She had noticed him earlier. He'd been dancing with a very obese woman who'd been light on her feet as he'd expertly twirled her around. Now she, too, could join in the fun. As she spun she spotted her aunt frowning and trying to catch her attention. Not yet, Dani thought. She wouldn't look in her aunt's direction just yet. First she wanted to finish this one perfect dance. She looked up shyly at the man holding her in his arms. He was of medium height, about five feet eight inches, his eyes were a lovely brown and he had a build that promised to remain slim and trim. There wasn't a man in Ruda nearly as good-looking as he, nor a man in this tavern either for that matter. His eyes seemed to be smoldering as he looked down at her and his hands held her protectively. She wanted to press herself closer, but she didn't because everyone was watching. She had never felt this way before and she couldn't decide whether it was agony or pleasure to be held in his capable arms. He was a graceful dancer and seemed to be in demand with all the women on the floor. Dani noticed earlier that several had called out to him. "Save me a dance, Roman." "Don't forget you promised me a polka." Dani saw no ring on his finger so she guessed he was still single,

123

unusual for a man who looked to be in his late twenties. He dressed well, in a sparkling white shirt, a navy blue suit and tie, and highly polished shoes. No wonder he is so popular, Dani thought. And to think he asked me to share a dance. Why it's a wonder he even noticed me sitting in the doorway in my old brown woolen dress. That thought brought a blush to her cheeks and the man called Roman pulled her closer as the dance ended.

"We'll do this again before the evening is over," he promised as he returned her to her seat. "Can I get you anything to drink before I have to dance with these other cows?"

"No, thank you," Dani answered as she laughed up at him. None of the women present appealed to this charming Adonis. That made her feel much better even though she was dressed rather shabbily compared to the other women in the room.

"Then we'll talk again later," he whispered. "I'll be back again as soon as I can break away." Roman walked to the other side of the room, and Dani's reverie was rudely interrupted by Tekla who pulled her into the kitchen. She frowned at Dani as she sat her down on one of the kitchen chairs. "Why were you dancing with Roman Kawa? What madness possessed you to leave your chair and dance with that devil? Didn't you see me trying to get your attention?"

Dani was near tears. She had no idea why her aunt was so upset over such a trifling matter. "I didn't do anything wrong, Aunt. The music was so lovely and he came up to me and pulled me onto the floor. I didn't know what to say. It was all so unexpected. I thought it best just to dance the one time and not cause a scene by refusing. What's wrong with Roman Kawa?"

Tekla wiped the perspiration away from her brow with an unused towel.

"Forgive me, Dani. I didn't mean to scream at you but I have to warn you against men like Roman. Stay away from him for he's nothing but an evil womanizer. He's twenty-nine years old, has a job of sorts when he feels like working, but he lives mainly off unattached women, sweet-talking them out of their money. That's why he's able to dress so handsomely and spend money at the bar like a well-heeled man. Oh, he's a charmer all right. He flirts with all the women, married and single, just for the fun of it. There have been several fights right outside this door over his escapades, but so far he's won every fight even though he's a slightly built man. One day someone's father or husband is going to kill him though. He has no conscience whatsoever when it comes to women. That's why I don't want you near him again. The only thing he's good for is breaking many a woman's heart. Please listen to me, Danuta. I know what I'm talking about. He's the rotten apple in the barrel."

"But he seemed to be so different from the other men, so polite and good-looking."

"He is. That's how he makes his living. I shouldn't have brought you here to the tavern. It was a big mistake and I'll suffer the consequences."

"No. Please, Aunt. Let me come here on Saturdays. It's been so much fun, even working in the kitchen and you can really use the extra help. You're too busy. I promise I won't dance with Roman again, I'll just sit and watch. Please."

"Oh, child, I didn't mean you couldn't dance. I'll find you proper partners if you like dancing so much. Just trust me to choose someone that just wants to dance and nothing else. All right. You can continue to come here. God knows we do need the extra help on Saturdays, but keep away from Roman Kawa and now and then I'll introduce you to someone suitable."

"I promise." Dani kissed her aunt on the cheek. "Thank you. You'll see, I'll make your work load lighter."

By the following weekend Dani's new dresses were ready so on Saturday she wore the pink one, although Tekla cautioned her to wear an apron while working in the kitchen. The dress seemed to shimmer as she moved changing from a pale pink to a dusty rose. As she tied her blond hair back with a deep pink ribbon, she thought that the new dress made her feel like a true princess. Even the dull work of preparing the food for the evening went quickly. As soon as the dishes were done she took off the now-soiled apron and sat in the chair outside the kitchen, listening to the same band that had played last week. At about nine o'clock she noticed Roman entering with a woman who appeared to be in her forties. Despite her age, his companion wore clothes suitable for a young girl. There were rows of flounces on her outfit and her wrinkled face was garishly made up. The tastelessly dressed woman clung tightly to Roman's arm until he seated her at a small table in the center of the room. Then she pulled Roman's chair around by hers so they could both watch the dancers while he went to the bar and brought back drinks. Dani caught glimpses of the pair now and then through the space between the dancing couples. They seemed to be huddled close, talking earnestly. After a while Tekla brought over a red-faced young man whose face was covered with pimples, and she introduced him to Dani. Evidently he was shy since Tekla did all the talking.

"Dani, this is Walter and he'd be honored to dance the next dance with you."

Somewhat embarrassed, Dani rose and danced with Walter, but she tripped over his feet and he tripped over hers. She felt that all eyes in the room were on her as she and Walter clumsily danced their way through an endless song while Tekla nodded encouragement from behind the bar. Finally it was over, and Dani gratefully sank back into her chair while Walter fetched lemonade, muttered a quiet thank-you, then left. After that she was content just to watch and keep time to the music with her feet. Please God, she prayed, no more Walters, but heaven forbid, was that Ziggy walking toward her? It could be no one else for Dani recognized the mismatched toupee immediately. But Tekla intervened before Ziggy made it to the back of the room and led him to the bar where she introduced him to another woman who beamed at the chance to dance. Ziggy's face was as round as a pie and as pink as a baby's, and he seemed to have a perpetual smile on it, which only made him look ridiculous. In addition he was very short, not much over five feet tall and very round. Ziggy didn't turn Dani's way again, probably because Tekla had warned him away.

At eleven Tekla decided to go home. Bolie and Martha would close up. She told Dani to get ready to go while she checked the storeroom for a liquor count. As Dani rose to smooth out her dress, Roman came close behind and whispered in her ear.

"You're stunning tonight, Dani, the most beautiful woman in the room. I would have asked you to dance, but word was passed along that your old dragon of an aunt doesn't approve of me and that woman I'm with is a relative who doesn't want me to leave her side. Will you be here tomorrow?"

"No, I only come on Saturdays, to help out and listen to the music afterward." Dani looked around nervously, expecting to see her indignant aunt about to pounce on her, but no one was paying attention to them. Martha was helping Tekla in the storeroom, and Bolie was working at a furious pace behind the bar, rinsing and refilling glasses.

"Then I'll see you next Saturday." Roman smiled wickedly. "You're a treat to the eyes, a soft pink cloud. You and I should be at a ballroom dancing the night away, not here with these peasants pounding and stamping. You were made to waltz through life capturing everyone's heart, especially mine. I'm attracted to you, little angel. You do something to me every time I catch you glancing my way. Do you have any idea of how enticing you look?"

Dani stammered out her next words. "I'm afraid my aunt says I can't be near you. She warned me last week that I mustn't speak or dance with you again. I'm truly sorry."

She felt utterly foolish saying these words. Instead she wanted to fling herself into his arms and dance wildly around the room with no thought of tomorrow or of her aunt's displeasure.

Roman put his hand lightly on her shoulder and then softly ran it down her back. "Never say you can't. You can do whatever you like. If not in one way, then in another. You only have to think about the proper way to avoid obstacles. I'll see you next Saturday, little angel." He crossed over to the other side of the room just as Tekla was locking the storage room door.

"Are you ready, Dani?" she asked, putting the keys back in her pocket.

As they walked home Tekla chastised herself. "If I decide to stay later on Saturdays I'll see that someone gets you home by ten or eleven. It's not right that you stay out so late. A tavern is not a proper place for a young unmarried woman."

"Aunt, I'm not a baby. I'm fourteen years old. Some girls are married by that age. You're unmarried and you owned a tavern when you were a young woman. There's nothing wrong with that, is there?"

128

"You're different. You'll wait a few years until you find a proper husband. My God there are many girls married at your age, but what kind of lives do they lead? Having babies when they're no more than babies themselves, looking haggard and old before their time. Don't even mention marriage for a long time. I hope you noticed Roman Kawa tonight and saw the foolish woman he's taken up with now. She's a widow with a nice amount of insurance money her husband left her. I'll make you a wager that most of it will soon be in Roman's pockets unless she comes to her senses soon enough."

Dani wanted to blurt out that the woman with Roman was a relative, but she shut her mouth just in time. She did not want Tekla to know that Roman had spoken to her. It was best to keep quiet or she'd never be allowed to return.

In late July and in August the heat was oppressive and tempers often flared on Saturday nights. Dani spent her free hours watching Roman dance and talk to other women, but occasionally he noticed that Tekla's back was turned and he came over for a quick word with her, always managing to touch her in some way, on the cheek, the shoulder, the arm. Each touch aroused a tingling fire on her flushed skin and tempted her to brazenly ask for more. She couldn't understand what had come over her. She had always obeyed her elders, but now she wanted desperately to forget all that Tekla had told her so she could be in Roman's caressing arms again, dancing to slow haunting music.

In the heat the customers brought their drinks out into the large yard behind the tavern and made use of the small tables and benches set up for those who wanted to catch a cool breeze. On one extremely hot and humid night in August, Dani went out back when she saw no trace of Roman inside. Evidently he wasn't coming, and she felt it was stupid to sit on a chair in that stifling room waiting for her weekly glimpse of him. She was disappointed for she had waited all week just to see Roman and to hear his few hasty words, to feel his light touch. Now that he wasn't here the whole evening seemed empty and wasted. Tekla often introduced her to other young men, making her dance with them, but it wasn't the same. Either they were too clumsy or too exuberant. Some pumped her hand up and down in time with the music until she thought her arm would be wrenched from its socket by their wild dancing maneuvers. To her, they were all dull clods in comparison to Roman.

She sat on a bench in a dark secluded corner, wishing for cooler weather and avoiding a particularly bothersome man that was Tekla's latest contribution to a long and dreary list of acceptable partners. Suddenly lightning streaked across the sky and the thunder that followed sent the patrons scurrying back indoors. Dani lingered, fascinated by the patterns the lightning made in the black sky. The cool wind that rushed in from the north felt so refreshing. Drops of rain splashed down, but not enough to send her back into the hot room. She was somewhat protected in the arbor by hanging vines so she lingered a moment longer to savor the fresh wet air. The next clap of thunder was quite close and she jumped at the mighty sound, but suddenly there was Roman in front of her and she found herself in his arms, her heart throbbing violently at his touch, threatening to burst. He lifted her face to his with one hand and put his cool lips against hers, pressing her so close she could feel his entire body welded to hers. Their kiss lasted a full minute before she came to her senses.

"Roman, please. We musn't. Tekla will be furious. She'll kill me. We'll ruin everything and then I'll be locked in the house on Saturday nights. I'll never get

130

out except to go to school."

Roman stilled her chatter with yet another kiss, this one more exciting as his tongue flicked the inside of her mouth sending new sensations through her body. He trailed a myriad of kisses across the hollow of her neck and pressed her closer still, his hands everywhere at once, touching her all over as she had wanted to be touched all these past agonizing weeks. Even in the cool breeze she was flushed and warm again, eager to indulge herself in more of these sensations. Her mind told her to get away from him, but her body was powerless to move. Her surroundings seemed to slip away. Nothing existed but the two of them and the deep ache within her that cried for fulfillment.

Roman broke away first and he immediately noticed the torn expression on Dani's face.

"Your aunt won't notice you're missing for a moment. She never even saw me come into the tavern, and she's far too busy inside waiting on customers to worry about you. Bolie and Martha had to leave so she has her hands full filling orders. Don't worry so. Do you expect your life to be filled with little stolen glances and an occasional quick touch to your arm? Don't you want more? Stop frowning, it will only make lines on your pretty face."

The rain began pouring down in a solid sheet and Roman held his jacket over her as she rushed to the back door. He pushed her gently inside and left through a side gate.

Unobtrusively, Dani mixed in with the crowd, slowly making her way to the bar where Tekla was filling mugs with foaming brew at a furious pace. Bolie and Martha were nowhere in sight, and Dani was puzzled by their absence.

"Where are Bolie and Martha?" she asked, pushing her way through the half gate to join her aunt behind

131

the crowded bar.

"They had to go home. Martha felt faint with the heat, and Bolie went to put her to bed with cold towels on her head. I told him not to hurry. I can manage. I have before. Where were you all this time? I confess I was so busy I didn't have time to think of you before the storm hit." Tekla talked as she worked, filling glasses and mugs, and Dani answered, filling more mugs, head down, ashamed to meet her aunt's eyes, afraid Tekla would notice her flushed face and guess what happened.

"I was out back with the others. Then everyone ran inside when the lightning began, but it was so beautiful I stayed to watch for a minute and came in just when the rain began to pour down. I didn't even get wet, only a few drops caught me as I ran in."

"Good girl. I'd send you home now for it's getting quite late, but I'm not sure how long Bolie will be with Martha."

"I can walk by myself. It's only two blocks and no one will bother me, but please let me stay and help you. Next week I'll walk home at ten and you can watch from the doorway. From here you can see almost all the way to your house. Let's try it for one week and see."

"I'll think about it," Tekla answered shortly. Even though it was at least twenty degrees cooler outside, the tavern remained hot and sticky. Only people sitting close to the open doors and windows felt cooler. By midnight the rain had slowed to a drizzle and everyone was ready to call it a night and get some sleep before the heat returned with a vengeance. Tired and sweaty, Dani and Tekla locked up, leaving most of the mess to be cleaned in the morning. Bolie never did make it back, and they guessed Martha was very ill for that conscientious man to shirk his duties.

Holding a huge black umbrella over themselves,

Tekla and Dani made their way home in the drizzle, walking slowly to take advantage of the cool night air. As soon as she was alone in her room, Dani slipped off her dress and underthings and sponged off her body with cool water. It would be delightful to fill the steel tub with water and take a complete bath, but it was far too late to begin heating water. She would only disturb Tekla who slept in the bedroom off the kitchen. A bath would have to wait until morning, but she was far too excited to sleep. She lay naked on top of the coverlet letting the breeze waft over her, remembering the new and strange sensations she had felt earlier. Roman loves me, she thought with wonder. He really loves me for didn't he show it tonight? She retraced the trailing path Roman had made with his fingers and closed her eyes, reliving the magical moments. How she wanted him. How could she possibly convince Tekla that her opinion of him was wrong? Every man must sow wild oats before settling down. Her aunt was so old-fashioned in her ideas and ways. She should have married after a decent mourning period when her fiancé died. Then she would have had someone to comfort her in the night, not just prayers and thoughts of a man taken in his prime. To Dani, Tekla seemed the typical dour spinster when it came to her attitude toward eligible men.

Dani remembered how much her father and mother had loved each other. When they spoke they always touched each other with loving hands, and Mama had always sent Papa off in the mornings with a warm kiss and a hug, and she had welcomed him home at the end of his long days the same way for as far back as Dani's memory could reach. And after dinner, while Papa had sat in his chair, Mama had massaged his back, lovingly loosening the kinks brought on by so many hours of stooping in the mine. Even when her parents had

133

walked they had held hands. Aunt Tekla must have forgotten long ago what it was like to love a man or else she would be more sympathetic. It wasn't necessary to marry for wealth and position. Look how happy her parents had been, and they had never had many of the material things in life. Their love had sustained them through good times and bad. If Roman really loved her she would find a way of talking her aunt into accepting him. And he had to love her or she would die of longing and jealousy whenever she saw him with someone else. He must have been waiting for someone just like her to come along or else he would have been married by now. Most of the men she knew in Ruda, and here, were wed in their late teens or early twenties and Roman was quite a bit older than that. She knew she could change Tekla's mind, for hadn't Roman told her anything was possible? Oh, she wanted to spend the rest of her life being loved by this handsome, fun-loving man who could make her blood run hot with just a touch. She would ask for nothing else in life.

On Sunday she wore her new white dress with the multicolored bands at the hem and a new white straw bonnet. Heads turned as she and Tekla walked down the center aisle of the church to one of the front pews. Heart beating wildly, she spotted Roman seated across the aisle. Throughout the mass he kept glancing in her direction, his eyes pleading for a smile, teasing her with a frank, open gaze that sent goosebumps down her arms even though the church was warm. He glanced her way every few moments until she was sorely tempted to cross the aisle and join him in his pew, but instead she dutifully kept her head bowed and occasionally stole a fast look in his direction. Stop, she pleaded silently. Everyone sitting in back of us will notice that he is staring and they will be sure to tell Tekla. Nonetheless, he continued to look at her,

134

oblivious of the gossip that could quickly spread. Dani had no idea what was said during the gospel or homily. She had responded to the prayers automatically. As she and Tekla left the church, Roman jauntily tipped his hat to the two women, said a polite good-morning, and then walked briskly away down Thirty-second Street.

Tekla made the sign of the cross at his departure. Her head came closer to Dani's as she began whispering. "I thank the Good Lord that the bricks of the church didn't fall down on our heads when that sinner entered. I daresay this is the first time he's gone to church since he left school, although his mother, God rest her soul, was a good woman. Takes after his father, Roman does. His father was a good-for-nothing lout who was abusive. They only had the one child because Roman's father always beat his wife when he was drunk and he caused God knows how many miscarriages. Poor woman, she's resting in peace now, and I'm sure she looked forward to an eternal sleep. Roman's father was killed in a tavern brawl so you could say like father like son."

"Maybe Roman's turning over a new leaf," Dani said brightly, hope creeping into her voice. "He might be repenting the wrong he's done in the past."

"Not him. I'll never believe that. He's up to no good that one. The nerve of him sitting right up in front as though he were a religious church-going Catholic. He looked our way often enough too. Dani, you haven't been speaking to him lately have you?"

"No, I haven't. But you're committing a sin you know. You're supposed to be forgiving. Didn't Jesus forgive even the worst of sinners?"

"Hush, child, and don't speak to me of forgiveness. All the saints combined couldn't convince Roman to change his ways. I tell you he's up to no good, and I suppose we'll find out sooner or later what dreadful plans he's conjuring up in his mind. He'd better not be thinking of adding you to his string of conquests. If he dares think he can force himself on you, I'll have Bolie break his bones like matchsticks. Bolie can do it too."

"Aunt, please don't excite yourself so over nothing."

They went home and Dani, in the early afternoon, caught up on her letter writing. A letter to Jan and her father was long due, and she expected one from them any day. By the end of September the harvest would be in, and Jan had written that she should expect him soon. He was eager to join her after hearing of the wonders of Chicago and couldn't wait to get there. He had given up the idea of becoming a sailor and wanted to try his hand at working on the new automobiles. He predicted in his last letter that they were the most revolutionary invention to date and he wanted to learn all about them, to be able to take them apart and put them back together again. But there was a hint of unease in his letters. The Russians and Germans were up to their old tricks, disrupting lives in Poland, and he was constantly nagging Casimir to give up on farming before it was too late. Although Casimir remained stubborn, Jan felt he was making some progress in prying him loose. Farming was backbreaking work, prices weren't very good at the marketplace, and Casimir was beginning to miss his daughter, especially when her letters came describing her life in the big city where Tekla could easily open doors for him to get work in one of the factories. Jan promised to keep on doing his best.

Clara Smentek wrote twice telling of her full life with her family. They, too, lived in a close-knit neighborhood, and she spent her days with the grandchildren getting to know and love them all. She loved all her daughters-in-law and couldn't have matched up her

136

sons with any better. All three were good mothers and exceptional housewives. Samuel took to his work with no problems and actually found it much easier here. His workday consisted of ten hours and he had Sundays and half-Saturdays off, and he even made more money than in the old country. Clara thanked God that they were fortunate to have good sons who insisted that they come to this prosperous land.

Carmella wrote almost every week, despairing because neither of them owned a telephone. It would be so easy to pick up a phone and call, but her family couldn't afford the luxury; and Tekla said there was no one of importance that she had to waste money on, everyone she knew lived within walking distance. Carmella had found a job sewing in a small factory but she said the job was monotonous. She spent the whole day putting sleeves on shirts until she wanted to scream with boredom. But her co-workers were all Italian, and she made enough to pay her sister board and have something left over for herself. Later, after she settled in, she would try to find other work, but for the present sewing would have to do. They promised to meet soon, maybe for the Christmas holidays when the stores downtown would be bedecked with tinsel and glitter. Both longed to see that sight.

After dinner Tekla left to check on her business. She had managed to lay her hands on a few schoolbooks the children in the upper grades used and she diligently worked on English every day with Dani. By the end of August Dani felt she made great progress. She could actually hold an intelligent conversation in English although many words still eluded her. But each day brought more knowledge and confidence, and her young supple mind kept adding words to her hoard that grew larger by the minute. War had broken out in Europe two weeks earlier. The streets were abuzz with conflicting reports, but it all seemed so far away. Never having been involved in fighting, Dani supposed it would be over soon without too many casualties. She supposed Poland would be resectioned by the victors, but she did not care who took over Poland if her father and brother were coming to America. They would all owe allegiance to America then, and America was strong enough to defend its territory. According to Jan's last letter, Papa was just about ready to say goodbye to farming and the lost cause of freeing Poland. Besides, when Papa came he would surely give her permission to see the man of her choice since he firmly believed in marrying for love.

The next morning breakfast was interrupted when a boy delivered a telegram.

"It must be from Papa," Dani cried joyously. "Who else would spend the money to send us an expensive wire? They must be on their way at last. I can't wait to see them. You'll love Jan when you get to know him. He looks just like Papa only he's quieter."

Tekla opened the envelope. As she quickly read the contents her face paled alarmingly, then she dropped to the floor in a dead faint, the telegram fluttering down beside her. Frantically Dani ran to the sink, wet a towel in cold water, and dabbed at her aun't face. She knelt on the floor, cradling Tekla's head in her lap, hysterical, thinking her aunt dead. Tekla opened her eyes slowly and began a bone-chilling wail, saying words that made no sense. Frightened, Dani glanced down at the telegram lying near her on the kitchen floor. It was signed by Father Czerny, their parish priest in Ruda.

MY SAD TASK TO INFORM YOU YOUR FATHER AND JAN KILLED BY GERMAN SOLDIERS. BE OF BRAVE HEART. THEY ARE WITH OUR LORD. LETTER EXPLAINING FOLLOWS. FR CZERNY.

138

"What evil joke is this?" Dani cried aloud. "They're not dead. They're coming here. The devil himself must have possessed the old priest to send such horrid news. Aunt, pay no mind to the wire. Father Czerny is old, his mind is senile. Papa and Jan are not dead, not both of them. It's ridiculous to say so and frighten us."

They both knelt on the floor, huddled together, the older woman with no hope in her eyes, the younger with disbelief.

Dani had no recollection of the next few days. At the end of the week a letter came from Father Czerny's brother Louis, who owned the farm next to Papa's. It was true after all. War had begun. But her father and brother hadn't died as soldiers defending their country. They had died needlessly, killed by soldiers who set fire to the farm when they were dissatisfied with the small amount of foodstuff that could be confiscated. Papa had already sold most of the meager harvest at the market, so the soldiers had seized only a few animals and some vegetables. When Casimir had denounced their thievery he had been shot down by those coarse untrained German pigs. Naturally, Jan had run to his father's defense. He, too, had been stopped in his tracks by a single bullet. By the time an officer came to apologize for the behavior of his men it was too late. Jan was dead and Casimir was slowly dying of a mortal wound to his head. The officer ordered a German doctor to try to save him, but there was little he could do for such a massive wound. The soldiers left quickly, marching on to other destinations, and Louis and Lottie Czerny were left to bury the two unfortunate victims. There wasn't anything left to send Dani; the army took everything that wasn't nailed to the floor. Ordinarily Louis would have tried to sell the farm so he could send Dani the proceeds, but because of the war there wasn't much hope of getting a good

139

price. Instead of settling, people were fleeing to safer parts of the country. Louis knew Casimir had money hidden somewhere but he had no idea where to look for it, although he would try to find it. Their letter ended with several sentences expressing their condolences and their hope that the letter would reach Dani. Louis had personally ridden to Gdansk and had asked a sympathetic captain to carry it to America.

Dani cried uncontrollably. She had just begun to understand her brother and now they would never be together. Too late she had realized how dear he was, how intelligent beneath his cloak of silence. There were so many things she wanted to talk to him about. She'd been saving the more important matters until he arrived, but now he would never hear them. She wailed in frustration and then sat motionless, staring at the walls, seeing her father's and Jan's faces. Tekla sat with her rosary beads until Father Stefan came. A neighbor had heard their wailing and had run to get the priest. Father Stefan brewed a pot of strong tea and took some biscuits from a tin, but the tea only made Dani gag and she pushed her cup away mournfully. It isn't fair, she protested silently. Nothing in life is fair. I should have been with Papa and Jan. If they were going to die in some senseless fashion I should have been there so we could all go together. I don't want to be alone.

At last Father Stefan pounded angrily on the table. "Enough. Of course you must grieve for your loved ones, but not by wishing for death. That is a grievous sin. Life must go on. Casimir and Jan are in heaven now and know what's happening here. Think how you're hurting them by acting so foolishly, wishing for death. God has a purpose in all He does and it is not for us to question Him. Wipe your faces, both of you. You're coming with me to church. I'll say a special mass of mourning for you in private, and then you're going to carry on as usual. I'm not saying you should forget. You can remember them at mass, in your prayers, and in your charitable work. Remember, soon enough life is over and you'll be joining them. Time passes by swiftly and before you know it, we're old and ready to meet our Lord and our loved ones. Cling to that thought and life will be bearable again. Now let's go to church."

In a trancelike daze they followed him. Being in church did seem to help slightly.

When they returned home Tekla dressed in black, but she insisted that Dani should not wear somber clothes.

"It won't bring them back," she declared. "If it would, I'd wear black the rest of my days, even paint myself black but it won't help. They're gone. Father Stefan is right. We'll be together soon. I'll join them before you do but we'll be reunited again. We'll not waste what's left of our lives. It would be a sin."

Dani was glad her aunt had found comfort in God, but she still felt bitter. She felt like smashing all the dishes in the house. She had to work to control her rage to remain calm and collected.

During the second week of September Dani registered at St. Mary's school, in an upper grade, to learn English, history, and mathematics. Religion was a regular morning class but she didn't feel religious anymore; not after her personal tragedy. She answered the questions and said the prayers mechanically with the rest of the class in a monotonous drone, her thoughts elsewhere. Although she studied and was an excellent student, her mind wasn't on the books laid out in front of her. She was learning, but automatically, and she didn't feel inclined to mix with the others at recess or lunch. The other students were too carefree. She didn't feel that way at all. How could she play games and sing? After classes were over for the day she went straight home to do her homework, clean the house, and begin supper; therefore she had no friends. Although Tekla was deeply saddened, she had her business to occupy her mind, and because of it, she couldn't remain morose and sorrowful. Drinking people didn't want to be bothered with mourning. They wanted to be cheerful and they expected the woman who ran the tavern to be cheerful too, unless they wanted to unload their problems on her. A few of Tekla's close friends were sympathetic, but they all had their own troubles. Life did go on, whether you liked it or not.

Saturday nights were the only bright spots in Dani's life. In October Tekla finally relented and let her walk home alone at ten, having been assured by her friends that nothing could possibly happen on the short two-block walk. Consumed by grief and forcing herself to appear happy, Tekla didn't notice that Roman was no longer around on Saturday nights. Little did she know he waited for her niece in the small park just beyond her home. There Dani met him every Saturday night. They sat on a bench in a dark unlit corner and his intense passion brought her the magic of forgetfulness. By late October it was getting chilly. The trees and bushes were now leafless and so the pair was exposed to inquisitive passing eyes. They kept their hands warm under each other's coats, and Dani's senses throbbed as Roman expertly slid his up and down her body. Through the material of her dress she could feel the indelible marks he made along her breasts and thighs. For an hour or more her mind was rid of sorrow and filled with Roman's sensuous probing. She didn't bother to confess these sins to the priest, she felt no remorse for something beautiful enough to make her forget Papa and Jan for a short while. Even the war news held no interest for her. What did it matter how many others were killed? They were all strangers. Not a drop of pity for them could be squeezed from her.

One particularly cold night at the end of October, Roman kept his hands in his pockets not touching her. "You realize we can't continue this silly pretense of love," he declared hotly, anger etched in his eyes. "Whenever I'm near you're constantly glancing over your shoulder to see if anyone is watching. It's ridiculous. I'm a man, not a lovesick schoolboy waiting to steal a kiss or two. I think we should stop seeing each other. I've certain needs and I refuse to leave you on Saturdays unfulfilled. I go home to my small flat and lie awake all night wanting more than you're willing to give. It would be best for both of us if we went our separate ways. I know I love you, but I can see you don't know anything of love. You're only a child wanting to be petted and cuddled. I've no room in my life for a foolish schoolgirl."

Dani's eyes opened wide in shock. "Please, Roman, don't say anything so terrible. I do love you. You're the only one who helps me forget my sorrow, but I loved you long before that. You and my aunt are all that I have left to love."

He grabbed her roughly by the shoulders. "Then show me. It's early. Tekla won't be home for at least two hours. Take me into your home where we can be warm and comfortable and show me how much you love me."

"Roman, I can't do that. What if she should decide to come home early?"

"She never comes home early. Not on Saturdays. What else do you suggest? That we stay out here all winter and freeze to death? Do you have a lock on your bedroom door?"

"Yes, but I don't understand you." Dani became

agitated at his impossible demand.

"We lock your bedroom, and if Tekla should come home and knock at your door, you just pretend you're asleep and don't want to be disturbed. We can be together in privacy for as long as we like, but if my staying all night makes you nervous, I promise I'll be gone by midnight. If necessary, I can always leave by your bedroom window. Let me show you what it's like to be a real woman. What we've been doing so far is only children's fondling. You have so much to learn, to experience. If you love me, then prove it to me tonight."

Dani pressed her hands to her temples. "Roman stop. You're confusing me. You're asking me to commit a mortal sin. I don't know if I can go that far. I'm frightened."

"Then let's say good-bye here and now. I see I've only been wasting my time while you toy with me, lead me on, tease."

Dani was distraught at the thought of losing him. She couldn't bear living if he left her life too. Her nerves were frayed. Good and evil pulled her apart. Hesitating for a moment, she finally relented.

"All right. But let's go through the back. Someone is sure to see us if we use the front door."

Roman pulled her close. "My lovely angel, you won't regret a minute of the time we spend together I promise you. You'll experience something so wonderful it will take your breath away." He held her face in his two hands and looked deep into her eyes, and his passion soon transmitted itself to her. "Dani, I've been longing for this moment since the first time I saw you. I knew it would happen—willed it to happen. I must be inside you, know your whole body; not the bits and pieces you've allowed me so far. Let's go now."

Soon they were climbing the few stairs to the back porch.

"Where's your key?" Roman asked, groping for her hand.

"Hush. Be quiet or the people upstairs will hear us."

There wasn't a glimmer of light so Dani felt her way along the wall, searching for the door like a blind person trying to locate the keyhole. After a few minutes she finally found the knob, Roman urging her to hurry. At last they were inside where the flickering gaslight at the front of the house enabled them to make their way across the kitchen without bumping into furniture.

"Where's your room?" Roman asked, holding her close. She could feel his hardness pressing against her thigh, sense his impatience. She led the way into the dining room and turned left into her bedroom. Roman closed the door behind them and turned the key.

"At last we're alone," he murmured, his lips close to her ear. "Do you realize the time I've invested in courting you? And to think you thought our being together was impossible. Didn't I tell you every obstacle could be overcome with proper planning? Nothing is impossible if you want it badly enough." Expertly, he undid the buttons at the front of her dress, and before she could protest his haste her dress was lying in a heap around her ankles. Next he removed her petticoat and underdrawers, leaving only her shoes and stockings. Pushing her onto the bed he had those off in a matter of seconds and himself undressed in a few more. Dani lay on the bed, staring at the outline of his body in the dim light coming through the curtains. She wasn't totally ignorant about what happened between a man and a woman. The other schoolgirls in Ruda had talked of it, and basically she knew what was about to happen. He was going to put that huge thing she saw in

145

the dim light inside her. She couldn't imagine how it would feel, only that it might soothe away the agonizing ache that seemed to consume her whenever he was near. This was her first shadowy glimpse of how a man was built and she was awed. Questions raced through her mind, almost making her laugh. Why didn't it look this big when Roman had his pants on? When he was dressed he always looked flat down there. Nothing stuck out. Now here he was in his nakedness, looking utterly ridiculous. If it weren't happening to her it would be funny. She had a vague notion that it was going to hurt terribly, but she put the thought aside, curious to know the result of abandoning herself with the man she loved so recklessly.

Roman couldn't wait a moment longer. For months he had contrived for this moment. Without any further preliminaries he thrust into her, pushing deeper and deeper until he penetrated the stubborn obstacle barring his way. Dani wanted to cry but instead she bit her lips against the searing pain. In a few seconds it was over and Roman rolled off her body, spent, breathing hard. A tear trickled down Dani's cheek. Was this it? She had yearned for this to happen, had felt all the new sensations Roman had aroused . . . and then this. Nothing but pain. She jumped up as she felt a hot stickiness between her legs. Shakily, she lit the kerosene lamp and, holding her discarded dress in front of her, saw several drops of blood on the coverlet. Anxiously she scrubbed them with the soap and water in her basin. Roman laughed at her frantic attempt to clean up the evidence of their intimacy.

"It will come out in the wash. Don't be so upset over something so natural. Now you're no longer a virgin. Tonight you've become a complete woman." He casually rolled a cigarette, then opened the window to let the smoke drift outside. After taking a few puffs, he threw the cigarette out the window and walked over to Dani and wiped the tears from her face with his hand. "Don't cry, my little love. Only the first time is painful. From now on you'll enjoy lying with me, and as soon as your aunt changes her opinion of me we'll be married. We both have to work very hard to convince her that I'll be a suitable husband for her precious heiress."

Dani looked at Roman puzzled. "Roman, what are you talking about?" I'm not an heiress. Tekla isn't wealthy you know. She makes a good living and is quite comfortable, but she's not rich by any means."

"Richer than I am," Roman retorted sharply. "She owns this house with no mortgage on it. She owns the tavern, and I'm sure she puts tidy sums in the bank each week. Don't let her fool you. Most likely she's set aside a nice dowry for you. It will be enough to give us a good start in life."

The clock in the living room struck midnight as Roman finished dressing.

"Let me out the back way. It's best not to take any chances until we're sure she's on our side." He kissed Dani lightly on the lips and was gone.

In a frenzy, Dani took lukewarm water from the back burner of the stove and dumped it into the tin bathing tub standing in one corner of the kitchen; then she added more cold water from the sink. Shivering, she climbed into the tub and washed away the traces of her lost virginity. Although she was chilled to the bone, she didn't emerge until every part of her body had been scrubbed vigorously. Then, putting on her warmest flannel nightgown, she emptied the tub quickly and hurried into the bedroom to see that the coverlet showed no trace of blood and to make certain nothing was on the sheet beneath. It was clean. She closed the window, turned out the lamp, and huddled under the down comforter in an attempt to get warm. A few minutes later she heard Tekla's key in the front lock and feigned sleep. She could not face the good woman after her transgression with Roman. She waited, tense, until she heard Tekla close her bedroom door, and then she spent the night turning from side to side, unable to sleep because of mixed emotions. Was Roman right? Did it get better after the first time? Because if it didn't, there was no use going on with this madness. It was too risky. She wanted to feel shame, but she couldn't quite reach that point even though she knew men had no respect for girls who gave in easily. Two years ago there had been a scandal in Ruda when Zoysia, a girl of Dani's age, had found herself pregnant. No one had been willing to take the blame and wed her. It was said that Zoysia couldn't name the father for she'd been involved with at least three different men. Anyway, Zoysia was three months pregnant, and her parents hid in shame from the other villagers. The local midwife was finally called in and performed a successful abortion but at the risk of the girl's life. Zoysia finally recuperated weeks later, after almost bleeding to death and suffering from an infection. She was then banished by her parents, sent to relatives in Chelma with orders never to return. The disgraced girl begged and pleaded to stay, but one morning in June she was put bodily from her home with a small pack of clothing and food, and made to walk the distance alone with only general directions on locating Chelma. Dani had slipped a few zloty into the girl's hand as she had passed. It wasn't much but it would keep her from starvation on the long trek. After that, her parents never forgot their shame. They walked daily with heads bowed and became more stern with their younger offspring, not permitting them to laugh and play with the other children anymore.

But for Dani it was different. Roman had proof she was a virgin and they would be married. She would start planning how best to get Tekla to look more favorably on Roman. Nonetheless, one thing puzzled Dani as she slowly drifted off to sleep. Was it possible that Roman thought she would have money to bring to him? She would have to make it clear that she came with nothing. She had pride, and they could live a good married life on what he earned for she certainly knew how to be thrifty, knew how to conjure up a meal from practically nothing and how to make their clothes if need be, not fashionable attire but good sturdy items that would last. She hadn't come to America to sponge off her dear aunt. Tekla had worked hard for her money, and Dani had no intention of taking a single penny. A man was supposed to support his wife, and a wife's job was to see that every penny earned was put to good use. But tomorrow was another day, a day for formulating plans for the future.

Chapter Five

For weeks Dani made every effort to bring up Roman's name casually, at breakfast, during supper and at any other moment she and her aunt were together, all to no avail. In a rare burst of anger one evening, Tekla forbid her to mention his name again.

"Dani, what's come over you? I ask you about school and you ask me about Roman. I talk about business and you bring up that *djabel*'s, name. He is a devil and I forbid you to talk of him. It's been so peaceful at the tavern because he hasn't been showing his face. Good riddance. The dog is running with his own as they say in the homeland. He's staying away and that's fine. There hasn't been a fight over a woman since he's found somewhere else to hang his hat, and I feel no sympathy for the ninny he's taken up with now. It must be some chit from another neighborhood where he isn't known well. The last time Bolie saw him, on a Sunday I think it was, Roman had a smug, self-satisfied grin on his face, so Bolie thinks he's struck it rich this time and found a plump pigeon ready for plucking." She looked at Dani sternly and her niece hung her head woefully. "You miss seeing him, don't you? You're like a lovesick schoolgirl. Since that first night, when he asked you to

151

dance, I've watched you mooning over him, following his every movement with your eyes. I wanted to say something to you long ago but I thought it would wear off in time, especially after I explained what a vile person he is. Now I can see none of my words sank into your head. He's attracted you with his false cloak of charm and looks. I'd rather see you back in the old country, grubbing in the dirt, than worshiping Roman Kawa from afar."

"But, Aunt, I know people can change. Please listen—"

"No. You listen to me. Sit down. We're going to have some plain talk. Let me tell you some of the things I know about Roman. At first I thought you were too young and delicate a girl to hear such talk, but now I suppose it's the only way to put this matter to rest and be done with it. Where shall I begin?" Tekla gathered up her thoughts at random. How should she begin to tell a naïve innocent girl that the young boy she had watched grow up to manhood had been a bad seed from the moment of his conception. How could he be anything else when his mother was too soft-spoken to rule her house and was constantly browbeaten by her husband who treated her as though she were dirt beneath his feet? She remembered first noticing Roman when he was about twelve and the scourge of the area. Gentler parents pulled their children away from Roman, knowing he would lead them into trouble, not the minor everyday trouble young boys usually got into but truly wicked misdeeds. When he'd been expelled from school in the sixth grade, his father had boasted of his misconduct while his mother had wrung her hands in sad anguish hoping, as she did until her dying day, that her son would be the opposite of his father. Now that he was grown Roman hid his wickedness behind a veneer of polite manners and false cour-

152

tesy, for he had learned somewhere along the road that he could gain greater rewards by practicing deceit. But in his younger days he had just taken what he wanted no matter who had been hurt in the process. His father had paid off the police several times to keep his son from being charged with stealing, and afterward the two devil's replicas had grinned at each other over their successful bypassing of the law. Neither father nor son had any respect for God, man, woman, child, or beast. It was time for Dani to know some of the truth.

"Four years ago," Tekla began, "Roman got a young girl pregnant. Naturally her parents were outraged when their daughter came home crying with the news. They went to Roman and insisted he marry her immediately. Of course the foolish girl was in love with him and the parents loved their daughter, so they were willing to see her marry a man they disliked with all their hearts. They wanted her to be happy you see. Roman, after he was cornered by the girl's parents and brother, admitted he was the father and the wedding was to take place that same month, but the girl committed suicide a week later. She drowned herself in the river near Iron Street. Her parents were positive Roman drove her to it, and when her body was found after two days, there were suspicious bruises on her face. Unless she had hit some object when she'd fallen into the water, which was unlikely since the water's deep, those bruises were Roman's work. No one knew for certain. Did they have a fight before she went to her watery death? Did he hit her in anger? That would be typical of Roman. It was thought he didn't actually push her into the river, but he may as well have. Almost everyone believed he drove her to her death, but nothing could be proved. Her family wanted to kill Roman. But their friends stopped them because Roman had said he was not around the week it happened. He'd said he was visiting friends on Milwaukee Avenue and even brought back the couple he was staying with to back up his story."

Tekla took a sip of water and continued. "About seven years ago when Roman was twenty-two, he left a girl waiting at the altar. On the very day of the wedding, with family and friends assembled in the church, he never arrived. The wedding was scheduled to take place at nine in the morning, and the poor bride waited until ten, thinking there was a horrible accident. The priest finally persuaded the wedding party to wait at home while friends checked on Roman's whereabouts. He was finally found that evening in a drunken stupor crying out that he wasn't ready to be pushed into marriage. The poor girl was so shaken with embarrassment that she joined a convent a short while later and, thankfully, was sent to another city for her novitiate studies. At least she didn't have to live with the stigma of that shame in her own community. A few years later her parents moved to the same city, for they felt if they had to continue seeing Roman's mocking face they would kill or maim him. There have been rumors that at least two other women have gotten rid of unwanted babies for which it was said Roman was responsible. Personally I think he's a sex-crazed fiend. An old widow in her seventies who lived on the very next block used to invite Roman over to keep her company and run errands. When she died a few years ago her nephews knew for certain she had money hidden away somewhere in the house but it never could be found. Roman must have put his hands on it, but again, nothing could be proven. I'm not saying Roman went to bed with the old widow, only that he took advantage of an unfortunate lonely woman who needed someone to talk to. Now are you beginning to see how many lives this man has ruined? Most likely what I'm telling you is only the tip of the iceberg. Only God knows what other misery he's put good people through."

Tekla poured herself a cup of coffee, embarrassed by telling the truth about Roman Kawa. These stories were not meant for a young girl's ears, but she had to find a way to shock Dani out of her fascination for this depraved man with whom she thought she was in love.

Her beloved niece looked up sorrowfully. "And there's no way you think Roman can change, become a good person?"

"No. Nothing will change him. You'll have to trust my judgment in this, my dear. I'm older and, in this case, wiser. I've known him most of his life. You've only seen his charming side. If I thought there was a chance of his turning over a new leaf, even a small chance, I would let you see him. I don't want you marrying someone you don't love, but I beg you to put him out of your mind. You're so young. The right man will come along one of these days and you'll be glad I intervened. Give yourself time. There's so much to see and do here. In the next few weeks I'll start showing you around the city and you'll be so impressed. I should have taken you out before now, but I'm always so busy. I thought I couldn't spare the time, but I'll make time. We can go to Jackson Park. I'll show you the one building that's still standing from the Columbian Exposition, the Fine Arts Building. I'll show you the very spot where the Ferris wheel was erected, and we can stop and have lunch at one of the restaurants in Hyde Park. Once you can find your way about you can use your spending money to explore on your own and it will be so thrilling. Roman will leave your thoughts when exciting new sights fill your eyes." Tekla stood up. "Now I must get back to work, but tell me first how you like school. You speak English so well. I'm amazed at how quickly you've learned. It took me a

155

great deal longer."

Dani carefully kept her disappointment from her voice. "School is just fine. The nuns are all so kind and the work is easy. I like it very much. The principal said my grades are high enough for me to graduate with the class in June. She complimented Mama for teaching me so well when I was young and for making me read so many books. As soon as I learned the language the principal decided I was evenly matched with the other eighth grade students so I can graduate in June."

"You're a good girl, Dani. Keep on learning. Next week we'll go sightseeing then I'll give you a regular allowance so you can be on your own more often. I feel you can be trusted as long as you're home before dark."

"Thank you, Aunt. I'll clean up the kitchen before I get back to my homework. Say hello to Bolie and Martha for me. Tell them I'll be in this Saturday."

"They miss you, Dani. Bolie has no one to tell funny stories to. Since school started you haven't been coming in on Saturdays, and they would like to see you once in a while. I'll tell them you'll be in this weekend. Good night. You'll be sleeping by the time I get back." She kissed Dani good night and left.

As Dani washed the supper dishes in the soapy hot water, she realized she had better start going to the tavern for a while on Saturday. Roman was coming to the house more often, through the back as usual, three and sometimes four times a week. Naturally, he didn't settle for anything less than taking Dani to her bedroom and teaching her what he liked a woman to do. She was thrilled, as in the beginning, with the preliminaries and the excitement his kisses aroused, but the ultimate act of love still gave her no pleasure. Just when she thought she would experience total joy, it was over. Too soon, Roman lay on his side completely spent while she was left with an empty feeling, an expecta-

tion of much more than he had given. Still she loved
him, especially when he uttered wild and exciting compliments in bed. She was his precious *aniol*, his angel,
the woman he'd been waiting to find all his life. His
words alone sent shivers up and down her spine. She
imagined, given enough practice, she would feel the
same fulfillment he did. Roman was coming tonight,
and she trembled, wondering how she could tell him of
Tekla's latest reaction. It seemed there was no hope for
their getting married, not if her aunt remained so drastically opposed to the union.

Precisely at nine, she heard his light tap on the back
door and she rushed to open it, smiling with pure joy.
Oh, how she needed someone to hold her close and
assure her everything was all right. She could find no
solution to their dilemma, but surely Roman would
think of one. He always did. He shut the door quickly
behind him, sealing out the chill night air.

"Well, little love, have you had a chance today to
sway your aunt in our direction?"

Dani shivered. She might as well get the bad news
over as quickly as possible. If she waited it would only
make her more nervous and frightened about losing
him.

"Roman, I have bad news. It seems my aunt will
never change her opinion of you. She told me some
rather horrid stories about you. I'm not saying I
believed them, but she does. There's a lot of gossip
going around the neighborhood, and it seems there has
been for years. Being in business, my aunt hears most
of it."

"What stories?" he interrupted, a tight angry look on
his face.

"Oh, she said something about your leaving a girl at
the altar and that another girl committed suicide some
years back. All the blame was laid on you. She claims

you'll never change, never find a decent job. She went on and on for so long I can't even remember everything she said."

"Didn't you tell her I'm working steadily now at the soap factory? For you I'm working ten hours a day at that foul-smelling, back-breaking job. Did you tell the old crow that?"

"No, I didn't have a chance. Once she started I couldn't get a word in. She wouldn't let me. Roman, I don't know what we'll do. She's not about to relent. I can't talk her into seeing our side."

Roman paced back and forth in the kitchen.

"The old bitch. She's jealous because she never found the right man to warm her bed. She'll die a cold-hearted virgin and expect you to do the same."

"Please, Roman, don't call her such vile names. She's a good woman who only wants what's best for me. Truly she does."

"Then you agree with her? Do you want to call it quits, because if you do, I'm willing. There are a lot of women waiting to marry, and I'm sure, with your aunt's help, you can find a reputable man. Should we say good-bye tonight?"

"Roman, no. Can't you see I'm only trying to help. I didn't mean to hurt your feelings. Of course I don't want you to leave. I just thought you could find a way for us to be together always, night and day. You're much smarter than I when it comes to solving difficult problems."

Roman took off his overcoat and caught her up close, nuzzling his mouth across the side of her neck and running hot kisses down to the swell of her breasts. "Then you're willing to do anything to be with me? I can count on you to be on my side?"

"Yes," Dani murmured happily, "whatever you say."

He pulled her to their regular trysting place, her bedroom, and locked the door. Once again tension mounted high until Dani thought she would burst with desire for a yet-unknown fulfillment. She was certain she would reach the peak she sought tonight in his loving arms, but another pang of disappointment set in as Roman let out a long soft moan and pulled himself away. She didn't dare ask him to prolong the thrusts and be a little gentler, fearing his wrath, for he did have a terrible temper that was better left unaroused. Soon, she felt, she could force herself to speed up the culminating of the forces in her own body; then everything would be perfect.

Roman left within the hour, with a sly grin and healing advice. "We'll be married soon, believe me. I predict we'll be man and wife in a few months." With that he let himself surreptitiously out the door promising to meet her late on Saturday since she was going to put in an appearance at the tavern. "I'll come there at six or so, eat, and then say I'm going up north to see my friends. This will allay Tekla's fears then I'll meet you at ten on the back porch. All right, little dove?"

"Fine," Dani whispered, content. She kissed him a passionate good-night wishing they had the whole night to spend together. Perhaps if she didn't always feel so guilty she would enjoy their lovemaking as much as he did. That was it, she decided. Guilt was preventing her from experiencing the full joy of Roman's lithe body.

Thanksgiving came and passed, but Tekla still steadfastly refused to discuss Roman. Bolie and Martha were invited for Thanksgiving dinner along with another couple from across the street and their two small children. The gathering feasted on barley soup, duck browned in a tasty crispness; mashed potatoes with gravy; lightly browned cheese-filled pierogi; and an assortment of beets, pickles, and creamed cucumbers. When Father Stefan joined them for dessert and a glass of brandy, he praised Dani's singing in the church choir and her excellent grades in school. He warned her that the choir would begin practicing Christmas carols soon and then sat down at the piano, a recent acquisition of Tekla's, to play the most popular carols while everyone joined in song. Dani sang the beautiful *"Dzisiaj Bethlehem,"* "Today in Bethlehem," by herself in a clear soprano that left the assembled group with misty eyes, anticipating the coming joyful holiday. Christmas seemed to be everyone's favorite holiday from toddlers to the oldsters. Work would begin in earnest in most of the households now. Women would be knitting at a furious pace, trying to complete scarves and hats for gift-giving. There were handmade rag dolls to be stuffed for the children, clothes to sew. Pennies and dimes must be hidden away to buy special small gifts at the store. Geese and ducks had to be fattened for the butcher block, platters of cookies baked and stored away. Yeast was fermenting in crocks, waiting to be used for the hot, fruit-filled paczki that would be fried by the dozens on Christmas Eve. Each housewife attempted to set a superior table at least during this time of the year.

As Tekla's guests departed, a light sprinkling of powdery snow began to fall, turning the deserted street into a fairytale scene. The tiny flakes glistened like diamonds, and no one wanted to be the first to mar the pristine whiteness with foot marks. Father Stefan slowly took the first step out onto the front stairs.

"You won't think it so pretty when you have to get up early in the morning and go to work. Tomorrow you'll all be complaining that you can't wait until summer."

He guided the couple and their children across the street to their home and waved good night to Bolie and Martha who walked behind holding hands as they shuffled through the snow, sending sprays of it right and left. They laughed as it caught the light and sparkled.

"Pick all you like," Bolie joked to his wife as he flung a handful of snow up to the light and watched it cascade down in a radiant shimmer. "Pretend it's all the diamonds I would like to buy you if I had the money."

Martha flung her handful away. "Silly goose, what would I do with diamonds? We'll have our own home soon and that's all I want; to be able to say we own property. No one in my family owns property. We'll be the first."

Bolie hugged his wife tightly. "That's one promise I can keep. We'll have our house, never fear."

"I wanted to give you babies," Martha said regretfully, "but God doesn't seem to answer my prayers."

"Ah, Martha, if we had babies then you would have no time for me. You'd be too busy taking care of the little ones and you'd forget all about your husband. We don't need babies to be happy, not as long as we have each other."

"You're right, Bolie. I need no one else, only you." Martha abruptly changed the subject "Bolie, do you think we should tell Tekla that something's up between Roman and Dani? I'm sure of it. I have this feeling something is going on between them and it worries me."

"No, my love. Stay out of their lives. You have no proof. You only see Dani looking at Roman with soulful eyes. He knows he can't get around Tekla; she's too strong willed. And I'll kill him if he gets to close to Dani. You're worrying over nothing. At Dani's age she's just learning about love, not in love. It will be over soon."

"I pray you're right, Bolie. I pray every night you're right."

Just before Christmas Dani was sure she was pregnant and Roman was overjoyed when she told him of her concern.

"Wonderful. This is the best gift you could give me, my beloved," he said immediately.

Deep inside he was relieved. He had come to her house three times a week just to make sure something like this would happen. It was about time too. He was beginning to think she was barren and he was wasting his precious time. At least five other women were pursuing him, asking him repeatedly where he was keeping himself these days although on some nights he had gone to one or two of them after leaving Dani. This courtship was cutting into the time he could spend with experienced, sensuous women, the kind of women who evenly matched his voracious sexual appetite.

Dani was terrified by the thought of having a baby without being properly wed. She hadn't had morning sickness but she did become nauseated whenever she thought of how Tekla would react to the news.

"She'll banish me from the house," she cried distraught. "She'll ship me away to Poland for punishment."

"Don't worry so, darling. Listen to me. I'll be here on Christmas morning and we'll tell her the good news together. You won't have to face her alone. When she hears of your condition she'll have to relent for she's a good Catholic woman. If necessary, we'll spend the whole day pounding it into her head that this is what we both want. She won't throw you into the streets. You're her only living relative. She'll get used to the idea little by little. She won't be overjoyed but she'll come around I promise you."

He was far more gentle that night, and Dani felt herself burst with pleasure for the first time. The thrill was overpowering, and after he left she lay in bed, filled

162

with wonder at the throbbing culmination she had just experienced. Everything would work out, she knew. Christmas Day would be the beginning of a new and glorious life; a life of freedom and closeness with Roman.

Tekla slept late Christmas morning and then they went to the noon mass. Although Dani had sung for the midnight mass, she joined her aunt for another hour in church. Tekla explained that the tavern was filled to the brim after the midnight mass and she couldn't close until nearly three in the morning. After church they came home and ate a leisurely breakfast, breaking the traditional *oplatky*, the thin wafer given by the church in the promise of a plentiful, blessed coming year. The wafer, similar to that used for Holy Communion, was square in shape, and it was the custom to "break bread" with friends and relatives each Christmas.

Dani and Tekla had trimmed the tree the previous afternoon, hanging on it precious hand-crafted ornaments and chains of cranberries. Although candles dotted the branches, Tekla lit them for only a few minutes; she was deathly afraid of a fire. Two days earlier Dani had walked to Morgan Street to buy the tree in a lot, usually vacant, that was filled with trees which ranged in size from two feet to a majestic fifteen feet. She selected a medium-size one and paid a young boy a nickel to help her drag it home. Now on Christmas morning as she walked into the living room, the tree shimmered with glossy beauty. A manger nestled in white cotton lay beneath it, and Tekla proudly admired the carved baby Jesus, Joseph and Mary, the three wise men, the shepherds, and the ornately worked stable and animals. A carpenter who

163

had been out of work for a few months had hand carved the whole set, and Tekla had paid a pretty penny for those figures, but now she decided they were worth every cent. Suddenly merry, she began handing presents to her niece. Amazed by Tekla's generosity, Dani sighed and exclaimed excitedly as each present was opened. There was a new brown wool coat lined with fleece to keep her warm this winter. In the next package she found a long robe and slippers, bright red ones. Two new dresses—one a soft plaid, the other a beige wool—were next, and the last gift was a pair of ice skates. A few boys would begin to try the ice soon and then scores of children and grownups would skate round and round on it, Tekla explained. She was much too old to join them, but she promised Dani she would sit by the roaring bonfire built nightly to warm the skaters and the onlookers, and she would watch her learn how to skate.

Tears sprang to Dani's eyes at the realization that she would be hurting her dear benefactress in such a short while. Roman was due at any minute, and together, they would break her aunt's heart. A sick feeling churned in the pit of her stomach while great tears ran down her cheeks.

"Don't cry, Dani." Tekla said comfortingly. "I know how much you must be missing your brother and father today, but they're both watching us from heaven, happy for you. It's a beautiful day. Be happy too."

Dani wiped her eyes and brought out the gifts she had for her aunt. Then she gave the older woman a great hug.

"It's not much, but they're given to you with all my love. I love you most of all the people I know in the world. Please remember that always."

"Stop crying, Dani." Tekla laughed. "You'll make me cry too."

She opened the two presents Dani handed her. A becoming black hat with a stylish veil rested in an ornate hat box. It was expensive. Dani had used a good part of the money her father had given her to pay for the hat, but it was the best Beckman's department store on Morgan Street had to offer. Mr. Beckman himself had said it came from an expensive milliner in New York City and that the design originated from Paris. The hat made her aunt appear very fashionable and years younger. Tekla was overjoyed and preened before the mirror, admiring her new acquisition. Dani's second gift to her was a water color she had done at school—a picture of St. Mary's church in the summer. The green foliage of trees outlined the building. One of the nuns had given Dani a frame and she had set the water color behind glass.

"It's truly beautiful," Tekla cried, delighted. "You're so talented. Your gift shall hang right here in my living room," she said as she removed a rather ugly picture of a horse and threw it aside. She put Dani's picture in its place and immediately it brightened the room and became a focal point to admire as one sat on the sofa. Tekla sat down, beaming with pride in Dani's water color. "Dani, I know I've been promising that we would go sightseeing, but with the holidays there's been too much of a rush. Work will slow down somewhat now and after the New Year we'll begin exploring."

Suddenly a loud knock sounded on the front door. Dani jumped at the noise and nausea churned up from her stomach. It's Roman, she realized. Can't I warn him to wait a few days? She dreaded spoiling Christmas Day. How could she do this to Tekla on this holiest of holidays?

Roman burst into the living room, holding a box of candy for Tekla, and swept his hat off regally, dusting off the few snowflakes that stubbornly clung to his dark gray homburg.

"Merry Christmas, my dear ladies," he declared as he took off his coat.

Dumfounded at his rude entry, Tekla was speechless for a moment; then her face flushed red with rage.

"How dare you come into my home as though you're an invited guest? Get out," she hissed. "How dare you!" She rose from the couch, her face becoming mottled as her anger mounted.

Dani stood in the middle of the room glancing from left to right, from Roman back to Tekla. She walked over to Roman and took his hand in hers. He gave her hand a slight squeeze of encouragement.

"My dear Tekla, I come to your house today in good faith. You must forgive us, but Dani and I are going to be married as soon as it can be arranged. We love each other deeply."

"Over my dead body," Tekla raged. "Never. Dani, what in God's name is going on?"

Dani's throat felt paralyzed. She couldn't manage to say a word. Her aunt stood directly in front of her, looking as though she'd been mortally wounded, and her life was draining from her body. In all her wild imaginings Dani had never thought that Tekla would be so stunned, so drained. Oh God, she prayed, take these past few moments back and I'll be different. I'll change; I'll even stay away from Roman only don't let her look like this anymore. A picture of her father suddenly flashed in her mind, and she remembered her promise to him that she would come to this new country and make him proud for she was being offered a chance to change her destiny and make something of herself. She hadn't been here a year yet, and what had she done with her life up to this point except to hurt someone who loved her?

"Please sit down, Tekla," Roman said quietly. "You

must force yourself to stay calm because, you see, I'm afraid your niece and I have to be married, and when I said as quickly as possible I meant just that. You see, we're going to have a child in July so the sooner we're wed, the better. Your gossipy friends will start counting the months on their fingers and I'm afraid there's no way to avoid the facts. Maybe if we're lucky we can pass it off as a premature birth but even so there will still be talk. It's best we go to the priest soon and see if we can get a special dispensation from the usual three-week banns. I thought a quiet wedding with no fanfare would be appropriate. Just the three of us, and perhaps Bolie and Martha as witnesses. You can always tell your friends we were married sooner to save face. Martha and Bolie will keep their mouths shut as I'm sure the priest will."

Tekla sank back onto the couch, her face now ashen, her hands trembling.

"Danuta, is this true?" she asked in a whisper.

Dani swallowed hard and let go of Roman's hand to sit beside her aunt on the couch.

"I'm sorry," she cried, tears streaming down her face. "Yes, it's true. I tried to tell you how I felt about Roman but you wouldn't listen. He truly is a changed man. He loves me you see and even has a steady job at the soap factory. He'll be able to support us both and the baby too. Oh, how can I make you realize he's the man I love? I'm sorry it has to be this way, but I'm not sorry about having Roman's baby. Please don't turn against us now. Roman and I are going to be very happy I promise you. Aunt, please say something. Don't just stare at me like that."

Tekla stammered out her words. "So you fell for this conniving fox and his promises. You've made your bed and there's nothing left but for you to lie in it. Get your coat. We're going to the priest's house right now

167

even if we have to upset his holiday dinner. But let me say one thing to both of you." She stared at Roman, hatred in her eyes. "You're on your own. Dani, don't come to me in the months to come crying over your mistake." She turned to look Roman straight in the eyes. "There will be nothing from me as a wedding gift. Do you understand? Dani leaves with only her clothes. Nothing else. Since you're going to be such a marvelous provider, she won't need anything from me." With these words she stormed out of the living room to put on her hat, coat, and gloves. "Are you ready?" she asked icily a moment later.

Tekla left the house in front of them while Roman muttered to Dani. "Don't worry, angel. She'll change her mind. If not now, when she sees the baby. Stop crying."

Father Stefan was surprised when the grim trio rang the rectory bell. Tekla stood in front, stony-faced, while Dani and Roman stayed behind glancing at each other nervously.

"What's wrong?" the priest asked, leading them into the office. "I can see by the look on your faces that this isn't a social Christmas visit."

"How soon can you perform a wedding?" Tekla asked quietly, shamed in front of this man of God. "Can you do it this week?"

"I think I understand," he answered. "But it's against all rules of the church."

"Then call the pastor and see what he can do about changing the rules," Tekla answered shortly. "It must be done now for my niece and her chosen partner have been living in sin. Surely you can perform the wedding this weekend so as not to put shame on their unborn child."

Father Stefan hurried to bring the pastor into the room, and after much discussion it was decided that

Dani and Roman would be married on the coming Saturday in the priest's office with only the bride and groom present and Bolie and Martha as witnesses. If questions were asked by curious parishioners the truthful answer could be easily evaded. A priest had the right to change the subject if he wished without being rude, and Father Stefan was very close-mouthed as was the pastor. If need be, he could always tell a little white lie, God forgive him, and say the banns had been posted in a church to which Roman belonged, one on the north side. But no one would question him that closely. Tekla flatly refused to attend the makeshift ceremony. She pressed a wad of bills into Father Stefan's hand as they left. "This is a donation, Father. Thank you for your help."

Roman left them at the front door, promising to return a good hour before the ceremony. He kissed Dani on the lips in full view of Tekla, but she only turned her head and left the room.

"It won't be long now," he said quietly. "Just a few more days and we'll be alone. Be strong, little one. It will all be over soon."

In the following days Tekla was gone before Dani rose for breakfast and didn't bother to come home for supper. By the time she did get home, Dani was fast asleep even though she tried to force herself to keep her eyes open so she could at least talk to her aunt before the wedding day. She dreaded leaving the house under these sad circumstances. She regretted not being able to graduate with her class too. Soon they would all know why she wasn't coming back after the holiday recess. Dani went to the tavern twice but Tekla made sure she was surrounded by jostling customers, and Bolie and Martha stared at her coldly, not joking and asking questions as they usually did, so there was nothing Dani could do but leave. She couldn't bring herself to broach the subject of Roman in front of strangers. It would be too humiliating if her aunt caused a scene in front of all these people.

On Friday night, she managed to stay up until she heard the key turning in the lock at three in the morning. Jumping out of bed before Tekla could escape into her room, she cornered her in the kitchen, eyes pleading for understanding.

"Please," she begged. "Please listen to me. I'll only keep you a few minutes, I promise. Just let me talk to you for a little while. Don't turn away from me."

Tekla sat down at the kitchen table, still wearing her coat, a look of impatience clearly etched on her face. Dani pulled another chair next to hers and took Tekla's hands into her own warming the chill out of them.

"You must say you forgive me, Aunt," she began haltingly. "I couldn't help myself. I was drawn to Roman from the first night we met, and even if you never brought me here, I feel I would have met him somehow and fallen in love with him. For some reason I was put on board the *Destiny* and brought here against my will. You know how I wanted to stay with Papa and Jan. Not that I don't love you, I just felt my place was in Poland with them until we could all leave together as a family. But no matter how hard I tried to stay, I had no choice. I was brought to you, and I believe deep in my heart I was meant to meet Roman. Please try to understand. I know the bad things Roman has done. He admitted leaving that girl at the altar but only because he didn't love her. He swore he had nothing to do with the other girl's suicide, and I believe him. He would have gone through with the wedding as promised and was shocked when he returned home to discover she had taken her own life. He even admitted to me that he took the old lady's money. He never did anything bad with her, only kept her company and talked when she

170

was lonely. Her nephews never bothered to visit her except on Christmas and once in a while on her birthday. She was hungry for companionship so he told her funny stories and went to the store for her and stayed for supper once in a while. He firmly believes he deserved the money she had hidden. I think he did too. Roman told me he found about three hundred dollars and he thought of it as repayment for the time he'd spent catering to her whims. He's going to change though. He has already. Don't turn away from me in disgust, for I don't think I can bear that. Say you'll forgive me."

Tekla's tortured eyes softened in the dim light. She sobbed convulsively and took Dani into her arms.

"I couldn't turn away from you. You're my only brother's child. You're like the daughter Józef and I would have had if only he'd lived long enough. Dani, you can turn to me whenever you're in need, but please don't tell that to Roman. I'm afraid if he finds life too easy he'll remain steadfast in his wicked ways. Maybe you're right, who knows? Perhaps you're the one who can make a man of him. Dani, I'll be right here if you ever need me, but please understand that I can't see you married. I just can't. You may keep the key to my house, and if you ever have need of a few peaceful hours or some food feel free to come home and help yourself. But don't bring Roman here, not yet. I have to see with my own eyes that he's a changed man. That's all I can promise for now."

Dani cried as she hugged her aunt. "Thank you. Thank you for forgiving me."

Then they went to their separate rooms, the elder woman distraught with worry, the younger happy and at peace.

Dani's wedding day dawned black and ominous. Dark clouds raced across the sky and a cold sleet

171

tapped at the windows threatening to crack them open with its steady assault. Roman came to get her, carrying a corsage of carnations to pin on her new brown coat. She pulled her mother's fur hat over her head and put on warm mittens. Tekla stayed in the kitchen until she heard the door close and then she prayed aloud, imploring the Blessed Mother to watch over her misled niece.

"Take care of her, dear Lady," she pleaded, her eyes turned upward. "Her life is going to be a living hell. Give her the strength to bear it."

The ceremony was short, no longer than ten minutes, and Martha and Bolie witnessed the hasty affair with silent and stern faces, neither offering congratulations as they left the rectory. They owed their allegiance to Tekla and felt any joy on their part would be tantamount to treason.

When Bolie first heard the news from Tekla's own mouth he had to be restrained from leaving the tavern, ferreting out Roman, and beating him severely. When he was asked to be a witness along with Martha, his face turned such a bright crimson that Martha thought he was on the verge of a stroke and she forced him to sit down and remain calm. Later, after Tekla left, he confided to his wife.

"Only for Tekla would I consent to being a witness to this monstrous marriage. That *bekarci,* that bastard, should rot with the worms in the bowels of the earth. You were right. I should have known you were right when you felt something was amiss. I should have trusted your judgment. A woman always knows when there's plotting afoot."

"Please, Bolie," Martha begged. "Tekla's heart has been pierced by the sword of deceit. Don't make it worse for her. She pinned all her hopes on Dani and they've been dashed to the ground. She has no one to comfort her but us. Please go along with her request. It's all we can do for her now. After the wedding, when Dani leaves, we'll keep her company and although we won't be able to cheer her at least she'll have someone to turn to. Do it for me and Tekla, Bolie, please. It will only take a little while."

Bolie took a straight shot of whiskey, unusual for him for he didn't like to drink, and patted Martha's hand. "You know I'd do anything you asked. I'll do it but not of my own free will."

Now the deed was done, and Dani and Roman were back at the house, Dani's pink corsage coated with ice that started to melt as soon as they entered the heated room. Roman hoisted up the packed suitcases waiting in the hall. They were going back to his one-room flat to live until Dani could find something better. She hugged her aunt in silence, and Tekla pressed some bills into her hand, putting one finger to her mouth.

"Shush," she admonished quietly. "Use it for the new things you'll need for your home." Gently, she pushed Dani away.

Roman's miserable room was cluttered. In it were a bed, a small greasy stove, a rickety table, two broken-down chairs, and a chest of drawers. Roaches skuttled away to hide as Roman lit the kerosene lamp and a mouse scurried off to escape the unwelcome intrusion on its foraging. Dani shuddered at the first sight of the dingy room with its cracked green walls, but she didn't allow the distressing scene to eat away at her happiness. Tomorrow she would start looking for a better place. Roman stoked up the coal-burning stove and some of the dank chill dissipated. Their wedding supper was cold cuts and bread. Dani couldn't bear cooking at the stove that was encrusted with years of old grease and

173

food splatters. They ate their meal and toasted each other with glasses of water. Then, as dusk darkened the room, Roman took her to bed where he violently tore the clothes from her body, ripping the buttons off her best winter dress. She started to protest but he cut off her words with a bruising kiss as he fumbled out of his own clothes. As her senses throbbed and she welcomed Roman into her body, she decided she had been right after all: throwing guilt to the winds did help. She was mad with desire for her husband and thought she always would be. But these stray thoughts vanished as quickly as they had come for now there was only Roman, bringing her wildly intoxicating ecstasy for a few brief moments. Warmed by the heat of their movements, they stayed in each other's arms all night while the room slowly grew cold and the fire in the stove waned away to pale ashes.

Ice frosted the one window in the morning, and Dani shook Roman awake. "It's freezing in here, sleepyhead. Get up and show me where the firewood is."

Teeth chattering, Roman grumpily wrapped an old robe around himself and went to the stove, shaking out the cold ashes and getting kindling wood from a pail. After fifteen minutes the room became warmer and Dani left the heat of the fire to explore the possibility of breakfast. In the wall cupboard she found a half-dozen eggs and set them on the table. She put a pot of water on the stove and, when it became hot enough, scrubbed off some of the grease from the grates. Luckily, she had found a fairly new pan, and she broke the eggs into that, one for her, two for Roman. There was half a loaf of stale bread, and it would have to do until she could get to the bakery to buy more. She toasted it over the fire to make it more palatable. Roman sat at the table, drowsily staring at the glowing stove with sleepy eyes.

"You don't have to work today do you, Roman?"

Dani asked, setting the eggs on the table.

"Are you stupid? Today's Sunday. You know the factory is closed on Sunday. No, I don't work today."

She ignored his surliness. "Good. Then we can go out to see if we can find a better apartment. We can go shopping too for some groceries for dinner. The little store on May Street is open till two."

"We don't have to go looking for an apartment. If that old bitch of an aunt of yours practiced the charity she always preaches we could be living comfortably with her. She has more room than she can use. Three bedrooms, a kitchen, a dining room, and a living room. The old bag doesn't need all that space for just one person."

"Roman, please don't start the day arguing. Tekla promised she may feel differently once she sees you mean well. Just give her a chance. You haven't lived an exemplary life up to now."

Roman pushed his plate off the table. It shattered and the yellow egg yolks splattered and congealed on the cold floor.

"Don't throw your big words at me just because I didn't finish school. Don't throw your intelligence in my face. I won't have it, do you hear?"

Dani put her fork down on the crooked table and began to cry softly.

"Dani, I'm sorry," Roman apologized. "I'm at my worst in the morning. I'll try to change, but as the day goes on my mood always improves. It's just that I hate getting up in this miserable dreary room. It depresses me for I want something better for us."

She smiled her forgiveness at him, and dutifully he helped her clean the room until it looked fairly decent. Then, in the afternoon, they went shopping and brought home enough to feed them for the next few days.

The following morning Roman woke with only minutes to spare. He had to get to work on time and left without breakfast, afraid he would be fired if he checked in late one more time.

Dani hated to use any of the hundred dollars her aunt had slipped into her hand after the wedding but the purchase of an alarm clock took priority over her reluctance. They had to wake up at least an hour before Roman reported for work so she could prepare him a nourishing meal and send him off to his job with a full stomach and a packed lunch. She didn't want to spend any of the money until they found a better place to live, but a clock was a necessity and Roman hadn't given her any money to shop with. That first morning she scoured and cleaned the room. She was relieved to note that the coal and wood peddler drove his wagon down the street daily. She was glad she wouldn't have to trudge for blocks lugging the heavy heating materials. Roman didn't have an icebox, but for now one wasn't needed. It was cold enough in the closet to keep anything from spoiling. Now that the stove and sink were sparkling clean, most of the roaches scampered away and she only glimpsed an occasional one now and then. Next, she plugged up the holes in the baseboard with old rags and wood splinters, praying the makeshift job would keep out the mice.

At six when Roman trudged up three flights of stairs, Dani had a hearty pot of stew bubbling away on the stove and she had bought a loaf of freshly baked rye bread at the bakery. A pot of strong tea was brewing, and while he washed in a basin of warm water she set it on the chest of drawers.

"I have to find another job soon, Dani," he said as he sat down to eat. "The odor of the factory is driving me insane. I can smell it even when I'm sleeping. Mixing those vats of foul-smelling soap is going to kill me, I

176

know it. I wish our baby could be born sooner so your aunt would relent and perhaps let me run the tavern for her. Now that's a nice clean job. She has a good business, and it could be made even more profitable with me assisting." He noticed the clock ticking on the dresser. "Where did that come from?"

"I bought it today," Dani answered brightly. "I didn't want to use any of the money Tekla gave us until we found an apartment, but we had to have a clock so you won't be late. I bought it for a quarter at the hardware store."

"Your aunt gave you money? Why didn't you tell me sooner?"

"With all the excitement of getting married and then coming here with you I forgot. It just slipped my mind. I want to talk to you about how we should spend it. When we move we're going to need just about everything: a decent bed, a new chest of drawers, a kitchen table and chairs, dishes, pots. Maybe we can even buy an icebox if there's enough left over. With what you make I'm sure we can get it all. The furniture can be bought at the secondhand store. They have some good quality merchandise and it's cheap."

"How much did Tekla give you?"

"A hundred dollars."

"Well then, you let me hold the money. I'll keep it in a safe place and give you half my paycheck every week so you can pay the bills and buy food. The rest I'll put away for our nest egg."

"But when are we going to look for another place?" Dani asked. I thought perhaps we could walk around after dinner. I think there are four rooms for rent right next door. Can't we go over and see what they look like? The man at the hardware store told me he thought they were still vacant."

"Forget about the flat next door," Roman snapped.

"I know those people and it's far more than we can afford. They're a pompous couple who think they own a palace. That's why the tenants never stay long. We'll stay here for a short while. It's cheap and we can save more money that way. Dani, could you possibly bear to live here until the spring? As soon as the weather turns warm a lot of people move and we can find a much better place at a price we can afford. No one likes to move in the winter when it's freezing. Everyone waits for the milder days. Look"—he pointed to the cleaned room—"you've worked wonders here already. It looks far better in two days than it ever did when I lived here by myself. It just needed a woman's touch. Another three or four months won't kill you, will it?"

Dani hesitated. "I guess not. All right. If you think it's best, I guess we can be happy here for a little while."

"That's my Dani," Roman praised. "You're truly the most wonderful wife a man could have."

Dani beamed at his praise, her disappointment forgotten as he cradled her in his arms and whispered passionate pleas in her ear.

The days turned bitter in January and February, and Dani couldn't afford to heat the room and pay the bills with the money Roman handed out at the end of each week. Somehow she thought he made more than he actually claimed, but then again, maybe not. She found it far more economical to let the fire die down to embers during the day and only rekindled it an hour before Roman was due home. Lately he'd been stopping off for a beer or two with his fellow workers and Dani felt life was easier when he did. At least he stopped complaining about his job after he had a few beers in him. Her father would have found the factory a haven compared to the mine, but she didn't dare mention that. She knew several other men who did the same work as her husband and they seemed happy

178

enough. They were glad of their weekly pay, and they managed to eat well even with several children to support. Roman must be putting aside a nice sum every week for their new home if they had to live so frugally now. At least they didn't have to worry about clothes. Dani had more than enough with all the things Tekla had bought her before she was married, and the small closet was stuffed with Roman's things. They had enough to last for many years to come, so clothing wouldn't be a major expense for a long, long time.

One afternoon Dani was surprised to see Tekla at the door, carrying a large bag. Tekla was aghast as she looked over the room.

"Is this how you live? Is this the best Roman can do for you?" As she set the bag down on the table, she noticed Dani huddled in a long bulky sweater. "Don't you have enough money to buy coal?"

Dani hurried to the pot-bellied stove and threw another shovelful into its hungry bowels.

"Yes, there's enough coal, but it's so expensive. I keep the fire low until Roman gets home. We're trying to save as much money as we can so that we can buy everything new in the spring when we move from here. This place is only temporary."

Tekla made no comment but began pulling purchases out of the large bag she'd brought. She took out a huge cut of beef—five pounds at least—two chickens, fresh vegetables, apples, and oranges. Dani hadn't tasted fruit since she'd left Tekla's house. It was priced far too high at the market so she'd put off buying any until summer when prices were lower and fruit was plentiful. She set water on the stove to boil for fresh tea in honor of her aunt's first visit. Dani wondered if Tekla was at last resigning herself to their marriage.

"Are you content, Dani?" Tekla asked. "Is Roman good to you?"

"Yes, I'm very happy. Roman's been wonderful. We don't go out much now because it's so cold, but when it's warmer and after the baby comes, we're going to go on picnics or we'll take the baby walking. He's even promised to go to church when it's warmer. Now he's always so tired after working all day. He's going to look for a better job soon, but even now he puts aside half his pay every week. In the spring, everything will be much better."

Tekla went back to the door and opened it to bring in yet another bag.

"Oh, Aunt," Dani chided. "This was too heavy for you to carry, especially up three flights of stairs."

"Nonsense. It wasn't all that far. You only live four blocks from me." Tekla took a huge chocolate cake from the bag and two loaves of bread, one rye and one white. "You don't use the key I gave you. I told you if you needed food you were free to come home and get whatever you wanted. I was expecting you to come and visit me but you haven't so here I am."

"Aunt, I'm bound and determined that we're going to live on what Roman makes," Dani declared firmly. "I wanted to come and see you in the mornings, but it's been freezing and by the time I get the fire lit and breakfast made I know you've left for the tavern and Roman doesn't want me to go there. He won't let me go out after dark either." Dani laughed. "At times he's more strict than you were. At least you used to let me walk the two blocks home from the tavern alone at night and explore Morgan Street by myself. Now I'm fortunate if I get to the corner grocery store. Roman doesn't want me out wandering the streets. He says it's dangerous for a woman walking alone; anything can happen."

"I agree," Tekla answered. "I never should have let you walk alone. Look what happened when I did. Roman put one over on me then. I should have

180

uspected something was amiss when he wasn't at the tvern on Saturdays. Oh, what a web he was spinning, apping you in the center with his threads of deceit. our father, God rest his good soul, must be writhing a his grave in frustration over my neglect. That's nother thing I'll have to answer for when I meet my Maker."

"Please," Dani begged. "Let's not go into that again. t's too late for recriminations. Papa would have nderstood. He would want me to be happy. Even if he tated Roman he would have allowed me to make my wn choice. Remember, Mama's parents disliked him."

"Maybe you're right," Tekla agreed reluctantly ipping at her tea. "What's done is done. No sense rying over spilt milk." She took off her coat now that he room was getting warmer and reached into her oocket. "I have two letters for you. One is from the Smenteks, I believe. The other must be from that trange Italian girl you met on the train. I don't see vhat you have in common with her or why you even oother to write."

Dani brought her hand up to her mouth. "Look at tow forgetful I'm getting. I've been so busy I haven't even had a chance to write them about my good news. I ust kept putting it off, waiting until we're settled at a oermanent address, and now almost two months have gone by."

Tekla noticed the tiny bulge at Dani's stomach. "You're starting to show already. Good. It should be a trong healthy baby. When did you say it was due?"

"Sometime in mid July."

"I can't wait, Dani. I'll soon have a great-niece or -nephew. Our family will grow again. Some good has come from all this madness."

"I know. Won't it be wonderful? A baby and a wife

181

are all that Roman needs to settle down."

"Dani, I hate to ask but are you holding the money you say you're saving? I can clearly see nothing was spent on this place." She glanced around disdainfully at the peeling, cracked walls and the rickety furniture.

"Roman's holding it. He's the man of the house, and it's only right for him to be in charge."

"Then do you know where he puts it? Do you count it together and see how it's growing?"

"No I don't. I think Roman puts it in the bank."

"You think? What's happened to the intelligent girl you were? He should have a bankbook lying around somewhere shouldn't he? Have you ever seen it? Surely you must clean the drawers and if he has one it should be there. Dani, I hate to sound so suspicious, but before you leap into renting another apartment you should check out the money. I hate to tell you this, but Roman's spending a good deal of money on drinks for his friends. He can't be doing that well. I know what most of the men make, and I know how much Roman makes. Darling, please check up a little. You're too trusting. I have to leave now because the liquor will be delivered soon and I have to be there to pay the bill. Check up on Roman, Dani. Don't leave everything in his hands. It's too great a temptation for Roman to have money in his hands. He enjoys spending it too much. Come to visit when the weather breaks. I'm home in the mornings."

Dani spent the afternoon answering her letters, but she didn't mention her marriage to her friends. As soon as they were properly settled she would share the good news. She was nervous when Roman came home, so immediately she told him of Tekla's visit and her generosity, about the letters from the Smenteks and Carmella. The Smenteks were doing well; they had another grandson and Carmella had a better job as a salesgirl in

182

large department store. After she ran out of news she couldn't bring herself to ask him about their savings.

Roman barely listened to the news of her friends. "Your aunt came here?" He rubbed his hands together. "Well, now that's good news indeed. It looks like she's beginning to miss you, doesn't it? It wouldn't hurt for you to visit her in the morning before she leaves for the tavern. Forget about my breakfast. I can manage. I think it's more important that you see her, spend an hour or so with her at least a few mornings a week. Yes, yes indeed. I think that's an excellent idea. You might even stay at her house a few hours a day and keep warm. You must keep the baby healthy and strong while it's growing inside you." He patted her rounded stomach. "You shouldn't be working so hard here in this flat. Go see Tekla and rest. You can keep her stoves going all day. She won't mind."

Dani was overjoyed with Roman's reaction. He seemed to have lost some of his early morning surliness. He usually went to work whistling a gay tune and he wasn't ever late. She made sure of that, carefully setting the alarm clock each night.

Her happiness was short-lived for on Saturday when he came home he was carrying a box with a new brown suit, a tie, and a tan shirt. He casually tossed a smaller box over onto her lap. She opened it and saw a delicate red silk scarf, something she had no use for with only household worries on her mind. She clamped the cover back on the box.

"Roman, how could you buy another suit? You have six hanging in the closet. Most men in the neighborhood only have one decent suit for Sundays and special occasions. You have more clothes than anyone we know. Now it's seven suits, at least twenty shirts, six pairs of shoes. It's so wasteful. We could use the money for something useful." She looked down at the box on her lap. "I love your thoughtfulness in buying me a gif but I don't need this. I have more than enough cloth to last for the next five years. Just what did all this cos anyway?"

Roman's sunny smile turned into a snarl. "It's non of your business. I buy what I want when the moo strikes me. You get half my paycheck. What else do yo want, every penny I earn?"

"Roman, did you use any of the money we're saving I have to know how much there is so I can plan."

"What if I have used some of the money?" h shouted. "Is it a crime? What's yours is mine now isn it?"

Anger surged through Dani. "Roman, answer me How much is left?"

He shoved her roughly down on the bed. "Nosy littl bitch aren't you? You're getting just like your preciou aunt. You want to know how much is left? All right, I' tell you. There're about ten dollars left and I' probably spend that tonight so there's nothing left."

Dani was horrified. "Ten dollars? We had almost hundred and you said you were putting aside mor each week. What have you done with it?"

Roman slapped her soundly on the face, leaving livid red splash on her left cheek. "Don't ever questio me again. I won't stand for it. Do you understand me I'm perfectly happy living here. It suits me fine. I'v lived here for more than five years and there's nothin, wrong with the place. I won't spend the rest of my lif penny-pinching just because you want a nice place t live. You'll live where I do. If this flat bothers you s much, ask your aunt if we can live with her. I'd b willing to sacrifice and live with the old crow. Then w wouldn't have to pay any rent at all."

Dani turned her face into the pillow and cried softly "I'll never ask her for anything. Never, even if you kee on hitting me. It would only prove to her that she was right all along."

"Then make up your mind that we're staying here and shut up. I'm tired of hearing about your stupid furniture, pots, and pans. It's disgusting. That's all you ever talk about. You've turned into a dull clod with nothing on your mind but housekeeping."

She kept her face buried in the pillow but she could hear him walking from one end of the room to the other. She dared a small peek and saw him putting on his new clothes, straightening his tie before the cracked mirror over the sink, dusting off his shoes.

"Where are you going?" she mumbled.

"Out to find some pleasant company. It's getting too gloomy here. All I hear is crying and moaning. I'm going to spend a few hours with my friends. They at least know how to laugh and enjoy life." With that he picked up the box containing the scarf and slammed out the door, closing it so hard the dishes in the cupboard rattled in the racks.

Dani continued to sob quietly. How could he do this? Spend all their money carelessly.

She didn't know what time Roman came home that night. It had to be after three in the morning because she had awakened then and he still wasn't in bed. When she opened her eyes again it was seven and he was asleep beside her, reeking of stale beer, cigar smoke, and cheap perfume. Why was he doing this to her? Was it because she was losing her figure slowly but surely? Did Roman find her ugly now with her protruding stomach and fuller breasts?

She visited Tekla the next day, and went to see her almost every morning after. Her aunt couldn't help but notice her pitiful attempt at gaiety.

"Dani, what's wrong?" she asked one morning in March. "Something is troubling you and I'd like to know if I can help in any way."

Dani was quick with her answer. "Why nothing's wrong. It's just that I'm not feeling very well lately. I'm starting to get even bigger and it's so uncomfortable."

Tekla let the matter rest; she was almost afraid to learn the truth. Roman didn't come to her tavern now, nevertheless she heard stories from some of her regular customers. She heard tales of his new clothes, that he'd been seen at another tavern with the loose women who hung about there. She didn't have the nerve to bring up the subject with her niece. There was no sense upsetting Dani in her condition. But Tekla had noticed the dark circles beneath Dani's clear blue eyes, and sooner or later, she felt that Dani would confide in her. At least Dani is eating better, Tekla thought. She kept her shelves well provided and made sure that at her house Dani ate well and drank plenty of milk to keep the baby strong. Every morning that Dani came, Tekla pushed aside the plain toast and coffee Dani made and forced her to eat a good breakfast: bacon and eggs, french toast, or oatmeal loaded with cream and sugar.

In May, Dani didn't visit for an entire week so Tekla decided to check on her, wondering if she was ill. After Roman had left for work, she briskly walked the few blocks and pounded on the door to Dani's flat.

"Who is it?" Dani asked quietly.

"It's me, Tekla. Dani, let me in."

After several minutes the door opened. The shade was drawn but Tekla could still see the dark bruise near Dani's eye. It was purple and ugly. Anger made her flush red.

"What happened? Has Roman done this to you? Tell me the truth."

"No, no," Dani answered nervously. "I bumped into the door the other day. That's why I haven't been over to see you. I know you would only think the worst and say Roman did it."

I know he did this, Tekla said to herself. You're covering up for him, you little fool. And at that moment she made a decision.

"Dani, the couple upstairs are moving. Their sons have put money down on a house on the north side. They'll be leaving at the end of the month and I want you to move upstairs. I'll feel better knowing you're close and I can keep an eye on you. I don't like to know you're living in this hellhole. Why sunlight never enters this room. How do you think you'll manage with a baby in this rathole? A baby needs sunlight and fresh air. You take the flat upstairs and I won't charge you any rent."

"Aunt, please, I couldn't do that. I can't be a leech and live off you."

Tekla saw the stubborn pride that crept into Dani's face. "Dani, how much do you pay here?"

"Eight dollars a month."

"Then I'll charge you ten dollars. That's a fair price."

"Aunt, it's far too low. The flat is worth much more than that."

"Nonsense. I'll feel better knowing there's someone in the building I can trust. You'll be home all day and in the evening so I'll know no one can break in and rob me. You can feed the chickens and ducks for me. It seems I don't have time to do that anymore now that we're so busy at the tavern. Say you'll come or I swear I'll have Bolie move you out bodily. I even promise I'll try to get along with Roman."

Dani knew this was a great concession on her aunt's part since she disliked him so.

And, Tekla thought to herself, with Dani upstairs Roman wouldn't be quite so brave about hitting a defenseless woman. She would make it her business to be home early in the evenings and to listen for anything

187

amiss. Sooner or later, she promised herself, she would win the battle against Roman.

Dani was genuinely happy for the first time in weeks, thinking about how bright and airy the new apartment would be. Just to get out of this dreary place would be a godsend. Whenever she paid the landlady the rent, she was given sullen jealous looks. Was it possible the woman was jealous because Roman had married her? She owned the building and she was married, but her industrious husband worked two jobs and was hardly ever home.

No doubt the landlady had been one of Roman's conquests, even though she was gross and ugly. Dani wouldn't put it past him. It would be good to get away from her eavesdropping and her sneering looks the mornings after she and Roman had had a fight. More important, Dani wanted to get away from the filth that could never be properly cleaned away. No matter how much she cleaned, roaches still scuttled from their hiding places and several had even crawled onto the bed, onto her clean white sheets, making her shudder with revulsion. The mice were back too, gnawing through her makeshift barriers searching for crumbs of food. So she threw pride to the winds and gratefully accepted her aunt's offer, then looked down, ashamed to meet her eyes.

"Now what?" Tekla asked.

"I won't have any furniture to bring. All the things here belong to the owner. None of it is ours except for our clothes."

Tekla deliberated for a few minutes. She knew Dani would accept no money for furniture. And from what she could gather by looking at her niece's crestfallen face, the couple had no money in the bank. "I'll get my friend Leon who owns the furniture store to extend credit. You'll buy the basic furniture you need, and I'll

188

see to it that you only pay a dollar or two a month. Have you forgotten the money I've been holding for you? The money your father gave you for your dowry when he didn't get on the *Destiny?*"

"But that was yours, not mine. That's why I returned most of it to you."

"No, it is your legal dowry." Tekla brushed aside the matter, waving her hands, and would not hear another word. "I have enough linen, dishes, pots, and pans for more than one family. You'll just use mine until you're ready to buy your own. There, that's all settled. You'll be moving in two weeks. I can't wait."

Dani brightened, her smile making her beautiful again. "Neither can I. I'll feel so much better there too. I can work in the yard. It will be heavenly."

Dani hesitated to tell Roman of the plan, but when she finally found enough courage, he was pleased and whirled her around the room in a wild dance. He kissed her on the forehead, the nose, the cheek, and finally gave her a long kiss on the lips. "Good for you, my darling little wife. Of course you told her we'd be delighted to take the flat?"

"Yes," she answered. "We can move in two weeks. Tekla will have the rooms painted and as soon as that's done it's ours."

Roman was exceedingly good to her for the next days, coming home right after work and taking her for long walks in the evening. He treated her tenderly and she lost her fear of his terrible temper, believing the move would change their lives and make them a happily married couple.

On moving day, Roman went to work as usual, first making two trips with their clothes, and leaving them in the front hall. Dani came an hour later carrying the food that was left in a market bag. When Tekla led her upstairs Dani was delightfully surprised at the sight of her new home. Gone were the dark walls the other tenants had admired. Gone was all the dark heavy furniture that had previously cluttered up the rooms. The walls were freshly papered, the living and dining rooms in a pink flowered pattern. The kitchen was painted white and each bedroom had been painted a different color: one white, the second pink, and the third a cheerful sunny yellow. Clean carpets were on the floors in the living room and the dining room, and fresh ecru curtains were on every window. Dani's brass bed, the one from her room downstairs, had been placed in the largest bedroom, the one off the living room, as had her dresser and washstand.

"Aunt, I don't understand."

"Now don't get all in a flutter," Tekla announced proudly. "The couple left the carpets and curtains. I just had them cleaned. As for the bedroom things, you know I can't possibly sleep in three beds. The one I have is just fine. Who else will use them if you don't? Leon should be here any minute. He had a good buy on a table and chairs for the kitchen. He'll also be bringing an icebox, a couch, and two tables for the living room. For good measure, because I'm such a good customer, he's thrown in a cradle for the baby, free. Now wasn't that nice of him? You must remember to thank him properly when he comes."

"What is all this going to cost?"

"No need to worry. You can afford a dollar a week. Actually the things are secondhand but they look almost new. No one will know the difference."

Tekla didn't dare tell Dani that she'd bought the carpets and curtains from the couple before they'd moved. Nor did she mention that she'd had Leon mark the prices down to a fourth of what they actually were and was making up the difference herself. What Dani didn't know wouldn't hurt her. Tekla hadn't bought the

190

most expensive items but had carefully selected cheaper furniture even though she had wanted to buy the best the store had to offer. She knew Dani would only cry again if she realized the truth and would stubbornly refuse the whole lot.

That afternoon she had Dani carefully select enough dishes, pots, sheets, pillow cases, and towels to "borrow" for a short time. The icebox was already stocked with a fresh block of ice, milk, meat, and butter, and the pantry held an assortment of vegetables, fruits, and bread. Tekla waved away the largesse.

"It's a welcoming present. You know it's impolite not to accept a present so don't say a word. Welcome to your new home."

The women hugged each other, both happy to be together again in the same lovely building.

Dani couldn't find the right words to express her gratitude. The flat looked absolutely beautiful with everything in place. Now she had all the essentials to begin homemaking, and the rest would come later, little by little as she could afford things.

"Thank you." She said over and over. "You're too wonderful. What would I do without you?"

Tekla got up to leave.

"Rest a while before supper. I have to go to work now; it's getting late. Take a short nap. I'm sure both you and the baby could use a little sleep." Tekla lowered the shade in the bedroom and tucked Dani beneath the covers. "I'll see you tomorrow child."

Within minutes Dani was fast asleep, a smile of contentment on her face.

Roman came home promptly at six to find her still sleeping, and after he fixed dinner himself, he woke her cheerfully. "Get up, lazy. Dinner is on the table, but I warn you I won't be doing this every night—just this once because you looked so peaceful sleeping in our

191

new bed. It's a beautiful flat, my dear. Just right for raising a family."

Dani rubbed the traces of sleep from her eyes. "Roman, what time is it?" When he told her she exclaimed "I've slept for over three hours."

"That's quite all right, little love. Now come. There's cold beef I found in the icebox, and some hot chicken soup Tekla must have made for us. It's time for our first dinner in our new home."

Until the beginning of July Dani was totally happy with Roman. He went out of his way to make life pleasant, even inviting Tekla up for Sunday dinners. Although Tekla came, she left immediately after the meal, distrusting this new facet of Roman's personality. He wasn't changing, she was sure, only masking his true character for reasons yet unknown.

Tekla pondered over the new Roman as she left their kitchen. She knew something was afoot in his devious mind, but she had no inkling of what would come next. She was positive he'd wanted to live in this building all along—in her flat—but it had been an unexpected bonus when he'd found that they would have the upstairs all to themselves. That was keeping him content for the time being, but knowing Roman, she was sure more mischief was in the making and she wondered what form it would take. Since she had no clue, there was nothing to do but wait to see what was in store. Thus far she hadn't heard any arguments, no loud voices; she'd seen no traces of tears on Dani's face. To tell the truth Dani was blooming since she'd made the move out of the vermin-infested room, and she was now a sight to behold. Her gaunt, downtrodden look had disappeared after a few days, and she looked herself again even though her waistline was expanding.

That was the only way you could tell she was pregnant for she hadn't gained weight anywhere else.

Tekla decided to ask Dani some questions the next day after Roman left for work. First, she had to convince her to put money away for herself if it was possible to do so. One never knew when Roman would go on a spending rampage again, and it was best to take proper precautions.

On the following morning, Dani laughed with her aunt, giggling at the puzzled expression on her aunt's face.

"See, I told you he would change in the right surroundings. He's happy now. We finally have a decent place to live, and he hasn't even bought anything new for himself. You know how wild he is about new clothes, but he seems content with what he has and he's been giving me a few extra dollars to put aside every week for when the baby comes. It can't be long now, only another three weeks or so."

Dani was very large now. Her rounded stomach was straining against her shapeless dresses. She was uncomfortable when she tried to clean the house, but she went about her tasks happily, singing the mornings away. In the afternoons she worked in the yard and went for short walks. She enjoyed the sight of flowers blooming, of new mothers pushing their babies around the park, and of older children sitting on swings or playing tag. Not too many young mothers stopped to chat with her, and when they did, only a few words were exchanged. Why? Dani wondered. Was there talk that she had had to get married. If that was the case she could live with it. It had happened to women since time began. Soon they would forget her hasty marriage. Most of them weren't sure of the date of her wedding anyway. Maybe they looked down at her for not having the usual three-day wedding feast when they knew

Tekla could certainly have afforded it. That was none of their business, Dani decided, holding her head up high. She was proud to be carrying Roman's beautiful baby.

The following Sunday afternoon found Tekla and Dani happily gossiping in Tekla's living room. Tekla hemmed diapers while Dani sewed tiny shifts for the baby. Roman had gone out for a few hours to visit friends, but he'd promised them he would be home early. Dani laughed anew every time the baby gave a mighty kick. Tekla could see the movement through Dani's cotton dress.

"It's certainly an active baby. My, it looks like he, or she, can't wait to get out."

As they sat, sipping lemonade and sewing, a light tap sounded on the front door.

"Now who can that be?" Tekla asked. "I'm not expecting visitors."

"I'll get it," Dani answered, being closer to the door. "I'm tired of sitting."

She opened the door to the hall, then the outside door. An emaciated man in torn clothing stood there, a stubble of dark beard covering his face. He was hanging on to the porch railing for support and swaying as though he were ready to faint. Dani closed the door part way, afraid this might be some tramp looking for a handout, then she opened the door wide and continued to stare at the unkempt person who stared back at her. The eyes, there was something about his eyes that caught her attention. No. It couldn't possibly be.

"Jan?" she whispered. "Oh, no. Is it you, Jan?"

"Dani," he mumbled weakly and clung to her shoulders.

"Jan," she screamed as they both fainted dead away, one from exhaustion and hunger, the other from shock

194

at seeing a loved one she'd thought dead for many months.

Tekla ran to the door and gasped at the sight of Dani's prostrate form. Jan. Had she heard Dani scream out Jan's name? That was impossible. How could Dani think this was Jan? Not this dirty bedraggled young man lying on the floor. Weak with excitement Tekla knelt down and lightly tapped Dani's face to bring her around.

"Dani darling get up. Wake up please."

Tekla paid no attention to the intruder whose dirty arm lay halfway across Dani's body. Impatiently she brushed it off. Dani's eyes fluttered open. Slowly full consciousness returned to her.

"Aunt, it's Jan."

Dani pushed herself up to peer closely at the prone man lying face up on the floor. "It's Jan I tell you. I should know my own brother."

"It can't be," Tekla answered. "We got the letter and the telegram saying he was dead. How could it be Jan?"

The man opened his eyes and moaned softly. "Dani, it is me. I made it. Didn't I promise you I'd join you in Chicago? I'm here."

Dani hugged the pitiful creature, her tears dropping on his dirt-streaked face.

"I told you it was him. Help me get him into the house, hurry."

They each took an arm and dragged him into the living room. Their jostling forced his eyes open again.

"Can I please have some water? I'm so thirsty."

Tekla ran into the kitchen and brought back a glass of cool water and a wet rag to wipe off his face. Jan revived somewhat after taking a few sips, then he struggled to sit up on the floor.

"Jan." Dani hugged him again. "Don't explain now. Let's get some food in you and then we can talk."

"Yes, of course," Tekla added, "but a bath after the food. Dani run upstairs and get something of Roman's for Jan to wear. The pants will be too short but they will do till we find out what's happened. Go, I'll heat some soup."

She helped Jan to stand and led him slowly to a chair in the kitchen. By the time Dani returned, Jan had a bowl of hot vegetable soup in front of him, and he was greedily spooning it into his mouth along with hastily dunked bread. But before he could tell his tale, Dani clutched her stomach and cried aloud as a sharp pain sliced through her midsection. As she gasped for air, another pain made her double over.

"Oh, my God," Tekla cried. "The baby's coming."

For the first time, Jan seemed to notice his sister's condition. What was this? His sister ready to have a baby? Impossible. Confusion made him blink his eyes rapidly. He couldn't comprehend why his sister was so huge and or why his aunt was wringing her hands and crying.

Tekla ran to the front door and spotted a small boy listlessly bouncing a ball along the sidewalk.

"You, lad. Do you know my friend Martha who lives next door to the tavern two blocks down?"

The boy nodded.

"Well, run as fast as you can and get her here quickly. Tell her it's an emergency, that she should come right away. Hurry." Reaching into her apron pocket, she tossed a coin to him. "Hurry."

The lad ran off, his ball forgotten as it bounced into the gutter. Tekla ran back into the kitchen and hoisted Dani to her feet; then she put her on the nearest bed, Tekla's own, off the kitchen. When she returned to the kitchen, she put pots of water on the stove to heat. "Forgive me, Jan, I'll be back with you in a minute. First things first."

Jan cringed at the moans coming from the bedroom, but before he could offer what little help he was able to give, Martha came bursting through the door breathing heavily. She tossed a hasty look at Jan who was still sitting at the table and then rushed into Tekla's bedroom when she heard another loud moan.

"Is it the baby?" she asked in a calm voice.

"Yes." Tekla answered shortly. "Help me."

"And who's the strange young derelict sitting at your table, looking so bewildered and dirty? Another poor stray you managed to pick up and feed?"

"No, it's my nephew."

"Your nephew? But Jan is dead. He died in Poland. You told me so yourself."

"Later, I'll explain later. There isn't time now. You stay with Dani. I don't think she's ready to deliver just yet, but it won't be long. The shock must have brought on early labor."

Martha stayed with Dani while Tekla lugged the tin tub into the spare bedroom originally intended for Casimir and Jan. Jan helped her carry some of the hot water from the stove and pour it into the tub. Then they added cool water until the tub was half full.

"Jan." Tekla kissed his dirty face. "I'm astonished. I can't believe it's really you, but you understand your explanations will have to wait until Dani's baby is born. Wash yourself and put on the clean clothes Dani brought down. They're right on the bed. Then lie down and get some rest if you can. We'll have a chance to talk in a while."

Jan obeyed silently, fatigue causing his mind to whirl in an incomprehensible muddle. Three hours later a daughter was born to Dani, who had valiantly kept her mouth shut tight in order not to scream out with pain for she knew Jan was sleeping in the front bedroom. Not for anything in the world would she cause him any more sorrow. It looked as though he had seen enough of that already. After the birth Martha cleaned out the room, gently washed the baby, and placed her in a tiny clean robe. The baby settled in to sleep nicely next to her mother.

Tekla, wiping perspiration from her brow, sat down heavily on the chair next to the bed. The kitchen was steaming from all the water that had been boiled on the stove, and it was in the upper eighties outside.

"I've never been so nervous in my entire life. My heart is fluttering like a bird's wings from all the excitement. Dani, sleep now while I see how Jan is doing."

"I can't sleep," she answered. "Not until I know how Jan came to be here. If he's awake promise me you'll bring him here so we can all hear his story together. If you don't, I swear I'll get up and go to his room and hear it for myself."

"I promise, I promise. Just stay where you are. We'll come in here. Just rest while I get him."

When Tekla softly crept into the other bedroom Jan awoke, instantly alert. The deep short sleep had done much to restore him, as had the first food he had eaten in days. He felt stronger already and was anxious to find out about his sister.

"Dani?" he asked sitting up.

"She's fine and you have a healthy niece. Are you strong enough to get up?"

"Yes." Jan swung his legs off the bed and stood to his full height, six feet.

Tekla looked up at him, awed. "My, I must say you look like a entirely different person all cleaned up. And to think I thought you were a tramp knocking at my door. You look like your father."

She studied his face, seeing her brother's eyes, his straight nose, the same chiseled cheekbones. Thin as Jan was she could see Casimir's good looks burgeoning forth. What was Jan, seventeen now? Yes, that was right. He was seventeen, but he appeared older. His eyes had a haunted look, as if he had seen something horrible.

"Come, we'll go to Dani now. Everything is in order, and if we don't get to her soon I fear she'll get out of bed just to hear your story firsthand. Your sister's as stubborn as a mule, as stubborn as your father."

Martha placed three chairs alongside the bed and they all sat down to listen to what Jan had to say. First, he kissed his sister tenderly and proudly looked down at his new niece. What a tiny red little thing she is, he thought. Brown fuzzy hair barely covered the top of the baby's head. Suddenly she yawned beguilingly, opened her eyes briefly for a quick look, and then fell asleep again. Jan took the chair nearest the bed.

"Dani, a baby? Are you married? So much has happened in such a short time."

"Never mind the baby. I want to hear about you first."

"Well, I'll start explaining, but what I'm going to tell you is rather unbelievable. I sometimes don't believe it myself. It all seems like a horrid nightmare, and I find myself wishing I would wake up so it would end. Dani, you said I was dead after you opened the door. Who told you that?"

"Father Czerny sent a telegram, and then Louis Czerny, his brother, wrote a letter explaining that soldiers had shot you and Papa."

Jan laughed sarcastically at her explanation. "Yes, there were soldiers everywhere, but they didn't shoot our father. It was Louis Czerny himself."

"What?" Dani cried. "Louis Czerny? He was a friend. He helped Papa settle in at the farm."

"Yes. It sounds impossible doesn't it? But I saw it happen with my own eyes. I was sitting up in the apple tree, daydreaming as usual. The sun had set and it was fairly dark. I saw Louis go into our barn and thought he was helping Papa with some work, but when he came out he was carrying the steel box we had buried there. I was just ready to leap out of the tree and confront him when I noticed Papa and a young homeless lad we'd hired that day walking toward the barn. When Louis spotted them, he set down the box and shot them both. It happened so quickly, I was still up among the branches, and the tree was fifty yards from them. First Papa and then the lad he thought was me. You see, he didn't know we'd hired Adam. Adam was an orphan, making his way out of Poland by doing odd jobs wherever he could find them. We still had some vegetables to pick so Papa decided Adam could help us for a good supper and a few zloty. He was supposed to work for us for a week or so. Anyway, Louis thought it was me he shot. It all happened so fast, not more than a minute or two went by. He shot our father first, and in that short span of time, Adam was stunned. He didn't really understand what was happening until a bullet hit him. I tried to shout but my throat was frozen. I couldn't utter a word. It was almost night by that time, very dark, but I could see that Louis was returning to the barn and I heard him rummaging among the tools. Both Papa and the lad were dead, shot at close range. They never had a chance. I can see now why Louis thought I was Adam. He was about my height and he was wearing some of my clothes while his were drying inside the house. There was nothing I could do to save either one of them. It was too late. Blood was gushing out of Papa's head. I'll never forget the sight as long as I live. Blood was everywhere. Pools of it."

Jan didn't have the heart to mention that his father's brains were splattered across the yard, a sight that would sicken him until his dying day, nor could he describe the look of surprise in Adam's eyes as he lay in the dirt, a massive hole in his chest pumping out a geyser of blood. Jan shuddered violently as he recalled the grisly scene for the thousandth time. No, he never would tell them everything.

Snapping back to the present, he continued. "I hid behind some crates and saw Louis carry a shovel out of the barn. He was still carrying the gun, and I watched him walk behind the barn and start digging a grave. I waited until he was done and then I watched him carry Papa and then Adam around the barn and toss them into the pit. I must have been half insane by then. I should have confronted him as soon as I saw how he'd murdered Papa, but he had a weapon and I was unarmed. You remember," he said to Dani, "Louis was as strong as an ox. I couldn't fight him on even terms. I'm sure he would have killed me had I shown my face for he had reloaded the gun. While he was digging the grave he was facing in my direction, and he would have gone for his gun again quicker than I could have run up to him. When the bodies were covered and his back was turned, I found an iron crowbar standing outside and hit him on the head with all my might. All the while I'd been crouching behind the crates, I hadn't realized it was there just beyond the reach of my hand. I meant to kill him, but evidently he lived, seeing he wrote you the letter. I wonder who he thought it was that hit him? Will I ever find out?

"Suddenly I heard horses at the front of the house. It seemed as though there were hundreds of them, and I heard men speaking German. A troop of soldiers was looking for a place to camp for the night. I was going to run out to them and explain what had happened, but something stopped me. I knew then they would never believe me. I thought they would accuse me of killing both Papa and Adam because we were relative newcomers to the area. They would call in the local people, and naturally, they would believe I killed them in a fit of anger. Louis was a respected farmer in the community. They would have questioned me and then killed me to save the bother of further explanation. You left just in time, Dani. I've seen horrors perpetrated in Poland. The armies are ruthless in their march across the land. The atrocities stick in my mind, but I'll not go into that now. Let me finish telling you about the murders. I knew I was covered with Papa's and Adam's blood because I could feel it soaking into my shirt, feel it all over my hands. There was the smell of it too, like when you kill pigs or other animals, the nauseating smell of blood."

Jan didn't tell Dani or Tekla that when he had lifted his father's head, the back of it had fallen onto his arm putting him in a state of shock. It was better they didn't know all these details.

"Instead of going to the soldiers I rushed back into the woods behind the house. I couldn't get to the strongbox in front of the barn; the soldiers would have seen me. They must have been overjoyed when they found it. For weeks I wandered around trying to get out of the country. I couldn't go into Gdansk; there were too many military people there. Somehow, a few months later, I finally made my way over the border into Germany. I had no papers and hung about a small seacoast town, hiding during the day and looking for a way out at night. At last I was able to steal a small fishing boat, and God surely was with me since I don't know how to handle a boat. I had to get away after all the ghastly sights I'd seen. I saw two old grandmothers who'd been raped by a troop, and then left bleeding and dying, with the enemy's slime covering their bodies. What turns some soldiers into such animals?

"While I was in town I ate what food I could find in the garbage bins and what I could steal. On the boat I found a few tins of biscuits and several cans of water so I headed out to what I thought was open sea and tried to follow some stars. I only knew I had to get away, as far as I could from that hell. After a week or so there was nothing left to eat, so I caught some fish with a net left on board and ate them raw. Then a week later I gave up. I couldn't manage to find the strength to even steer the boat. It rained and I tried to catch the drops in an old piece of canvas but I didn't get enough water. The next thing I remember, a small English freighter picked me up, but by then I was incoherent and the seamen couldn't understand a word I was saying. They surely must have been in danger too, with a war going on, but they pulled me aboard. This ship wasn't large, not as large as the one I later stowed away on. They couldn't seem to understand how I'd drifted that far after the engine had stopped running—there'd been no fuel to restart it—but they took me back to England with them and turned me over to the port authorities, thinking I was German since the boat I stole had some German papers on it. There I was fed and placed in a locked room until they could find someone to translate. The next night I managed to open the nailed window and jump to the ground, spraining my ankle in the process. Then I became a fugitive. I could understand only the few words I remembered you studying at home, Dani. I knew at least those. It was easier to steal food there too. The people in England were more careless. I've been bitten by at least four dogs, and beaten once by an irate innkeeper when he found me in his kitchen snatching a loaf of bread. A month later, I spotted an American ship in port and I stowed away in the hold. Don't ask me how I managed to stay hidden the whole time. I think fear made me overly cautious. Anyway I slept in snatches between the rounds of the men checking out the ship. The slightest noise woke me; I was frightened of being caught. In the hours before dawn I sometimes managed to find a few scraps of food, and one night I even drank a half bottle of whiskey left on deck when one of the crew forgot to take it below, but it only made me deathly ill and I thought for sure someone would hear me vomiting. There were rats in the hold with me, but I never was bitten, thank God. They just stared at me from several yards away and then left to forage elsewhere. I kept a long stick in my hand and waved it around madly when they were near.

"We docked in a city called Boston where I stayed aboard ship till four in the morning. I couldn't get off on the side facing the dock—there were still people about—so I jumped off on the far side and swam until I could see a deserted area. I never thought I could make it. Here I was so close to you and yet so far away. I never did swim in an ocean before, only in the river that ran alongside Ruda. The waves kept splashing over me, and I swallowed so much sea water I thought I surely would drown. At last I managed to reach shallow water, and the waves washed me onto a beach. It seemed like I lay there for hours coughing and spitting up salt water. I can only say God was still by my side. I think it was March then and still cold.

"I crawled to a fisherman's shack some yards up the beach, and they took me in immediately, took off my wet clothes and nursed me back to health. They were Portuguese people and we managed to get by with sign language. The man seemed to know I was in some sort of trouble, for he never told even his neighbors that I was staying in their home. I managed to make it understood that I was looking for Chicago, and one night the man brought me a raggedy map and showed me how far away Chicago was. I somehow thought I could get here in a few hours. I didn't realize how vast America is. Two weeks later I felt well enough to travel, so the man and his wife packed smoked fish and bread for me and pointed west. I still have the map they gave me in my pocket.

"I started walking, some of the time heading in the wrong direction. Once in a while I would meet a kindly farmer driving a cart and by then I could say in English, 'I go to Chicago.' Most of them laughed at me. They seemed to think it was like saying I was going to the moon, but every few miles helped me get closer. When I found myself in a place called Philadelphia, a large bustling city, I knew I had to keep going in the direction of the setting sun. I hopped on board a train pulling out of a depot and the miles sped by. By the time they found me and threw me off, cursing and beating me, I was in Pittsburgh and when I looked at the map I saw how close I was getting. I came the rest of the way on foot with short wagon rides and almost cried when I passed through Indiana.

"There I met a Polish man and he gave me explicit instructions on how to finish my journey. Outside of the Portuguese fisherman he was the kindest man I met all the while, and it was even better for we could at least speak together. He fed me that night and explained he was going back to Detroit. He works on automobiles, promised me a job at the same factory if I ever wanted one. He apologized over and over because he had no extra money to lend me for train fare but it didn't matter. Finally, two days ago, I was on the outskirts of Chicago, and I kissed the ground with happiness. I could actually feel your presence then, but for a whole day I couldn't remember the street you lived on.

"After sleeping in a field Friday night it came to me. Of course, how could I be so stupid? It was Fox Street. I cursed my stupidity and asked people I met where Fox Street was but none of them knew. They told me to ask the police but I couldn't. I'm here illegally and the police would throw me in prison. I was still in southeast Chicago so people told me I should go farther and ask again. I wasn't expecting a city so large. Early this morning a man in an automobile pointed me this way, and after walking for hours and asking again and again, I found you at last. When I came to Morgan Street I could hear people speaking Polish and then it was simple. So here I am just as I promised."

Jan's throat was parched after talking for such a long stretch. Exhaustion dulled his eyes.

"Enough for now," Tekla commanded, tears streaming from her eyes. Martha and Dani were quietly crying too, suffering along with Jan as he finished.

Dani held him close. "You kept your promise. Oh, Jan, I don't know how you managed but you kept your promise."

Tekla intervened then. "We all need some rest. Danuta, you go to sleep. Jan, come back into the kitchen. You'll eat another bite more and then go back to sleep." Tekla clasped her hands to her breast looking upward. "Thank you, dear Lord, for bringing him safely to us and for giving Danuta a fine healthy daughter. God has surely smiled on us today," she said to Martha. "There are truly miracles still happening to ordinary people like us."

An hour later Roman came home slightly intoxicated and was greeted with the news that he was a father and that his brother-in-law was alive. As he walked upstairs after seeing his wife and daughter, he spat on the steps. He cursed Jan's arrival as he threw off his clothes and sprawled across the bed. Just when he thought life was going according to his plan fate had slapped him in the face.

"Damn, damn," he muttered and then fell into a drunken sleep.

Chapter Six

"What shall we name our gorgeous daughter?" Dani asked when Roman came down in the morning. She was mesmerized by each movement the baby made and had spent half the night just watching the marvelous little creature move her fingers, yawn, and greedily suck her fill of milk. Even her daughter's crying seemed a special event. Dani was too entranced to notice the look of impatience Roman gave her when she asked about naming the baby.

"Name her what you like," he answered, shrugging his shoulders. "It makes no difference to me. If it were a son I would have called him Roman, but it wasn't so any name will do."

Dani waved away his early morning surliness. Was this going to start again? You never knew where you stood with Roman, he was so changeable. One moment he was happy, the next indifferent or angry, but even Roman's attitude couldn't spoil her day. The future could only be good. Jan was safe, her long pregnancy was over at last, and she had a beautiful daughter to show for the months of discomfort. She looked down at the precious baby in her arms.

"I know. Eleanor is what she'll be. It sounds regal

and stately and she does look like a tiny bundle of royalty. Roman, do you want to hold her for a moment before you leave for work. She's not fragile."

"God, no. She looks very ugly to me, like a tiny red chicken." He backed away slowly. "I don't know anything about babies. That's your responsibility. Where's your long-lost brother? Still sleeping?"

"Oh, Roman, isn't it exciting? After I'd given my father and brother up for dead, Jan turns up on our doorstep. Seeing him at the door was such a shock, I still can't get over it. You can't imagine how good I feel having Jan here. Wait until you get to know him. You'll grow to love him as I do. Most of the time he's quiet and doesn't say much, but when he gets to know you he opens up marvelously. I'm going back upstairs today. I've inconvenienced Tekla long enough, poor dear. She had to spend the night on the couch since I'd taken her bed, and I know she must be uncomfortable. As soon as everyone's up, they'll help me upstairs, then we'll all have dinner together tonight."

Roman pulled on his cap and turned away. "Eat without me. I have things to do this evening. I might not be home until late. By the way, was that a pair of my pants I saw Jan wearing last night? Does that mean he's come with nothing in his pockets and he'll sponge off your aunt?"

"Roman, he had a dreadful time getting here. Be charitable." Dani told Roman a short version of Jan's trials and of her father's death, but he seemed uninterested. When she finished he let himself out the back door without further ado. No kiss, no sign of happiness over their daughter, their creation—nothing.

Dani guessed he was disappointed by not having a son first. Men were so conscious of their masculinity. Most felt they had to have a son to prove themselves to their peers. Goodness, you would think this would be heir only child. She knew others would follow and Roman would have a son—or sons—if he'd only be patient. She nuzzled her lips to the baby's soft cheek.

"Don't worry, little Eleanor. You'll get enough love from me to make up for the lack of it in your father."

The baby opened one eye, stared at her mother, and then fell asleep again, unconcerned with the soft words.

Breakfast was a gay time. Tekla, Jan, and Dani laughed merrily all the while. It was more like a celebration than an ordinary meal. They ate their oatmeal and sweet rolls, and drank coffee, spending over an hour at the table, talking, each trying to get a question in before the other. Tekla, at first, insisted Dani stay in bed while she was served breakfast, but Dani was indignant.

"I feel wonderful. Nothing hurts. I don't even feel as though I've gone through childbirth."

"That's a real peasant for you, Aunt. She's just like the women in the fields back home, giving birth one minute and up and working the next. My sister has no class whatsoever."

Jan merrily tweaked his sister's nose and Dani made an attempt to get up and chase him but Tekla interfered.

"None of that. I don't care how well you feel. You stay right where you are, young lady. I don't need or want any more excitement for quite a while. Yesterday was enough to last me a lifetime. After breakfast I insist you get back into bed."

"Yes, mother hen, but I'm going up to my own bed. I don't imagine you relish sleeping on the couch so I'm taking myself and Eleanor upstairs where we belong."

"No," Tekla protested. "You should stay here for at least a few days. It won't kill me to sleep on the couch. It's quite comfortable and—"

"It's not and you know it. I can manage the stairs if

211

someone will carry the baby, and you're both to have dinner with me tonight if you'll do the cooking that is. don't want to miss anything, and I won't have the two of you down here talking without letting me hear. By the way, Roman won't be home for dinner. He has other plans so it will be just the three of us."

Jan turned serious. "I must say from what I've seen of your husband he doesn't strike me as a particularly adoring mate. Dani, why did you get married so young and to an older man? Somehow I imagined you would wait until you were at least eighteen. I didn't think you would meet someone so soon when there were so many new sights to take in. Is there something I should know?" Jan asked, puzzled. "Roman looked sullen and angry last night when he should have been proud and happy that your ordeal was over. He barely said two words to me; then he stamped upstairs as fast as he could. What's wrong?"

Tekla gave Jan a warning glance.

Dani's eyes were downcast. "No. Roman is just Roman. You have to get used to him, get to know him a little at a time. He was a bachelor for too long, and it's taking him a while to accustom himself to married life. I mean, most of the time he is satisfied, but sometimes he feels suffocated by his job and his new responsibilities. When he gets gloomy it's best that he get it out of his system in his own way. He'll be fine in a few days, as soon as he gets used to the idea that he has a family."

Jan looked at his sister dubiously. "I should think he's had more than enough time to get used to the idea. You didn't get pregnant and have a baby all in one night. He's had months to get used to being a father."

Tekla gave Jan a look meant to silence him.

"Let's get Dani settled upstairs if she insists," she ordered. "While she's resting I'll take you to my place of business and show you around. You can meet my

vo dearest friends who help me run the place. I know
ou met Martha yesterday but it was all too hectic then.
oday we can relax and talk. Dani, I promise Jan will
e back at lunchtime to help you. He can bring you
nch from the kitchen at the tavern. I know Martha
ill have something ready."

They settled Dani in the brass bed. Then Jan carried
ie cradle from the baby's bedroom and placed it
eside her while Tekla opened the windows. A fresh
arm breeze wafted lightly through the room parting
ie soft curtains. Jan patted Dani's golden hair.

"Rest now, little sister. I'll be back in a few hours to
ee how you're doing." He looked down at her again.
You are absolutely beautiful this morning with your
air all shining and your face glowing. Motherhood
vidently agrees with you. You don't look like a pesty
ttle schoolgirl anymore but like a lovely woman. I'll
e back soon."

Jan didn't seem at all embarrassed by his strange
ttire. His borrowed trousers were four inches too
hort and his boots, torn in several places, barely
tayed on his feet. In addition, the laces were knotted in
everal places where they had frayed. Although his
hirt was freshly laundered, it, too, was frayed and
orn. His jacket had been beyond repair so Tekla had
hrown it in the trash. But when Tekla insisted he
ccompany her to one of the stores to be outfitted
roperly, Jan protested. She became adamant.

"I won't have you shaming me by looking like a poor
astoff relative. Just look at you. Your shoes are worn
own to practically nothing and your clothes are in
atters. You look like a clown in Roman's pants; they're
ar too small. Let's get started. We've much to do
efore I can present you to my friends, not that I'm
shamed of you but I want them all to see what a hand-
ome nephew I have. I've been telling everyone about

213

my family for so long, and now they'll have an idea of what my brother looked like because you look exactly as he did when he was your age." She took Jan by the arm. "Let's go."

In the few hours before lunch Tekla filled Jan in on what manner of man his sister had married. She omitted nothing, glad to have the opportunity to unburden herself at long last. She had told Bolie and Martha some of her feelings but not all. Such discussions only made Bolie rant and rave and want to fight Roman, and his reactions worried Martha to tears. Tekla's other friends knew what Roman was like before he'd married her niece, but Tekla kept her mouth tightly shut when any of them asked how Roman was behaving himself. Naturally, anyone could see that Roman stayed out late, drank to excess far too often, and boasted of his affairs with countless women, but Tekla attempted to paint a different picture. Neither she nor Dani needed anyone's pity. Somehow life went on for better or worse, and what a blessed relief it was to share one's thoughts without holding back.

"He beats her?" Jan asked outraged. "He has other women? What kind of man is this? How did my sister get involved with him to begin with?"

"I'm not sure about the beatings," Tekla answered. "I've seen bruises, but Dani won't admit anything to me. She still thinks the sun rises and sets only on Roman. At first I went along with her when she explained that she bumped into a door or into a cabinet, but, Jan, she's not a clumsy girl. What else can it be? For a while, after they moved upstairs—I thank God I persuaded her to do it—Roman improved, but if I'm right, I fear he's going to get worse. He wanted a son and got a daughter. He wants to worm his way into my savings, but you arrived and that made him furious.

can't fight him openly, but I can almost read his mind. Don't forget I've known him for years. No doubt he thought Dani would inherit my money and he would sit pretty for the rest of his life. Tomorrow I must make a legal and binding will. I'll see a solicitor to draw up the document. I do have a nice healthy sum put away, and that scoundrel isn't going to get his slimy hands on one penny, I promise you."

"But, Aunt Tekla, you're not old. You have years and years ahead of you, God willing."

"I'm almost forty years old, well past my prime. It's better to be safe than sorry. I'd like to be able to out-live Roman but that's not likely."

"You can still get married," Jan stated matter-of-factly. "It's not too late. You're still a fine-looking woman, and I'm sure you've had your share of men asking for your hand. There must be a number of widowers or single older men who never married who would be good to you, make you happy."

"Heaven forbid." Tekla's face flushed crimson. Never. There was only one man for me and that was Józef. When he died I vowed there would be no one else. You wouldn't understand, Jan. You're too young. After my Józef was killed in that freak accident, I seriously thought of joining the convent, but the mother superior warned me if there were any doubts, then the sisterhood wasn't meant for me. Well, there were some doubts. Even in my grief I realized I couldn't spend my whole life praying and living a cloistered life. I think my destiny was to be a surrogate mother to you and Dani, and I'm glad for that. At least I can help the two of you, if only in small ways. Try to get Dani to confide in you. She has too much stubborn pride, and she thinks she can make a silk purse out of a sow's ear. Tell her she must stand up for herself, not let Roman trample all over her. She has to be tougher if she means to stay married to him. Jan, I confess, if Dani wanted t[o] leave Roman, even though it's a sin, I would help her i[n] any way I could. I'd condone a divorce, an annulment[,] or I'd even put her on a train or ship to get her free. That's how much I despise him—so much that I'd g[o] against my religion to have Dani rid of him."

Jan promised solemnly that he would do his best. Hot anger surged through him as he thought about h[is] sister being abused, but Tekla cautioned him again an[d] again that Dani wouldn't be swayed against Roman. I[t] was going to take much more time for her to see he[r] husband as he really was, but eventually the day woul[d] come.

Supper that night was clouded by a somber atmos[-]phere. Jan had decided earlier that he would write t[o] the authorities in Poland to explain how his father ha[d] been murdered. He intended to write to Father Czern[y] in Ruda as well, even though mail wasn't always gettin[g] to its destination. If he wrote several letters it was likel[y] that at least one would get through.

"Louis must not be allowed to remain free afte[r] committing those murders. It's unthinkable. He mus[t] be punished, and if it takes years, I'll see that he pay[s] for his crime. I'll start writing tonight," Jan vowed.

After they ate, Tekla left brother and sister alone t[o] talk. She gave Jan a look that clearly told him to gai[n] his sister's confidence. He wasn't quite sure how to d[o] that so he plowed right in.

"Dani, does Roman treat you well? Is he a good husband?"

Dani smiled up at him, seeing through the charade.

"I see our aunt's been talking to you. Jan, deep inside Roman is a good man. Aunt Tekla doesn't realize it's going to take awhile before Roman gets used to married life but he will settle down. She forgets that he stayed single until he was twenty-nine, so he was used

216

to seeing other women, spending his money without concern for tomorrow, and having the freedom to come and go as he wished. A man so popular and sought after doesn't change overnight. It takes time to adjust, but he will. I'm sure of it. He has his faults, I'll admit, but so does every man alive. He's grumpy in the mornings, but only because he hates his job, mixing vats of smelly soap. He goes out to drink with his friends and that helps him forget the factory. He's much better since we moved here. Tekla's slowly coming around too. She comes up for Sunday dinner. Months ago she loathed Roman, but now she's making an effort to understand him. I suppose Tekla told you everything Roman did when he was single, but he can be kind too. He buys me presents now and then, we go out walking when the weather's nice, and soon we'll be taking little Eleanor along. Jan, I love him. Please don't interfere with my life. It's what I chose."

"But, sweet Jesus, Dani, you're still a baby. For Christ's sake you're only fifteen, even though you do look older."

"Jan, have you forgotten I've been keeping house since Mama died? I helped her since I was a baby, and when she died I took over almost all of the household duties. I'm not a baby. A lot of girls my age are married and have families."

Jan took his sister's hands in his own. "All right, little one. I won't intrude but if you ever want me to talk to Roman or if you need any help, you know you can always count on me."

"Yes, dearest, I know." Dani rose and kissed his cheek.

"What a touching sight," Roman said as he stumbled into the kitchen. "I come home a little earlier than planned and find you and Jan huddled together like lovers. Is that what you are?" Roman swayed. He

217

reeked of cheap whiskey.

Jan rose, clenching his fists, ready for a confrontation.

"Please, Jan," Dani begged. "Do go back downstairs. I can handle this. Roman didn't mean anything. He's just had too much to drink. I can manage him."

"Yes, Jan, go back downstairs and get the hell out of my house. I want to be alone with my wife if you don't mind."

"It's all right, Jan. I'll be fine. Please go now."

Jan hesitated at first but Dani gently pushed him out, locking the door after him.

"I'll see you tomorrow."

Roman would have to come home in this condition just when she had almost convinced Jan that Tekla had painted a false picture of Roman. Now Jan would never believe that Roman was trying to mend his ways, especially after the vile accusation he'd made. She turned to her husband who stood leaning against the wall.

"Roman, please come to bed. You've had too much to drink and you'll be sorry in the morning when you have to get up for work."

Roman weaved his way into the bedroom, took the alarm clock, and smashed it down on top of the dresser. It shattered loudly, the bell clanging as it broke into many pieces.

"I don't have to get up in the morning because I quit my lousy job today."

The noise woke the baby so Dani picked her up and gently rocked her back to sleep in her arms.

"Oh, no. Roman, why? Jobs aren't easy to find. There are too many men out of work."

The baby settled back to sleep and Dani placed her in the cradle.

"I'm sick of it, do you understand?" Roman

218

thundered. "Sick to my stomach of the foul smells. I wasn't meant to spend the rest of my life in a stinking factory sweating like all the other halfwits working their asses off for minimum wages."

He fell heavily into bed, the springs protesting loudly at the sudden impact of his weight.

Dani lay beside him quietly, knowing she should wait until morning to ask questions, but she was too afraid for their future to postpone her misgivings.

"Roman, what will we do for money until you find another job?"

"You nagging bitch," Roman growled. "Leave me alone. You're irritating me to my grave." He pushed her roughly out of bed. She landed on the floor heavily and winced with pain. "Sleep on the floor where you belong, bitch, or go sleep with your darling wonderful brother. You make a fine pair—two prim and prissy clods."

He threw a pillow down at her, turned over and fell asleep.

Crying, Dani lifted herself up and pulled the cradle quietly out of the room. She carried it into the living room, intending to sleep on the couch, the baby next to her. The strain of pulling the cumbersome cradle started her bleeding anew so she padded herself thickly, hoping it would stop if she lay quietly and kept her legs tightly clenched. After an hour she fell into a fitful sleep, and by the time the baby cried for her feeding, Dani noticed the flow had almost stopped.

"Oh, little Ellie," she cried as the baby fed, "is he ever going to change? We must make him change, you and I. He can be a good man if we work at it hard enough. He has to change for the better soon or I'll lose my mind. I can't continue making all these lame excuses. We have to do our best to turn him around."

Roman woke after ten still belligerent.

"Then you really have quit?" Dani asked, setting toast and coffee on the table.

"I told you that last night, didn't I?" he answered shortly.

He made no mention of his cruelty the night before, just acted as though nothing untoward had happened. Just once, Dani thought, I would like to hear him say he is sorry. She sat, sipping her coffee and hoping the impossible would happen this morning.

"I think I'll take my time looking for work," Roman said, yawning. "No sense rushing into just any job. I'll walk around today and see what some of the men have to say. Maybe I can be a salesman. I might even take the trolley downtown and see what's available. I have some friends on Milwaukee Avenue and they know a lot of influential people. Perhaps I can get into the restaurant business there. We'll see."

He went back to bed till noon, then he dressed and left the house without another word. As soon as he was gone Jan and Tekla came up, concern on their faces.

"What happened?" Jan asked. "I heard a loud crash last night. I wanted to come up, but Tekla stopped me. Did he lay a finger on you? Tell me the truth."

"No, no," Dani protested. "Roman was drunk and he bumped into the dresser and knocked the alarm clock down. It shattered into a million pieces and woke the baby. He was only celebrating the birth of his first child with some of the men he knows."

"And is that why he didn't go to work today?" Tekla asked.

Dani looked up forlorn. "He's quit his job. He's out looking for another."

"No good bastard," Tekla shouted. "Now, with a family to support, he quits his job as though there are hundreds to choose from. Times are hard, men are out begging for work and he quits his job. God should strike him off the face of the earth. If I were a man I'd break every bone in his body. I should have sent you up, Jan, so you could do the job for me."

"Aunt, please," Dani begged. "He'll find another. It's not easy working in a factory. He's not suited for that kind of work."

"Excuses, excuses. You always manage to find another excuse for him. When are you going to see the light, when you're lying in your grave?"

Dani was on the verge of tears so Jan interrupted. "All right. Let's forget about Roman for now, shall we? Let's talk about baptizing Eleanor. When will it be? Who will the godparents be?"

Dani silently thanked her brother with her eyes. "I thought a week from Sunday would be best and Jan, you will be godfather won't you? I'm going to ask Carmella to be godmother."

"Carmella? Who is Carmella?"

"That strange Italian girl Dani met on the train to Chicago. Dani, I wish you wouldn't," Tekla began, but she noticed the set look on her niece's face. "Well, at least she is Catholic, but people will think it most unusual."

"Dani, I was hoping you would choose me," Jan beamed. "I'm proud to be godfather and I'll be a good one too. Eleanor will be just like my own daughter. She'll never want for anything."

Tekla offered to go to a pay phone and ask Carmella to be godmother to the child. There was a telephone at the tavern, but Tekla had never had occasion to use it— she'd only answered its persistent ringing when Bolie was busy—so she was a bit nervous about making the call.

"But you never told her you married," Tekla protested. "What will she think? Will she be able to understand me? Will they let her take a phone call at work?"

"Of course she'll understand you," Dani chided. "You both speak English, don't you? She knows I'm married. I wrote a few weeks ago and explained everything. She said I could call her at work during her lunch hour and gave me the number. Just tell her the date and what time to be here. Explain that I can't leave the house and phone her myself until after the christening. I still think it's a foolish superstition that I shouldn't leave the house until after I've been blessed in church along with Eleanor. Whoever started such nonsense anyway?"

Tekla was horrified when her niece questioned tradition.

"It's not a silly superstition. Bad luck will haunt you if you try to leave the house sooner."

"But what happens when a mother can't baptize her baby immediately—let's say the baby is ill—and she has to go out if a crisis comes up?"

"You don't have a crisis," Tekla answered. "If there's an emergency that's different."

Eleanor was baptized the following Sunday. Fortunately, she slept throughout the ceremony even when Father Stefan poured holy water on her head and put the few grains of salt on her tongue. She only smacked her lips at the strange taste and settled back into blissful sleep. Roman stood proudly in front of his friends, nattily dressed for the occasion in an almost new tan suit. He invited many people to the house after the christening, and the party lasted till well past midnight. By the time everyone left, Dani was exhausted from serving food and drinks to the people gathered in her home. Tekla and Jan helped, but it seemed there weren't enough hands to keep providing refreshments. Carmella helped too. But right in the middle of the party, Carmella suddenly decided to leave, just when they were all enjoying themselves. Strange, Dani thought. She was supposed to spend the night. Then Dani decided Carmella probably felt ill. It was rather hot and Carmella wasn't used to eating Polish food. When someone had told her she was eating kishka, blood sausage, Carmella had turned rather pale and had gone out on the back porch alone. Soon afterward she had made a hasty departure, claiming she had forgotten she had something very important to do at home. Neither could afford a telephone, so Dani couldn't call her, but she would write to her. They wrote to each other once a week and that would have to suffice until Dani was able to get a pay phone and call Carmella during her lunch break. Later, when the baby was older and more manageable, she would take the trolley and visit her friend occasionally on Sunday afternoons when Roman was usually out.

Meanwhile, Dani stood looking at the messy aftermath of the christening. She decided to wash the enormous stack of dirty dishes in the morning. Jan was a trifle tipsy and Tekla was flushed and overtired from doing the cooking with the help of Martha so Dani told them to leave and get to bed.

Just as she laid her head on the pillow, Eleanor woke. It was two o'clock and she was hungry. Dani fed her and then dropped off to sleep as soon as her head hit the pillow, happy to have four or five hours to rest before Ellie woke again.

The rest of the summer passed quickly. Eleanor was a satisfied, compliant baby who never fussed overly much, except when she was hungry or had dirtied her diaper. Roman was still looking for work and left the house at noon each day, confident that some intriguing job would fall into his lap soon. Where he found carfare for his jaunts around the city Dani didn't know, for she was forced to accept food from Tekla despite her protests that she didn't want any charity. Every few

223

days Roman threw a few dollars on the table. Dani didn't dare question its origin for fear of making him fly into a rage. He didn't have the money he needed for drinking, so the shortage of funds made him unbearable most of the time. Dani was relieved when he left the house, for then she could play with the baby or catch up on housework instead of listening to his unattainable plans for the future.

One Sunday in September she had a few extra quarters and Tekla urged her to get out of the house with Eleanor. Tekla tried to slip a few dollars into Dani's purse, but she pushed them back into her aunt's pocket.

"No, you've done too much for us already. I can't take more. I have carfare, Eleanor and I will visit Carmella."

She braved the trip on the trolley without knowing for certain if Carmella was home, but luckily, Carmella was. She gave Dani a warm welcome as did her large family. It was so different in Carmella's neighborhood. People seemed to know each other, to get along. The front steps were filled with laughing dark-haired women and children who smiled a greeting as she passed. Carmella coaxed Dani into staying for dinner and she couldn't refuse the kind offer, not when Carmella's relatives begged her to stay so everyone could have a turn at holding the baby. Fourteen adults and children sat around a huge oak table eating strange dishes called antipasto, linguini, agnellino. Dani enjoyed every morsel she tasted, and everyone joined in the laughter when she repeated the names of the various dishes with her funny-sounding accent. She tried to remember everyone's name that afternoon but couldn't. Angelina, Franceso, Matteo, Concetta, Rodolfo—it was impossible to remember everyone at one meeting, and when she told them some popular Polish names they were aghast at the spelling and pronunciation. As a result when the meal ended everyone was trying to think of the most unpronounceable name he or she knew. Dani won hands down with a neighbor's name, Aloysius Kaczmarkiewicz. No one could top that, so they held their sides and laughed. Dani's eyes sparkled for the first time in months. She was really enjoying herself, but when she invited Carmella to her house, she noticed the reluctance that immediately appeared in her friend's eyes.

"What's wrong?" Dani asked. "I meant to ask you why you left so suddenly at the christening, but it slipped my mind. Did someone say something to hurt your feelings or insult you? Polish people are very clannish, but they'll get used to seeing us together."

"No, no," Carmella protested. It's just better for you to come here to my sister's house. It's more fun here, right?"

"No, it isn't right," Dani answered. "Carmella, something happened at my house and I want to know about it. Someone did upset you. Who?"

"It's nothing, Dani, really. It's just that when some men drink too much they act stupid."

"It was Roman wasn't it? You can tell me, Carmella. I should know him by now. He did something to you, didn't he?"

"Dani, please."

"Never mind, Carmella. I understand. You're right. I'll come visit you instead. Then there'll be no problems."

Carmella wouldn't say more. How could she tell her friend that while she was on the back porch getting a breath of cool air, Roman had crept up behind her, put his hands up her dress, and sloppily tried to fondle her. When she had resisted he had pushed her up against the wall, had torn her underwear, and had tried to kiss her.

Carmella had felt his wet tongue, slimy and repugnant, on her face and neck. With all her strength she had shoved him away, sending him sprawling backward until he almost fell over the railing. What a scandal that would have caused. Carmella shuddered from thinking about it. She still had felt the humiliation, as though everyone knew that Roman had torn her underdrawers, had violently attempted to seduce her, had slid his hands up and down her body before she could make her escape. If he'd been sober Carmella was sure he would have managed to drag her into the yard or the shed unless she had screamed. But she hadn't wanted to do that, to make a scene and hurt Dani. "Pig," she had spat out as she had run to the trolley that night. How could Dani have fallen in love with and married such a pig? Carmella had been in tears all the way home, and uncomfortable because of the strips of underclothing flapping around her legs even though her dress hid the damage. That night she had promised herself she would never go back to Dani's house. In the future they could meet at her sister's or somewhere away from both homes. Never again would she subject herself to such shame.

Now Carmella wondered if Roman even remembered his absurd actions that night. Was he always so detestable or was the christening the only time he had made such clumsy advances? She couldn't be sure so it was better not to take a chance. Roman might think she was looking for him. What if Dani had happened to step out on the porch that night? What if she had seen them? Today Carmella was doubly shamed to see the despair creep into Dani's eyes when just minutes ago they had both laughed so freely.

"Carmella, please." Dani put her arms around her. "It's all right. We're still the best of friends. It will be good for me and Eleanor to get away for a few hours at least once a month. I'll love coming here if you'll have me."

Carmella hugged her tightly. "Of course we'll have you. Whenever you like, just come. You'll never need a formal invitation. Almost everyone's home on Sundays. I'm always here."

After the Christmas holidays Dani realized she was pregnant again.

"It's too soon," Tekla grumbled. "Eleanor will still need too much attention and you'll have another baby to care for. Why couldn't you make Roman control himself a while longer?"

But Dani didn't mind having another baby as long as it was just like Eleanor.

"There won't be any problems. Eleanor will have a playmate. Besides, Ellie's such a good baby and I had no problems having her."

Tekla refused to be placated.

"It would be better if your husband found a steady job then I wouldn't be so worried about your being pregnant again. How will he support you?"

Roman had been searching for something suitable for months. He'd been a dishwasher for two days but had decided the job was degrading. Then he'd tried his hand at housepainting and, after one day, had come home in an abominable mood. It had taken Dani days to clean the paint out of his hair. He'd become a chauffer and had been pleased with the job for a week. Then he'd smashed up the owner's brand-new automobile. Being a salesman hadn't worked out either. Roman had insulted a female customer who'd been unable to choose between a brown and a red sofa. The store owner had had no choice but to dismiss him for his insolence. When the soap factory rehired him to

227

work in the packing room, he complained that he could still smell vile odors even though he was far away from the mixing vats. He left. And so it went.

During the winter money was very short so Dani took in sewing to make a few extra dollars a week. At least it put food on the table, although she was months behind in the rent. Tekla didn't want the money, but Dani kept insisting she would catch up with the bills soon. She began to take in ironing to help make ends meet, and often Tekla found her, late at night, heating irons on the stove grates and sweating away at the menial work. Jan and Tekla begged her to stop, but she stubbornly refused to listen to their pleas.

"I'll manage," she told them. "Roman will find something steady soon."

Since Eleanor amused herself most of the day, Dani was able to get large stacks of mending and ironing done weekly, and she didn't nag Roman about his nonchalance at finding work. It was more peaceful if she kept quiet.

Jan was helping a mechanic repair automobiles, and he became fascinated with the work. As soon as he learned where every part went, he planned on moving to Detroit to work at assembling the cars. He wrote regularly to the man who had helped him in his search for Chicago and was repeatedly promised work whenever he decided to go to Detroit. Jan answered that he would be moving in August after his sister had her second child. Most of the time Jan stayed out of Roman's way because Dani pleaded with him to do so. The brothers-in-law hated each other, and you could visibly see sparks fly whenever they were in the same room for over five minutes. Jan was learning English as fast as he could and whenever he spent a few hours with the new friends he'd made he overheard one story or another about Roman's misdeeds. He would have liked nothing better than to smash his fist into Roman's face, to dissipate his bottled-up rage. He couldn't figure out what Dani found so attractive in the man she'd married. He had to admit Roman was rather good-looking, but that was all there was to him—that and a fascination for anything that wore skirts.

Since Roman couldn't afford to drink as often as he liked, he was sober most of the time, only meeting his cronies on Saturdays. Dani couldn't decide whether she liked him better drunk or sober. When he was drunk he became abusive and ornery, but at least he dropped off to sleep after a few minutes. Sober, he was becoming unbearable. He constantly complained, saying that he should have stayed single, that Dani brought him bad luck. When he was single, he said, he'd always had money in his pockets. Once in a while he came home with a new shirt or some other expensive finery, and Dani guessed that another woman had given it to him for services rendered. At these times she cried herself to sleep quietly, her head buried in her pillow. Nightly, she prayed, asking God to send Roman a good job, something that would make him content. But by the time her second child was due, he was still wandering from one odd job to another, not satisfied with any of them.

Dani's labor began on the hottest day of August, but this time she agonized for over twenty hours before another daughter was born. When the midwife placed the baby in her arms, Dani was too exhausted to really look at the wrinkled red-faced child and she dropped off to sleep having noticed only that the girl had a head of soft reddish blond fuzz, ten fingers, and ten toes.

Roman took one look at this added responsibility and left the house to get roaring drunk. When he didn't bother to come home for three days, Tekla wanted to go after him with her meat cleaver, but as she had in the past, Dani made excuses for him.

She named her daughter Lydia, and Bolie and Martha were the godparents. Eleanor played contentedly with her wooden blocks, took her nap at midday and went to bed regularly every evening at seven o'clock; but Lydia was a demanding baby. She slept in half-hour stretches and then screamed at the top of her lungs. Dani and Tekla tried to calm the child. They put warm compresses on the baby's stomach to relieve what they thought was colic and they fed her strained rice water to calm her. Neither worked and Dani's nerves were frazzled from lack of sleep. She constantly had to rock the baby during the night to keep her quiet so Roman wouldn't wake up in a rage and rouse the whole building.

One night, in desperation, Tekla put a spoonful of brandy in some warm water and, for the first time in months, Lydia slept seven straight hours. Dani was sorely tempted to use this ploy more often, but she and Tekla agreed it would be bad for the baby so instead Dani learned to sleep in snatches, never getting a full night's rest. On Sundays Tekla would take Lydia to her place for a few hours while Dani and Eleanor took a nice long nap together, undisturbed by the shrieks and screams of the red-faced Lydia. When Lydia was a year old and finally settling into some semblance of normalcy Dani found herself pregnant again. She no longer made a pretense of paying Tekla even a token rent for money was almost nonexistent, at least for her. Although Roman was working steadily as a bartender at a beer garden on Milwaukee Avenue, his wife and family saw very little of the salary and tips he made. He threw down three or four dollars every Monday morning, just enough to buy the food for the week. Dani tried to keep on doing sewing for neighbors, but it was hard to work at it with two small children, especially with Lydia who whined and fought for attention all day. The cantankerous child refused to take a nap and Dani finally gave in to her because the child's wailing and screaming resistance was exhausting. During this pregnancy she was too nauseated to care much about her youngest daughter's sleeping habits and manners. It was hard enough trying to keep food down. Only after dinner could she sip some clear soup and, if she was lucky, eat a slice of plain bread. Instead of gaining weight, she kept losing it, until finally she appeared almost skeletal except for her protruding stomach.

Tekla was frantic with worry but none of the tempting dishes she or Martha cooked would stay down. After forcing herself to take a bite or two, Dani always made a mad dash to a handily placed bucket. It was lonely with Jan gone too. He had put off the move to Detroit for months after Lydia's birth, but it was obvious that he was anxious to go now that he knew the inner workings and parts of an automobile. The auto industry was growing by leaps and bounds. It seemed that everyone was buying a car; even middle-income families found owning one a necessity. Jan was eager to make a start in what he felt was going to be a multi-million-dollar industry. In the short while he'd tinkered with the autos in Sam's garage he'd felt an affinity with the machines he worked on. He even spent all his free time dreaming up ingenious innovations to experiment on when he had the proper tools and schooling. He felt sure he could learn much more in Detroit, the hub of the industry. Finally, amid tears and sorrowful good-byes he left. He was nineteen and strongly resembled his father. Three good meals a day had put twenty pounds on his lean frame, and he had the assurance of a man who knew what he wanted and was determined to get it. Going away to start a new life seemed to take his mind off vengeance against Louis Czerny. Numerous letters had been written to Poland but only one answer was received. The new priest in Ruda wrote that Father Czerny had died. He said he knew nothing of his brother Louis and had problems enough coping with the parishioners in Ruda. Jan promised he would continue to send letters to the authorities, and when political matters were settled in Europe, he planned to have enough money saved to go back to Poland so he could confront Louis even though Tekla pleaded with him to let the matter rest.

"It would be futile Jan," she told him. "Too much time has elapsed and no one would believe you."

"We'll see," was Jan's answer.

He intended to become an American citizen, after which he would apply for a passport and make the long trip back to see that Louis suffered as much as he did whenever he thought of his father. Jan drove himself, keeping constantly busy, for when he was idle the nightmare of his father's mutilated body came to the forefront of his thoughts and left him sleepless and shaking with rage. His sister's marriage added to his mental anguish, but there he was frustrated too; for every time he made an attempt to deal with Roman, Dani interceded, begging Jan to leave him be. He had been unable to convince his sister that her marriage was unholy. She knew he was right but wouldn't admit it. She was too stubborn to acknowledge that she was never going to change Roman. Jan decided it would be best if he left before he killed his brother-in-law and lost the freedom he'd worked so hard to attain. He departed Chicago with only two regrets, that he was leaving Dani with the kind of man she had married and leaving his aunt to bear the brunt of the turmoil in Dani's life.

But Dani would have it no other way. She lived in

232

her own fairytale world waiting for Roman to change from a frog into Prince Charming. He guessed some-day she would be rudely awakened and he hoped that day wouldn't come too late for her to enjoy a few happy years. He couldn't bring himself to stay and watch his sister change from a beautiful intelligent woman into a haggard one who had become old before her time from worry and childbearing. No amount of pleading would coax her into accepting financial help from him or from Tekla. Dani had always been stubborn and willful. It had been a major battle even to get her to accept the fact that Tekla did not want her to pay rent. She'd only conceded because she couldn't possibly pay it and she dreaded moving into whatever dark hole Roman would drag her to, probably their old shabby flat. She only accepted presents from them at Christmas or on birthdays, and even then she cautioned them not to overspend. One gift each was more than enough, she insisted, and they had to abide by her wishes because if they gave more she would return it.

Jan and Tekla had decided that their gifts would have to be thought out very carefully. For Christmas, Tekla would buy the girls a new winter coat each year for they were constantly growing. Jan would buy each of his nieces a dress and he would sneak in one small toy each. For birthdays the girls would receive sweaters or shoes. Dani refused to accept clothes for herself. She wanted something practical, if anything. The past Christmas Tekla had bought her a sewing machine, and Dani had been aghast at the price, insisting this would be her gift for all the Christmases to come. She marveled at the machine's speed. After taking a few lessons from a neighbor, it became her lifeline. With it she could take in mending and get the work done in less than half the time. She could even sew a whole dress for a customer in one or two days and save the scraps for her growing children. Her daughters surely had the strangest underwear imaginable. Petticoats made of several different materials; sometimes a striped top with a flowered bottom or vice versa. Their stockings were always knit by Dani and were passed down from one to the other until they were past mending.

Dani bore her third daughter, Irena, in October, 1918. Roman was away from the house as usual during the birthing, and this time he didn't bother to come home until a week later, at which time he swore loudly when he found out he had another daughter.

"Damn you to hell, woman, is that all you're good for?" he shouted. "I'm surrounded by female bitches who will all nag me into my grave. You're completely useless, presenting me with daughter after daughter. I curse the day I met you. I should have known from the beginning you'd only produce sniveling female brats."

For months the only thing that pleased Roman was Jan's absence. He was even fired from his job at the beer garden with no notice. Dani learned later that the owner of the jovial meeting place had caught Roman and his wife in a very compromising position. This time Roman had met his match and he came home bleeding because he had been hit on the head with a full bottle of whiskey. The doctor who had been summoned to stitch up the wound advised Dani that Roman had a concussion and should remain in bed for a few days. Dani paid him with her last dollar.

With Roman around the house the days became progressively worse. He constantly hounded her to come to bed with him, in the afternoons and again during the night, sometimes in the mornings. He expected her to leave the children to play and to give in to his demands whenever he felt the urge. She protested that the children were getting older and that it was unwise to leave them unattended in the middle of the day, but when she told him this she got a beating instead of understanding. It was easier to acquiesce to his repeated demands. Once again Tekla began to notice bruises and hollow circles beneath Dani's eyes and that upset her. Why was God sending her these crosses to bear when she abided by her religious beliefs faithfully? She was torn between putting in longer hours at the tavern to get peace of mind or staying home to ease her niece's burden. What would it take to make Roman leave her beloved niece alone? When Dani became pregnant for the fourth time Tekla made her move. Was this pig insatiable? She would give Roman what he wanted but only on her terms. One evening when Roman was sitting on the front porch and Dani was putting the children to sleep, Tekla made her offer, feeling only revulsion for this swine she nonetheless spoke sweetly. She opened the front door.

"Roman, please come into my house. I have to talk to you in private for a few minutes."

Roman grumpily stood up and followed her into the living room, scratching his unshaven face.

"What now? Are you going to tell me I owe you rent? You can't squeeze juice from a prune. I don't have any money. Do you want us to move? I can always get my old apartment back, the room Dani lived in when we were first married. Is that what you want?"

Tekla grated her teeth. "No, Roman, that's not what I wanted to see you about. I have a proposition to put to you. How would you like to be half owner of my tavern? The work's getting to be too much for me and I've decided to slow down. It's a profitable business and the two of us can earn a decent living."

"I don't believe it," Roman said hotly. "You hate my guts. Why are you offering me a half of your business? Are you sick or have you gone mad?"

"Neither, you imbecile. There is something you

would have to do to earn your share. That's why I wanted to speak to you in private. You can be half owner if you leave Dani alone. You're killing her with too many pregnancies in too short a time. I don't ask that you give up your husbandly rights completely, just give her a chance to have some breathing space in between pregnancies. At this rate you'll have a child every year and she'll be worn out and useless in no time. Leave her alone for a nice long time and part of my business is yours. Is it a deal? Isn't this what you always wanted?"

Roman strutted over to the mirror and smoothed back his hair. "Half interest you said? I have a general idea of how much the tavern brings in and that's not too bad. How long do I have to leave your precious niece alone? Forever?"

"No, give her at least two years after she has this baby and then promise me you'll only take her once a week or even less after that."

"And what do I do for two years? Fondle myself like some schoolboy in the shed?"

"I don't care what you do for the next two years, just be discreet and don't let her hear of a scandal or anything that would hurt Dani any more than she's been hurt already."

"You're right in a way, Tekla. All I get from her are more females. She's probably carrying another daughter in her belly now. What good is that?"

"If you were a decent man you would be proud of your daughters. All three are beautiful and will grow up to be good women. Other men are proud of their children, girls as well as boys. Martha and Bolie would give their eye teeth for any child."

"Bah, spare me your sermonizing. All right. We've made a deal. I'll be happy to join you at the tavern. As long as there will be two of us we can think of

236

expanding, put in a proper beer garden for the summer, bring in better polka bands, enlarge the dance floor to draw more customers."

"We'll talk about that later. Then you agree to my terms?"

"Yes, yes, I agree," he said impatiently.

"If you cross me in any way, Roman, if you go back on your word or steal from me, I promise you I'll have Bolie break every bone in your body and I assure you he can do it. He'd be only too happy to if I gave the word for he knows you for the dirt you are."

Roman looked up nervously. "There's no need to get violent. I agreed to your terms, Tekla. You'll see. We'll work very well together, you and I, and we'll both make good money. You see a changed man in front of you."

"Do I?" Tekla muttered to herself after Roman left. "I'll believe your promises when wolves stop howling in the night but it will help for a while; I'll have time to think up some other tricks." She looked upward. "Oh, God, why must I resort to devious plotting in my old age? All I want to do is work and enjoy the rest of my life, yet here I am thinking up plans to spare my niece from hell on earth."

Dani's fourth delivery was a very difficult one. The baby was in the breech position and the midwife, unable to turn it for proper birthing, wrung her hands in desperation. Dani screamed agonizingly for a whole day and night, then into the next morning. Finally Tekla called in a proper doctor who ordered Roman to carry Dani downstairs and place her on a kitchen table. It was larger than the one upstairs. Roman couldn't take the shrill cries another second and left the house as soon as he'd placed his wife on the table, barely looking at her in his haste to escape. Tekla ran after him, intending to make him watch the misery he was putting Dani through, but she let him go. What good would

237

that do? He cared for no one but the devil himself. He had no conscience. Between spasms of excruciating pain, Dani saw Roman leave and clasped Tekla's hands in hers, panting with effort as the doctor turned for a pan of boiling water to cleanse his instruments.

"You're right," she whispered, forcing the words from her mouth. "All the time you were right and I was wrong. He's not a man and never will be. He's a weak godless fool; he's worse than a fool, he's nothing. I'm the fool for believing in him."

She began to sob out her years of pent-up hurt; then she screamed again as a stabbing pain caused her to lose her breath, while the room spun around crazily. All Dani wished for now was a quick death to end this ceaseless torture. If she could reach a knife she'd stick it into her own heart just to feel blessed painless relief.

"I'm going to have to cut her a little; there's no time to get to a hospital," the doctor decided. "It's the only way we're going to get the baby out. We'll lose them both if I don't." He took a sharp scalpel from the water and cut a large incision in the vaginal area to work the baby around. Dani let out one last scream that reverberated throughout the house and then she fainted, a relief to Tekla after seeing her hours of anguish. Neither Tekla nor the doctor noticed Eleanor huddled in a corner of the kitchen, frozen in shock at seeing her mother's suffering, and terrified when blood poured from Dani's private parts. She stood stock still, watching a bloodied baby emerge. She winced when she heard the red ugly thing cry and watched in horror as the afterbirth slid out onto the table and down to the floor with a wet sickening thud. The doctor took up a needle and began stitching. Mama's insides are pouring out, Eleanor thought wildly. The doctor is cutting away all her insides. She stared with glassy eyes, expecting a heart to fall out next, beating and pumping madly. Blood was everywhere; on the doctor, on aunt Tekla; dripping from the table to the floor; on the ugly thing that resembled a baby that the midwife was wrapping in a towel. Eleanor gagged and vomited on the kitchen floor. Only then did Tekla notice her.

"Oh, God. No," she moaned. "The children were supposed to stay upstairs. Why didn't Martha keep a closer watch?"

Martha ran down just then, searching for the missing Eleanor, and she took the child back upstairs. Eleanor stared vacantly into space all that day. In the evening she finally gave way to a burst of tears.

"I'll never have a baby," she declared vehemently. "Never, never, never."

"Poor child," Tekla comforted her. "Why didn't you stay here? What made you sneak away?"

"I wanted to help Mama stop screaming," Eleanor answered. "She stopped when the doctor cut her. Is she with the angels now? Is Mama dead?"

"No, darling, she's going to be just fine, but she has to rest for a long time and you and I are going to have to help her. I'll take you downstairs now so you can see that she's better, but only for a minute. Come darling."

Eleanor gripped Tekla's hand tightly and walked into the bedroom where her mother was sleeping. She was so white, almost the color of the sheet she lay on. Eleanor was relieved to see her mother inhale and exhale softly, but she still had to hear her speak—just one word—to really be sure she was alive.

"Mama," she whispered next to Dani's ear, "Can you hear me?"

Dani opened her eyes slowly and smiled faintly at her eldest daughter. "What is it, Ellie?"

"Oh, Mama, I'm so happy you're all right. Do you hurt? Can I help you?"

"No, Eleanor. I only want to sleep for a while. Be a

239

good girl and help Martha with your sisters. You'll have to help with the chores until I feel better."

"Yes, Mama, I know. Good night." She kissed her mother's cheek tenderly.

Dani patted her head. "Good night, little love. I'll see you again tomorrow when I'm rested."

Eleanor lay in the bed next to her sister Lydia and watched rain trickle down the windowpane and form zigzag patterns on the glass. Why, she wondered, did God make Mama suffer so? God was supposed to be good and kind, yet she had heard her mother beg and plead with Him for merciful relief. Eleanor was five and already very intelligent, but she couldn't comprehend why God could be so cruel, like her father was most of the time. Hours later, she slipped out of bed and, carrying her doll gingerly in one hand, opened the back door. She flung the doll that used to be her favorite treasure into the garbage bin. "Bad baby," she whispered. From that day forward she never asked for or touched another doll. Babies only brought pain and hurt their mothers. She wanted no part of them.

As soon as she awoke Dani named her new daughter Celia, but this time Dani was very weak and could not get out of bed for several weeks. Tekla helped as much as she could, but the better part of her day had to be spent at the tavern watching over Roman to see that he wasn't cheating her. Then came devastating news. Bolie had accepted a job at a steel mill in East Chicago and could only work for her on Saturdays. Although he had to travel over an hour and take three different trolleys to get to his job, he felt it was worth the time since the pay was so good. Tekla knew, though, that the real reason he had done it was that he couldn't stand working side by side with Roman, who barked out orders like a drill sergeant. She knew Bolie's feelings were deeply hurt, as were Martha's. When they'd found out that Roman was a full partner in the business and therefore their boss too, they had been shocked and outraged. Tekla had explained why she'd made such a move, but Bolie was a proud man and he decided to get himself out of an impossible situation. Loyalty had its limits when one had to choose between independence or domination. He and his wife both loved Tekla dearly and would remain her friend, but they weren't getting any younger and had to plan wisely for the future.

Bolie was a strong man so working in the sweltering heat of a mill didn't seem to bother him much. With the increase in salary, he was that much closer to buying the home he'd always dreamed of, and he soon found it in a Polish-Croatian community in East Chicago. It was a good bargain that he couldn't pass by. It had four large rooms, a full basement, and an attic. It cost only three hundred dollars. The owner had died a year earlier and his widow intended to move in with her married daughter. Tekla was glad to have Bolie working on Saturdays when the crowd was heaviest, but on Sundays Bolie wanted to stay home and work on his new house. As a result, Tekla had to watch Roman more closely than ever. She knew he was slipping some of the profits into his pockets, but by overseeing him carefully she tried to keep his theft to a minimum.

Dani was flabbergasted when she heard that her aunt had freely given away half of her prosperous business to Roman. Purposefully, she walked to the tavern and confronted her aunt in the kitchen.

"What's come over you?" she asked. "What possessed you to let Roman come in with you? Has he threatened you in any way? Aunt, tell me the truth. I'm shocked at what you've done."

"Dani, please. It's time I slowed down. I've worked hard for well over twenty years, and I don't enjoy it as

241

much as I used to. All of a sudden I find myself too tired to take care of all the details so I went to your husband."

"But why him? You told me countless times he shouldn't be trusted. Why him of all people? You could have sold half to Bolie. He would have loved to be your partner."

"No. Bolie doesn't want to own a tavern. His savings are all going toward buying a home. It's my place of business, and I can bring in whoever I want. I'm just trying to give Roman a chance to prove himself. Even with only half the profits the business is prosperous enough for two. Trust me Dani, I know what I'm doing. Now I don't want to talk about it anymore."

Dani wasn't satisfied with the explanation but she left anyway, knowing Tekla wouldn't explain further. They were both stubborn women.

Dani was as content as it was possible for her to be under the circumstances. There was a steady income coming in, enough to begin paying her aunt rent again and to improve the food situation. They could afford meat a few times a week whereas before she'd had to concoct meals with starches: potato soup, beet soup, pancakes, and the like. The girls could eat fruit again, and she did not have to depend on Tekla's bounty. It felt satisfying to walk into a store and pay for her purchases rather than put them on a running bill. Slowly she was able to pay off the debts that had mounted over the past few years. She couldn't understand Roman's sudden lack of interest in sex, but she was grateful for the respite since it was taking her so long to heal after the birth of Celia. A week or two after her other children were born, she'd felt fit and able, but this last birth had left her sore and aching for months. Dani had no free time, not with four small children to care for. She was constantly cooking, washing, cleaning, and preventing arguments between the children. Lydia, she was sure, would become a willful woman, for she always insisted on getting her own way. Perhaps the good sisters at school will discipline her properly, Dani thought as she bent over the steaming washtub one morning. She looked forward to Lydia's fifth birthday for she was eager to see what the nuns could do with this child.

Roman continued to abstain from having sex with her and she grew more puzzled, not that she didn't appreciate the discontinuance. Now she could fall asleep at a decent hour for Roman usually didn't come home until two in the morning. Now when he got in, even if he was intoxicated, he lay down on the bed and turned his back to her. Did he have another woman right under Tekla's nose? It was possible. Anything was possible with Roman. Let him have as many women as he liked. It didn't bother her, not anymore. There wasn't an ounce of feeling for her husband left in her. She had been a blind fool and had to live with her mistake. Still, life was more bearable without him mauling her at all hours.

The bloom slowly came back into Dani's cheeks, and she found a few minutes a day to brush her long flaxen hair and to relax despite Lydia's whining tantrums. While Eleanor was a real help and did little chores like dusting, wiping the dishes, and folding freshly washed clothes, Lydia was becoming more troublesome. She would purposely sit in dirt and mud just to spite her mother. Belligerent, she defied all the rules, young as she was. Irena and Celia were more like Eleanor and settled into regular eating, playing and sleeping periods, but they were exposed to Lydia's behavior and at times they tried to imitate her. Lydia was somewhat afraid of her father, but Roman wasn't home enough to discipline her. When he was, she changed into an acquiescent child, fetching his slippers or a glass of water without protest.

"Two of a kind," Tekla warned. "I'm sorry to say this, but I believe the devil takes care of its own."

"Aunt, you should be ashamed of yourself. Lydia's just a baby. She'll be like the others once she's enrolled in school."

"I'll believe it when I see it. You're too lenient, Dani. Some children sense this and act accordingly."

By the time Celia was a year old she had blossomed into a beautiful child and Dani had finally lost the haggard look that had plagued her for so many months. Dani had discovered that sound spankings made Lydia a little less demanding, although she still devised tricks to play on her younger sisters and tried to get them into trouble whenever she could. However, Eleanor appointed herself Irena's and Celia's protectress when Lydia stole their toys or their special treats and the girls turned to her more and more when Dani wasn't nearby.

With Bolie away during the week, Roman became more bold in his attempt to take over the tavern. It was all Tekla could do to keep up with him, to watch every move he made. When she came home at midnight she carried the day's profits with her and cursed Roman the next day because she was sure there should be more. And Tekla had noticed that Roman was drinking more during the course of the day because the liquor was now free. His hand trembled in the morning if he didn't have a shot of whiskey in his breakfast coffee. In addition, Roman had taken it upon himself to hire a new barmaid, a young girl in her late twenties, who helped out now that Martha was gone. The girl was a plump blond, slovenly in her dress. She did bring in more customers, but not the kind Tekla wanted or needed. One of the girl's duties was to help in the

244

tchen with the cooking, but at that work she was slow and careless. However, at the bar she glowed with happiness when the men told lewd jokes and paid her extravagant compliments, and when Roman talked to her, it was obvious that she idolized him. Tekla had to handle all the major cooking chores, and she found herself spending more hours than she liked at her place of business. She wanted to spend a few hours with her great-nieces on Sundays, but Dani couldn't help but notice her yawns so after dinner she always sent her own to rest. The tavern closed early on Sundays, and as usual Tekla took the day off to go to church and catch up on her housework even though doing so meant losing more money to Roman's greedy hands. Tekla was sure he was sleeping with the barmaid, Sophie. She could tell by the way the girl smirked whenever she was told to finish her work. Sophie lived with her aged grandmother and Tekla knew Roman was sneaking into her house after closing hours. Soon, Tekla promised herself, she would get rid of Sophie and hire someone older. There were a number of widows in the neighborhood who would be eager to earn enough money to support themselves. She tried to talk Dani into leaving Roman again, but she couldn't sway her.

"I can't do it, Aunt. I realize what Roman is, but I married him for better or worse and I must stay married to him. Marriage is a holy sacrament, and it's my duty to stay with him even though I realize I'll never change him. I was gullible and stupid. I let him charm me into loving him when all he wanted was to live easy on your money."

"Does he bother with you, Dani?" Tekla asked, concerned.

"No. He hasn't touched me since Celia was born, and really don't care how many women he has as long as

he leaves me alone. Strange, isn't it? I can't bear th
thought of him laying his hands on me anymore and
loved him so much. But was it really love I felt? I don
know anymore. It couldn't have been love or I'd lov
him still, and I don't. I don't hate him either. I fee
nothing for him. Nothing at all. But is it my fault? Hav
I done something wrong somewhere along the way
Perhaps if I were a different person Roman would hav
been good to me and his daughters. I just don't know
anymore if I was right or wrong."

"Yes, he would have been a different person if yo
were a slut hanging around taverns all day long an
drinking with him. He's attracted to that kind. Then h
would do as you say for I told you long ago that was th
kind of woman he preferred. He doesn't want a decen
woman, only whores. You didn't do anything wrong
Don't blame yourself. We have to keep our eyes o
Lydia though, for I feel she's going to follow in he
father's footsteps. Somehow I get that feeling when
ever I look at her. Punishment and spankings accomp
lish nothing. She's going to get her way whatever i
takes. Be careful with her, Dani. She's too indepen
dent for one so young. She may break your heart some
day if she doesn't change before it's too late."

"I know, Aunt. She is defiant, but I'm hoping that i
the fall when she starts school the nuns can help. Mos
of the children are in awe of the sisters with their black
habits. They do their homework and their extra tasks
willingly enough. I'm praying Lydia will change for the
better then."

Tekla sighed and reflected that she sorely missed
her friend Martha. It would be good to talk to her
and if she were back at the tavern things would be
running more smoothly. But Martha preferred to stay
in her own home now and make things nice for Bolie
Tekla thought it was a good thing that Dani had her

246

riend, Carmella.

Two or three times a year, in the spring and summer, Dani got a chance to visit with Carmella who worked or the telephone company now and had had a phone installed in her sister's home. Dani felt she, too, could afford a four-party line so she had one put in. When the friends couldn't meet, especially during the long cold winter months, at least they could talk to each other. Carmella had fallen in love with a hard-working man named Giovanni who owned a small store in her neighborhood, and she spent most of her free time with the man she was planning to marry. Dani had met Giovanni once and she was happy that her friend would marry a man who treated her so well.

"Giovanni has a terrible temper." Carmella laughed. "But deep inside he's soft-hearted. It's not too late for me to start a family either. I'm only thirty-three. I've years left to have babies, but he had better set the date soon for I'm getting impatient. I like my job at the telephone company but I'd rather be spending all my days at the store where I know everyone. Giovanni has a good business, and with the two of us working there we can make a good living. He wants to branch out and sell more American food. I can mind the store while he goes to the market in the morning to select produce, meats, sausages, and the like. Someday we might even be prosperous, who knows?"

Dani was somewhat relieved that her friend was getting married for it was rather difficult traveling on the trolley with four children in tow. On the way Lydia often created a scene. Once the child left a piece of gooey candy on a seat, and a man dressed in an expensive business suit sat on it and then raved at Dani about her ill-mannered child. On another occasion Lydia threw up on the woman next to her. Dani wondered if she had done it on purpose by sticking her finger down her throat, for the girl wasn't sick before they left home or afterward when they were at Carmella's. There she had whined until she was allowed to sip a small glass of wine because she wanted to be like the grownups. Impossible child. She was in school now and so far hadn't noticeably improved.

On the other hand Tekla was happy to be able to get about a bit again. She had fired Sophie at long last and had replaced her with two good women, one married and one widowed. They cooked and helped at the bar They were good clean women in their late forties and they lifted much of the burden from Tekla's shoulders She had breathing space once again. Roman roared when he heard Sophie was gone and in retaliation went home in a rage, threw Dani down on the bed, and savagely violated her all through the night. This continued for days until Tekla heard the commotion early one morning and confronted Roman later.

"You promised me two years Roman," she declared. "The time's not up yet. You've six months to go. Dani's feeling better so I warn you to leave her be for a while longer."

"You warn me. How dare you warn me to leave my wife alone? For that I could go see your precious confessor and have you taken down a peg or two. Don't you know you're committing a sin coming between a husband and wife? You didn't warn me that you were going to fire Sophie, did you? The men are teasing me that I'm not man enough to have a son, and I'm going to have one no matter what. My wife has had enough rest. It's time she started being productive again."

Two months later Dani was pregnant. She carried the baby to full term only to have it stillborn. The umbilical cord had been wrapped around the mite's tiny head and neck, choking out life. Dani cried over the loss. She didn't need another baby to care for, but she had nurtured this one for nine months only to have it taken away from her. It was a girl so Roman wasn't concerned over its death, nor did he pretend to be. He just didn't care.

When Dani had married Roman he'd been a neat handsome man. Now he was turning into a sloppily dressed alcoholic. He refused to change his underwear and went for days without bathing or shaving. He didn't bother buying new clothes anymore although his old ones didn't fit properly because he had put on a great deal of weight in the last few years. Food stained his undershirt when he ate, but he seemed to find some sort of perverse satisfaction in wearing dirty clothes, if only to annoy his wife. When he was near her his breath smelled foul for several of his teeth were decaying; yet he refused to clean them or see a dentist. He drank steadily and heavily, and came home weaving on his feet to sink into bed, pulling Dani along with him.

Please, she pleaded silently, each night, let it be over quickly for I can't stand him to touch me anymore. Let me bear him a son so he'll leave me in peace and get his satisfaction from someone else.

"Dani, this can't go on," Tekla stated one Sunday afternoon when they were together in Tekla's flat. The children were in the kitchen eating cookies and drinking glasses of milk. "Something has to be done about Roman. He can't go on mistreating you like he has."

Dani looked up dismally.

"Nothing can be done. I talked to the priest and he told me it was my duty to submit to my husband. He said Roman was the man of the house, and my job was to be a good wife and to comfort my husband when he came home after a day's work."

"Did you explain how Roman treats you? Did you tell him what a vile man you're married to?"

249

Dani pushed her hair out of her eyes.

"Yes, I told him everything and he advised me to pray to the Lord for patience and understanding. He said all men had faults and women were born to suffer. Some men drink, some gamble, some won't work, some abuse their wives. I'm to pray for guidance. It's no use. Nothing can be done without my being excommunicated from the church and damned to hell."

"Good Lord," Tekla answered. "Yes, all of us have faults, but Roman has all of them rolled together. He drinks, gambles, carouses with loose women, and beats you. Don't bother to deny it. I do have ears."

"I won't deny it any longer," Dani said. "He's worse than ever. Nothing I do pleases him. Maybe a son would. He really wants a son. I've got to keep trying until I do have a boy because if I do he'll dally with someone else."

"Don't tell me you're pregnant again?"

"No, but I probably will be soon."

Even Eleanor was aware of Dani's situation.

"Mama, you have to stop getting babies," she said one morning. "It only makes you sick and sad. You have enough children now."

"But you don't have a brother yet, Eleanor," Dani answered. "All girls should have at least one brother."

"We don't need one," Eleanor pouted. "He'd be just like Papa and we don't need another man like Papa."

"From the mouths of babes," Tekla chided.

Meanwhile Roman continued to accuse Dani of being able to produce only daughters. "You'll give me what I want," he raved, "even if it kills you. I must have a son. I will have a son."

"No more," Tekla shouted to Dani one day. "This madness has to stop. You're not a brood mare in pasture waiting for the stud. You realize no amount of praying is going to help?"

250

"How do I keep him away?" Dani asked. "This is his home."

Tekla ran her hands through her hair. "Let me think for a moment." She put her hands up against her forehead. "He always takes you when he's drunk doesn't he?" she asked.

"Yes, but then he's always drunk."

"Then you must learn to become as crafty as he."

"How? You know I'm not a schemer."

Tekla's face blushed a bright red. "Dani, this is going to be difficult for me to say. Please bear with me. How can I begin?" The flush deepened and ran down her neck. She had been long alone and was extremely modest. How hard it was to say such things to a young married niece, embarrassing but necessary. Quickly, she gathered her wits and began, trying to be as brief as possible. "When Roman is on top of you and almost ready to reach his peak you must somehow slide his organ out of you and finish the job with your hand. It can be done. I heard one woman talking at the tavern once. She did this for years, but only when her man was in his cups. She didn't dare do it when he was sober. Since Roman's always drinking you can try to do it. You must if you want to be a good mother to your four girls. How much time will you have for them if you have a dozen children or if you're constantly worn out from being pregnant? It's worth trying, Dani. Think about it. Roman won't use anything to be safe. Maybe he uses a protector with his other women, but he has this insane desire that you must bear him a son. Try what I suggest the next time and see what happens. If he suspects anything is amiss you can always come up with some kind of answer. Say it slipped or . . . I don't know what else you can say, but you'll think of something." She hurried from Dani's apartment totally ill at ease because of their frank talk.

251

That night Roman woke Dani at three in the morning. He was ready for another bumbling effort at begetting a son. His breath made Dani shudder with revulsion. And he thought the soap factory smelled foul, she thought hysterically. Doesn't he realize he smells far worse? How do his whores stand him? I'd rather be smelling soap night and day than smelling him. In his stupor his thumping and pounding lasted no more than a few minutes. Dani wondered what she would do if he went on for almost an hour as he had when they were first married? She would probably scream out her frustration and despair till the doctors put her away in an asylum. Maybe there I'd find peace, she thought. No one would bother me and I could sit all day and stare at nothing or rock in a rocking chair, unaware of the outside world. Stop it, she commanded herself sharply. The girls need me. If something happened to me there would be only Roman, God forbid, or Tekla who is overworked already.

Roman began to emit a loud guttural moan and she deftly repositioned herself sliding her right hand between them. To her utter amazement, Tekla's ploy worked. His seed gushed harmlessly on her leg. Dani was elated by her first successful attempt to put something over on him. It could be done. By practicing a little variation on the ploy each night, she just might avoid becoming pregnant for a while. As Roman rolled off her body and fell asleep, Dani's eyes glittered in the dark room. She congratulated herself over and over. I need not confess this to the priest, she thought. It wasn't a sin. Roman was satisfied. I did my duty and that's the end of it.

Not wanting to embarrass her aunt, Dani simply told her the next morning that her plan had worked splendidly.

Tekla smiled. "Good. Don't forget to do the same

every night."

Now Roman had something else to rant and rave over.

"Are you a barren women so soon? I come to you every night and there's no sign of you bearing my son."

"They say alcohol makes a man sterile."

Dani wanted to laugh at his outraged face, but she bent her head down instead because she was smiling. Now only the occasional beatings hurt her, and this pain she could take. She was used to it.

The children were getting out of hand though. Not Eleanor. She was a help, but Lydia was getting harder and harder to manage. And now that Irena and Celia were getting older, there was always turmoil. The three fought constantly, Lydia usually being the instigator. At least twice a month Dani was called to the school to listen to a sermon from the principal because of Lydia's misdeeds: fighting in the halls, stealing someone's lunch, hiding in the boy's washroom, even cutting off a large clump of her classmate Adeline's hair. Lydia had calmly snipped off as much of Adeline's long black tresses as she could in one try. She had managed to sneak her mother's scissors out of the house, just for that purpose. After that incident Dani had dragged her home and spanked her soundly.

"Why do you do these things? Can't you behave like the other children in school? What possessed you to cut off Adeline's hair? Now she'll have to have it cut short because you sheared away such a large piece. Answer me. Why?"

Lydia never cried when she was spanked and now she looked up at her mother with no remorse.

"Because I don't like her. She's always walking around like a peacock, admiring her long curly hair in the mirror. All the girls hate her, she's a show-off. Now she'll look ugly and everyone will laugh when they

253

see her."

"Lydia, that's no excuse. It was wrong to do what you did. I'm taking you over to her house so you can apologize."

"Never, I'll never say I'm sorry to her, even if you whip me with Papa's belt! Not even if you kill me!" Lydia screamed.

"I've never hit you with a belt, Lydia. Stop screaming."

God, what am I going to do with her? Dani asked herself. She stood in the middle of the floor shaking. Finally she sent Lydia to the bedroom she shared with Eleanor, but when Irena came home a fight erupted over something trivial. The noise woke Celia who was taking a nap and she started crying. Dani ran out onto the back porch, unable to hold back her tears. She was shaken by great racking sobs.

"I'm going mad," she said aloud. "What have I done to deserve all this? A lunatic husband, three children who constantly bicker and fight from morning till night, the pitying looks of other mothers who think I can't control my children or my husband. I wish I were dead. Right now I would like to be struck dead just so I could have some peace and quiet."

On her porch downstairs Tekla heard the dreadful sounds. She ran up to Dani.

"Dani, what's wrong? I came home to get some eggs and I find you hysterical. What happened? Shame for wishing you were dead. Come down and talk to me. How long has this been going on?"

Dani followed her aunt like a small child, crying all the while. "I'm sorry but I can't take it anymore. The fighting between the girls, Roman, everything. I can't stand it another minute."

Tekla poured her a cup of tea and laced it liberally with brandy.

"Here drink this," she ordered. "We'll find a way out of this predicament. Come now, take a few sips."

Dani drank the hot mixture down in great gulps.

"You must have some time for yourself," Tekla said sympathetically. "You must get away from the house and the children. I can see that now. Why didn't you say something to me sooner? I had no idea it was this bad. You keep telling me everything is fine. Of course I know about Roman, but not about the constant fighting between the girls. You only told me they argue once in a while. Listen to me. Every Friday you're to go out for the day. Go wherever you like. You can come home just before Roman does."

"Where would I go?" Dani asked in despair. "Walk around like a crazed woman? Go to Morgan Street and back? Visit Carmella? I can't do that. She's too busy now that she's married and helping her husband. She has no spare time to spend visiting with me. Friends? I have no friends. I can't have any. Roman would only flirt with them, so everyone stays away from me as though I have a disease. He pays all the bills. I don't have any money and I can no longer take in sewing. I try, but there's never enough time. I'm lucky if I can keep up with my own mending. One of the girls is always tearing something or outgrowing her clothes. Maybe I should work at the tavern one day a week. I would too, but Roman is there."

Tekla shook Dani hard.

"Stop talking like a fool. There are hundreds of places to go. The streetcars run all over Chicago. You've never even seen the city, just the few blocks here where you live and the short ride you take to see Carmella. There are fine department stores, the lake, museums. Try someplace new each week. You'll be surprised, and you'll have the money for your excursions from me. I insist on it. Tomorrow is Friday, and you'll go every Friday. I promised you when you first came that I was going to take you to all these places, but I never found the time. Had I kept my promise you would have forgotten about Roman."

"Aunt, please. It's not your fault. I'm totally responsible for what's happened to me. I can't bear it if I've made you feel guilty. Please don't say that. Oh, what a burden I've become. You never should have insisted that we come to America. Look how peaceful your life would be. At least Jan never gives you any problems. He's doing well, already a foreman in Detroit. He'll make you proud some day."

"Stop," Tekla insisted, "or I'll slap you soundly! It's all settled. Stay here and finish your tea while I check on what's going on upstairs."

There was a loud crash. Dani shuddered. One of the girls must have dropped something heavy.

Again Tekla hurried up the stairs. She found a crock shattered in the pantry. The earthenware pot and its contents, old grease and lard, were splattered along the floor and on one wall. Lydia and Celia stood by the door, Lydia looking defiant, Celia frightened.

"Which one of you did this?" Tekla asked sternly.

"I was getting a glass down from the shelf and stumbled," Lydia said. "It was an accident."

"Oh, I see," Tekla replied calmly. "Well then, since it was a true accident, you can clean it up."

"I can't," Lydia answered. "It's too messy and greasy."

"Yes, you can. Get a bucket of soapy water and start right now. Hurry up. I mean what I say."

Lydia looked up, eyes blazing. "No. You can't force me. Mama will clean it. I'll get too dirty."

"Your mother's not here. Now you'll do as I say." Tekla grabbed Lydia by the shoulders. "Either you'll clean up this mess yourself or I'll do it for you by wiping it up with your dress, with you in it." She pushed Lydia's face down toward the middle of the grease, even pressing her nose down into it. "Should I wipe it up with your face instead?" she threatened.

Lydia started to scream and as she did Tekla pushed her whole face into the mess. Sputtering and shocked, the child stopped bellowing and looked up at her great-aunt in shocked surprise. Tekla made a move to push the girl's face down again.

"All right, I'll clean it," Lydia said sullenly.

"And do a good job," Tekla commanded. "Get the spots on the wall too. I'll wait in the kitchen until you're done so I can inspect your work. Then you can wash out your dirtied dress."

"Where's my mother?" Lydia cried in alarm.

"There's no use running to your mother. She's down-stairs and won't be up for a while. If you don't wash the dress you'll have to wear it to school tomorrow. I'm sure all your classmates will be highly surprised to see you with grease all over your pretty dress."

"Mama won't let me go to school wearing a dirty dress," Lydia answered, putting soap into a pail.

"But I would and I'm going to be here tomorrow to see you off. I just might be here every morning to see that you all get started off to school peacefully, and I promise you I don't care how you look when you go."

Lydia took off her dress. Darting quick looks up at Tekla, she put it in the washbasin to soak while she scrubbed away at the mess on the pantry floor. What was happening? She didn't want her great-aunt up here all the time making her work. She didn't like cleaning and washing. Mama was supposed to do all these things.

257

Chapter Seven

The morning dawned sunny and mild for March and held a note of unexpected excitement as Dani helped her daughters off to school. When they left she started washing the dishes.

"No, no," Tekla objected, snipping off thread from the blue wool dress she was mending for Dani to wear. "It's your free day. Here's your dress looking almost new with the collar I've sewn on. Now go pretty yourself while I finish here in the kitchen. And by the way, there's ten dollars on the table. You're to spend it on yourself."

"That's too much," Dani protested. "We can eat for two weeks and more on ten dollars."

"All right, little mule. The ten dollars is only for today, your first time out. Next Friday I'll only leave a dollar. Does that make you happier?"

Dani dressed quickly and, pulling her hair back into a chignon, looked at herself in the mirror. She was almost twenty-four; how fast the years went by. Her face was still smooth and when she found reason to laugh, her eyes became a deeper blue as they were today. Her hair was still long and pale gold, and it shone with shots of silver after it was washed and brushed. Faint stretch marks crossed her stomach but that couldn't be helped after having children and miscarriages one after another. She pinched her cheeks for color and walked into the kitchen where Tekla was busy putting away the dried breakfast dishes.

"My, you look pretty." Tekla complimented her. "I suggest you buy some decent shoes today. Yours are beyond repair."

"Where shall I go?" Dani asked. "I feel so stupid. I don't know my way around the city and I've lived here for nine years. I'm just like a newly arrived immigrant."

"You're not an immigrant, Dani. You speak the language. They don't. If you would like a suggestion why don't you see one of the big department stores downtown? They're huge compared to our tiny neighborhood shops. You can spend a whole day in one just browsing and time will fly by."

"But I don't know how to get there."

"You have to learn to be more independent," Tekla said with exasperation. "Stop putting yourself down all the time. You'll learn your way around the city in a few weeks. Just ask the motorman for directions and he'll be happy to help. Now off with you. It's already nine o'clock and by the time you get downtown the stores will be open for business."

Dani walked the one block to the Thirty-first Street line with trepidation. It was strange to have no children holding her hand or clinging to her skirts. She felt almost naked without her daughters at her side. To her surprise and relief, the motorman on the trolley was helpful just as Tekla had said he would be. The morning rush was over so he took time to explain where she should get off to transfer and how she could get back home. After thirty-five minutes Dani was in the heart of the city, oblivious to the crowds around her as she stared up at the tall sleek buildings lining State

260

Street. Does one have to walk all the way up if one wants to get to the top? she wondered. Slowly she made her way to the first department store she saw and foolishly went through the revolving door twice before an elderly gentleman pulled her out just in time to avert a third spin. Shaken with embarrassment she mumbled her thanks to the gray-haired man in a quivering voice.

"No need to thank me," the man said, delighted at her awkwardness. "You looked as if you were having fun going round and round. Always wanted to try that myself but never had the nerve. I thought I should rescue you though for there's a line of customers waiting to get in. In another minute, I'm afraid they would have been shoving you aside and shouting at you to get off your imaginary carousel." He laughed again and pulled her off to the side so they wouldn't be in the way of the eager shoppers making their way into the store.

While the crowd plowed by, her new acquaintance winked.

"Let me give you a word of advice, young lady," he said. "By your slight accent—and personally I think it charming—I gather that you were born in another country. I think it brave of you to come to our land. We can always use new blood. But don't be ashamed of your ignorance. If you make a mistake, laugh it off. Don't be frightened. Thousands of people make mistakes every day. It's no big deal. If you're lost, ask for directions. Nine times out of ten, people will be willing to come to your aid. Hold your head up high and flaunt yourself. You're just as good as the next person."

Dani smiled and a dimple rarely seen suddenly appeared. What a kind merry old man she had bumped into. "You've been most helpful. Thank you again."

"Remember what I said. You're just as good or

better than anyone. Now forgive me, but I'm late for an appointment. Is there any particular department you're looking for?"

"I'd like to see the shoes," Dani answered.

"Shoes? Let me see, I believe they're on the third floor."

"And the stairs, where do I find them?"

"No stairs, my dear. You don't have to climb up scores of stairs tiring yourself." He pointed to the back of the store. "There are elevators that will whisk you up to whatever floor you desire. You simply enter the cage, tell the operator which floor you want, and presto, he takes you up, announcing the floors as he goes along. Have a good day." He was gone in a second, nimbly disappearing through the perplexing revolving door.

Dani stood where she was for a few minutes watching the people go in and out. How adroitly everyone managed to get through the door. There were no accidents, no one bumped into anyone. As one person left a partition, another entered. I think I can do it now she said to herself and swept to meet this challenge. The deed was done with no mishap, and she made her way back through the door, laughing aloud at her new experience. Several shoppers stopped to stare as she smiled at everyone. She looks like a little girl playing games, several thought as they passed and they smiled in return.

Dani made her way to the bank of elevators and entered one as though she had done so a thousand times before. "Three, please," she told the young man operating the strange-looking mechanism. Several other shoppers crowded in and the doors clanged shut. She heard a whirring noise and then the elevator swept up, making her tremble with fright.

262

"Two," called the operator, then "Three." This was her floor. As she took several uncertain steps forward a floor walker approached to assist her.

"Can I help you, miss?"

I must not be awkward, Dani told herself.

"Yes, where are your shoes?"

"Down the center aisle to your left." The middle-aged man gestured in that direction. It was all so easy she thought, walking down the center aisle. Her initial shyness left as she confidently made her way through the coat section and came to a large area set aside solely for the sale of shoes. Dani stood, amazed. There must be hundreds upon hundreds of shoes here. The tiny store on Morgan Street sold only sturdy everyday shoes, nothing so fancy or glamorous as those displayed on the gleaming racks before her.

An eager salesman hurried up to her.

"What can I do for you?"

She wanted to cringe as she looked down at the shabby shoes she wore. Was the salesman looking at her disdainfully? She mustered up a little more courage as the kind old man had told her to do.

"Yes, I'd like to see a pair of shoes in black."

"What kind were you interested in?"

"Oh, I don't know," Dani answered. "What kind do you have?"

"Would you like dancing slippers, sandals, oxfords, pumps?"

"Just show me a pair of everyday walking shoes, please."

"Yes, miss. Please have a seat while I measure your foot."

After checking her size he disappeared for a few minutes and came back with several boxes piled on top of one another.

263

"I don't want all of these," Dani cried alarmed.

"I'm bringing out several styles for you to choose from."

"Oh, all right."

She tried on several pairs and finally decided the black low-heeled style would serve her purpose.

"How much are these?"

"Eight dollars," the salesman answered as though he were offering her the greatest bargain in the world. "They're on sale, and at a good price. These shoes will last for years."

Now Dani was truly humiliated. She had ten dollars in her purse. How expensive this store was. Why back on Morgan Street she could get a good pair of shoes for two dollars or less. Better to tell the truth so the young man wouldn't waste any more time with her.

"I'm afraid I won't take these. They're much more than I can afford."

The clerk looked up, deflated. He would have liked to spend more time waiting on this attractive young lady. He had had several dates with customers in the two years he'd been a salesman, and this lady looked like she'd be fun to be around. He experienced a vague yearning to take her dancing or perhaps to an amusement park, but she wasn't offering any look of encouragement. Oh well, there would be others. Still it wouldn't hurt to be polite; she might be back one day. "Well, it was a pleasure waiting on you. I think I can be of help. There is a store three blocks south where you can find the shoes you're looking for. It's called the Boston Department Store. Ours are rather expensive." He put Dani's shoes back on her feet. "Maybe another time you'll favor this store again. I'll look forward to waiting on you."

"Yes, maybe," Dani answered apologetically. Thank you." She walked dejectedly back through the coat department and looked at some of the prices. They

264

were outrageous. It was a certainty she wouldn't be back to squander hard-earned money here. Making her way back to the elevator, she practically ran from the store and walked south to Boston's. Some of her depression lifted when she found a good pair of serviceable shoes for two dollars, and after purchasing them, she walked leisurely through the store taking in most of the departments. As she walked she noticed how well dressed most of the shoppers were. Women were practically showing their knees and here she was in a dress almost down to her ankles. Most of the women her age wore chic short dresses banded at the hips. Smart-looking little cloches adorned their heads, and they walked with a free and easy air as though they hadn't a care in the world. My clothes are so outdated she thought as she continued looking at the styles. She came to the conclusion that although she wasn't too shabbily dressed, except for her shoes, the clothes she wore were rather matronly. While she had an egg salad sandwich and coffee, in a cafeteria in the same store, she continued to observe the details of the various styles adorning the female shoppers.

Then, having eaten, she headed for the yard goods department, where she bought enough white lawn to make a blouse similar to the type many women were wearing, and some soft rose-colored linen for a skirt.

"Will you need a pattern, miss?" the saleswoman asked courteously.

"No, I don't think so. I think I can make it exactly like the ones I've seen."

"Then you must be an excellent seamstress."

"I hope so for if I ruin this material I don't know what I'll do." She wondered what Roman would say if she made herself a short flapper dress trimmed with spangles and beads. She decided she'd have to wear the dress in her coffin for Roman would certainly kill her. Wives, according to him, were supposed to stay home

265

in aprons and house dresses, and not venture out of the house except to go grocery shopping or to attend a special event like a wedding. Even then they were supposed to wear dark somber colors. But I'm still young she told herself. What delicious fun it would be to dress like the women I've seen and perhaps even be daring enough to smoke a cigarette encased in a long holder. She imagined herself slithering past Roman, dressed as a vamp and casually blowing a puff of smoke into his outraged face; then she came to her senses when she thought of the aftermath. She didn't feel quite that daring after all.

Back on the first floor again, she purchased a pale pink lipstick and a deep pink silk rose to wear on the blouse she planned to make. Her eyes lit on a black leather purse, and she longed to have this luxury to complete her outfit. Not one woman she'd watched today carried a handmade knit purse. But counting her change she found she only had enough money left for carfare and a little extra to buy the girls chocolate candy before boarding the trolley. The purse was out of the question. I've spent ten whole dollars, she chided herself on the way home. I should have bought some clothes for the girls, not spent everything on myself.

But her guilt disappeared as she delightedly described her day to Tekla. There was a new sparkle in her eyes as she told her aunt everything that had happened from the revolving door incident to the guilty ride home.

"Good, I'm glad," Tekla said, pouring them coffee and slicing a piece of cake. "It's right that you spent money on yourself for a change. The shoes are stylish. We have nothing like them at Beckman's, and I can't wait to see the blouse and skirt you sew. The girls will be pleased with the candy. That's enough for them."

Celia was sitting at the table, happily munching on a part of her share.

"Next Friday," Tekla continued, "you can go somewhere else and you must take the money I give you. If you don't spend it all, fine; but I don't want you stranded without enough to get home. It would be an embarrassment for you to have to ask a stranger for carfare like a beggar when there's no need. I won't be poor and destitute without it. If you don't take it, I swear on Józef and Casimir's souls I won't speak to you again. Today has been good for you. You look like a different person from the one I saw this morning who was afraid to go out all by herself. Don't worry, I'll take the money out of Roman's share. He won't know the difference."

"All right," Dani consented. "But not ten dollars, that's too much." She busied herself preparing supper, already longing for the next morning to come so she could begin making her new clothes. She had the styles committed to memory. The girls noticed her cheerful attitude and were surprised to hear her humming as she fixed supper.

"Why are you so happy?" Irena asked.

"Where did you go today?" Eleanor queried.

"I went sightseeing and if you behave and help with the dishes and do your homework without any arguments, I have a surprise for you after we eat. It's some very special candy I bought downtown today. Celia's had some of hers already and it was good, wasn't it, Celia?"

Celia nodded her head up and down, glad there would be more of the delectable chocolate later, and much to Dani's surprise there were no arguments or fights that evening.

Roman came home just after ten while Dani was trying to sketch the blouse she planned on starting in the morning. She reheated the oxtail stew, and after he washed his hands he glanced down at her crude

267

drawing. "Where were you today and where was your aunt? She never takes a day off."

"Tekla was kind enough to stay home and watch Celia. She's going to do the same every Friday so I can get out for a while. It was so nice today, Roman. I went downtown for the first time and had a chance to see a part of the city I've never seen before."

"But you didn't ask my permission, did you? I don't want you going out roaming the streets. I told you, your place is at home. There's enough here to keep you busy."

"But, Roman, the girls were at school and Tekla was very happy staying home with Celia and having a chance to rest for a change."

Roman pushed his plate aside roughly, ready to start a heated argument, but suddenly he stopped himself, a sly grin on his face. He had wondered why Tekla hadn't shown up, but in her absence he had pocketed an extra twenty dollars and had had a chance to visit Sophie in the afternoon when her grandmother was taking a nap. He lowered the hand that was about to strike Dani and thought about the money he could steal if Tekla was away every Friday.

"All right. You have my permission to go shopping on Fridays but just for a few hours. You'd better be home by the time the girls get out of school and see that supper is ready. I'll be home myself at six just to make sure you're where you're supposed to be then I'll go back to the tavern."

The successive Fridays proved to be more pleasurable than Dani could have imagined. Wearing her new blouse, skirt, and shoes she went downtown for the second time to browse from store to store. She was fascinated by the variety of goods to be bought if one had enough money. After careful scrutiny she did manage to find a fairly good purse for seventy-five cents at a bargain sale. How courteous the salespeople were, just as though they had waited all day to see to her needs. It was embarrassing at first but easy to get accustomed to, a real luxury. No one had treated her this grandly before, as though she were woman of means and could afford anything she set her eyes on.

Her next outings included a trip to the Museum of Natural History which had opened a few years earlier. Dani was so enthralled with the huge building she hated to leave. It was so cool and peaceful there. By the end of summer her eyes and mind were filled with so many new sights she was able to brush Roman's cruelty out of her mind. While he was forcing himself on her she found she could switch her thoughts to the new and exciting places she had visited that spring and summer: the movie houses, Lake Michigan, Bolie's new house. She had even watched an airplane take off and actually fly high above the buildings. She knew the Smenteks would be impressed with that. And to think they had laughed at her when she had predicted that in the future travel would be faster and faster. She could imagine bigger and better airplanes crowding the sky someday just as automobiles now crowded the streets. She rode the trolley to the north and south sides of the city, asking directions and getting lost occasionally, but it was fun and she learned to cope.

In July and August, she took the girls with her so that they, too, could see some of what bedazzled her, but in a way she couldn't wait until fall when they would be back in school and she could roam the city by herself again. Her pleasure was far greater with no heads to count, no constant checking to see that they all held hands and stayed close. Lydia created several scenes. Once she knocked over a mannikin in a department store and, as the model's head rolled down the aisle, screamed hysterically that she had killed a lady.

The store manager was most disturbed and whisked Dani and her offspring out the door as quickly as possible. Dani was mortified but thankful she didn't have to pay for the damage. On another occasion, Lydia had a tantrum in another store when Dani said she couldn't afford a particularly expensive doll Lydia had her eye on. The child sat down in the middle of the floor and held her breath until she almost turned blue. Dani's only recourse was to throw water in her daughter's face. Luckily, the water fountain was only a few feet away and not too many people witnessed the episode. Each time she misbehaved Lydia was punished, and during the next outing she stayed home with Tekla. Once, however, Tekla came with them and they picnicked at the beach. The girls seemed to like this best, for by the time they came home late in the afternoon, their heads nodded with fatigue and they went to sleep very early without fighting.

Roman naturally put a damper on their happiness with his grumblings, but he was less abusive now that he was pocketing extra money every Friday and seeing Sophie regularly. He still forced himself on Dani but less frequently. Each month, as she saw the beginning of her menstrual flow, she silently thanked God she wasn't pregnant again.

On a quiet Monday morning the first week school started, Dani heard Tekla give a great whoop of joy in the front hall. Who or what could make her that excited? It wasn't Jan. Jan visited every summer in the last week of August and for a few days at Christmas time. He had just left several days ago. It was always a happy week when he came, even though he was so serious and so immersed in his work it seemed he hated to leave Detroit because he felt he was wasting time. Tekla and Dani had been forced to resort to sharp comments to get him to change the subject when he talked incessantly about automobiles and the hundreds of parts that went into their making. He was now in charge of the drive-line assembly department and neither his aunt nor his sister had any idea of what he was talking about when he mentioned shafts, bearings, or countless other technical items. His work had forced thoughts of revenge from his mind temporarily, but he did mention that he was still putting aside money each week for his trip back to Poland. He already had half of his passage he said matter-of-factly, and when Dani or Tekla brought up the subject of marriage he always changed the conversation, saying he had no time to consider it yet.

"Later," he protested. "I'm still learning too many things to be thinking about wedding bells. I go out to dinner once in a while with a girl from the office, but we're just good friends. She lives near where I do. I don't have all that much free time to waste."

During his visit Jan had stayed away from Roman, and had been adamant about not speaking to his brother-in-law; anyway Tekla had taken the week off and Roman would have slept in the tavern if there'd been a bed in the stock room, so covetous was he of every penny he could steal.

But Jan was already back in Detroit so why was Tekla calling her name so loudly?

"Dani, come down this instant. I have the most marvelous surprise for you."

Dani hurried to Tekla's, not bothering to comb her hair, but she stopped short when she saw the man who was grinning at her.

"Raymond. Raymond Patek. I don't believe it. Not one word have we heard from you in all these years and here you are on our very doorstep." She threw her arms around him and squeezed tightly. "Where have you been all this time? You promised to write and never did.

271

I tried writing you but had no idea where to send the letter. Come in. Sit down and tell us everything."

Raymond certainly looked distinguished. The gray at his temples and his tanned face and arms gave him a cosmopolitan air. He was handsome enough to turn women's eyes in his direction and he probably did in every port. Dani had never seen him cross or angry on the voyage over. He'd always seemed to be happy-go-lucky and this had added greatly to his charm. His eyes had been etched with crinkly little lines of laughter. Now there were a few added lines, but not enough to detract from his merry appearance. Raymond put his arms around them both as they walked into Tekla's kitchen to enjoy a second breakfast. Over steaming cups of coffee and buns, he brought them up to date on his life.

"I can't believe the years flew by so fast. I did mean to come sooner, but something always came up to delay me. After I came back from South America I joined the army and spent two years in Europe, and let me tell you I didn't enjoy soldiering one bit. As soon as I mustered out I tried to get back on the *Destiny*, but the ship had been dismantled. It was on the scrap heap. The old tub just gave out I guess. It took me months to track down Captain Murow, and now we're together again on board a brand new freighter. In fact, we just returned from an extended voyage around the African coast. I have two weeks shore leave. For the hundredth time the thought crossed my mind to visit you two. I felt I had to learn what happened to you. I'm here. And what do I find? My little fascinating princess married and the mother of four children. Well, I didn't think you would wait for me anyway, but are you happy? Did you marry a wonderful man? One fit for a true princess?"

Dani and Tekla exchanged glances, and Dani gave Tekla a warning look.

272

"Yes, Raymond, I'm happy. I didn't marry a wealthy man, but we have everything we need. My life is running smoothly."

"Good. I'm glad to hear it. I only have a few hours to spend with you. I have to leave on tonight's train, and if I found you hating life here I swear I'd take you with me and bring you to my beautiful island to live. You see, I have a home of sorts on Jamaica and someday that's where I'll settle down in my old age. It's not much, just a three-room house but it's absolutely fabulous. Flowers bloom all year long. A far cry from the cold wet winters aboard ship or in New York. A native watches over the place while I'm gone, but I do get back there once or twice a year." Playfully, he danced Dani around the kitchen. "If you were free, I would spirit you off with me and set you down—plunk—on the beach by my house; and you would have a servant to clean and cook for you, fruit to pick right out in the yard, fish to catch and eat, and swimming all year round. It's a paradise, but I don't have anyone to share it with yet. In five or ten years I plan to retire for good and just take life easy. With my savings I can afford to be a beachcomber or maybe open up a little place of business. But forget about that. I can see I'm too late."

"Raymond, you fool," Dani laughed. "Do you possibly think I believe your tall tales? Oh yes, I believe your story about your wonderful home, but do you think for a minute I thought you were waiting and pining for me? I was a silly adolescent when you left me at the train station in New York."

"But I saw your possibilities," Raymond answered, letting his hand touch her hair. "Even then I knew you would grow into a beautiful woman and you have indeed. Your husband's a lucky man, Dani. I hope he appreciates you. Will I get to meet him?"

Dani wanted to laugh in his face. Let him think

Roman is the perfect husband and I'm his adoring wife, Dani thought. There is no sense getting him involved in the travesty of my marriage.

"No. You won't meet him, Raymond. I'm afraid he's very busy lately."

Raymond met her children instead and quickly had them eating out of his hand, enthralled by his funny stories. For once, Lydia sat quiet as a mouse listening to every word he said, as did the others. He spent the whole day with them, talking and laughing over the past, and he left promptly at five to hurry to Union Station and catch his train. He kissed Tekla and Dani soundly at their parting.

"If you ever want to come to Jamaica, just get on a ship and I promise you'll be made most welcome. Everyone on the island knows where I live. You can see the harbor from my front window."

At the door, alone with Dani for a brief moment, Raymond said, "I meant every word, sweet one. I'll have you whenever you say the word, married or not. In Jamaica no one would know or care if we lived together. I could tell Tekla doesn't like your husband and I trust her judgment. You can't fool an old shark like me. I see glimmerings of unhappiness behind those beautiful eyes. If you can't make a decision right now, at least think about it."

He kissed her again as he had that last night on the *Destiny,* but Dani felt nothing. She wondered if she was dead to all feeling after being immersed in Roman's tyranny.

Upon Raymond's departure, Dani became moody. The girls were out in the yard so she sat down at Tekla's table, her thoughts far away.

"Well, there was a good man you passed by." Tekla spoke sadly. "Even though he would be gone most of the year he would have made a good husband. I wish he

274

had seduced you on the ship. Your life would have been much happier."

Much to her dismay, several weeks later Dani found herself pregnant, even after she'd tried so hard to avoid it. Her outings stopped when she was in her fifth month, for Roman forbade them, saying she looked slovenly parading around in public with her stomach protruding. She dreaded delivering this baby after her last painful experience. But this time all went well and finally they had a son, Roman Jr.

He was a terribly thin and fretful baby who didn't seem to gain weight as the other children did, vomiting up almost all the milk he drank, even when they tried goat's and cow's milk. When he was two months old he developed a respiratory ailment and had great difficulty breathing. Roman even accompanied Dani to the doctor on Morgan Street, but after a long examination the doctor declared the baby to be seriously ill. Various medications were prescribed, but none seemed to help little Roman keep his food down, nor did they clear the congestion in his tiny lungs. Two weeks after visiting the doctor Dani woke one morning and glanced at the cradle placed next to her bed. She screamed when she looked at the baby whose face was blue and mottled in death. She held him in her arms while Roman went for the doctor, but when he came he stated sadly that he had expected this to happen, that it had only been a matter of time. He couldn't pinpoint the cause of death, but he surmised that the baby had been born with some defect.

Roman stormed out of the house and remained absent while his son was buried the next morning after a private Mass of the Angels at St. Mary's church. Dani didn't miss him for she was immersed in grief. The girls, especially Eleanor and Celia, tried their best to stop the tears that poured from her eyes for days. Her poor little son had been so helpless. He had needed her so desperately, and though she had tried so hard to put strength into his little body, she had failed . . . he was gone. He had been a beautiful boy with golden curly hair. As his undersized coffin was placed atop Józef's at the Resurrection Cemetery, Dani had fainted upon hearing the dull thuds of dirt covering it, knowing that the gravediggers were sealing her son in total darkness for all eternity.

Prohibition was now in full swing and Tekla had converted the tavern into a restaurant although she suspected Roman sold home-brewed liquor illegally—not when she was there, but late at night after closing hours. He started buying himself stylish clothes once more and began taking greater care of his appearance. He never mentioned his son's name and looked at Dani coldly whenever he was in the house, his eyes accusing as though it were her fault that their son wasn't born perfect. Then he took to drinking more than ever and sometimes slapped Dani, blaming her for the child's death, not caring or noticing that she too was filled with despondence and grief.

When Tekla urged her to resume her outings, Dani protested, but she changed her mind after a particularly cruel episode with Roman. He'd come home late one night, staggering, and Dani had been up till dawn, cleaning up after him as he vomited and urinated in their bedroom. Nauseated and disgusted, she made up her mind to escape him even if only for a few hours a week. He was such a beast. She thanked God his daughters didn't see too much of him for he certainly was no example of fatherhood.

With a heavy heart she resumed her Fridays out, mostly riding on the trolley back and forth across the city, hardly seeing what was going on in front of her eyes. She was twenty-eight, but she often felt ancient.

One rainy morning, rereading the letters her mother had written Tekla years ago, she came across several that mentioned her great-uncle Anton, the historian. She wished desperately she had known him, for he seemed to be a marvelous man. One Friday she decided she wanted to see what a large university looked like and so she went for a walk around the University of Chicago in Hyde Park. For several weeks she walked down the halls of the noted school or sat on a bench on the grounds and watched the students as they rushed to their classes. Twice she found the nerve to sit in on a class, placing herself in an inobtrusive seat at the back of the room where no one noticed her presence. It was a history class and the professor was a striking man. She wondered if Uncle Anton had seemed just as knowledgeable to his Warsaw classes and she felt closer to him even though she'd never seen his face. Bringing herself back to the present, she studied the teacher who stood behind a desk. She had to come to this class once more to sit entranced while he kept the students engrossed for the entire lecture.

He was telling them of the cold-hearted Anna Ivanovna, Empress of Russia in 1740, and of the elaborate ice palace she had had erected during one particularly bitter winter. The edifice had been built of ice blocks but had seemed to be sculpted from one massive square. Ice trees and birds had been created to suit her fancy, and the bedroom had had furniture completely carved from ice, even to the pillows and nightcaps lying on the frosty bed. Because one of her royal princes had dared to defy her by marrying a woman not of her choosing, he was punished by having to spend his honeymoon with a new, hand-picked ugly bride in that icy cold palace as a cruel reminder that only the empress could arrange marriages between the aristocracy. Evidently the chastised prince survived the humiliating ordeal for he lived to a ripe old age, married till his death to the ugly crone who was his long-term punishment.

The professor glanced at her several times during his lecture so when the bell rang for dismissal Dani quickly made her way out before anyone could question her. The next week, sitting outside on a stone bench, she decided not to chance another intrusion. Surely someone would grow curious if she continued to sit in a back seat with no pencils or books. But it was so restful on campus, walking among the fallen leaves during the mild weather of October. A half block away, facing the lake, there was an intimate cheery tearoom, and when she finished her walks she went there to relax before going home. It was virtually empty at two o'clock so she could get a window seat and watch people stroll by: students, arguing or playing silly games; teachers, frowns creasing their faces as they seemed to be debating the problems of the world; and occasionally a woman taking a child out for exercise. There were many homes and apartments around the University, and Dani often wondered what the insides of these opulent homes looked like. From the street, the rooms appeared to be large and filled with the finest furnishings. This Friday, as she sat in the tearoom she was aroused from her musings by a man's voice.

"Mind if I share your table?"

She looked up, startled. Most of the tearoom's twenty or so tables were vacant. Why was this man bothering her? She blushed as she recalled the man's face. It was the professor who taught the history class. God, was he going to make a scene here in this quiet shop? Was he going to voice his disapproval before the few customers quietly talking in corners and demand that she pay a class fee? It would shame her if he denounced her in front of these well-dressed sedate people.

He saw her look of dismay and quietly calmed her fears.

"Never mind. If you prefer, I'll take another table. It's just that I would much rather share my tea with a beautiful woman than sit alone thinking my own thoughts. Please say yes. You see, I noticed you in my class twice and you intrigued me. I couldn't place you. Were you a fellow teacher sitting in on my lecture? Did the dean send you to spy on me? Were you just a figment of my imagination? I wasn't sure. I tried to get to you the last time but you disappeared down the hall, and when I ran outside, you weren't in sight. A week went by and you didn't come back. By then I was sure I had dreamed you, but here you are in person. You do speak, don't you?" he asked playfully, touching her lips.

Dani was at a loss for words.

"Yes, of course I do," she stammered.

"Good. Sarah," he called softly to the waitress. "Bring us a fresh pot of tea, please." He turned again to Dani. "I've never seen you in here before. I usually come at two or so."

"I always come here on Fridays," Dani answered, "but I get here a little later, just before I have to go home. This is the first time I've been this early."

"What a pity. Think of all the times I've missed seeing you, just by a few minutes."

Dani was unsure of herself. How could she talk to this man, a learned teacher, and not sound like a fool? He seemed to sense her uneasiness again and put forth an extra effort to get her to relax.

"You're in safe hands with me, you know. Ask Sarah. She can vouch for my behavior. My name is

Alexander Pritzkin and my friends call me Alex. Now you must tell me your name, or I shall think you are a nymph that vanishes at will."

"It's Dani. Danuta Kawa actually, but everyone calls me Dani."

Looking directly at him, she saw a man who was probably in his late thirties or early forties. At his temples gray smudged his coal-black wavy hair. His eyes were such a dark brown they almost appeared black, and his skin seemed tinged faintly by the sun. His mouth was full and sensuous. He wasn't handsome exactly, not like a movie star, but he was extremely attractive. Compelling. Yes, that was the word. She couldn't look away. She felt hypnotized by his deep low voice, quiet yet masterful. It compelled one to listen intently. He was tall—nearly six feet—and lean, and was dressed in dark pants and a tweed jacket with leather patches at the elbows. At first glance he appeared serious but his eyes held a devilish twinkle.

He, in turn, saw a lovely woman who seemed to be in her twenties. Beneath the hat she wore he could see wisps of white gold hair and he had a strange desire to see it floating unbound around her shoulders. Her mysterious blue eyes looked older as though they had seen much pain and disillusion somewhere along the way. From her hands, which held the tea cup, and her plain clothes, he could see that she wasn't wealthy or idle, but she was married. A thin gold band encircled her finger. Those hands, with the nails trimmed short and neat, were used to hard work. Could she be a maid, he wondered, or perhaps work in a factory? But no, there were no factories nearby. He settled on the former profession. Yes, that was it. She must work as a maid or cleaning woman in one of the large houses on Lake Shore Drive. A sudden urge to protect her overwhelmed him, and he had to shake the feeling from his mind. How was it possible that the appearance of this strange pretty girl could affect him so? There were hundreds of pretty girls. He saw beauties almost every day, so why did this one cause an unusual sensation in the pit of his stomach. Strange, he had no answer. He stopped staring at her and selected several tea cakes from the cart Sarah offered.

"Have a Napoleon," he offered sliding one onto her plate. "They're delicious, melt-in-your-mouth pastries."

"No please," Dani protested mildly. "I've already had cinnamon toast."

"That's all? Then surely you can have another bite. One slice of toast can't possibly assuage anyone's hunger. Just try a bite or two. I hate to eat alone."

Being thrifty she was unable to let the pastry lying on her plate go to waste. It looked delicious and expensive. She took a forkful of the Napoleon. It was delicious. She licked her lower lip to catch a stray crumb.

"See I told you you would like it. There's something irresistible about a well-made Napoleon."

They both laughed. Then he invited her to sit in on his class whenever she felt she wanted to do so.

She told him of her great uncle Anton, who had written several books on the history of Poland, and he had actually read an English translation of one of them. He admired Anton's candor and his refreshing style.

"There now." He laughed again. "We have a common bond for I can even quote several passages from your uncle's book. Is that why you're here? To soak up some of the same atmosphere that surrounded your uncle?"

Surprised, she answered, "You must be a mind reader. Yes, some of my mother's letters fascinated me, and it was because of him that I came to this university."

281

"You must promise me you'll be back next week," Alex said, calling for the check. "We'll have more time to talk then. Come about one if you can. I'll have two free hours, and I'll think of a million questions to ask you. Right now I have to dash to make another class in time."

"I don't know," Dani answered, flustered.

"You must promise or I'll not leave this spot. Then I'll be severely reprimanded for failing to perform my job properly. Now you don't want to see me in big trouble do you?"

"No but—"

"Just say yes. Hurry, I've got to run."

"All right, yes then. I'll try to be here."

"Not try, will. Thank you, little princess. You do resemble one you know. I knew from the start you reminded me of someone. I know. Cinderella in the ballroom—a drawing of her I saw once in my preschool days. I thought she was most beautiful. You look exactly like the drawing. Till next Friday then." He hurried out of the tearoom and she could see him running along the leaf-strewn path to the building where he taught.

She gathered her sweater and purse from the adjacent chair. All the way home she was in another world. She argued back and forth with herself. mustn't see him again. I've no right. I'm a married woman. There's no reason whatsoever to see him again. But another part of her wanted to see him very much, to talk to him, get to know him a little better. There's nothing wrong in just talking she finally decided. Talking can't hurt me. Tekla said I should try to meet new friends, and that's what Alex can be, a friend when I'm away from home. Someone with other things on his mind than raising children, cleaning, washing, or dreary household tasks. He is a man of the

282

world who can surely drive away my frustrations and make life more interesting and bearable. Just once or twice more, she promised herself. Just long enough to see what he has to say.

By the time she walked into her flat, she knew she couldn't possibly tell Tekla anything about the strange encounter that had taken place. She had already told her aunt that she had sat in on the class at the university and Tekla had been pleased to hear the story but frightened that Dani could get into trouble. Dani hadn't told her anything about the man who taught the class, however, and she wouldn't tell her anything now. That would be her secret. It isn't possible that such a striking man is interested in me, Dani said to herself over and over. If only I were single and a career woman . . . Then I wouldn't feel any guilt, she thought. She put the idea from her mind. That's enough, I'm not single, I'm a mother with four children.

Roman, as was his custom on Fridays, came home for dinner. He sneered at the meal of baked fish and vegetables.

"I should have eaten at the tavern. We have a good cook there who doesn't mind making meat for me. I don't go along with the rules of the church on not eating meat on Friday. It's unreasonable."

He pushed his plate angrily off the table and sent it smashing to the floor. The girls bent their heads down, expecting one of his sudden fits of unreasoning anger. Eleanor felt her bile rise and, in an effort not to throw up, clamped her lips shut tightly. It was so pleasant when her father wasn't home. Why didn't he stay away for good? Then life would be fun, with just them and Tekla. She decided as soon as she was of age she would leave home and live somewhere on her own, some place where she didn't have to listen to this. Yes. As soon as she was old enough to work she was going to move far, far away. Celia reverted back to thumb-sucking whenever trouble started. Irena shut her eyes tightly, and Lydia stared at her mother with a smirk. These scenes really weren't arguments for Dani never answered back, but today her response was unpredict-able.

"Roman, if you don't like what I make for dinner then stay at the tavern. You only upset the girls with your crude way of expressing yourself, and I won't have them made nervous because of you." She picked up her plate and sent it flying across the kitchen to shatter in the sink and then ran into her bedroom, locking the door. Roman sat stupefied. Eleanor, Lydia, Irena, and Celia looked at him, their eyes wide, unable to comprehend their mother's unprecedented fit of temper.

Roman rose and walked to the bedroom door. He turned the knob back and forth violently, but it didn't give. Giving the door a resounding kick, he strode out-side, barely containing his rage. If these little outings were going to make his wife defiant, he would just have to put a stop to them. Enough was enough. He would take care of that in the morning.

And he did. He dragged Dani away from the sink where she was washing the breakfast dishes and struck her across the face again and again.

"You little spoiled bitch," he roared. "How did you dare to do what you did last night! You acted like a filthy slut." He pushed her against the wall. "Do you hear me?" He shook her back and forth. "No more Fridays out roaming the city. It's made you too inde-pendent. You dare to throw a dish?" He picked up the wet dishes draining in the sink and threw them across the room one by one, breaking every one he could lay his hands on. "I'll break your neck just as easily if you go out again."

"Then kill me," Dani cried, thrusting out her neck defiantly. "Kill me right now, for the only peaceful moments I have are when I'm away from you. You're a crude coarse pig and I hate the sight of you. You repel me. You smell of liquor and sleazy women. Kill me and go to your whores. Do you think I don't know about them? Get it over," she screamed. "Now. So I can have some peace."

Tekla ran into the kitchen, out of breath, her heart pounding from the commotion that she had clearly heard downstairs. She grabbed Roman's hands as he was about to put them around Dani's neck.

"Stop this at once," she shouted, hanging onto Roman with all her strength. "Dear God, what's happening?"

Roman shook her off easily. "Your bitch of a niece is never to be away from the house unless she has the children with her from now on. I forbid it. I don't want her roaming the streets like a whore."

"Roman, surely you won't deny your wife a little free time? It keeps her happy. It's all she has to look forward to."

"She should look forward to bearing me a healthy son. All she's given me are girls and one sickly son she couldn't take care of properly."

"Roman, come downstairs with me . . . please. Give Dani a chance to get her wits together. She's having a breakdown."

Tekla literally pulled Roman from the room.

"Mind your business," he told her as he sat in her kitchen. "Sometimes I wonder if it was a mistake moving upstairs. You hear too much and interfere more than a mother-in-law would. Dani will stay home where she belongs."

Tekla had to find a way to sway him from this rash decision. Without her outings, Dani would fade away

285

to nothing again. Since she had started going out after little Roman's death she had picked up some of the weight she'd lost and she wasn't so despondent. It was obvious that the outings were keeping Dani sane. Tekla decided the only thing that would force Roman to change his mind was money. That was his only god.

"Roman, I'm not a fool. I know when I'm not at the tavern on Fridays you pocket quite a bit out of the cash register. I've known it from the first. Remember, I've been in business for a long time and I know how much I should take in day by day. If you let Dani go out shopping and sightseeing as usual on Fridays you can keep all the money made that day. Every penny."

Roman's surly look changed to one of greed. She could see him mentally adding up the figures. There was a hefty amount to be made on Fridays—payday. His decision was quickly made.

"All right. I don't want to go back up now or I'll choke the life out of her, so you tell her she can continue. I have to leave. I'm busy."

Tekla breathed a sigh of relief and went upstairs to tell Dani the crisis was over . . . for the time being.

Dani was sitting in the kitchen staring down at the broken crockery without seeing it. The shards almost covered the floor.

"I have to go out Friday," she said wistfully. "There's something very important I have to do."

"And so you shall. Roman just told me he acted too harshly. He's changed his mind."

Dani looked up startled. "He didn't. He never changes his mind. Did he really say that?"

"Yes, he did. Now let's clean up this mess. I'm proud that you finally got the gumption to stand up to him, but now I'm not so sure it's wise to do so. When he's angry he's a crazy man. He might have killed you if I hadn't come up in time. Perhaps it would be best if you

286

just kept quiet when he acts up. The children were very upset yesterday. They told me what happened before they went to the park this morning."

"I don't know what came over me," Dani explained. "He made me so angry, I wanted to smash his brains out. At least I threw the dish at the sink, not at his head."

Dani was fifteen minutes late on Friday and she ran from the streetcar, afraid Alex would think she wasn't coming. Pushing open the door of the tearoom, she was dejected when she didn't see him sitting at the table near the window, but she brightened as he waved to her from the corner. He rose to escort her to the nook they would share.

"It's more private here and we have quite a bit of talking to do. I decided not to eat until you came."

"I'm late," she gasped, out of breath from running. "I thought you wouldn't be here by the time I arrived."

He took one of her chapped hands in his. "I knew you would come. There was never a doubt in my mind. It was a certainty. You see, I've had a rather difficult week—problems with a student, some personal trouble—yet I know the sun has to shine after a storm, I felt that it surely would shine for me on Friday when I saw you."

She laughed, and he poured the tea and set a whipped cream tart in front of her.

"You're going to make me fat. I was very satisfied with my cinnamon toast."

"Ah, but these Austrian delights are food for the gods. We won't stoop to common fare when we meet. It's too demeaning. You shall have the best Ye Olde Tea Shoppe has to offer. Besides you're far too thin, like a starving orphan."

"Alex, I'm truly flattered"—she smiled—"and I'll accept your treats. You see, I can't quite afford these,

287

but they can become habit forming."

"My poor little waif. Then I shall have to spoil you, won't I? Tell me about yourself. What do you do? Where were you born? Are you in love with someone? I'd like to hear from the very beginning."

Dani sat silent, not knowing what to say.

"You don't want to do the talking? Then I'll tell you about myself. It will give you a chance to catch your breath and gather your thoughts. You're far too tense. I promise I won't ravish you right here in front of God and everyone."

The dimple appeared in her cheek as she looked into his eyes.

"You should always laugh. It makes you look like a charming schoolgirl without a worry in the world. Let's see, where should I start? Ah yes, with my parents naturally. They were born in Kiev, Russia. They grew up together and knew they would marry since they were twelve. It was a hard life in the Jewish ghetto and my father dreamed of becoming a doctor, but Jews weren't allowed that privilege, at least not poor ones. My grandparents, aunts, and uncles scrimped and saved enough to send my father to America where he would be free to seek a profession, but before he left, he and my mother were married. My grandparents knew it was the last time they would see him and they wanted the wedding ceremony performed in Russia. From what my mother and father told me, it was as lavish an affair as they could afford, which wasn't much; but they were happy. In New York my father studied hard. First he had to learn the language. Then he attended medical school, where he wasn't welcomed, but he persevered. Meanwhile my mother worked in a garment factory to support them. Times were very hard indeed, and my father told me he often pilfered a little of the hospital food because there wasn't enough money for decent meals, not with only my mother's earnings.

"After he became a full-fledged physician he decided there were more opportunities and less prejudice in the Midwest; so they came to Chicago, where my brother and I were born. He's an attorney, by the way, and two years my senior. Little by little my father prospered. He was an excellent dedicated heart surgeon, and after a while he won recognition for his skill with a scalpel. He saved countless lives, and he wrote numerous articles that were published in medical journals. At medical conventions, he was always in great demand as a speaker for he always managed to jolt the audience with his innovative ideas, most of which were very effective when put into practice. When I was fifteen, my mother died of consumption and the loss nearly did my father in. You see, skilled as he was, there was nothing he could do to save her."

"My mother died of something similar when I was young," Dani said quietly. "She had a painful disease in her lungs."

"Then we have a common grief, don't we, Dani?"

"You're Jewish then?" Dani asked, not wanting to linger on the subject of death.

"Yes, I am. You look surprised. Have you never met anyone Jewish before? We're not any different you know. We're men and women just like everyone else. Our rituals are just as holy and sacred as those of any religion. We eat and breathe the same air as everyone else."

"I didn't mean anything by my remark," Dani apologized. "I've only met one Jewish man, but I'm delighted to be with another now. You see, I only knew Mr. Beckman who owns a small store near my home, and he wears a funny little hat and talks so strangely I can barely understand him. For some reason I thought all Jewish people talked that way."

289

Alex laughed and took her hand. "No, my dear. We aren't all the same, although I'm sure your Mr. Beckman is a fine person. Now, where was I? My father worked long hard hours to put David and me through school. He would have liked one of us to follow in his footsteps, but I'm afraid neither of us were inclined toward medicine. I was always poring through history books and was fascinated with anything pertaining to the past. After high school I knew I wanted to teach history, to put life into what many people think is a boring subject. And I love my work. When I was twenty-eight and well settled in my career, my father began wondering when I would settle down, marry, and make him a grandfather. My brother was already married and the father of two children, but that wasn't enough for my father. He wanted my life settled too, and he felt he was getting too old to wait for me to make up my mind and choose a wife. He began throwing what he thought were proper girls at me, pointing out their excellent traits as though he were showing thoroughbred horses. The last one he introduced me to, Rebecca Rubin, was his favorite. He repeatedly invited her to dinner. Soon Rebecca had him wrapped around her little finger. Before I knew what was happening they began making plans, and I went along with them. It was easier that way for I liked to see my father happy and easing up a bit in his work. He used to put in fifteen hours a day until Rebecca coaxed him into relaxing over her home-cooked meals. Working so hard, he earned a good deal of money, which my brother invested wisely for him, but my father never seemed to figure out what to do with it. He was comfortable in the apartment he and my mother had shared and wouldn't move to anything larger. David's home on the north side only overwhelmed him, so most of the time if we wanted to see him, he insisted that we come

290

home. Well, he became used to Rebecca's chicken soup, her latke and streudel; and I, immersed in my work, was pleased to have discussions of subjects other than medicine at the dinner table. Just before my father died of a heart attack, he begged me to marry Rebecca to ease his mind. I promised him I would do so. Now I'm happy that he died when he did, before he got to know what manner of woman Rebecca is. At least he was spared that hurt."

Alex shook his head and ran his fingers through his hair.

"What's come over me? I must be insane telling you the trials and tribulations of my life. Forgive me, please. I was supposed to make you smile and laugh, not preach gloom and doom. What must you think of me? I've never confided any of this to a soul, not even my brother. Dani, please say something."

"Alex, I don't mind listening. Honestly. Please finish. Why would your father have been so unhappy? What is wrong with Rebecca? Is she ill?"

Deep inside she was happy that Alex was married. Perhaps now her heart wouldn't flutter so furiously when she looked at him or thought about him. She would begin to put him out of her mind, knowing they both had commitments. Or perhaps they could be friends, friends who met once a week or so and poured out their inner feelings, then left cleansed and refreshed.

"Well, if you really don't mind, I'll finish and never bring the subject up again. I might as well not leave you wondering what happened. After Rebecca and I were married, six months after my father died, she had great plans regarding spending the money he had left. At first I was happy to let her decorate our apartment. She liked new furniture and constantly changed the decor, seeking a style that pleased her. Two years after our wedding, she became pregnant and I was elated by the news. But a few weeks later she had an abortion because she couldn't stand the pain of childbirth or the disfigurement of her elegant body. She had already stopped cooking the delicious meals she had prepared for my father and me, and had insisted we hire a maid to do that menial work. She was too engrossed in having a good time to act the typical housewife. I was furious at her calm announcement of the abortion and never asked if our baby had been a boy or a girl. I doubt whether she herself asked that question of the back street butcher she paid to perform that disgusting task. For months I wanted to kill her as she had killed our child, but finally the feeling wore off. I worked longer hours for I could stand the sight of her no longer. Not after what she had done. We still live together, if you can call it that; she spends most of her time traveling. I haven't handed over all of my inheritance. No. She, too, was left a substantial sum so she can afford to flit about most of the year. She does come home now and then, and she does a superb job of entertaining because she likes to be recognized as a perfect hostess. When she's here she presses me to seek the dean's position or the presidency of some other university. She still doesn't realize I intend to remain a teacher because I love teaching. I'll never get enmeshed in the administrative end of education.

"So now you have my life story, such as it is, and I apologize again for inflicting it on you. You see, Rebecca just left for London yesterday and I'm still furious at her latest ploy. She'd had a little too much to drink at a party we attended this past week, and she went around telling those present that I'd be a much more competent dean than the one we have now. Of course the dean was there and heard her. Before I could shut her up and take her home, the damage was done. Now you can see why I said I've had a bad week. She has forced me to convince everyone at the gathering that I'm not eager to advance up the academic ladder."

"Alex, don't apologize. I'm glad you confided in me. It makes me feel very important to share your inner feelings. When I came here today I said to myself this would be the last time we'd meet, for I'm a married woman and it isn't right that I look forward so much to seeing you again. All week I've waited just for today. Something happened and for a while I thought I wouldn't be able to come, God heard my prayers. Now we can be friends, can't we? I really don't have any close friends, except one and I don't see her often since she married."

"But you must have friends. Everyone has some. You're too intriguing not to have friends."

"I don't. There's no possibility of that. But I do have one now, don't I?"

"Yes." He looked at her tenderly. "Yes, you have a very good friend indeed. Next week, Dani?"

She nodded her head affirmatively.

Alex looked down at his watch. More than two hours had sped by.

"Looks like this time I will be late for my class. Next week you'll tell me all about yourself. It's only fair that I know about you too, isn't it? Walk with me as far as my class, please?"

As they walked together through the late October chill, he pointed out the various buildings around them, not caring that he slowed his pace and was more than a little late.

Fridays became Dani's reward for a grueling, impossible week. She went about her daily chores in a daze: cleaning, washing, helping the children with their schoolwork, ignoring Roman's incessant loud words. The girls' arguments caused her less concern because she blocked them from her mind whenever they occurred. **Now and** then Roman came to her late at night and she blocked this out also, wondering how it would be if Alex were with her instead. She conjured up pictures of them together in bed, his full lips kissing hers passionately, his smooth tan hands running up and down her body setting it afire, his strong arms encircling her. She knew she would respond, matching him kiss for kiss, an eager partner in anything he chose to initiate. Repentant, she wiped the pretended scenes from her mind. Making love to Alex would be one of the major sins.

She never forgot Tekla's advice about getting pregnant and she practiced the ploy each time Roman came to her. He still had his obsessive dream about fathering a son. However, someone had told him if he saved his strength for weeks, he had a better chance of realizing his dream. Dani briefly wondered who had told him this fairy tale but she really didn't care. If it kept him away, all the better.

Through November and December she opened up to Alex, telling him all the details of her life, for Alex was a man who insisted on knowing everything and he had the knack of prying out her pent-up thoughts. Although she'd never meant to tell a soul, Dani found herself describing her first meeting with her husband and their life together afterward.

Alex was outraged.

"How can your husband be such an animal?" he cried in alarm. "It isn't fair to you, Dani. You can leave him, you know. There's nothing shameful about a divorce these days. You must divorce him."

"What is fair in life, Alex? A divorce isn't possible. I married him for better or worse; divorce is against my religion. My church doesn't recognize divorce. I'd be banished to hell, never able to receive the sacraments, a shame to my children. No, it's not possible. I'm married until the day I die or until the day Roman dies."

"And you thought my religion had strange customs when I tried to explain it to you. Yours is barbarous. Listen to me, for God's sake. The Lord won't abandon you if you throw him out. God is not a monster; He's kind and forgiving."

"Please, Alex. Remember we promised never to talk about religion again. We never agree on the subject. Let's not waste our time."

Alex had reshuffled his schedule so they could be together for four hours, the entire afternoon. It had taken some conniving on his part, but he had arranged to have an associate cover one class a week for him, with administrative approval. He had begun to wait in his car at the trolley, to save her the walk in the cold, biting weather. They drove, never too far, to unusual little hideaways where they could be together for a few hours of talking, of incessantly pouring out their feelings. When it was time to leave, he would drive near to her home so she would have only a short ride on the streetcar. She insisted he not bring her any closer, for if someone saw them that would put an end to their meetings.

The Friday before Christmas, Alex gave her a silver pin shaped in the form of a slipper. On its buckle was a small ruby.

"It's for you, princess. Someday our lives will change and we will be happy. Dani, come with me to my apartment today. Just this once."

"Alex, no. We've discussed this before. I wouldn't feel comfortable. Why your wife could come in at any minute and get the wrong impression."

"Rebecca's in the south of France. I've had a telegram from her saying she wouldn't be home for the holidays. She asked that I join her there, but I've no desire to waste my time with her frivolous, empty-headed friends. Come, it's holiday time and this makes me lonely. Let's sit by the fire for the next few hours. I'm tired of driving around in this abominable weather. Let's be comfortable and cozy for a change. You've nothing to fear; I won't ask anything more of you."

"I know that, Alex. I trust you, but I don't think I can do it. It would make me feel guilty as though we were planning something dreadful."

"Dani, have pity on me. I detest driving and only find it bearable in the spring and summer. Besides I can't look at you when I'm behind the wheel. I have to concentrate on the traffic. Change your mind?"

Two forces pulled at her. How she wanted to see him in his personal surroundings.

"All right then, but just for a little while. I have wondered where you lived, what your apartment looks like."

"Oh, you'll find it very fashionable. I'll give you the grand tour but then we'll go into my den. It's the most comfortable room. There nothing gets disturbed; the room is totally mine."

He drove a short distance to an expensive-looking apartment building on East Fifty-fifth Street and they rode the elevator in silence to the fifth floor. Dani followed Alex into an elegant foyer done in pale rose and white. A sparkling crystal chandelier sent forth brilliant shots of color from its prisms. The living room was enormous. She could fit four of hers into this one room so tastefully done in pale green and deep rose. Dani stared at the furniture. It's style was completely unfamiliar. Alex explained it was French. Next they entered a dining room that could easily seat twenty people. Dani walked slowly around the apartment examining every object. "It's beautiful Alex, just like a mansion."

"No, dearest, hardly a mansion yet too much room

for one person. Come, let's get a fire started in the den. I'll mix us some Christmas punch and we can toast the holidays."

"That's right. Poor Alex, you have no Christmas, do you?"

"No, we've just had our holiday. I'm afraid I'm getting lax in my religious practices. I spent Hannukah at my brother's, now I'm ready to spend part of Christmas, or most of Christmas with you, even though it is a few days off. Too bad I didn't think to put up a small tree to make the holiday complete."

"Alex, I don't need a tree to remind me it's Christmas. And thank you for my pin. I'll treasure it always. But I didn't get a gift for you. You should have warned me."

"Darling, I don't need a gift that money can buy. Your company these past months is enough." He kissed her then. Never had she imagined a kiss could feel like this. Not even when she'd thought she was in love with Roman years ago had she felt this way. Alex's mouth searched hers hungrily, and from that moment she was lost completely. How could she ever have thought Roman was the most desirable man alive? This kiss wasn't a kiss at all, but a union of two separate entities that together constituted a perfect whole.

Time hung suspended as they clung together, each dreading that the moment would end.

Finally Alex pulled away. "I promised you this wouldn't happen, but I couldn't help myself. I love you, Dani. Surely by now you realize it. A new year is on its way, and we're going to find a way to be together for the rest of our lives. Either we'll both get a divorce or we'll run away. You and I and your daughters. We'll go to another country, far away. I can always get a teaching position in Europe or even Canada. I want you with me forever. It's no good going on like this, only talking, when I want all you have to give a man."

Dani trembled in his arms. "Alex, I never meant our meetings to go this far. Can't you see it's impossible?" She cried then, giant tears running down her face. "Yes, there is a new year coming and we'll have to stop seeing each other. I love you too. You make me feel like a woman, something Roman's never done. Oh, once I thought I knew fulfillment with him, but it was a sham. I realize now that I was an infatuated child when I met him. It wasn't love I felt then, just a crazy childish lust. I thought he would fill a void in my life. He didn't, of course, but it's too late to change things."

"Dani, it's never too late. We can have a good life together. I know we can. I'm not saying it will be easy, but in the long run, everyone will be happier. Your daughters will learn about a happy marriage. If you like, your aunt can come with us wherever we go. Your brother is settled in his career, but I'm sure he would wish you well. You told me yourself he detests Roman. You've no one else left to worry about. Let Roman go his own way. It's probably what he wants. His pride will be hurt for a short while, but that is nothing compared to what he's put you through."

"Alex, stop it. Don't you realize the meaning of the word 'no'? I can't marry you or run off with you, but please take me now. If nothing else, I want to know what it feels like to have a man I truly love inside me. It's all I can offer you, all I can give. It will be my gift to you."

He knew better than to insist. He could see a stubbornness changing her eyes to a deeper blue. Perhaps in time he could sway her to his way of thinking, but not now so he conceded.

"There won't be any turning back once we begin. If it's all I can have, then I'll take it."

"Now, Alex, we've so little time. Let's make every

298

minute count."

He led her into his bedroom, where they undressed each other slowly. Alex slowly explored every inch of her slender body until she was in a frenzy, unable to wait a second longer for the consummation of their love. Hers was a beautiful body he thought as he kissed the faint stretch marks on her hips and stomach, giving each one he found special attention. She flushed with embarrassment, considering them deformities, but he silenced her with his mouth.

"You've a beautiful body," he murmured, "that of a complete woman. Don't close your eyes in shame when I look at you."

His tongue trailed everywhere leaving her feeling euphoric and suddenly devastated. He urged her to match his every move, so she let her eyes feast on him. It wasn't tan from the sun that covered his frame, but a natural golden tint inherited from past generations. As she ran her hands over his muscular thighs and along his taut stomach, his body shook with tremors of anticipation. She wanted him desperately. It was impossible to deny her need for another second.

"Please, Alex, now," she moaned.

"Yes, love, I know it's time. Dani, I love you more than I've loved anyone in my life. I promise you won't regret this because I'll devote my life to making up for what your husband's done to you."

"Hush," Dani whispered. "No more talk about the past. Let's concentrate on now." They lay back on the soft comforter and explored each other as though this were their last day on earth. He filled a void in her, a void she'd never known existed. She wasn't immune to arousal after all. This was how it was then to love someone completely and to be loved in return. She said his name over and over as he brought her to the highest peak of pleasure, and wantonly, she caressed him with her hands. Waves of pleasure consumed her and she shuddered with delight. Roman, at his best, when they were first married, was nothing like this. She pushed Roman out of her thoughts. Someone so corrupt didn't belong in this magical time. She strung tiny kisses along Alex's arm, then on his neck, whispering to him, "How can I not see you after this?"

The trail her lips laid aroused him again. He couldn't have enough of her. He pulled her on top of him and again they joined in perfect unison, two lost human beings who up to this point had missed something special in life. This time there were no words. They weren't needed.

Afterwards, they lay coupled together, not wanting to break the spell. Finally Dani looked lazily at the clock on the bureau and jumped up.

"I'm late. Where has the time gone? I'll never be home in time to start supper and Roman will be furious. I must hurry." She began putting on her clothes haphazardly.

"Dani, let me drive you all the way home. It's snowing out. I'll take you to the front of your house. No one will see us. You won't have to get out of the car until we're sure no one's around. I insist."

"Well, just this once," Dani relented. "We must watch the time from now on."

"Then you'll keep on seeing me?" Alex asked. "Somehow I was under the impression that this was your goodbye gift to me."

She threw her arms around him. "At first I thought it would be but not anymore. You've cast some sort of spell over me. Will you settle for just Fridays? It's all I can manage."

He kissed her mouth hungrily, holding her against him, wishing she could stay the night—no, stay forever. It would be impossible agony for six days until she was

300

with him again, but he couldn't risk losing her completely.

"You have a deal. Every Friday we can pretend we're an old married couple. I suppose it's more than some people have."

"It is, darling. I'll make up for the other days, I promise you. Now hurry, please."

Just before six Dani hurried into the house, afraid Roman had come home ahead of her and there would be a disastrous scene. Tekla looked at her questioningly.

"There was an accident," she explained breathless. "The streetcar went off the track and I had to wait forever until they could right it. I'm sorry." She noticed supper ready on the stove. "Oh, thank you, dearest Aunt. I was so worried that Roman would come home before I did. Thank you for everything. I'm so glad I have you."

Tekla noted her glistening, bright eyes. It was well worth giving Roman more money to see her niece this happy. The outings were doing her good for she looked almost like a child again tonight.

Lydia came running out of the bedroom and noticed the silver slipper pinned to her mother's dress. "Mama, where did you get the pretty pin? Can I have it?"

"No, I'm afraid not, dear. I bought it in a second-hand store. It's a Christmas present from me to me. It's the only piece of jewelry I have except for my wedding ring, and I fell in love with it as soon as I saw it. I'll buy you another pin someday soon."

"But I want that one."

"I said no. Maybe St. Nicholas will bring you one if you behave yourself. There are much prettier pins than this I assure you. Now, all of you, quick. Help me set the table before your father gets home."

She changed into a cotton housedress and was doling out food as Roman walked through the back door. It had been a most profitable day for him and he knew the evening would be even more lucrative. He had another barrel of bootleg liquor hidden behind a false wall in the cellar, and he had passed the word around that it would be for sale after closing hours. He could hear the extra money jingling in his pocket already. This was an excellent batch, and it would bring in a good price, which put him in a generous mood. After dinner he threw ten dollars on the table.

"Buy something for yourself and the girls for Christmas. A friend of mine will be bringing over a tree tomorrow."

Dani was stunned. "Thank you, Roman. I made the girls a new dress each, but now I can get them a few things they really need."

"Get something for Tekla too." In a fit of generosity he threw another five dollars on the table.

When she'd come home late after spending a sinful afternoon in Alex's arms, she'd felt as though God would punish her in some horrible way, but instead she'd been blessed. Roman was in a rare good mood. His behavior made her feel disoriented; he was so seldom pleasant.

"Don't forget to buy the presents," Roman said. "I have to get back to work. It's going to be a busy night."

"Roman, I know business hasn't been good lately, just selling food, and I appreciate this extra money when you're making so much less without the liquor."

"There's a card game in the back room tonight, and I feel lucky. I'll make up whatever I've given you."

When Dani went downstairs after the girls were in bed and informed her aunt of Roman's generosity, Tekla only smiled.

"Will wonders never cease? St. Nicholas must have hit him with his magic staff."

Tekla knew another batch of bootleg alcohol must have come in. Someday, she expected, the police would barge in and smash up the place, leaving her with no way to make a living or, worse yet, some Black Hand thug would come and force them to pay an exorbitant protection fee. With careful planning, she could afford to sell the place to Roman outright, but that would leave no money for emergencies. What if she needed a large sum of ready cash someday? She would have to remain in the business for a while longer. Even with Roman's thievery, she was still putting money aside each week, although a lot less than before.

Throughout January and February, Dani continued to see Alex at his apartment every week, except one Friday when he said Rebecca was home for a short stay between trips. These past months had more than made up for a lifetime with Roman. As familiarity released Dani from her initial shyness, their lovemaking blossomed until the days she spent away from Alex were unbearable. She wanted him so. Being deprived of his body made her more passionate when they finally did meet.

When Rebecca's presence interrupted their bliss that one week, they drove listlessly around the south side of the city unable to make love because Dani refused to go to a hotel where she felt all eyes would be watching her, seeing her as a fallen woman, a common mistress.

Rebecca stayed for an entire week and by the time she left for Italy to be a guest at a noted palazzo, Alex's face was grim and his nerves were strained from controlling his desire to prod her into an earlier departure.

"Darling," Rebecca purred, "if I didn't know better, I would think you can't wait to see the last of me. Are you by any chance up to no good? No, I don't believe

303

you are. You're always too busy studying or grading papers." Languidly, she blew a cloud of smoke in his direction.

"I see you've taken up a new disgusting habit," he answered, evading her last question. "What other vices have you acquired?"

"Really, Alex, it's not my fault that we aren't the perfect couple. You are aware that we can afford to live a luxurious life, especially if we combine our investments. Haven't I begged you to give up your thankless job and join me? You could meet all sorts of important people if you would just take the time to travel and socialize."

"Yes, Rebecca. I know. You've asked me hundreds of times and I'm not interested. Please excuse me now; I'm swamped with work. You'll have to go to the Smithfield dinner party by yourself. Offer them my apologies."

"You're becoming a bore," Rebecca accused. "I was planning on staying longer, but life is so dull here. I'll be leaving in the morning with you or without you."

"Thank God," Alex muttered to himself as he closed the door to his private sanctuary.

By March Dani was certain she was going to have Alex's baby for she had taken no precautions when they were together. Now, she thought, if we have to part for some unknown reason I'll have something of his to cherish. She looked at herself in the mirror and ran her hands around her still-flat stomach. Let it be a healthy baby that I can raise, she wished fervently. She would have to tell Alex soon but not yet, not until her pregnancy started to show, for she knew he would insist they marry. The situation was too complicated, and she couldn't face that just yet. As it turned out she didn't get an opportunity to tell him, at the beginning of May as he softly plied his hands along her body in

304

the bright sun streaming into his bedroom window, he knew.

"Dani, why haven't you said anything?"

"Said anything about what?" she teased, laughing up at him.

"Dani, I know the signs of pregnancy. Your breasts are suddenly fuller, your stomach is beautifully rounded with our child. I know it's ours. It can't be otherwise. Didn't you think I had a right to know?"

"But I was going to tell you," she replied soothingly. "Any week now I was going to say something. Oh, Alex, I'm so happy. I'll have something of you for the rest of my life."

"And what will I have? A chance to see our baby on Fridays, maybe only while he's young. Then what? Will I never see our child when its older because it might come out that I'm the father? No, Dani. I won't allow that. I lost one child, I refuse to lose another. Get used to the idea of leaving Roman, for you're going to if I have to kidnap you and your daughters. I swear that I would do it. I'll come and get all of you. So it's settled. We're going to Europe. I've had several offers to teach there, and we can file for our divorces from there as well. I've money enough so I don't have to rush into just anything. I think we'll settle in Switzerland. You'll love it there, the scenery is breathtaking, the people mind their own business, and they welcome newcomers. Start making plans to leave the first week in June—as soon as the term is over."

"Alex—"

"Not another word. Do you want our child to grow up thinking Roman is its father? Watching Roman abuse you, seeing him drink constantly, knowing he whores around with any woman that comes along? Do you think I'll subject my child to such a life when I can well afford to raise it properly? No, we'll be a real

305

family, you, Eleanor, Lydia, Irena, and Celia. Tekla too, if she wants to join us. We won't be poor my love. Oh, I've a million things to do: convert my holdings to a Swiss banking firm, resign my position here at the university, and talk to Rebecca and rid myself of that albatross hanging about my neck. Dani, you've made me the happiest man in the world today. Thank you, darling. I can't even tell you how much I love you, I can only show you."

"Alex, your career is here. You love this school, your students."

"How can I love a school? It's an inanimate object. I love you. There are other schools, other friends to be made, other students to teach. There's a whole world to see and enjoy, and I'm going to love showing it to you and our four four daughters and my new aunt. You'll see, darling. Eleanor will forget her promise to run away from home, and Lydia will straighten out when we're both there to help her see how beautiful married life can be. Celia and Irena will lose their fear when they're not witnessing abuse. Remember, the first week of June. Start getting ready, the time will fly by."

The decision was taken from her hands. There was no choice, not between the man she worshiped and the one who had made her life hell. She would die before she hurt Alex or denied him access to their child.

Dani dreaded telling Tekla what was going to take place, but she put aside her qualms and confessed the next morning after the girls left for school. She candidly told her aunt everything, omitting only the exquisite moments she'd spent in Alex's arms. Their love was a private thing to be shared with no one.

At first Tekla was overcome with shock at her confession, but then she wept with joy.

"Dani, Dani, it's the best news I've heard in years. I never suspected anything like this was going on. You

306

looked so happy lately I didn't want to question you. I
thought you'd found a new interest to keep you
amused, a new building to explore, a new section of the
city you'd never seen, that you were spending more
time with Carmella. I never suspected it was another
man. Why on earth were you afraid to tell me? You
know I only want your happiness—always have.
Didn't I want to help you run away with Raymond just
to get you away from Roman? Your happiness and
health have always come first with me. I don't care
what people say or think as long as you benefit. Didn't I
tell you there was a man who would make you happier
when you insisted Roman was the only man you could
love? So at last you've finally found him. I weep with
joy."

"You were right, but I was such a young fool. Now I
realize what you meant, and according to Alex, it will
work out for the best. I can't fight him any longer. I'm
carrying his child, and he wouldn't think of Roman
raising it."

"Then I must help you make plans. The girls must
suspect nothing. Otherwise they might make a slip in
front of Roman. You'll need passports, suitcases. How
will you get away?"

"Alex will come one morning, after he sees Roman
going off to the tavern. We'll take as little as possible,
one or two suitcases, and I'll tell the girls we're off on a
holiday. Once we're on the train to New York I'll tell
them only what I think it best they know. Most likely
they'll be frightened, but they will get used to the idea.
God knows they're frightened of their own father.
Eleanor's almost fifteen and can't wait to get away
from the house. Lydia will love the excitement, and
Alex is just the man to handle her outbursts. Irena and
Celia are younger. They'll adjust. Oh, I wish I could
have brought him to meet you, but then you'll have

years and years to get to know each other. You are
going with us, of course?"

"Dani, you know I can't leave Chicago. My Józef is
buried here. My home is here, my business."

"But you know how Roman will act after I'm gone.
I'm going to leave him a letter explaining what I've
done. He's sure to take it out on you somehow. Aunt.
Józef isn't really here you know. He's waiting for you in
heaven not here. Talk to your attorney. He can sell the
house after we're gone and forward the money to you in
Switzerland. He can sell the tavern too. All you have to
do is withdraw the money you have from the bank, or
you can just leave everything as it is. Alex will be only
too happy to support all of us. He really wants to. He
knows all about you and loves you just as I do, even
though he's never met you. Please change your mind."

"I don't know, Dani. It's a hard decision. Let me
think about it for a while. My mind's awhirl. I don't
know if I can make such a drastic change at my age.
You've shocked and surprised the daylights out of me. I
never expected this to happen. It eases my mind. Now I
can die peacefully knowing you'll be taken care of, you
and the girls. That's been my main worry for years, but
I'm not sure if I can just go and leave everything."

"Yes, you can. We're your family. You don't want to
be alone do you?"

Tekla looked up thoughtfully. "No. I was alone for
too many years before you came and I didn't like it. All
right. I'll come, but I won't sponge off your Alex. I'll
withdraw my money and see an attorney. I have more
than enough to support myself for the rest of my days."

Dani hugged her tightly. "Everything is going to be
beautiful. I just know it. I'm so happy I don't know if I
can contain myself for the next few weeks."

Mentally Dani made a list of what could be taken.
Only one extra set of clothes for each, to change until

they arrived in New York. There Alex would buy them enough for the ocean voyage, this time on a luxury liner, not a freighter. In recent weeks, their love had become even more meaningful. Instead of being in a frantic hurry and watching the clock to be sure Dani got home on time, they both relaxed and enjoyed every minute together, comfortable in the knowledge that soon they would have all the time in the world to do as they pleased. After making love, as they lay spent in his warm familiar bed, he kissed the small mound of her stomach that held the new life they had created, the child that would be the foundation of their new home. Once they were in Switzerland, he told her, they would find a comfortable house and furnishings. He phoned Rebecca and asked for a divorce, and she was surprisingly agreeable. She didn't know about Dani but she had become involved with an aristocrat in France. If she were free she felt sure he would marry her, and life with him would be exciting since he was the center of a smart group that spent the year traveling the world. His continental circle didn't look unfavorably on divorced women, and he was wealthy and had no family to hamper their union. The phone crackled with static, but Alex could hear the gist of the conversation.

"I think it's a wise move, Alex. I've decided to buy a small villa in France. Your university people are so boring I can't even stand to visit any longer. Life is here—in France. The excitement is exhilarating. I've begged you to join me time after time and you have refused so you can't blame me for seeing another man."

"No, Rebecca, I can't blame you. Yes, it's a wise move. I agree. Then you'll start the proceedings?"

"Yes, Alex. I'll leave for New York in the morning and see a lawyer there to start the ball rolling. I don't have to come back to Chicago; there's nothing I want at the apartment except my clothes and some personal items and you can ship them to me in France. The sooner this is over, the sooner we can both get on with our lives. In New York a divorce can be gotten quickly if you grease the right palms, and I do have connections there. I don't want to lose Armand although he's a very impatient man. I'm glad you brought up the subject first. I didn't want to hurt you unnecessarily, darling. Good luck. I have to hang up so I can book passage immediately."

"And good luck to you, Rebecca. I'm sorry things didn't work out for us."

"Yes, Alex, so am I, but that's life."

One hurdle out of the way, he murmured happily. One step closer to Dani.

It was the last Friday in May—their last Friday together in Chicago. Dani sang as she readied herself to meet Alex. Before another Friday came, she'd be on the train headed for a new life. She knew she should have agreed sooner. They would have had that much more time with one another. Why am I so stubborn? she asked herself, combing her hair. How could I ever think I could live without Alex? The girls and Tekla will love him as much as I do. Luckily this was the final day of school. The girls would get their report cards and then be off for the summer. But why wasn't Tekla upstairs yet? She always came up early on Fridays. Impatiently Dani went down, only to find Tekla crying, a folded newspaper lying on the table in front of her.

"Aunt, what's wrong? You're getting too nostalgic. I promise you we'll send for the Chicago newspapers in Switzerland. You'll have new friends there too."

Tekla didn't answer, only moaned and sobbed loudly as she pushed the paper across the table to her niece.

Dani looked down at the paper, frowning. What was

so disastrous that it had put Tekla into such a turmoil? What was Alex's picture doing in the paper? Had he won an award? Dani peered closer and blinked rapidly. No! It couldn't be true. It wasn't happening. This was a monstrous joke played by some fool. She read the column under Alex's picture. "Alexander Pritzkin, distinguished professor of history at the University of Chicago dies in fire. Faulty electrical wiring was found to be the cause of an inferno that raged through an exclusive apartment building in Hyde Park. Luckily most of the building's occupants were brought out safely, with the exception of an elderly couple on the third floor and a child that Professor Pritzkin went back to save. The boy, Arthur Anderson, who lived with his parents in the apartment next door to the professor, had run back into the building to get his dog and heroic Professor Pritzkin had run after him. Their bodies were found in a stairwell between the first and second floors. . . ." The column ran on listing Alex's achievements, but Dani couldn't read another word. Suddenly there was no feeling in her body. She fell to the floor, her head bursting with pain. Tekla didn't have the strength to come to her aid.

Roman already knew Dani was expecting another baby, but he was undisturbed by her illness for he didn't believe she would ever deliver a healthy son to carry on his name. He was resigned to producing only girls. For two days Tekla expected Dani to miscarry, but she rallied enough to get out of bed on the third day to attend Alex's funeral. Tekla's protests would not dissuade her. The ceremony and the burial had been postponed so Rebecca could arrive by train from New York. Dani had received that information from the university when she'd called regarding Alex's last rites.

She dressed carefully that afternoon, washing away the traces of her tears and sewing a veil over her black hat to hide her reddened eyes. Roman had wondered why his wife had spent the last two days in bed either crying or staring vacantly at the wall but Tekla had told him this was only a symptom of her pregnancy and he had accepted her explanation with muttered grumblings.

"I know it will be a sickly child. How can it not be with her carrying on so? She never did this before."

"Every baby is different, just as every pregnancy is," Tekla answered shortly. "Just leave her alone and she'll feel better soon." She wanted to wail loudly along with Dani—her own dreams of living happily had been dashed too—but someone had to have the fortitude to see them through this disaster.

When Roman left the house, he soon pushed thoughts of Dani and his forthcoming offspring from his mind. Sophie was waiting for him in the bedroom of her newly rented apartment, a short ride away. Her brazen wantonness made him ache even though it was getting rather expensive to be with her. He was the fool who had advised her that as long as she enjoyed men she should be paid for her services. She had listened intently to his advice and had begun to charge him, but her prices were getting higher and higher. In the past two years she'd mastered every trick that she could to drive a man wild, yet Roman still felt he hadn't experienced everything Sophie had to offer. Avidly, he wondered what ten dollars, instead of the usual three, would buy him and licked his lips in anticipation.

Dani arrived, shaky, at the Bernheim Chapel in the early afternoon, a short while before the funeral was to take place. It was strange to be going into the chapel for her people held wakes at home where the departed was laid out to rest amid familiar surroundings. A chapel ritual was new to her, and it seemed very cold and impersonal. At first she was startled to see that the men were wearing little round hats on their heads; then she remembered Alex telling her about the custom of wearing yarmulkas. She gathered up her courage to make the long walk to the casket which held her Alex. There was a crowd of mourners in the chapel. Alex had been known and loved throughout the university circles. Coming closer, she noticed there were no kneelers to rest upon and say a prayer. Waiting in the short line and finally standing in front of her love, she steeled herself to look down at the body which such a short time ago was so alive and so full of love for her. Staring down at Alex's peaceful face, she saw no trace that he had been touched by flame; then she heard someone behind her say that smoke inhalation had killed him and the boy. He seemed to be sleeping as he sometimes did after they had made love. She put her hand on the edge of the coffin while waves of dizziness coursed through her, and the casket rocked ever so slightly under the pressure of her unsteady hand. She heard a startled voice coming from her right.

"David, who is that woman? She's been standing there far too long. There are other people waiting to pay their respects. David, please do something. Is she going to faint or create a scene? Who is she?"

"I'll handle it," a man's voice answered. "It's a friend of mine. She knew Alex and me long ago."

"Then hurry, please. People are beginning to stare."

David took Dani by the arm and walked her to the rear of the chapel, where there was an empty couch and no one nearby to overhear their conversation.

"You must be Dani. I'm David, Alex's brother. He told me about you and about his plans a few weeks ago. There's nothing I can say to make you feel better, only that I know he loved you. He was truly a happy man for the first time in years. I was helping him settle his affairs before this dreadful accident. If it's any conso-

313

lation to you, he told me he loved you and I knew it was
true. Dani, I hate to bring this up at such a sorrowful
time, but I still have power of attorney over some of his
investments—Rebecca knows nothing of them—and
I'd like to tell you there's no need to worry about
finances. I'll see that you get a fair settlement, enough
to raise the child as Alex would have wished. If you
prefer, I'll finish making all the arrangements to get
you into Switzerland and see that you're settled there
with as little fuss as possible."

Dani pulled up her veil.

"No, David. Absolutely not. There's no need for
that. I won't be going away with Alex now, and I wasn't
after his money. Thank you but I'll manage, and I
promise you I will raise our child as he would have
wished. Not in the Jewish religion of course. That
would be impossible under the circumstances."

David looked into her eyes and saw in them what his
brother had seen, the heart of a loving woman. She
would have been an ideal partner for his unhappy
brother, for even though Alex had always laughed and
joked with everyone he met, he'd been bitter and
cynical about women since his marriage to Rebecca.
Dani was nothing like Rebecca. The conniving bitch,
David thought. He pounded a fist into the palm of his
hand. If nothing else, his brother had deserved a few
happy years with someone sweet and tender. He had
deserved to know the child he wanted to badly. How
could anyone stoicaly accept God's will? Was he
supposed to go into the synagogue later and thank God
for the loss of his only brother?

"Dani, what will you do? Where will you go?"

"Why . . . nowhere," she answered calmly. "My
husband thinks the child is his. He has no suspicion
that I was about to leave him. We'll be just fine."

"Dani, please, if you ever need money or help you've

314

only to call me."

"No. That would only bring back memories. At first I wanted to die too so I could be with him, but then I realized that was the coward's way out. I'll have his son or daughter and I know he'll be with me somehow—in my memories I guess."

"David, there are friends waiting to speak to you." A cool arrogant voice intruded on their conversation.

Dani looked up to see a striking woman in her late thirties. She wore an elegant black suit, and huge diamonds glittered on her ears and on her fingers. Her black hair was drawn into a perfect chignon beneath the black feathered hat which set off her perfect features.

"I'll be with you in a minute, Rebecca."

So this is Alex's wife, Dani thought. For all her elegance and beauty she looked cold and aloof, like a hostess at a cocktail party not the bereaved wife of a remarkable man.

Dani stood up.

"Thank you, David. Thank you for everything. I did feel faint at first. I must get home to my children now. Good-bye."

She held herself proudly erect and walked out of the chapel not looking back. Alex's face, his touch were burned into her memory forever. It wasn't Alex lying there. It was a shell of a man. Alex was walking beside her, and would be from now on.

In October, Alexander Kawa came into the world easily and with hardly any pain. After an hour of mild labor and a few sharp contractions, he was set into her waiting arms. Dani looked down at her son. He had pitch-black hair just like Alex's, and from what she could see when he opened his eyes, they were going to be dark, maybe just as dark as his father's. His nose was identical to Alex's. How different he looked from her other children. Eleanor had light brown hair, Lydia's was reddish blond, and Irena and Celia had pale yellow tresses.

"He will look just like his father," Dani whispered to Tekla. "Can you call the church? I'd like the christening for next Sunday."

"If he looks like his father," Tekla replied softly. "then Alex must have been a handsome man indeed. But will you feel well enough in a week?"

"Yes, I feel well enough now. Alex gave me no pain coming into the world just as his father gave me no pain—except the pain I felt when he died but that wasn't intentional. I know how he must have felt in those few minutes before it happened. He thought of me I know and cursed himself for putting me through what he knew was inevitable. We could almost read each other's thoughts, you know. From now on, we won't mention Alex, my child's father. We'll only speak of Alex my son and your great-nephew.

Roman came home a few hours later when someone happened to congratulate him on the birth of his son.

"At last," he beamed. "This time I hope you can manage to care for him properly."

"You have no need to worry, Roman," Dani answered coolly. "I'll care for him as no mother ever has before."

"Good." He peered at the baby. "Such black hair. Who does he take after? No one in my family had black hair."

"My mother," Tekla answered abruptly, giving Roman a withering look of hatred. "She had hair as black as night."

Roman appeared satisfied with the answer.

During the christening Roman's mouth hung agape when he heard the priest read out the baby's name. He looked at Dani suspiciously and whispered in her ear

"My son's first name should be Roman not Alexander. I took it for granted you were naming the baby after me."

Dani looked up from her prayerbook.

"We already had a son called Roman. Have you forgotten so soon? He lies in Resurrection Cemetery where we buried him."

Abashed at Dani's spiteful answer, he sat quietly through the rest of the ceremony.

Chapter Eight

As Alex passed through the stages of infancy, he was treated, without exception, as an unexpected gift. He was fondled, teased, and loved but Dani brooked no spoiling of her offspring. The family could cuddle the baby, hug him, or sing to him, but when he cried for more attention at bedtime she sternly put her foot down.

By the time Alex was five he could already read simple books quite well. He begged Dani to get him others, for he was bored with the nursery rhymes he knew by heart. Holding his hand, Dani set off gaily to the library, where Alex learned to choose what he wanted to read. She took out books for herself as well, and at bedtime he pleaded with her to read a few paragraphs of the history or geography books she loved, especially the ones depicting Switzerland. They pored over them together, both delighted by the pictures that opened up vistas for them: mountain scenes, quaint villages, beguiling capital cities. Through the magic the library had to offer, they traveled to different countries or cities each week, but Switzerland always remained Dani's favorite and the librarian searched out books on that country, knowing how happy they would make her.

"Why do you love Switzerland so, Mama?" Alex asked once.

"Because," she answered, "everyone has a never-never land to dream of. Switzerland is mine. It's my idea of heaven on earth. One day you'll probably have a favorite place too."

"Mine is home, but my next choice will be Switzerland too," he answered, snuggling up to hear the next chapter Dani would read to him. He couldn't comprehend the more complicated words and stopped her countless times to ask their meanings. Patiently she answered his every question, and soon he began to print letters and short words with a sure hand. Then Dani spent hours teaching him to spell correctly.

Sitting by his bed one night after he'd fallen asleep, she relaxed and began to think of the past five years. So much had happened that her despondency over Alex's death had eased. Nightly, before dropping off to sleep, she had a one-sided conversation with him, telling him the myriad details of his son's progress. She pictured his face smiling encouragement at each report. Some might think her crazy, but she looked forward to these respites after a hard day. "Alex, our son said his first word today. Darling, it was 'Mama' he said but he'll learn to say 'Daddy' too in no time, I promise you." Or, "Alex spelled the word house today." And so it went night after night until sleep overtook her. This was a necessary ritual that made her days worthwhile.

During those years, Jan married the lovely girl he worked with, the one he occasionally took to dinner—her name was Elizabeth, Beth he called her—and they had a son, John, who helped keep Jan's mind occupied with thoughts other than those of work. And a year before his marriage he had taken the long delayed trip to Poland, a waste of time and money, Dani now thought. He had found Lottie and Louis Czerny. Their children had gone off on their own, with the exception of one. Lottie had welcomed him with open arms, but she had cautioned Jan to wait in the kitchen while she prepared Louis for the exciting news of his return. Pouring him a cup of coffee, she had prattled about how surprised she was.

"When we heard the soldiers took you and Casimir off to work in their labor camp, we were desolated. One of our sons was killed in the war, and the other is left without a leg although he can walk again with the use of an artificial limb. Our two daughters fared better. One, we managed to send to Cracow, where she married a merchant. The other is in a convent. That life is poor and bleak, but she seems content. Poor Louis had a stroke several years ago, and the doctor warned him that he shouldn't get too excited. I'm not even sure I should tell him of your return, but maybe it will put a little sparkle into his tired eyes again. He's been feeling very lonely and helpless with the children gone. We have two nephews working on the farm, but it's not the same. Only Henryk, bless him, is here, but he goes through periods of deep depression over the loss of his leg. Sometimes he won't talk to us for days or weeks."

"Your farm looks prosperous," Jan said, finishing his coffee. "I see you've added a brick addition to the house and you have more cows and pigs than when I left."

Lottie patted her hair and beamed at Jon proudly. "Yes, at least we're not hurting financially, although there are dreadful shortages. Louis was left a bit of gold by a relative, and he hid it until after the war. Thank God the army didn't get it. They vandalized everything and everyone. Just when the war started, one of those vile soldiers hit him on the head, the very same day they captured you and your father. For several weeks Louis

321

wasn't right in his mind. It's a miracle we weren't sent away on a work program. Those pigs only took our food and animals, and decided to let us be. I believe that head wound had something to do with his stroke even though the doctor tells me no. We didn't have it easy either, Jan, not till years later. Louis worked hard when the war was on and when it was over, trying to recover what we'd lost. The work almost killed him. You see, he's a bedridden old man now and must be content to watch the fields from our bedroom window. Well anyway, after the soldier hit Louis, he never completely regained his senses. I remember him screaming in the middle of the night with terror. I hope seeing you won't be too much of a strain." She turned to walk down the hall to the bedroom, then faced Jan again. "How stupid of me. I haven't even asked about your father. Is Casimir well?"

Jan's vocal cords knotted with tremors of hate.

"No, I'm afraid he died, Lottie. I wasn't captured by soldiers. I managed to escape and make my way to my aunt's house and Dani. My father never made it out of the country."

"Poor Casimir. But how is my darling Danuta? Is she doing well?"

"Quite well," Jan answered, impatient to see Louis, the murderer, thief, and liar.

"I'll be right back," Lottie said, walking softly in slippered feet down the long hall.

After five minutes Jan began to pace across the kitchen floor. Evidently Lottie was innocent in the affair and knew nothing of her husband's treachery. No wonder Louis had had a stroke. His guilt must have put him through hell, but Jan felt that to be a just retribution. Still, from what Lottie said, somehow Louis had managed to keep the gold. The soldiers hadn't gotten it

322

after all. In their rush to be gone from the farm after raiding it, they must have overlooked the steel box lying on the ground in the darkness.

Lottie came back holding a finger to her lips.

"I think you can see him for a short while, Jan. I only told him I had a surprise, that an old friend was here to visit him. But please don't stay too long. It will only overtire him, then he'll be forced to take more of the medication he detests."

"Only a minute or two," Jan promised, seating Lottie at the kitchen chair she'd vacated moments ago. "Why don't you stay right here and I'll call you if anything goes amiss."

"Fine, Jan. That will be fine."

Jan stood at the closed bedroom door, fists clenched, as droplets of sweat trickled down his forehead and along the back of his shirt. Revenge was foremost in his mind, but what kind of revenge? He wanted to face a healthy Louis, not a man who couldn't fight back. Could he get out of the country in time if he choked the life out of him? No, that was impossible. The authorities would be after him long before his ship sailed for home, and the top management at the auto firm had had a difficult time getting him the proper entry papers. He decided to feel his way.

Louis lay propped up on two large feather pillows, anxiously awaiting his promised visitor. His eyes opened wide in disbelief while his face paled at the sight of the unwanted apparition before him. The dead were coming to claim him after all. Hundreds of nights he had dreamed of Casimir's bloodstained face which stared at him accusingly, but until now Jan had never appeared in his horrendous nightmares. Yet here he was, in person, to extract vengeance. Spittle gurgled in Louis' throat as he struggled to push himself away from

323

the specter closing in on him while he lay in the confines of his bed unable to move. A hammering began at his temples. The pounding reverberated throughout his head as he tried to escape the accusing eyes that came closer and closer, their hatred boring into him.

Dear Lord, he prayed silently. I've said I was sorry for my greed and for the murders a thousand times. I didn't mean to do it. I had a little too much vodka that day at the market and it made me insane. He slumped over seconds later, his eyes open wide in shock, his mouth agape with a silent scream, saliva oozing down onto his neck. Jan took one long look at the shrunken man. His revenge was over, there was nothing more he could do to punish Louis. A pity Louis couldn't have hung on for a few more minutes. To Jan's mind his death had come too quickly.

"Lottie," he called loudly, backing away. "Come quickly."

She ran into the bedroom and gasped at the sight of her husband half hanging off the bed, his face contorted.

"Oh, no. I should have guessed it would be too much. The sight of you finished him. Get out." She pushed at Jan, raking her nails across his face as he caught at her hands. "Get out. Your coming has done this. I would curse your father too if he were here with you. My Louis couldn't take the shock."

A slow smile spread across Jan's face.

"The sight of me didn't kill him. The sins of his past did."

"What are you talking about, you wicked boy? Why are you smiling like some gleeful demon?"

"My father's ghost must have haunted him for years. I didn't have to come here at all, my father took care of his own revenge." Jan laughed sarcastically.

324

"What evil are you mouthing? You're insane. The war unhinged your mind."

Jan turned away to leave.

"The gold didn't do much good after all, did it? Louis didn't inherit the gold from a relative, Lottie. He stole it from my father the night he murdered him, the night he thought he killed me as well."

Flushed with rage, Lottie struck at Jan again, but he caught her hand.

"Have someone dig up the ground behind our old barn. You'll find my father's decomposed body with a bullet wound in his head, a bullet from your husband's gun. You'll find another buried there too, a lad Louis mistook for me. Your husband, dear Lottie, was nothing more than a thieving killer who deserved every misfortune that came his way. I hope you live happily on your rebuilt farm that was paid for with my father's life."

Jan retrieved his coat from the kitchen and slammed out the door, hopping onto the wagon that would take him back to Gdansk. From there he would go home. This country was no more home than the moon. When he arrived in America he went straight to Chicago to tell Dani and Tekla of the results of his journey, but he refused to remain, leaving the same day to catch a train to Detroit. Beth was the only person who could help him to return to normal everyday living, but it took her many months to coax him out of his silence and depression.

As for Carmella and Giovanni, they were prospering. Their business kept growing and they moved its location several times, expanding with each move. They were on Taylor Street now, in the heart of an Italian neighborhood. Working ten or more hours a day wasn't a hardship because their days were filled with friendly camaraderie. Their neighbors came in every day to purchase something. The only disappointment in Carmella's life was that she had no children but that was an act of God. She and Dani found time to talk on the telephone once a week, but Dani hadn't the heart to visit her often. It was painful to see her two happy friends, very much in love, teasing and joking with each other as they worked side by side.

During these years the Smenteks had both died, within weeks of each other. They had been happy till the end, the love of their family enveloping them. One of their sons wrote a long letter after their deaths, thanking Dani again for being so good to his parents. That was the end of another chapter in Dani's life.

Dear Raymond Patek had written at intervals, usually at Christmas, always sending along a small gift for Dani. He was still roaming the seas, but he planned to retire to his island soon. She kept the treasures he sent on a shelf in her bedroom so she could look at them and remember her friend. Roman didn't object for he knew little of Raymond and thought him to be an old wizened sea dog, so in the open sat a carved mahogany box from the Philippines, a delicate porcelain music box from Austria, rosary beads purchased and blessed in Italy, a ship in a bottle—so many lovely gifts he'd sent over the years. In Raymond's letters to Tekla he reminded her of his invitation to all of them to join him in Jamaica. The offer finally became a family joke. Whenever Dani or Tekla had an unusually hard day or many things went wrong, one of them would say, "Let's go to Jamaica," and their gloom and worry would dissipate as they began to laugh.

Bolie and Martha had visited once a year, during the Christmas holidays, and always brought small gifts to the children. They usually had stayed for an hour or two, and then had hurried away before Roman came home. Martha had grown more plump over the years for Bolie was making a magnificent salary and she enjoyed staying home and cooking tasty dishes to keep up Bolie's strength for his job at the mills.

Eleanor, determined and self-sufficient, had gone to live at the nurses' quarters at Mercy Hospital for over a year. In another year she would be a full-fledged Angel of Mercy. She usually came home on Sundays to play with Alex and gossip with Celia and Irena but she made hurried excuses that she had to be back on duty whenever Roman happened to come home. She never talked to her father and when he asked an occasional question she answered him with a curt yes or no. Roman, often as not, stared after her, genuinely puzzled by her open animosity.

"She needed a few swipes with my belt in her early years," Roman often complained. "She's spoiled, with no proper respect for her father. Single young girls should be living at home, not be away six days a week. Does she think I'm stupid? I hear stories about doctors and nurses openly copulating in every available empty bed."

Dani only looked at him in disgust whenever he uttered his depraved remarks.

Lydia had run off with a salesman, another blow to Roman's pride. Lydia was his favorite daughter, although by his actions you would never know it. She had been working downtown as a receptionist at an insurance company, but when Tim Fitzpatrick, one of the commissioned salesmen, had said he was off to the west coast to get rich, Lydia had gone along, having no qualms over her reputation or the gossip that would follow her leave-taking. She came home one night after dinner and, while Tim waited outside in a ramshackle car, threw her clothes into a battered suitcase and a shopping bag. Then she had told her mother and aunt point-blank that she was off to California to try to make it in the movies. When Dani and Tekla had protested her rash decision, she'd become furious. But this time it hadn't been a tantrum but cold calculated anger.

"You can't stop me, you know. Even if you tie me to my bed, I'll find another way to leave."

Lydia always had acted as though her whole life was a tortuous road of abuse. Nonetheless, Tekla had tried to stop her determined great-niece.

"No decent girl travels alone with a man she's not married to."

"What's wrong with it? It's the cheapest way to get there. We'll share expenses, and when we get to California Tim goes his way and I go mine. I'll be glad to get out of this stupid nosy neighborhood. It's dull and boring, and so is my job. In California things are happening. There's money being made there, and I'm off to get my share of excitement and money before I'm an old hag. I refuse to be tied down by a husband and brats who hang on my apron strings night and day. This neighborhood is full of dull plodding gossipy hags. It's not for me."

"Let her go," Dani had said quietly after Lydia had kissed them each briefly on the cheek and left. "Lydia's always had her way and she's not going to change. Not now, not ever."

Poor Lydia, her flighty determined second daughter. She was always a problem. Would she meet someone in California who would cut her down to size? She was beautiful, with her red-gold hair and deep blue eyes, and she had a certain boldness that men liked. Will I ever see her again? Dani wondered.

328

At the time Tekla had reluctantly agreed with Dani. "I guess it's for the best. But she's not going to bring Hollywood to its knees. She may be pretty here in her own little pond, but there she'll be a very small fish indeed. She'll see hundreds of girls, beautiful girls, and she'll learn that the sun doesn't rise and set on her alone."

"You're right, Aunt. Some day she'll learn, but it must be the hard way."

Irena was working at a part-time job at a newspaper office. She typed on one of those fast little machines, but she wanted to get married and quit working. All she wanted out of life was a home, a husband, and one or two children in that order. She was lazy and on most mornings she had to be literally dragged from bed, but she thought marriage would be simply divine. Dani had no inkling how Irena had arrived at this ridiculous notion for she had certainly seen how miserable marriage could be. She decided Irena must have blocked her home life from her mind to fantasize about life, taking her cue from the movies where there were always happy endings. Dani had never seen a typewriter except in pictures, but she was proud that her daughter had mastered such a complicated piece of office equipment. On that machine the letters of the alphabet weren't even in any proper order but were randomly scattered all over the keyboard so that one had to memorize their positions. Dani could barely keep up with the new technological miracles being created each day. It was now true, as she had thought years ago it would someday be, that a person could get into a flying machine and be flown across a country, across an ocean, in hours. It seemed to defy all laws of gravity that the heavy odd-looking airplane could stay up in the air without crashing to the ground. But to

Dani the most wondrous of inventions was the refrigerator run by electricity, which kept food from spoiling for days. The iceman still made his daily rounds. He wasn't doomed yet because many people couldn't afford an electric icebox and many homes weren't yet wired for electricity. But soon the iceman would be a thing of the past.

Tekla had given in to progress and had had the house wired so they could use electric lights instead of candles or kerosene lamps. Now Dani could read or sew delicately under a bright glare instead of squinting in the semidarkness. She was going to save enough money to buy an electric icebox too. That was her goal, but she would wait until the price was more reasonable.

When Celia was fifteen she had insisted that she wanted to enter a convent, but Dani had refused to give her permission. She had thought Celia far too young to make a choice she might regret years later when she might want a family.

"Once you take your vows," Dani had warned, "they're unbreakable."

But Celia had not relented despite endless hours of discussion.

"Just give yourself a few more years," Dani pleaded. "If you still want to be a nun in five years, I won't stop you. I promise. By then you'll be a woman."

Dani knew Celia wasn't as mature as her sisters. Eleanor was aggressive in a quiet way. She had planned her life determinedly and wouldn't stray one inch from her set goals. Lydia was aggressive too, but in a bold calculating way. Those two would probably get what they wanted from life. At least they would make every attempt to do so, but Irena didn't put much effort into living. She just plugged along and was happy with whatever life held in store. Not ambitious, she would probably settle for a humdrum life, her excitement coming from gossiping with neighbors and friends. Of them all, it was Celia who worried Dani the most. She was too quiet and introverted, coming straight home from school and going to church every morning, rain or shine, in bitter cold or broiling heat. She seemed to have no need for friends, and this was what Dani wanted to change before allowing Celia to lock herself away from society. She tried to push the girl into going to parties and into attending the weddings where eligible men might congregate, but in social settings the girl just sat and looked forlorn as if she'd have preferred to stay at home.

Roman was Roman, older and meaner than ever. He would never stop chasing women, never ease up on his drinking, never have many kind words for his family. When Alex was five, he felt confident that his son would live to maturity, but that didn't stop him from assaulting Dani almost every night except on the weekends when he stayed with one whore or another. Sophie was long gone. She had left the neighborhood when she'd accumulated enough in savings, and rumor had it she had married a man with quite a lot of money who owned a good-size hotel on the north side. Someone on the block claimed to have seen Sophie once, walking downtown, sporting a mink coat and bejeweled fingers.

Upon hearing that news Tekla had shaken her head sadly.

"The good get punished and live hard lives while the worthless of the world get rewarded with material things," she had said. "Sometimes I think life is very unfair, but then, our good Lord must have a reason for His actions. We'll all know in good time."

Fortunately Dani hadn't become pregnant again,

and she'd been thankful to have more free time to spend with Alex and Celia. She guessed you could call Roman an alcoholic, for he could not go long without a drink. With other women, he boasted of his sexual prowess, yet nine times out of ten, with Dani he couldn't perform in bed, and he invariably blamed his wife. When this happened he cursed Dani and said she had lost all her appeal years ago. He told her that she was cold blooded and frigid, a woman who didn't know anything about keeping a man happy. The last time Roman had roared out his wrath she had laughed right in his face, for she knew the kind of women Roman was consorting with lately. The lowliest pigs clung to him in the hopes of making fifty cents or a quarter, their gaudy looks having faded away years ago. They were disgusting and sloppy, and would take on anyone for whatever they could earn. For her laughter Dani had received a severe beating. Roman had struck her again and again in the stomach and the ribs, and then he had kicked her in the back as she lay on the floor, searing pain shooting through her body. It had been almost worth it to see Roman's outraged face when her laughter told him he was a has-been. Dani had held back the pain the whole night, but in the morning Eleanor had come. Realizing the condition her mother was in, she'd had a friend drive her to the hospital where the doctor's examination had revealed three broken ribs. After they were taped, Dani had been able to breathe without experiencing excruciating stabs of pain in her chest, but the persistent ache in her back had lingered on. Eleanor had begged her to see the doctor again, but Dani had refused.

"It's not unbearable," she'd said. "I can live with it, so it can't be anything too serious."

In school, Alex continued to get the highest grades in

his class, but he did not have to bury his head in books. He found time to play with his friends and still maintain excellent grades. Indeed, of her five children, Alex was the most social. No one teased him because he was bright, instead his schoolmates were drawn to him like moths to a flame. Although Alex participated in most of their pranks, he never went too far. He always stopped them before they got into deep trouble.

Prohibition finally ended, and Tekla could again sell liquor legally. The restaurant was doing well so she expanded, keeping the former tavern as a dining area and building on a new bar and lounge as such places had become known. In her late fifties now, the years of hard work had etched deep lines on her face. She felt lukewarm about the business she had once loved but she persisted with it, not quite ready yet to give up something Józef had bequeathed to her.

Roman kept the profits from the bar, while Tekla took only what was made from the restaurant. It wasn't worth it to her to constantly watch him to see how much he was pocketing for himself. As long as he gave Dani enough to put food on the table, keep the children clothed, and pay the bills, she was satisfied. Many nights, lying in bed after her prayers, she wondered how many years she must wait before joining Józef. Not too much longer, she hoped. She was tired and she wondered what heaven would be like. Just to be at peace—without any aches, pains, and worries— seemed like paradise.

Dani's pain grew steadily worse, and finally Eleanor forced her to see one of the doctors at Mercy Hospital. The experience was humiliating. She did not like to have strangers probing her body. After three days of tests and X-rays the doctor diagnosed kidney damage and said an operation was the only way to lessen the pain. In terror, Dani released herself from the hospital. By sheer willpower she lessened the pain for a few months.

Then Roman came home in one of his fighting moods and hit Dani viciously when she asked him where he'd been for the past two days. She'd only questioned him to make some conversation at the quiet dinner table. He slapped Celia too for accidentally pouring hot coffee on his lap. Celia ran from the room in tears and then Roman pushed Dani against the sink, threatening her again. This time Dani screamed aloud, her cries bringing Celia back. Taking one look at her mother, she called Eleanor at the hospital and an ambulance arrived in ten minutes. Dani was rushed to the emergency unit as knife-sharp pains spread through her body.

Eleanor sat anxiously in the emergency waiting room while Dr. Emmons, the house surgeon, made a quick examination, took X-rays again, and prescribed morphine for the pain.

"Mrs. Kawa," he said, "I told you a long time ago you needed an operation and now there appears to be internal damage, probably to the kidney that was giving you trouble. I'm afraid there's no other alternative but to go ahead. I must get inside to see exactly how much damage has been done."

"I feel a little better now," Dani protested weakly.

"Only because the pain is deadened by drugs. It will be back in a few hours and we'll give you another shot, but it won't go away this time. I'll schedule the operation for tomorrow morning." He turned to Eleanor. "Talk to her, Ellie. Without the drugs, she won't be able to bear the pain and you certainly don't want to see her addicted to morphine. There's some serious trouble internally."

"I will, Doctor. She'll agree. Just let me be alone with her for a few minutes."

The nurses settled Dani in a ten-bed ward. She was placed next to the window through Eleanor's influence. Eleanor was fast becoming the most capable nurse in the operating room, coolly slapping the required instruments into surgeon's hands during the most difficult surgery. Most of the other nurses were in awe of her dedication and dexterity. It was whispered in the halls that she could probably perform an operation all by herself just as well as any of the doctors who practiced at the hospital. Eleanor smiled when she heard the rumors. I'll bet I could at that, she thought. After helping to settle her mother comfortably in bed, she stayed a few minutes until the sedative took full effect.

"Mama, by this time tomorrow it will be over and you'll be on your way to recuperating. I won't be in the operating room—relatives are not allowed—but I'll be waiting just outside the door and I'll be with you night and day until they let you get up. Please, Mama, you must have this operation. Think of it as a rest away from home. He did this to you, didn't he? My father's such a brave man. He's great at hitting women. Why do you put up with him? Why are you such a martyr?"

Dani shrugged her shoulders. In a drug-induced haze she could see that her daughter was right about the surgery, and she nodded her head in agreement. The pain had been getting worse lately, but that sudden shove into the rim of the sink was more than she could bear. Best get it over with so she could do some of the heavy work again instead of leaving it up to Celia during the week and Eleanor on Sundays. Irena was married and expecting her first child so she wouldn't think of asking for her help. Of all things, Irena had married a man who worked at the soap factory, but he was a good provider and very different from his father-in-law.

Pleasant dreams drifted through Dani's mind as the morphine took hold. Dreams of her and Alex, together again, walking through autumn leaves, making love before the fire. She was listening to his voice, that deep beautiful voice that held a note of love even when he spoke of trivial everyday matters. When the sedative wore off, a nurse was ready with another shot. Dani could continue to dream of Alex, to imagine their lives together, raising their son and her daughters in Switzerland, all of them happy in each other's company.

In the morning, the trip on the wheeled cart to the operating room wasn't as horrid as she had expected for she felt a cool detachment. She could see Tekla's sad face, hear Eleanor's words of encouragement, but they seemed far away and fuzzy as though everything was happening to someone else.

Eleanor and Tekla sat in a private lounge, nervously awaiting the doctor's return. An ominous feeling rested heavily on Eleanor, one that she couldn't shake. She had assisted at hundreds of operations, most successful, some not; but any Dr. Emmons performed were miracles of surgical perfection. Why then was she filled with dread? She remembered the pool of blood her mother lay in at childbirth so many years ago, and she cried out at the sudden vision. Tekla clasped her hand while Eleanor sobbed uncontrollably.

"Mama's had such a rotten life. Why should she have to suffer more? He should be lying there getting cut open, not her."

"Her life wasn't always bad," Tekla answered after a few minutes.

"When was it good? When my father wasn't home to harass and abuse her? When she was a young girl struggling to stay alive in a poor mining town? She's had a horrid life."

Tekla wisely decided to keep her mouth shut about Dani's small fragment of happiness with Alex.

"It can't be much longer now, Eleanor. It's been four hours. We should be hearing soon."

Eleanor seemed not to hear. "And where is my father? Is he out drinking to forget Mama's pain or is he with some whore? Does he even care that he's to blame for what happened? Does he care about anyone but himself?"

"Hush, child. This bitterness won't help. Just pray; it's all we can do. I'll think of some way to keep Roman away for good. I'll give him the tavern—lock, stock and barrel—if he'll take a room in the basement and leave your mother alone."

Eleanor muttered viciously, "You don't have to give away anything that's rightfully yours. You've been bribing him for years and don't bother to deny it."

Tekla could only remain silent. How much Eleanor had heard over the years she didn't know for sure, but Roman's voice did carry so she must have heard a great deal.

Another hour slowly ticked by before Dr. Emmons joined them, still wearing his green operating clothes stained with small patches of blood.

"Oh merciful God, no," Eleanor cried, seeing the look on his face. "She's dead, isn't she?"

"Eleanor, please calm yourself. No. Your mother's not dead, but it's touch and go. There was much more damage to the kidney than I expected. I had to remove one, and the other isn't in very good shape. We'll just have to wait and see what the next twenty-four hours bring. There's a small chance that her other kidney will function satisfactorily, but I can't tell yet. The orderly will bring her back to the ward soon. You can see her in a few hours."

"Not the ward," Eleanor said. "Put her in one of the best private rooms. I'll pay for it and make the arrangements with Sister Ludmilla." She ran from the room to inquire if the private room on the fourth floor was still unoccupied.

Tekla stood up, stiff from sitting so long. "Is my niece going to live, Doctor? Please tell me the truth."

He looked at Tekla sadly. "I'm afraid not. I did the best I could, but I'm afraid not. Best prepare for the worst unless a miracle occurs. I'm trying to soften the blow for Eleanor."

"So then, how long does she have?"

"It's hard to say. Perhaps a few days, maybe a few hours. She won't be in any pain, not with the narcotics I've prescribed. Her remaining kidney is so badly damaged I had a rough time deciding which to remove."

"Thank you, Doctor." Tekla shuffled out of the room, looking far older than her years.

Dani was wheeled into a private sunny corner room, where Eleanor and Tekla waited, tears hastily wiped from their eyes. Under no circumstances would Dani catch them crying.

A few minutes earlier Eleanor had called Celia to tell her to bring Alex to the hospital on the streetcar and they should be here momentarily. The nurses transferred Dani to the hospital bed and Tekla gasped with shock. Was this her beautiful Dani lying there? This couldn't be her lovely niece looking so gray, her blond hair matted and tangled, tubes hanging from her body. The woman in the bed looked twenty years older than her Dani.

Eleanor clasped one of her mother's hands. It was

cold and clammy, a lifeless piece of flesh and bones. Dani's eyes remained closed so Tekla and Eleanor sat in silence until Celia and Alex arrived. Minutes later, Irena rushed into the room, out of breath from running up the stairs. She hadn't waited for the elevator but had dashed up the stairs instead.

Alex came closer to the bed. "Mama, can you hear me? Do you feel all right?"

Dani's eyes fluttered open slowly. Why was everyone hovering over her asking if she felt all right? She felt just fine. They had interrupted a lovely dream about her mother and father and she wanted to get back to it, not be bothered to answer questions. She shut her eyes again, but the voices kept disturbing her. Oh, why didn't they leave her alone for just another minute so she could see her parents' faces again? Her mother looked absolutely stunning and her father handsome and strong. She thought she saw Alex standing just behind them and she wanted to make sure. She opened her eyes as someone grasped her hand, and then she focused clearly, the dream momentarily pushed aside. "Alex my son, what are you doing here? You weren't to come for a few more days, not until I felt better."

"Mama, your hands are cold, just like wet ice."

Dani looked at the faces surrounding her. Her lovely children, her dearest aunt. She could feel herself slipping away from them even though she tried hard to assure them of her recovery.

I'm not going to recover, she thought suddenly as her heart began to pound wildly. This is where it will end. She wanted to cry out to her father, to beg his forgiveness for being such a disappointment. He had sent her to this country to make something of herself and what had she accomplished? Nothing. His bright intelligent

339

daughter had squandered her life away. Would he be angry when she saw him? No, of course not. Papa never got angry. He would understand and forgive her.

Her words trickled out slowly and with great effort from her parched lips. Why was it she could think so clearly but it was most difficult to talk?

"Eleanor, Irena, Celia, come closer please." Each girl kissed her cheek. "I tried my best, honestly I did, but somehow things never worked out as I planned. Once there was a chance for a happy life for all of us, but it never came to be. You must know I love you all, even Lydia, although she never writes to us. If she comes, tell her I love her too."

The three girls couldn't control themselves and silently escaped into the hall for a few minutes to pull themselves together.

"Alex, my little love. You are my most treasured child. Always remember that. The future lies in your hands. Make me proud, Alex. You are going to be a great man, I know it."

"Mama, why are you talking so funny?"

Tekla gently pulled him aside. "Alex, wait in the hall with your sisters. I have to talk to your mother privately."

Tekla and Dani were alone in the room. Dani's voice was weakening. "Aunt, please take care of my Alex for me. Tell Celia to go into the convent as she wishes. I shouldn't have stopped her for so long, but Alex will need you for a while longer. Please be strong for him until he's old enough—another burden I'm putting on your shoulders. All I've ever given you are burdens. Forgive me."

"Quiet, Dani. You're talking too much. Try to rest so you can keep up your strength."

"It's no use, dear Aunt. I feel something terribly strange happening inside me. Something's not working right, it feels different." Suddenly her eyes grew brighter. "Behind you I can see Alex waiting for me, and he looks wonderful. He's calling for me to come. I mustn't keep him waiting any longer or he'll go away and I won't be able to find him. Goodbye, dearest Aunt. Mama?" she asked happily. "Papa, is that you?" Her eyes shut again and she smiled, at peace.

Chapter Nine

Two hefty patrons of the tavern, muscles straining their shirt seams, came early to Tekla's apartment to rearrange the furniture in her living room and to set out extra chairs, keeping one wall free for the placement of the casket. Eleanor opted for having the wake at the funeral parlor, but Tekla was adamant.

"I will not permit them to drain my niece's blood and disembowel her. Enough was done to her body. The mortician will arrange everything beautifully right here."

An overpoweringly sweet smell of flowers filled the rooms. Eleanor almost gagged at the heady fragrance. Although more and more people were holding their wakes at chapels, Tekla insisted it be done the old way, in her home where she felt Dani belonged. For two days and nights Dani's body would lie in rest, mourners free to visit at any hour of the day or night. The funeral would take place on the third morning.

Roman held court in Tekla's kitchen, presiding over a variety of hastily arranged bottles of liquor. The men congregated there with him and left the women to the

343

dining and living rooms. Each woman who quietly walked into the house brought an offering: a cake, a meatloaf, or a casserole. The bounty was piled high on the buffet so all could help themselves as the dismal hours dragged on. Dani looked at peace lying in the bronze casket inlaid with pink satin, the best Tekla could buy. She wore a deep rose silk dress, and her pale hands clasped a pearl rosary. A hairdresser had been brought in to arrange Dani's hair in a coronet of braids. The women, trickling in one by one, exclaimed over how beautiful the deceased looked, how peaceful she seemed lying there in her final receptacle.

Eleanor wanted to lash out at them violently for their pious condolences. Where were all these hypocrites when her mother needed them? Her mother could have used their friendship, yet they had shunned her. Oh, they did say a polite good-morning or talk casually about the children once in a while but none had ever come to visit—to hospitably welcome her into their homes, their hearts, because they considered her unworthy of their precious friendship, these pious matrons who thought their husbands were models of perfection. Eleanor could cause a few scandals right this second if she chose to. Smug Mrs. Nowak's husband was secretly having an affair with his own sister-in-law, for she spotted the pair huddled together one evening in a dark restaurant downtown and had retreated hastily before they could see her. And Mr. Lechna, who passed the collection plate in church, pocketed several dollars each Sunday when he thought no one was looking. And would Mrs. Dombrowski guess that her husband was attracted to other men? He had come to the emergency room once to be stitched up when his Saturday-night boyfriend had jealously decided to show him who was the boss. He must have paid a pretty penny to get out of that mess. The next day, Mrs. Dombrowski had wailed that her husband had been attacked and robbed while out with the men for a few drinks. They all thought themselves above her mother who had real class and real dignity.

Noticing the girl's anger, Tekla took her off to the side.

"Eleanor control yourself. They mean well. Your mother does look beautiful, peaceful."

"How can she look beautiful? She's dead. Dead is ugly and cold."

"Eleanor, lie down for a while. You're overtired."

"I can't lie down. Why did you have to hold the wake here, in your home? It's barbarous. Alex is upstairs crying his heart out. He refuses to come down. Celia looks like hell. Irena claims she's going into labor and I know she isn't. Did you see the empty bottles of liquor in the kitchen? What is my father doing, hosting the world's gayest party. He came into the living room once for a minute, looked down at his wife, and went off to fortify himself with another drink. Everyone's eating and drinking. They came for a party, not to mourn my mother."

"It's the way things are done, Eleanor. No one will really grieve except you, me, your brother, and your sisters. Go up and rest, please. It's getting late. The funeral is early in the morning and people will be leaving soon. A few will stay all night with me."

Eleanor walked to the stairs, paying no attention to the newcomers arriving with more sacrificial offerings.

"Tell them the party's over after the funeral tomorrow."

Tekla shook her head sadly before joining the latest callers. Being the eldest, Eleanor had seen the greatest portion of her mother's anguish. It had made her cynical and right now Tekla couldn't find the right words of consolation.

A dank, bone-penetrating fog enveloped the slow moving line of family and friends walking to the grave site. As they trudged along the sodden grass, the autos that had brought them to the cemetery disappeared into the thick murky fog, and everyone huddled closer seeking comfort as the ghostly outlines of tombstones hovered around them. Alex clung to Eleanor and Celia's hands sobbing quietly. No one close to him had ever died and he felt alone and lost. Tekla walked between Bolie and Martha, clinging to their strong arms for support. Next came Jan and Beth, who had arrived late last night, Jan still in silent shock at losing his sister when he'd had no idea of the pain she was in no idea of what had led to her death until the early hours of the morning when Eleanor had filled him in. Surprisingly, he hadn't gone upstairs to thrash Roman. Instead he'd withdrawn further into a shell of isolation. Roman walked by himself, first in line after the priest who chanted a mournful prayer. Irena was with her husband Stan, head bowed, stumbling on the slick grass. Although the three sisters had spent hours calling several information centers in California, no one could help them locate Lydia. Since she'd left, the earth seemed to have swallowed her up. Not one post card or letter had ever arrived. Frustrated, Eleanor had called a halt to the futile search while Alex had stared at her, in awe. He'd never seen her lose her temper before and it was a bit frightening to see the venomous expression on her usually calm face.

Another fifteen minutes brought a conclusion to the

somber proceedings. The workers lowered the casket into the ground. Holding sodden handkerchiefs to their eyes, the small group filed back to the cars, making their way cautiously to the cemetery entrance as dull thuds of wet earth covered Dani forever.

Driving home, the lead car was forced to stop at a railroad crossing by a slow-moving freight train. The cortége waited a full ten minutes before being allowed to proceed.

Tekla made the sign of the cross.

"This means another death soon," she predicted. "It never fails. An obstacle on the way home from a funeral always foretells the death of someone close."

Alex and Celia looked up, frightened, but Eleanor appeared unconcerned.

"Stop your superstitious nonsense, Aunt. How can a train be an omen of death? It's nothing but an old wives' tale started by someone long ago who ran into such a situation. We were stopped by several red lights too. Is that supposed to bring bad luck?"

Tekla looked at her balefully.

"You'll see. Don't make fun of a serious superstition. You'll summon the evil spirits."

"Aunt, for God's sake. You're frightening Celia and Alex with your absurd folklore. That's enough for now please."

The rest of the ride home went by in silence, Tekla's lips pursed tight with indignation.

"We have to talk," Tekla said, pouring tea as they sat around her table. "We have to make plans. Celia, your mother told me before she died that you should go into the convent. She realized it was what you truly wanted, so of course you can go whenever arrangements are made."

Celia shook her head.

"Not yet. I'll stay to help take care of the house and Alex for a while longer. My calling can wait for a few years. They'll still have me whenever I'm ready to join them."

"But there's no need to wait, darling. I'll be here. Irena's not far away and Eleanor will be coming home on her days off. We can manage."

"No," Celia protested again. "I'd rather wait. I have to do my share too. Irena won't be of much help. She's too busy starting her own family and spending her free time visiting and gossiping. Eleanor will be too tired after working to do all the cleaning. And you," she glanced at Tekla, "will have your hands full enough watching over our father. He's going to keep cheating you. He'll feel you're too preoccupied worrying about us and take advantage of you."

"You're right there," Eleanor added. "Isn't there any way you can get him out of the business? Mama's not here anymore for him to abuse. I doubt if he'll bother with us. If he does, I swear I'll call the police and have him locked up."

Tekla decided now was the time to lay all her cards on the table. Eleanor and Celia were old enough to understand. Alex was out in the yard feeding the chickens.

"There's no way to be rid of Roman unless I buy him out and give him every penny I've saved over the years and that would leave me with nothing. When I gave him fifty percent of the business, I had to sign it over legally. My lawyer drew up the papers, so you see, half is your father's. I definitely will not buy him out. There would be nothing left for emergencies, and I'm not as young as I used to be. For years I had Bolie and Martha to help me but they're gone, and they wouldn't come back even though they are my good friends. I can'

348

handle the tavern and restaurant all by myself. There's too much work, and my arthritis is getting the best of me. When I was younger I had the energy to see the business grow and prosper. Lately I don't care all that much."

"Damn him," Eleanor cursed. "He's ruined everyone's life."

"Who are you talking about?" Alex asked, walking into the kitchen. "Who's ruined everyone's life? Papa?"

"No, honey, we're talking about someone you don't know."

Alex sat down desolate. "I miss Mama. What are we going to do?"

Eleanor put her arms around her brother. "I know, Al. We all do, but we have to go on, make her proud of us. There's nothing else we can do."

Jan and Beth stood up. They had to catch the train back to Detroit.

"Alex, why don't you come back with us?" Jan said. "You can stay for a few months or for as long as you like. Would you like to get away for a while to new surroundings? We'd be happy to have you."

Alex loved his uncle and aunt, but he blanched at the thought of leaving everything familiar, even for a short while. "No, Uncle Jan. I have to stay here so the family can all be together. I can do the heavy work like carrying up the coal. I'm needed here more."

Jan understood the desperation in his nephew's eyes and held him close. "You do whatever you feel is best, Al. I'm only a phone call away if you need me." He quickly pulled Beth after him when they'd said their goodbyes before the rage building up in him erupted in a violent outburst against Roman. He could almost feel the satisfaction he'd know by squeezing the bone and tissue of Roman's neck—crushing them with his hands.

Worse yet, he could feel the pull of the knife that lay on Tekla's table waiting for him to pick it up, to find Roman, and to plunge it deep into the black heart that was his core. His hands shook so while they sat at Tekla's table that he had to get away. After Jan and Beth left, the rest of the day was spent in silence, no one wanting to put grief aside, not yet. It was too soon, too difficult to do.

Two weeks later there was a terrible row downstairs, and Celia called Eleanor at the hospital, her voice quaking with fear. "El, can you come? Something awful is happening. Aunt and Papa are shouting at each other. Papa is calling her vile names, and I heard dishes breaking. I'm afraid to go down; Alex isn't home from school yet. What shall I do?"

"Celia, stay put. I'll have someone drive me home. I shouldn't be more than ten minutes."

Eleanor slammed down the phone, furious. Does he think he's going to start on Tekla now? I'll kill him first and spend the rest of my life in jail if I have to. She was a few minutes short of going off duty so she asked one of the ambulance drivers to give her a lift home. He quickly agreed and had her there in less than five minutes, his siren screaming until they reached Fox Street where Eleanor asked him to turn it off lest the neighbors stare out of their windows. As she went up the walk, she heard her father ranting loudly.

"Damn it, woman, I couldn't help it. It wasn't my fault. I was cheated, I tell you."

Eleanor opened her aunt's back door. "What's going on? The neighbors can hear you with their windows closed, and you've frightened Celia out of her wits."

Tekla stood next to the table, anger making the blood rush to her face. She pointed an accusing finger at Roman.

"He's lost half the tavern. He's gambled it away, the bastard. My life's work he gambled away, playing cards. It seems that I have a new partner, Lefty Kemp, of all people. Everyone despises him, almost as much as they despise this fool." She pointed again at Roman who cringed in his chair. "How can I have a partner like Lefty? It's impossible. Jesus, what have I done to deserve this stupid fool for a relative?"

"I couldn't help it," Roman wailed. "He caught me off guard when I'd had a little too much to drink. He kept bragging that he was a better card player than me and so I couldn't back away from a challenge. I think he cheated me. Besides I have reason to drink. I just lost a good wife. Have you no feelings?"

Eleanor looked at her father with loathing.

"I'm sure you miss your wife. You always treated her so well; you made such a good life for her. I'll bet she enjoyed it every time you hit her, especially the last time, the time that killed her. You're no better than a murderer! As for Lefty, he's only better at cheating than you, admit it. You probably thought you were going to take him for all his money and he surprised you. You're a fool. No. Worse yet, you're a totally incompetent drunk. Everyone's laughed at you for years. You and your drunken ugly whores, swaggering about like you owned the city. You might have been the ladies' man years ago when you fooled my mother, but you've lost whatever touch you had long ago." Eleanor picked up a cleaver that lay on the sink while Roman hastily backed away his chair, then fell to the floor where he lay staring as the blade came closer.

"Merciful heaven stop!" Tekla cried. "Eleanor stop!"

Eleanor lowered the deadly knife to her side.

"Don't worry, I'm not going to kill him. That would be an easy end to his miserable life." She looked at her

351

aunt. "See if you can get two men to move some furniture into the basement. That's where he's going to live. It's all refinished. You were going to rent it out once as a small apartment years ago before you decided to use it for storage space. There's heat and a sink and bathroom. He can live in the basement from now on. You're not part of this family anymore. Do you hear me?" she screamed at her father. "Am I getting through to you, you miserable bastard?"

"What? What do you want me to do?" Roman cried. "Live in the basement like a dog? Your own father? I told you I didn't think all this would happen. I didn't want to lose my share of the tavern. I refuse to live in the basement!"

"That's exactly what you're going to do. Your bed, your clothes, a table and chairs will be brought down. I don't want to see your face here or upstairs again, or I swear on Mama's grave I'll slit your throat. Don't think for one minute I can't do it. I'll have hundreds of opportunities when you're asleep, when you're drunk. I'll bide my time, but if you're not settled down there by tonight you're a dead man and I don't care if I have to go to jail. It would be worth it just to be rid of you."

"I'm your father," Roman screamed. "You're insane, talking to me like this."

She came closer with the cleaver. "You're not my father. You're the animal who happened to get my mother pregnant. That's all you are, all you'll ever be."

Roman scrambled up, backing toward the door. "The tavern—"

"You have no tavern," Eleanor interrupted. "You've lost any claim you had on it. Fend for yourself now. You're always bragging about how well off you are. You'll have a place to sleep and three meals a day that someone will bring down to you. That's all. It's more than you deserve. If you prefer you can get out altogether and live where you like."

Roman shuffled out the back door, defeated. His first-born had turned into a raging violent virago and he knew by the look in her eyes that she would kill him without a moment's hesitation, without any qualms. He'd live in the stupid basement until he could find another job and get away from them all. He and his son would live together in some fine apartment once he was on his feet again.

Eleanor dropped the knife, hands shaking as she sat in the nearest chair. "Don't you dare give him a single penny, Aunt. I mean it."

"Of course I won't. God how could he do this? There's no way I can stay in business with Lefty. I'll be forced to sell out to him."

"I'm sorry, what else can I say? I know you let my father in with you just to keep him away from Mama. I always heard the arguments late at night. He was never satisfied, always wanted more. If you sell out, will you get a fair price? Will you open another place?"

"No. I haven't the energy. I'm not sure about the price. I am sure Lefty will want my place all for himself. He doesn't need partners."

"Well, I'll help. I'm making better money now. We'll manage."

"Eleanor, I do have money in the bank. We'll have more than enough to live nicely, at least until Alex is old enough to work. You need your money if you want to go on with your courses."

"No, I insist. I can do my share. Don't let Celia know just yet what happened. She's not the kind to go out looking for a job. She'll only be terrified of working, meeting strangers. First let's see if we can get someone to move his things. I can't believe all this is happening.

353

Will there never be an end to his conniving? I'd prefer to throw him out of the house bodily, but there would only be more scandal. I imagine we're the talk of the neighborhood already. Whenever I walk down the street I can feel the looks of pity the neighbors are giving me. Oh, poor Mama. How did she take it all these years?" Eleanor paused to think. "Don't let Celia go down to give him his meals. She's terrified of him. He knows it and relishes tormenting her. Alex can bring them down. He and Lydia are the only ones that never bore the brunt of his temper. He loves Alex in his own curious way, not as his son but as some sort of link to carry on his name. I suppose we can forget Lydia. I doubt if she's even thinking about coming back home."

"Eleanor, what do I say to Lefty?"

"Let him make the first move. I'm sure he'll be at the tavern today with several witnesses to prove he's your new partner. Just try to keep a clear head. Wait him out and see what develops. Aunt, I'll be back in a few hours. I'm going to the nurses' home to get my things. I think it would be easier if I lived here."

"Eleanor, no. It's too inconvenient."

"No, it isn't. It's only a short ride to the hospital and when I'm on nights I'll get someone to drive me home. I'm thinking of transferring to another hospital anyway. Come upstairs after you close tonight. Tell me everything."

Tekla walked with leaden feet to the business she had once loved. If only Bolie were still with her she wouldn't feel so alone, so powerless. Lefty Kemp was too much for her to contend with. Already he owned a coal yard, a brewery on Archer Avenue that turned out a mediocre beer, a hardware store, and a bowling alley where his followers gathered nightly. Undoubtedly he wanted to add a good-size tavern to his holdings so he could push his own private label brew. The only good to come out of this mess was that Roman had finally met his match. She smiled sardonically. After years of having his way, of being what could be called the neighborhood bully, someone more odious had come along to oust him from his perch. Too bad she'd had to be hurt financially in the process or it would have been funny indeed.

As expected, after the dinner rush, Lefty and two of his friends walked in to survey the premises. He shook her hand politely.

"Pleased to meet you. I'm sure you've heard by now that I'm your partner? Your nephew foolishly refused to keep the stakes within his means. He lost fair and square. I have signed papers to prove it and witnesses to testify it was a fair game. The witnesses aren't all my friends either, some of them are regulars here. I didn't even know them until last night."

Tekla gave the proffered papers a quick glance. There was Roman's signature bold as brass giving up his fifty percent. "He's not my nephew. He's related through marriage only."

"That's right. I apologize. I've heard you're a smart businesswoman, and I never could figure out why you shared a profitable place with the likes of Roman Kawa. But I guess it's none of my business. Can we sit down and talk for a minute? I'd like to make you a proposition."

Tekla joined him and his friends in a far corner of the lounge. "I'm waiting to hear what you have to say."

"Well, first of all, I'd like you to let me buy you out. I'm willing to offer you a fair price. Actually, I'll give you more than the place is worth because there's going to be a rougher clientele hanging round and I wouldn't like to have a lady like you involved. It's not right for a

355

refined woman. I've had the building checked out by a real-estate man, and with the liquor you have on hand, the fixtures, the furniture, and other miscellaneous items, it's worth about four thousand dollars. I'll give you double that amount."

Tekla was surprised but she kept a look of detachment on her face. "What if I say no? What if I want to stay on?"

"You can always do that if you like, but as I said before, more men will be coming in and they'll be a rough lot. Are you sure you can take it? I'll be glad to have you, but you'll have to work as hard as I do."

"And if I sell out to you?"

"If you do, I have some grand plans for the place. I'd like to take out the restaurant completely. There's no money in food unless you raise the prices a lot higher than what they are and we have enough restaurants in the area. It's inconvenient. You have prize property here. There're two hundred men working at the soap factory, and truthfully, though I don't want it spread around just yet, I hear there're going to be two more factories opening up soon. Naturally all the men aren't going to patronize this tavern, but we'll get a fair share of the business. It's going to be very lucrative with this building sitting in the center of action so to speak. There are plenty of men waiting to plunk down some of their hard-earned money on a drink before going home, to seek female company, or to sit here awhile on payday after they've cashed their checks."

Tekla was horrified at being linked with dishonest hustling of drinks and probably women. For years she had run an honest business and even Roman had never cheated the men openly. There seemed to be no choice. Never would she stoop to Lefty's way of doing business. Her good name would be lost in short order.

"Let me think about it," she said rising.

"Sure, Miss Mrazek. Take all the time you want. I realize it isn't easy selling something you've built up all by yourself. I'll stop by in a few weeks and you can give me your answer. Will that be enough time?"

"Two weeks will be fine."

"Good. It's been a pleasure talking to you." He left with his friends, without another look at the surroundings so sure was he of her compliance.

"He knows I'll sell," Tekla told Eleanor later that night. "He was polite enough, but then why shouldn't he be? He's sure I won't be part of his schemes to entice the kind of customers I never wanted, and he was generous. I expected him to offer far less than the place is worth, but he actually doubled the price."

"Have you decided to sell then?"

"Yes, but I'll make him wait the full two weeks. No sense rushing things. Is Roman settled in the basement?"

"Yes. The two men you sent over were great. I went down myself to check, and he'll be quite comfortable. There's your old potbellied stove for heat, a bed, dresser, table and two chairs. I've already paid the men. Actually it's a better place than some people around here have. Alex brought down his supper, but he wasn't in so I told him to leave it on the table. He asked me a lot of questions, but he seemed to accept the fact that his father wants to live alone. He thinks Roman can't bear to sleep up here because of Mama's death, but I don't think his love for his father runs very deep. He loved Mama so and tried to intervene whenever Pa came home drunk."

"Eleanor, you're a marvel. You were always so quiet I never dreamed you could take control so efficiently."

Eleanor laughed. "Neither did I, but necessity works

357

wonders doesn't it?" Two weeks later, Eleanor went to work at the Michael Reese Medical Center. Thoughts of her mother had intruded whenever she'd entered the doors of Mercy Hospital. It held too many sad memories, so it was best to leave, and Michael Reese offered more opportunity. It was expanding rapidly. Although she had requested operating room duty, she had to spend time on the floors in various buildings first to get accustomed to her new surroundings. She staggered O.R. shifts for a week then floor duty the next. Now she was on the four-to-midnight shift, but she would get a lift home from one of the interns or orderlies. There were so many employees it wasn't difficult to find a ride if you posted a note on the bulletin board.

Depressed by thinking of all the time and effort she'd put into her business over the years, Tekla agreed to sell but she couldn't get used to the idea of having time on her hands. Still, it did feel good to relax in the late afternoon and to take a short nap before Alex came home from school. She found herself helping Celia keep both apartments clean, and she cooked the meals for everyone, including the dishes that were sent down to Roman. She knew he was sleeping in the basement for she heard stumbling noises late at night and when she went down to bring him something for breakfast she could hear him snoring loudly behind the curtains that partitioned off the sleeping area. She always laid the tray down with a loud bang to awaken him. But he was never home for lunch so she only had to worry about breakfast and supper which Alex usually brought down.

On a chilly evening late in autumn Tekla lay down for a nap but wakened abruptly when she heard dishes rattling in the kitchen. Celia peeked into the bedroom.

"Stay in bed aunt. I'm getting supper ready. Eleanor's left for the evening shift and Alex went to a friend's house, so there will only be you and me. I've made pork chops and mashed potatoes. They should be ready in half an hour. Rest, I'll call you when it's ready."

"Thank you, child. I feel rather poorly today. I have chills and I feel a little feverish."

"Then I'll heat up some of yesterday's soup and bring it to you in your room."

"No, no," Tekla protested. "I can get up and eat at the table with you. But I will rest awhile longer as long as you've already started."

Celia came back with a glass of water and two aspirin.

"I called Eleanor and she said you were to take these."

"Don't fuss so, Celia. I'll be just fine, but thank you. You would make an excellent nurse too, darling."

"No, I don't think so. I couldn't stand taking care of seriously sick people. I'd feel too sorry for them and get everything all mixed up."

Tekla swallowed the pills and dozed off again. Later she woke with a start. It seemed that hours had passed, but when she looked at the clock on the dresser only forty-five minutes had elapsed. Celia should have called her by now. Why was it so quiet in the kitchen? Oh, no. Celia wouldn't be so foolish as to take Roman's supper down. She had told her time and time again that either she or Alex would take care of that chore. Most likely Roman was browbeating her over some inconsequential matter, and Celia, being an obedient child, was afraid to leave before Roman had finished with his latest tirade. Tekla's chills had abated somewhat so she slipped a housedress over her nightgown and pulled a worn sweater over her shoulders.

"Let me go rescue the child," she muttered to herself, pushing her feet into worn slippers.

There was enough light left to make out the stairs leading to the basement and she hung onto the rail, walking down slowly. Her arthritis was acting up again, making her wince with pain each time she put her weight on another tread. A dim light was lit over the table, but she couldn't see Roman or Celia. Puzzled, she stood on the bottom step; then, faintly, she heard a quiet sobbing coming from the front of the basement. Pushing pain aside, she ran across the floor, clearly hearing Celia's pitiful sobs again. Pulling the string for brighter light Tekla saw the girl standing against the wall frozen with shock as her father loomed over her, his grotesque hands fondling her exposed breasts.

The top of Celia's dress was torn open to the waist, and the buttons lay scattered across the floor, shining like so many accusing eyes in the dim light. Roman didn't seem to notice the light nor did he hear Tekla approach, so engrossed was he in his sordid attempt to seduce his own daughter. In the seconds it took Tekla to reach him, she could hear him mumbling obscenities and the name Sophie over and over. His mind is rotted with alcohol, she thought wildly. Doesn't he realize it is his daughter standing in front of him, too afraid to scream or run away. Picking up the nearest thing at hand, the heavy plate holding his dinner, she brought it crashing down on Roman's head with all her strength. It cracked in half with a dull thud as it hit the back of his head and he turned around in astonishment, his eyes glazed and bloodshot with drink. He tried to speak, but fell to the floor and lay there with his legs crumpled beneath him.

Tekla ran to Celia and pulled the torn dress up around her arms.

"Celia, poor baby. Come with me, darling. Don't cry, it's all over. Come."

She placed her arm around Celia's shoulders as they made their way upstairs, leaving Roman sprawled awkwardly on the floor.

Celia sat in the kitchen, quivering from shock, until Tekla poured a trickle of brandy into a cup and put it to her lips.

"Drink this down."

Celia sputtered but she managed to swallow a small sip, and slowly her shaking subsided but tears continued to roll down her anguished face.

"Celia dear, I told you never to go down with your father's supper. Only Alex or I do that. You know your father picks on you for no reason. Why didn't you listen to my orders?" She kept her voice quiet and low to calm Celia down.

"You were sick and I wanted to save you a trip. I didn't even think he was home; it was so quiet. But when I put the plate on the table he came up from behind and grabbed me. I tried to get away, honestly I did, but he dragged me back toward the wall. I was so scared I couldn't move. Then he started calling me Sophie, and he sounded angry at me for leaving him. He tore my dress. I tried to get away again, but he slapped me and said he would kill me if I moved. He started to choke me then. Oh Aunt, what was he going to do? What's wrong with him?"

Tekla noticed the bruises beginning to swell on either side of Celia's neck.

"Quiet now, darling. Your father's a very sick man. Something's terribly wrong with his mind. Most likely the liquor he's drunk over the years has damaged it.

361

You didn't do anything wrong, child. Your father is a perverted man."

Celia sobbed louder. "Did I commit a sin? Must I tell the priest what happened? I couldn't, I just couldn't."

"No. You did nothing wrong, I tell you. Celia dear, listen to me. You have your heart set on being a nun and you shall be. I'm making the arrangements this week and you shall have your heart's desire. I won't listen to any more protests. I've told you and Eleanor that I can manage. Why should you wait if you're sure you want to enter the convent? You're going soon, that is if you still want to. Without the tavern I have nothing but free time on my hands so taking care of the house will be simple."

Celia laid her head on Tekla's shoulder. "Of course I want to. I want it more than anything in the world, but I feel guilty leaving you alone with only Alex to protect you. Eleanor's not always home."

"Darling, I'm well able to protect myself, I assure you. Celia, I hate to say this, but how long do you think your father will last? I swear his insides are rotted by all the alcohol he's consumed over the years. I don't think he'll be around too much longer to plague us, and if that's God's will, it's for the best."

"You're sure? If you're sure then I'd love to go. I'll be so happy at the convent."

"It's settled. Now why don't you wash up and go to bed unless you want something to eat first."

"No, Aunt. I'm not hungry, just tired and scared. Thank you for saving my life."

"No one will hurt you ever again, I promise. Go upstairs and have Alex lock the door as soon as he comes home. He should be here any minute now. Celia, it would be best if we didn't mention this to Eleanor. Wear your blouse with the high neckline and she won't

362

notice the bruises. It would only upset her, so we'll keep it our secret. Good night, dear."

Celia kissed her aunt on the cheek.

"Good night. I love you and I won't say a word; it's too embarrassing."

Tekla sat at her table consumed with anger. She didn't dare tell Eleanor about this. Eleanor would kill Roman for sure. She thought she had heard a woman's voice down in the basement the other night. He must be bringing his whores home with him. Tekla could imagine the busybodies peeking out of their windows, scandalized at his debauchery. God forbid if they somehow got wind that he had tried to attack his own daughter. What perversion would he try next?

"This can't go on," she moaned.

Someone had to stop Roman. For too long he had gone through life hurting people unmercifully and he was getting worse. What little conscience he'd ever had was long gone. He was still strong, even while drinking, and he could drag some unfortunate child down into the basement one day. It was a possibility for he liked women, the younger the better, and he thought they all felt the same about him. He lived in a fantasy land, thinking himself still young and good-looking, and now he was without funds to pay for women.

Tekla climbed upstairs to tuck Celia and Alex in bed. After midnight she heard Eleanor climb the stairs and relock the door; still she sat in the same chair racking her brains for a way to get Roman out of their lives forever.

Help me God, please, she prayed. What shall I do? She walked into her bedroom to light a vigil candle for God's help and then her eyes fastened on the two drapery cords on her bedroom window. She stared at them for minutes before she took them off and slowly ran them between her fingers. No one will help me. It's hopeless. We must all learn to help ourselves. I can't ask God to make a man drop off the face of the earth.

Once again she made her way to the basement, the drapery cords held tightly in one hand. During her absence Roman must have regained consciousness for he now lay sprawled on his back in bed, snoring loudly. His bedclothes reeked with the odor of excrement. Vivid lights flashed before Tekla's eyes as she watched this demon at rest as though nothing had happened.

"Filthy pig," she moaned. "Useless pig. You've not done one decent thing in your whole life. You've killed my niece, hated your daughters—almost raped one— cheated, lied, stolen. It has to stop. Next time I may not be around to save someone you've violated or I won't have the strength. It must stop now."

Calmly she tied one of Roman's wrists to the bed post with one cord and then walked around the bed to tie the other. He lay there not moving, only snoring louder as yellow spittle ran down one side of his face. Tekla's fingers burned as she touched him. It was like touching a demon straight from the bowels of hell.

"Forgive me God, but I have to do this before some- one I love does it instead." She picked up the pillow that had dropped to the floor and held it tightly over Roman's face blocking out any incoming air, pressing down harder and harder. Roman struggled weakly at first and tried to scream but the sound stayed muffled beneath the thick down of the pillow. Tekla started counting, her mind a blank. She counted slowly to three hundred. His writhing leg movement had stopped long ago so she pulled the pillow from his face at last, not looking down. She put the pillow beside his head and untied his wrists; then she shut off the lights, her heart pounding furiously as the flashing lights dancing inside her brain subsided.

Upstairs, she put the drapery cords back in place and sat on her bed, her thoughts in wild disorder. I'm a murderess, she thought. I've committed the most deadly sin and will never be forgiven. I have no hope of meeting Józef in heaven, of being reunited with my family. I am a doomed woman from this moment forward with only the fires of hell to look forward to.

All that night she sat in bed staring at nothing, unable to pray, cry, or beg God's forgiveness. The first streaks of dawn broke, sending a glimmer of light into the room. Still she sat. At seven she washed mechanically and put on a fresh housedress. Thumping on the ceiling with a broom, she woke Celia and Alex as usual and started to prepare breakfast: oatmeal, toast, and coffee. Alex offered to carry his father's tray down, but Tekla shooed him off to school and Celia off to church where she spent her mornings cleaning and polishing the altar pieces after mass.

After they left Tekla fixed a tray for Roman as usual, setting out a covered bowl of hot oatmeal, a steaming cup of coffee, and several slices of toast. She covered the tray with a clean towel and went down slowly, careful not to spill a drop. Setting the tray down on the table and turning on the light she walked over to the bed. Roman lay as she had left him the night before. She touched his hand. It was cold and stiff.

She climbed up the two flights of stairs and woke Eleanor. "Ellie, get up. Something's happened to your father. I think he's dead."

"What?" Eleanor woke with a start. "Dead?"

"I went down to bring his breakfast and I think he's dead. Usually I just leave it on the table, but the room smelled so badly I thought he was sick in the night and I wanted to check. He's there, cold as marble, and won't wake up."

Eleanor bounded out from under the covers, throwing on a robe.

"Wait here. I'll be right back," she said.

She ran down the back stairs and sure enough Tekla was right. He was dead. She looked down at her father with no feeling and thought of the past. Somehow she had thought her father would live forever like the evil vampires who preyed on helpless people. She whispered her final words to him.

"So it's finally over. If you didn't beat my mother she would have been alive and happy to be a widow, but you saw to it she went before you. Did you think you would live to a ripe old age, drinking and whoring until you were in your dotage? The devil's finally claimed you for his own." She threw the cover over his face and left the basement.

"He's gone," she said to Tekla.

"Shall we call the undertaker first?"

"No, we'll need a death certificate signed. I'll call Dr. Sidney Levine. He's sort of a friend of mine over at Reese. Then we'll call the undertaker."

"I don't want him waked out in the house," Tekla said. "He can be at the chapel. Eleanor will you see to the arrangements? Just get what's necessary to bury him. No frills. The sooner it's over with the better."

Sidney came shortly after Eleanor's call and examined Roman's body. "El, my condolences. From our talks at the cafeteria I gather there was no love lost between you and your father, but I presume it's still a shock. With just a cursory examination I'd say it was a coronary. But if you like I'll request an autopsy."

"No, Sid. Do we have to go through all that? I'd rather not. It would be too upsetting for the family."

"Of course, El, whatever you want. I'll sign the certificate and you can begin making preparations. El, is there anything else I can do?"

"No thank you, Sid. You're a good friend. Thanks. How about some coffee before you leave?"

"No, not now. I'm sure you'll be busy. You have a few rough days ahead of you. I'll see you when you get back to work."

"Thanks again, Sid. I appreciate your help."

Roman was laid out for one night only, highly unusual in a community where the custom called for two or three days. Eleanor explained that one night was enough because Alex and Celia had lost both their parents within a few months and she wanted to spare them any unnecessary grief.

Tekla took to her bed.

"Eleanor, I don't feel well. Can you call your doctor friend and ask him to come over, please?"

Sid came again and diagnosed pneumonia. He ordered Tekla to stay in bed. He wanted to admit her to the hospital, but Tekla refused to budge, thoroughly alarmed at the thought of being in the hospital where she would probably be given drugs which might cause her to lose control and talk.

"Sid, leave her be," Eleanor pleaded. "She's frightened of hospitals ever since my mother died. I'll take two weeks off and care for her myself. A friend of ours can take over until after the funeral, and then I'll do the rest. Just tell me what medication to give her."

Sid left several prescriptions and promised to come back in two days to check on the patient. "It's not too serious, El. Only one lung is infected. It should clear up in a week or two. She'll be good as new."

Eleanor came home after the funeral and sent Anna, their neighbor, home with thanks for her help. She told Alex to stay upstairs until his aunt was better and asked

Celia to begin packing. The sisters of Notre Dame were expecting her in two days. She was to take a train to Wisconsin to begin her novitiate.

"Eleanor, I can stay home awhile longer until aunt's on her feet again."

"No, Celia. Absolutely not. If you put it off again something else will come up and you'll never have what you want. Everything's arranged. You'll leave as planned. I'm sure you'll be happier with the sisters. They'll be keeping you pretty busy and that will get your mind off mourning. Come on." She hugged her sister. "Start packing."

Downstairs, she gave Tekla her medicine and sat next to her on the bed.

"Everything went well. I hope you don't mind but I didn't bury him next to Mama. I couldn't. He's in another plot about fifty yards away. I couldn't bear to see them lying side by side. Some of the people seemed shocked, but I don't care. It will give them something to talk about for a week or two, I guess. Let them talk."

"You did right," Tekla said weakly. "If I were well I would have done the same thing. Where are Celia and Alex?"

"Celia's packing. I told her she was to leave as scheduled. Alex is cleaning out the basement with two of his friends. They offered to do it so I let them."

Tekla clasped her hands together under the covers. Good. From what she could gather Celia had no inkling of how her father had died. None of them did. They accepted the death as a natural one. At first Tekla had planned to turn herself in to the police so they could punish her. But then, lying in bed, feverish and ill, she had decided it would be better if her nieces and nephew never learned that their aunt was nothing more than a murderess. God would punish her instead.

Eleanor breathed a loud sigh of relief. "It's over. We

can pick up the pieces and go on. Guess what?" She laughed. "On the way home from the cemetery we weren't stopped by a single train. There were none of your omens of death."

"Don't laugh, Eleanor. That's a good sign. Your lives will run smoothly now."

Chapter Ten

"El, Tex." Alex bounded into the kitchen after school, eyes bright with excitement. "You'll never guess what happened today."

"Calm down," said Tekla. "What's all the shouting about? And stop calling me by that ridiculous name."

"But the name fits you. Tekla, Tek, Texas. You're just like the pioneer women who settled in the west, strong as the state of Texas." He laughed, giving her a big bear hug, and sat on a chair poking cookies into his mouth. "I can't tell you unless you both promise to keep it a secret. No one's to know but my immediate family."

Eleanor put her hands on her hips. "We are your family. What's wrong with you?"

"First, promise."

"All right, we promise," Tekla and Eleanor answered together.

"Well, remember when we were making plans about where I should go to high school and we decided it would be better if I went to the public school so it wouldn't cost so much?"

"Yes but—"

"Wait. Let me explain. Today the principal called me

371

to her office and said I had won a full four-year scholarship to De La Salle. A few of the kids whose parents have money are going there and now I can too. It's a full scholarship that covers tuition, books, fees—everything. All I'll need is bus fare. I can bring my own lunch."

"Alex, that's wonderful," Eleanor praised. "It's worth a great deal of money. How on earth did you manage it? I know you're a smart boy, but I've never heard of anyone getting a full four-year scholarship from St. Mary's."

"I know. It's the first time. Isn't it great news?"

"Then why are you to keep it a secret?"

"I don't know exactly, but it was one of the conditions. The man donating the money doesn't want any publicity. He's contributing a few scholarships, one to our school and two or three others. I don't know the names of the other schools involved."

"Well then," Tekla said, "congratulations. It's where I wanted to send you in the first place, but the tuition was rather high. Now that I have no business to fall back on and the cost of everything is going sky high, money is pretty tight."

Alex popped another cookie into his mouth. "Later I'll write Celia. I don't think we should tell Irena. She's got a big mouth and can't keep a secret. I have to go now. Baseball practice starts in five minutes."

Tekla and Eleanor looked at each other after Alex slammed out the back door in high spirits.

"Aunt, something sounds terribly suspicious. Do you know what a four-year complete scholarship is worth? I realize Alex is bright and probably deserves it, but why the secrecy?"

"I have no idea. Do you think you should go see the principal and ask some questions?"

"That's exactly what I'll do. In fact I think I'll go now."

Twenty minutes later, Eleanor found the principal, Sister Delphina, still in her office sorting through stacks of paperwork.

"Eleanor, how nice to see you. I suppose Alex came home and told you the good news?"

"Yes, and it's left us puzzled. Who on earth would give away a good deal of money and then ask that his generosity be kept a deep secret? Kids like to brag to their friends. Who donated this money?"

"Eleanor, I'm sorry but I'm not at liberty to say. I can only tell you it came from a highly unexpected source. The man is wealthy, I can tell you that much. He seems to be truly interested in helping several Chicago children; children who are bright and who he thinks will go far in life. Alex wasn't the only one singled out. I understand others received the same bounty. Personally, I think it's worth the secrecy to give Alex the benefit of a good education. He'll learn far more in a well-disciplined Catholic school than he would in a public one where there are too many distractions and they aren't strict enough."

"You've met this man then?" Eleanor asked.

"No, actually I haven't. He called the pastor and asked for an appointment. When he came he asked Father Lojak if he could look over the grades of this year's graduating class. Each student was asked to write a composition on what he wanted from life. Alex's turned out to be the best. Of course, that didn't surprise me. That, along with his excellent grades, earned him the reward."

"May I see the composition Alex wrote?"

Sister Delphina looked apologetic. "I'm sorry, but the gentleman took it with him. I can tell you though

373

that Alex basically wrote that he wanted to become an attorney and to help people in all walks of life. He outlined various ways he would do this given the chance, and his writing was very mature for a boy his age. Didn't he say anything about it at home?"

"No, he didn't, but he may have thought nothing would come of it."

Eleanor picked up her purse, thanking the principal for her time. She felt better about accepting a stranger's generosity. If a wealthy philanthropist insisted on helping some children better themselves, he must be a good man. If he was publicity shy and wanted to keep it a secret, that was his business. Alex would reap the benefits.

Tekla was in a pensive mood one Sunday afternoon a few weeks later. "Eleanor, why don't you marry one of those nice doctors you're bringing home to dinner every so often. Sid Levine has been here more than the rest, and even though he is Jewish he is a nice young man. You seem to like him a lot too. He makes you happy, your interests seem to be the same, and you make a nice couple."

"Sid is just a friend, my best friend. As for marriage, I'd rather be a spinster with no responsibilities except for myself. I like doing what I please. You have to follow orders at work, but not in your private life. That suits me just fine."

"Eleanor, there are good marriages. Just because your mother and father had one of the worst doesn't mean you'll find yourself in the same predicament. You're not a young girl but a mature woman who knows what kind of man will make a good partner."

"They all change after you marry them. The first few years might be fine but then everything goes downhill. Husbands make boring demands—iron their shirts, make breakfast, keep the children quiet—all because they bring home their paychecks and think the money

374

entitles them to be waited on hand and foot. That's not for me. I know there are happy marriages; Irena is well satisfied with hers. She dotes on Stan and their two children, but she's content to stay home cooking, cleaning and washing. I wouldn't be. Sid and I understand each other, understand that all we can be is friends. His parents are deeply religious and would sit shiva for him if they even thought he was going out with a goyim."

"Eleanor, you're saying words I don't understand."

"We're goyim, Aunt. That means we're not Jewish. His parents would treat him as dead and say mourning prayers if he married someone not of his faith."

"That's ridiculous. You're a fine woman. They should take you to their hearts and he happy for their son. I've never heard of such nonsense. I realize there are people here who would be scandalized if you married someone of the Jewish faith, but gossip never bothered you before. I certainly wouldn't turn against you. Why, Alex never gave his religion a thought."

"Alex? How does Alex fit into our conversation? Aunt, I love you dearly but I think your mind is beginning to wander a bit."

Tekla could have slapped her own face. She had almost let the first Alex's name out of the bag without thinking, and after all these years too. Thank God Dani had named her son Alex. Let Eleanor think she was getting senile. She probably would be soon enough. Age was beginning to creep up on her with distressing speed. She was in her late sixties and didn't relish dying. When she did, she expected to be cast into hell for her heinous crime and she feared hell with a passion, cringing at the thought of being with the dregs of humanity for all eternity. The thought of dying made her so nervous she fought to keep moving briskly, working in the house till every corner shone with polish, pushing away her arthritic pain and tiredness resolutely. If she kept moving she would feel healthier and therefore live longer, thereby prolonging the time until the day when the black angel came to claim her.

"My mind is not wandering, Eleanor. I was just wondering where Alex is. It's almost dinner time."

"He's baby-sitting for Irena. She and Stan went downtown to see a movie and a stage show at the Chicago Theater."

"What a waste of time. I've never seen a movie and don't ever want to. Everyone raves about how wonderful they are. They can't possibly be that fantastic."

"I'm going to take you to one right after dinner, and this time there will be no excuse to stay away. You should be ashamed of yourself, afraid of going to see a film. You'll have a marvelous time."

"I don't like sitting in the dark with a crowd of people. I'll suffocate. There won't be enough air. People were trapped in a theater fire years ago and they all died."

"There you go again. Let's eat. We'll leave something on the stove for Alex, then get dressed. If you feel faint I promise you we'll leave. Let's walk over to the Ramova. It's more elegant than the Eagle and the seats are more comfortable."

"I'm rather tired tonight. I thought I'd lie down after eating and rest for a while."

"You're not getting out of it this time. We're going."

Eleanor paid for the tickets while Tekla clung to her arm for she didn't know what to expect. They handed the tickets to the man at the door and entered a rather large lobby where two girls were busily selling something from behind a large counter.

"Something smells very good," Tekla admitted grudgingly.

"It's pop corn, I'll buy us a box."

There were five doors, all closed. Tekla wondered if the movie was taking place behind these formidable barriers. An usher announced that the feature would begin in five minutes and led Tekla and Eleanor down the center aisle to their seats in the middle of the theater. He lit his flashlight so they might seat themselves with the least amount of fuss.

"Good," Eleanor whispered. "We have aisle seats. if you feel like leaving after the movie starts we won't make a commotion and disturb anyone."

Loud music suddenly erupted and Tekla jumped in her seat.

"What's that? Where is it coming from?"

"Shush," Eleanor warned. "No loud talking. The movie's beginning."

Tekla stared around her. The theater was rather ornate, with wrought iron balconies. The tiny white lights high up in the ceiling looked like stars twinkling in the heavens. A large picture emerged on the giant-size screen, giving the title of the movie. *Gone with the Wind.* Tekla's nerves were shattered twice during the film. Once, when she thought the running horses were going to leap right off the screen onto the stage and trample them to death, she ducked behind the seat in front of her, but Eleanor laughed and explained it was all make-believe. Seeing no one else shrinking with fright, Tekla was ashamed of her stupidity. Then when Atlanta was burning and the flames were leaping high, she almost could feel the heat. She looked around suspiciously, but everyone around her was mesmerized by the unfolding drama so she settled happily into the story eating her popcorn slowly, engrossed in what was taking place.

"Well, did you like it?" Eleanor asked as they left the theater. "You didn't say a word so you must have."

"I never thought a movie could be so interesting. I don't know why I was frightened of going in the first place. Thank you, Eleanor. It was a real treat."

From then on Tekla was addicted. Week after week she went to the movies, whenever the feature changed. If the Ramova Theater held the same picture over for two weeks, then she walked to the Milda or the Eagle which was closest to her home, but the Ramova remained her favorite. She began collecting the dishes that were given away every Wednesday evening and soon the pantry shelves were crammed with plates, cups, and saucers until they could hold no more. She bought a china cabinet for the dining room and transferred some of her most prized treasures there. Eleanor helped her move the things on her day off.

"I didn't realize what I was getting you into when I took you to the movies for the first time. My God, you have enough plates to feed an army. You don't have to take them, you know. You can see the movie and decline the plates."

"Why should I? I'm paying to get in so I might as well accept what they're offering. They're beautiful dishes. Last night I saw *Dracula* and I didn't like it that much. I was scared all the way home, expecting a vampire to pop out of a gangway and attack me. It's a good thing I met Mr. Sidulski. He walked me the rest of the way home and I felt quite safe. Your mother used to tell me about the movies she saw on her outings, but they never sounded too exciting or maybe I just wasn't paying attention to what she was telling me."

"Well, you sure are making up for lost time now, aren't you?" Eleanor kissed her aunt. "I'm glad you've found some enjoyment. You can't keep working constantly. Everyone needs time to relax a little."

When Tekla was at the movies she forgot for a time the ever-present sword hanging over her head, and instead of nightmares when she went to bed, she usually dreamed about the leading men and women and the stories they portrayed on the giant screen. She fell in love with them all and saw everything: comedies, westerns, love stories, and musical extravaganzas. Musicals were her favorites. The colorful costumes, the singing, lulled her into a comfortable haze. Whenever a new one was booked she sat through two showings. Only then did she feel she was getting her money's worth.

Something called television was making its debut but Tekla refused to buy one on time payments. The screen was far too small and the picture was only a fuzzy black and white. In her opinion television would never compare to the rich dramas filling the movie theaters.

Jan still came to visit twice a year, before Christmas and in August. He and Beth were happy and their children, John and Susan, were well mannered, but he remained engrossed in his work. He was employed by the Cadillac division now as a design engineer after putting himself through countless hours of night classes. His family was indeed proud of him for he commanded a highly respectable salary. But he considered his present position only a stepping stone to something bigger and better.

When he came for his latest Christmas visit, he was stunned by a letter he'd received through various channels from Poland that very week, although the letter was dated months earlier. He showed it to his family after dinner.

"Do you believe this? Lottie Czerny died feeling guilty about her husband. There's two hundred dollars waiting for me in a bank in Gdansk. Whenever I care to go back I can pick it up. Can you imagine? It would cost me twice as much to get back there and only God knows what price in frustration and time wasted. What a farce! Lottie offering me money for my father's life."

"She didn't know what her husband did until you told her," Tekla stated quietly. "She must have felt very guilty indeed after you left, and this was the only way she felt she could repay you. Don't judge her harshly, Jan. She wasn't the guilty party."

"Then she never should have left me the money. It would have been far better had she forgotten us before she died."

"What will you do?" Eleanor asked.

"Nothing. There's a war going on and the money's probably been confiscated. Anyway, I'll write to the bank instructing them to give the money to the orphanage in Gdansk, that is if the bank's still in business. It's not worth the trouble to get it out. There are too many formalities, and the war makes it impossible."

Tekla took Jan aside as everyone was getting ready for bed.

"Jan, you must learn to forgive. For too long now you've kept bitterness in your heart and it's eating away at you. You have a lovely wife and family, and you're a good father and husband, but I feel something is missing from your life. You work too many hours for a family man. You drive yourself too hard to forget what's buried deep in your heart. You'll only find true peace when you can forgive Louis for what he did so many years ago. You have let your bitterness grow like a cancer, and soon it will eat all of you. What Louis did was terribly wrong, I know this for wasn't it my only brother he killed? But it's over and done with. Your resentment won't bring Casimir back so let it go, Jan, please. Forgive deep in your heart and forget. You'll find serenity."

"My dearest Aunt, how can you possibly expect me to forgive and forget? Why should I forget?"

Tears welled up in Tekla's fading blue eyes.

"Jan, I've done wrong in my life too, a terrible wrong, and it would be so peaceful if I could find forgiveness. That's why I ask you to forgive Louis. His poor tormented soul will be at rest if you'll only forgive him. I have."

Jan laughed.

"Don't be ridiculous. What terrible sin have you committed? Cheated a shopkeeper out of a dollar? Missed mass on a Sunday or, heaven forbid, did you weaken and eat meat on Friday perhaps?" He put his arms around his aging aunt's shoulders. "You're the most saintly woman I know. Don't tell me about your venial sins." He kissed her cheek. "Good night, love."

"I'm not a liar, Jan. When I say I've done wrong, I have. Don't mock me. Promise me you'll think of forgiveness?"

"All right then. If you insist I'll think about it, and when I make a decision you'll be the first to know. Does that satisfy you?"

"No, it doesn't but it's a beginning. Good night, Jan. Kiss the children for me and say good night to Beth."

The second world war was being waged, but Tekla's family was spared active involvement. Of course they bought war bonds, collected scrap metal, and gave up precious ration stamps to neighbors more in need, but luckily, the men in the family didn't have to go overseas. Jan was involved in essential war work and was granted a deferment even though he wanted to enlist and fight for his country. Stan, Irena's husband was classified 4F and felt bitter over the classification. He desperately wanted to prove himself on the battlefield, but he had been born with one slightly deformed leg, which left him with a permanent limp, and the government decided he would remain at home and work.

Stan, Irena felt, wouldn't be the same until the war was over and something besides the latest news of the struggle filled the newspapers and radio.

Although he volunteered as an air raid warden and helped raise thousands of dollars in war-bond money, he still felt he wasn't doing his duty. Irena and the children sympathized with him. They praised his efforts at fund raising and his diligent duty, and this mollified him somewhat. Not one person in the neighborhood called him a draft dodger because they knew him too well; he had been born and raised in this very section of the city. They admired him for the long hours he put in and they respected his patriotism. Strangers, seeing him walking, naturally thought he'd been wounded in the war so no spiteful names were whispered behind his back.

Alex, of course, was too young to join the army, although he did try to enlist once. A kind but stern sergeant brought him home, warning him in front of his sister and aunt that it was a serious offense to lie about one's age.

Eleanor was furious.

"Alex, how could you be so foolish? You're far too young to be involved. Didn't you stop to realize how we would worry about you? You've years ahead of you. When you're grown there might be another war. I pray there never is, but you will have your chance to fight. Perhaps not on a real battlefield, but in other ways as you grow older. Just keep on with your schooling and forget about this nonsense of joining up."

Alex's face lit with a stubborn light.

"When I'm of age, if the war is still going on I shall join up. You can't stop me then."

"When you're of age I won't try to stop you, but you're not old enough now so forget it." Besides working at Michael Reese Hospital, Eleanor volunteered twenty hours a week at the Veterans' Hospital. "I wish I could take you with me to the hospital and let you see how gory war really is. You should see how some of our men are returning from the fighting: blind, maimed, crippled. You wouldn't think war so glamorous then. You should smell rotting flesh, crusting wounds. It's horrid." Eleanor burst into tears. "You've no idea."

Alex was immediately sorry for being so cruel.

"El, I'm sorry. Please stop crying. I promise I won't do anything stupid unless we talk about it first. Okay?"

His sister dried her tears with her hand. "Thank you Alex."

"You're working too hard, El. You put in enough hours at Reese. You don't have to go to the Veterans' Hospital too."

"I know. I hardly get a chance to see you lately. Let's go on a real vacation, all three of us—you, Tekla and I. I'll take a week off and we can visit Celia at the convent in Wisconsin and relax for a few days on the lake. How does that sound?"

"That's great, El. When can we leave?"

"In a month when school lets out. We can celebrate the end of your first year in high school. You deserve a break for getting such good grades and not missing one day of school. We can ask permission from the convent for Celia to stay with us at the resort, at least for two days."

When the school year ended they enjoyed spending two days with Celia at a rustic inn deep in Wisconsin's heartland. From Celia's monthly letters they knew she was happy with her calling, and seeing her in person, this proved to be true. There was a serenity on her face that bespoke peace. Gone were the traces of fear that had usually strained her pretty face. She laughed with them, happy to see her family yet impatient to go back to where she felt she belonged.

Eleanor relaxed and renewed her strength so she could go back to her regular job and continue her volunteer work whenever she had time available. Alex loved swimming and horseback riding, and he learned how to play tennis. Tekla seemed to be the only disgruntled vacationer. She was happy to be with Celia for two days, then she became bored with the rural setting and eagerly awaited their return so she could go back to her favorite pastime, the movies. The inn held bingo games, but after one session Tekla hotly declared bingo a farce; one got one's hopes up to win only to lose when the caller cried out the wrong number.

Peace came at long last and the country celebrated the end of hostilities with rounds of parties. Neighbors whose sons had returned home safe and sound took their banners from their windows while those who had lost sons left the stars hanging for all to see so others might remember that not everyone was overjoyed.

Shortly after the war Alex graduated at the top of the class of 1947. As the school band played "Pomp and Circumstance," his family stood proudly in the audience. They gasped with surprise as the announcement of scholarships was made. It seemed their brilliant Alex had a choice of two universities, an honor won through his scholastic achievements. He could either go to the University of Chicago or DePaul University, both prestigious institutions, although the scholarship to the University of Chicago offered more benefits. Alex winked at his family during the proceedings, and they knew he had hoarded this secret for a long time, waiting to surprise them all.

In honor of her great-nephew's commencement, Tekla held a party at her old tavern, with Lefty's permission of course. He gallantly closed the place on Sunday from one till six while family, friends, and neighbors joined in the celebration. Jan, Beth, and the children came from Detroit; Carmella and her husband from the west side; Sid and several nurses and doctors from Reese. Food and drink flowed freely, but Lefty wouldn't hear of Tekla footing the bill.

"It's my treat," he insisted. "You sold me a very profitable business and I can afford to be generous."

Indeed, Lefty proved to be quite courteous and respectful to Tekla, which surprised her for she had heard many stories of his shady dealings. He made it a point to visit her at least twice a year, always asking if she needed anything and bringing small gifts. He even invited her to come and see the remodeled tavern several times, but she had refused every invitation until she needed more space for Alex's party. She didn't at all like the way the tavern looked. Dim lights and shiny chrome had replaced the highly varnished wood and a glaring jukebox poured out raucous music. Without its huge kitchen, the place looked like a totally new establishment. Food was brought in for the party by a caterer. Tekla knew it didn't taste as good as her home-cooked delicacies, but it was free and she appreciated Lefty's bounty.

Whenever Tekla looked at Alex she was stunned by his handsomeness, his vibrancy and enthusiasm for life. Alex now stood six feet tall, his hair so dark a brown it almost looked black. His eyes were a searching deep brown. Tekla imagined his real father must have looked remarkably like this when he was young, but with prejudice, she decided her Alex was much more handsome. After all, she had helped raise Alex.

Tekla had time to dwell on the past a great deal these days. Her arthritis had worsened to the point where she could barely hobble around the house, but she kept trying to do for herself. Her outings were curtailed to sunny dry days, for damp humid weather made her ache unbearably.

Alex earned extra money after school, despite the long hours of study he put in for his classes at the university. He helped the alderman, running errands. With that money and what Jan sent from time to time, he was able to buy a jalopy and he used it to go back and forth from school, even taking Tekla to the cemetery on some Sundays so she could conscientiously keep the graves of her loved ones neat and well planted with seasonal flowers. Not once did she go near Roman's grave. Alex repeatedly asked her why, but finally he stopped when she refused to answer time and time again. While he waited for her to trim weeds he would amble over to Roman's grave to trim the grass the caretakers had overlooked or to plant a fresh flower.

"You hated him didn't you?" Alex said accusingly one day. "I don't remember too much about my father, only that he drank a great deal and fought with Mama a lot. Why? Why did he always want to fight with her when she was so good to him?"

"Some men aren't happy with good women, Alex. Your mother, dear sweet thing that she was, wasn't meant for someone like Roman. She deserved a good man. No, Alex, I didn't like your father. I knew he was wrong from the very beginning, but your mother thought she loved him. By the time she realized she wasn't going to change him, it was too late. She didn't believe in divorce you know. She might have divorced him, given more time, but time was taken away from her. Such a shame. She was so beautiful and she loved all her children, even Lydia whom we've never heard from since the day she left, though they say a bad penny always turns up. I won't be surprised if one day she comes back."

"Where do you think she is now?" Alex asked, putting the garden tools in the trunk of the battered car. "I

386

hardly remember what my sister looks like."

"She left for California. That's all any of us knows. She could have had the decency to write once in a while but Lydia was always selfish, just like her father. She wanted excitement and money, and she couldn't find them here."

Alex became more and more involved in politics. Besides his law studies, political news was his main topic of conversation at the dinner table. Eleanor and Tekla were constantly told of the wheelings and dealings of politicians, and were sometimes shocked at what went on behind the scenes. Alex was promoted to screening phone calls, delivering campaign literature, even writing some of it himself. He helped escort voters to the polls on election day, seeing that they were safely brought in and returned home when the weather was foul. Alderman Flynn depended on him more and more, and Alex became his trusted confidant, getting deeply involved with the hundreds of problems in the 11th Ward. He declined the honor of becoming a precinct captain; yet many people needing political favors came to him, knowing if help were possible Alex would try his best to put the right word in the right ear. Through Alderman Flynn Alex came to know just about every other alderman in the city. He knew the boundary lines of the wards as well as he knew the streets of his Bridgeport neighborhood. He knew the ins and outs of city hall and could immediately walk to any office without once looking at the directory in the lobby. Politics was in his blood, politics and the law.

At school, his life was hectic. There never seemed to be enough hours in the day to accomplish all that needed to be done. Alex was one year away from getting his law degree; his goal glistened on the horizon. He was now certain that one day he would run for office. In what capacity he wasn't certain yet but, the seed of determination was well planted.

He had many friends at the university but saw them only during the day, often wondering why they even bothered with him for he seldom joined them for an evening out. Still, he remained popular.

Norm Sullivan, a fellow law student who was Alex's friend, hailed him one day as he came out of his last class.

"Hey, Al. You going to honor us with your presence at the faculty-student costume party tonight? Bailey's in charge of refreshments, and you can be sure he'll add some potent mixture to the punch that no one except a chemist will detect. He promises to put some spark into a usually dull evening."

"Sorry, I don't think I can make it. I half promised I'd hand out campaign literature in the ward tonight."

"Sweet Jesus. Don't you ever take time out to enjoy yourself? You could coast along till graduation on your marks. Why keep rubbing your nose to the grindstone night and day? If you're not studying, you're breaking your balls for the ward office. What the hell do you expect to get out of all this? They going to groom you to be alderman one day?"

"No way, Norm. I'm not looking to be alderman."

"Well, what then? There has to be a reason for your dedication to the Democratic party. Beats me what it is though. Sounds dull as hell."

"I haven't decided yet, but I give you my word you'll be the first to know my plans," Alex joked as they walked along.

"Then break away for one night and go to the party. Some of those gorgeous sorority sisters have some pretty snappy costumes in mind. One's coming as a belly dancer, and there's going to be a mermaid and a Cleopatra. That will knock the socks off some of those dull professors and their wives."

"And what are you going as? I'm sure your devious mind must have dreamed up something sensational."

"Well, I thought I'd be Jean Lafitte. Nothing turns the ladies on like a pirate. Deep down I think they all have dreams of being kidnapped and spirited off by a wicked swashbuckling rogue of the sea. Women adore villains."

"I don't have time to whip up a costume."

"Al, not everyone is getting dressed. A costume is optional. There'll be lots of guys dressed in street-clothes."

"Yeah, all the old staid professors and the guys too embarrassed to let down their hair."

Norm laughed. "Well, you can always go as Professor Pritzkin. You look just like the hallowed historian."

"Who's Professor Pritzkin?"

"I was in the library today killing some time in the archives, and while I was trying to catch a glimpse of Nancy Baker, I ran across an old publicity book. Nancy didn't show so I kept thumbing through the book, and lo and behold, I came across a guy with a face just like yours. He's a little gray, but the two of you could pass for brothers. With a little white powder at your temples and a different way of combing your hair you'd floor some of the older teachers who've been here awhile. Wait. I checked the book out. Come to my locker. I stowed it away there until I could find you. It's amazing."

As they walked down a long corridor Norman talked on about his find. "This professor taught here for about twelve years. Seems he was killed in a fire about twenty years ago. His first name's the same as yours too."

Norm fumbled with the combination lock and finally withdrew the book in question, riffling through the pages.

"Now take a gander at this and tell me what you think."

Alex looked down to where his friend pointed.

"Norm, you're crazy. I don't look like him. No way." He continued staring at the picture. "Well, maybe the facial structure is similar but that's about it."

Norm led Alex into the men's washroom, stopping at the sink.

"Part your hair in the middle and don't plaster it down." He took out his comb and worked swiftly with his friend's hair, then he picked up the book and held it against the mirror facing Alex. "Okay, now what do you think?"

Alex stared at the book and then at himself. The more he looked, the more he was convinced he was looking at himself, at what he would look like in another fifteen years or so.

"Now do you see what I meant?" Norm beamed. "With a tweed jacket you're Professor Pritzkin. Let's see. There are about fifteen or so teachers who were here at the same time as him. I'd like to see their faces when they see you walk in. You'll be the talk of the geriatric group."

Alex brushed his hair back to the side again with his fingers. "You're nuts. For God's sake do you think I want to walk into a crowded room dressed as a dead man? I mean it's all right to dress as Napoleon or Henry the Eighth but this guy's only been dead for a short time. It's bad taste. I'll pass on the party, but I promise I'll go to the spring dance."

"Well, I guess that's something. Who will you take?"

"Anyone. I don't care. Fix me up with a date will you?"

"Christ, you don't need me to fix you up. Just about any girl would drool at the chance of going with you if you took the time to ask. They all think you're pining away for some old childhood sweetheart."

"Norm, I don't have time to look around for a date. I mean it. Fix me up with anyone. What's the difference? It's only for one evening. You can even see if Selma Carruthers will go with me."

"I wouldn't fix my worst enemy up with Selma. She's too overpowering, too radical. She comes on like a Mack truck and she eats up little boys like you for a hobby."

"I think it's a great idea. Deep down she's probably dying to go. Never mind, I'll ask her myself in class. Mind if I borrow the book for a couple of days? I'd like to show it to the folks."

"It's all yours. Just be sure to have it back by next week. The librarian always looks at me with murder in her eyes every time I bring back one of her precious keepsakes late. I'm kind of afraid of old hatchet face. I think she has the killer instinct when it comes to protecting her charges. But you aren't serious about Selma, are you? Tell me you're joking."

"You know, you have a lot of hang-ups, Norm, but the worst is you don't dig deep enough. How the hell do you think you'll make a living being an attorney? You look at the superficial and never see what's beyond." Alex thumped Norm on the back and laughed. "I predict you'll marry a gorgeous woman and regret it the rest of your life because she'll bore you to death after one year. See you." Alex waved and was off, running back down the corridor and out of the building.

It was too late to show the book to Tekla or El that night because he didn't get home till after eleven, but at breakfast he laid it down on the table while El served freshly baked rolls and coffee.

Tekla caught the book as it was about to fall off the table.

"Alex, why can't you relax and eat properly? Must you always bring books and papers to the table? I swear

391

you're just like your Uncle Jan."

He poured cream into his cup and stirred in a spoonful of sugar. "But this, my dear Aunt Tex, is not a classbook. I want you to see something and give me your opinion."

Tekla grumbled but not too loudly at the apple of her eye, "I am not your Aunt Tex."

Alex playfully pinched her round cheek. Then he opened the book to the page where a marker was inserted.

"Here, have a look at this. Norm tells me I look just like this gent here on page forty. What do you say?"

Eleanor turned the book around to face her and looked down to where Alex was pointing.

"Norm's right. It's uncanny. Except for the touch of gray at his temples, he looks exactly like you. They say everyone in the world has a double and this one must be yours."

"Hand me my glasses," Tekla said, pulling the book over to her. Putting on the spectacles she detested, she stared down at the page and turned ashen.

"Are you all right?" El asked, concern marking her voice. "What's wrong?"

"Nothing, nothing. I just felt a little twinge of pain in my hip. It's gone now."

"Let me get you some aspirin."

"No. It's gone, I said. Stop babying me. It was only a little twinge."

"Well, what do you think?" Alex asked again. "Do I look like him?"

Tekla was slow to answer. "Sort of. But I wouldn't go so far as to say that you're identical. It's only a photograph. In real life he probably looked quite different. Pictures don't always do one justice." She shut the book quickly and sipped her coffee. "Is this part of your homework, finding replicas of yourself?"

"No, my love. It was only a joke. I have to run or I'll be late. See you tonight at dinner."

Eleanor rinsed off the dishes in the sink.

"I'd better get dressed myself or I'll never make it to work on time," she said and ran upstairs to get ready.

Alex had forgotten the book in his haste to leave, and Tekla opened it again with trembling hands. Dear God it was her Alex in person, a little older in years but unmistakably the same. She hadn't thought of Alex Pritzkin in years, not even of the yellowed newspaper picture of him printed when he died and long hidden in her old battered hatbox upon the highest shelf in her closet. The small box contained the picture and the newspaper article, the slipper pin Alex had given Dani, and their passports which were never used. Tekla remembered the day they had sat for the photos. They had sent the girls out to window-shop while Dani and Tekla answered questions, for they hadn't wanted the girls to suspect anything before it was time to leave. Dani had only told them that she wanted photos of her daughters and these were the most reasonably priced. Now Professor Pritzkin had come back to haunt them. If only they had gone to Switzerland . . . Then Dani would be alive and happy, loving Alex. Lydia, most likely would never have run away, and Tekla herself wouldn't have had to resort to murdering Roman. She would be at peace, ready and willing to join Józef and the rest of her family in paradise.

"Damn you," she swore at the handsome face smiling up at her. "Why did you have to play the hero? A few more days and we could have avoided all the useless suffering that followed your death." She made a mental note to get rid of the contents of the hatbox when she had the stamina to climb a high chair and get the box down from the shelf. She couldn't ask the children to get it for her; then they would want to rummage through the old cartons to see if they held anything interesting.

She no longer asked God for favors but now she silently pleaded with an unknown protector to let this be the end of Alex's questions. Let him please just return the book to its rightful owner and forget about it. How could she possibly explain to Alex that Roman wasn't his father? How could she tell the girls that their mother had had a chance for happiness and had lost it through a cruel twist of fate. Would they understand? She slammed the book shut and threw it on the floor.

Alex, without any qualms or misgivings, purposely tracked Selma down after class and asked her to the dance.

"I usually don't have time for these affairs" he said, "but I promised a friend I'd take time off to relax and have some fun. Would you like to go?"

Selma Carruthers was practically speechless, unusual for she never was at a loss for words. She wore thick framed glasses, was thirty pounds overweight, and kept her hair cut in a straight cap that molded her head and made her appear somewhat mannish. She never wore makeup, having decided long ago that it was too frivolous for her taste. Knowing herself to be an ugly duckling she hid behind a wall of belligerence, loudly castrating her fellow students. Selma's sharp tongue and negative wit caused the more squeamish to stay very clear of her. Few bothered to debate a point with her in class, and those who did often found themselves at the losing end of the stick. Even if they were right, they lost and the class laughed uproariously when Selma struck back with outrageous frankness.

"Is this some kind of a joke?" she said. "No one asks me to dances. If you're doing this to win a bet at my expense forget it."

Alex was taken aback for a moment.

"Selma, I'm serious. I'm honestly asking you if you'd like to join me, but if you're busy then I apologize. I just thought we'd have a nice evening together, dance, have dinner. I wasn't thinking of ravishing you in my car."

He turned to leave.

"Wait. I'd love to go if you're serious. I thought you were pulling my leg. I'll go if the offer still stands."

"Good. I'll pick you up at eight."

Selma was devoted to causes, and in the years ahead, long after school was over and done with, she championed Alex in any endeavor he attempted. By asking her out, when everyone else shunned this outspoken girl, he had won a friend for life. Furthermore, Alex spent an illuminating evening with her, for she was one of the most interesting people he'd ever talked with.

She was remarkably intelligent and had laid out a plan for her life that left him stunned. Her plan included various projects that all seemed attainable through some very hard work. She wanted to see women paid better wages, whether they worked in a factory, an office, a university, or at home. She wanted to start day nurseries so more women could get out and earn a decent living, even leave their husbands if they were being abused. Too many women, she explained, were beaten mentally and physically, but were afraid to leave home, afraid that no matter how hard they worked they would be unable to support themselves and their children. Good reasonable day nurseries would alleviate some of their fears, but women weren't yet being paid enough to support their families. She was going to try to change that if she could. And she wanted prisons investigated; she was certain the guards were milking the prisoners out of money by supplying them with overpriced goods. She wanted the government to provide soup kitchens for she knew there were many poor people who couldn't afford to eat decently. For every subject that Alex brought up, Selma had a plan in mind. She spoke quietly, not in her usual abrasive tone, and the oddly matched couple never stopped talking throughout the evening, not even while they danced to slow romantic music. The majority of the couples on the dance floor clung to each other and kept time to the steps, their eyes closed and vacant expressions on their faces. Not Alex. He and Selma danced without hearing the songs, so engrossed were they in trading serious concepts.

Norm looked on in wonder, puzzled at his friend's sincere interest in the strange girl. When Selma smiled she looked different, still overweight, of course, but more interesting.

When Alex dropped his date off at her door hours later he kissed her on the cheek lightly.

"Thanks, Selma. I wouldn't have missed tonight. Have you any idea what an interesting person you are? I have two favors to ask of you."

"What are they?"

"First, stop being so negative. People would jump at the chance to be your friend, but you hold them at arm's length with your barbs. You could have everyone on campus in the palm of your hand if only you would drop that façade you use so deftly. You're remarkable. Don't hid behind hate. I don't understand why you're so contrary."

Selma beamed under his praise. No one had ever talked to her like this, as an equal. All night she hadn't insulted anyone or retaliated with any unfair remark, but ever since she'd begun school she had been ostracized and had fought back in the only way she knew. Being an observant, only child she instinctively saw other people's flaws or fears, and whenever a classmate taunted her with ugly words, her quick mental processes heightened as her adrenaline flowed. Then sharp criticism spewed forth. She had discovered at an early age that it was her only means of defense, and she had learned that it felt far better to crush someone than to let her tears flow and run home to her overprotective parents. No, she would fight her own battles. Being sensible she knew Alex wasn't romantically interested in her, but she relished the camaraderie of a kindred mind.

"And what's the second favor?" she asked.

"If I ever run for office will you join forces with me, perhaps be my campaign manager or something similar? With you behind me I couldn't lose. That won't be for a long time, but eventually I'll make plans."

"It's a deal." Selma laughed. "Between the two of us we'll have the votes locked up. Thank you, Alex. I've had a wonderful time. In a few months we'll be done with school. Will we keep in touch?"

"Damn right we will," Alex promised. "I'll call you whenever I have a spare moment, but I warn you I'm going to be pretty busy for the next few years. I have to start building an image, but we'll get together."

"I guess I have some image building to do too. We both have a lot of hard work ahead, but it will be a little harder for me. I have more barriers to overcome."

The year Alex graduated there was freer talk of casual sex. *Playboy* had come into existence, and it's dynamite centerfold could be seen tucked between the pages of young men's textbooks. Hugh Hefner was envied for his access to the lovely young flesh that beat a path to his door, eager to be discovered.

Before graduation, Norm Sullivan organized a special weekend stag party that was held at his parents' summer home in Lake Geneva. The young men watched the latest in short-reel porno movies and then drove from lounge to lounge until they found a girl who looked like a Playboy bunny. They crowned her regally with a tiara of braided corn husks. Alex was glad when it was over for his head ached abominably and his stomach rebelled at the enormous intake of alcohol. It was his own personal lost weekend. Now he was an honest-to-God attorney, with the documents to prove it. It had been a long seven years but worth every minute, Alex thought, looking down at the degree.

His family celebrated with dinner at the Hilton Hotel. Tekla, with the aid of a cane, was overjoyed to be able to join them. It was a dry warm day so her arthritis aches had abated for the moment. Her hip and back hardly bothered her this evening and she walked straight as an arrow, discarding the hateful cane. She even summoned up the energy to dance a slow two-step with Alex in honor of his passing the bar. Just one. She didn't want to press her luck.

The dinner was Jan's treat—he insisted Alex's turn would come as soon as he won a big case—and the table hummed with merriment as the diners chatted away good-naturedly. Jan and Beth, Tekla, Eleanor, Irena, Stan, Carmella and Giovanni, Norm and his father, Bill, and Sid Levine were all enjoying themselves. Only Sid's recent bride, Reva, held herself aloof, refusing to dance with anyone except Sid. Her pert nose seemed to wrinkle with distaste when Bill Sullivan asked her to jitterbug so no one cared to extend another invitation. When an emergency called Sid away, a feeling of relief swept across the table. It was uncomfortable trying to talk to Reva who answered questions with a flat yes or no, offering nothing further.

She was a lovely young woman with dark wavy hair, and her evening gown was beautifully designed. However, she seemed more intent on displaying her three-carat diamond engagement ring than socializing. Her face came to life only when someone complimented her.

At home, after midnight, Tekla voiced her opinion over a late cup of tea. "Eleanor, I've watched your friend Sid come here to eat at least once a month for years. He's taken you out to dinner, to concerts. I was sure sooner or later both of you would come to your senses and realize how evenly matched you are, but you insisted you didn't want to be married and you told me Sid's parents insisted he marry a girl of his own faith. Well, so he has. You never even told me. I wondered why he wasn't around lately, but I took it for granted you still were seeing each other. As soon as he has a good practice on Michigan Avenue, suddenly he's married. Now can you honestly tell me he loves this girl and his parents have taken her to their hearts? She looks like a mighty cold fish to me. She's only happy when she's the center of attention or when she's staring down at her jewelry. She's much too young for your fine busy doctor, and I don't think she'll take it well when he comes home dead tired or when he's called out on emergencies if they have other plans for the evening. He worked hard to build up his practice and now I can see him spending every dime he earns trying to placate that greedy-looking girl. You've let the years slip by, but it isn't too late. You're thirty-nine and could still be happily married, but you throw away every prospect, not only Sid but the others as well."

"Aunt, please, I don't want to hear this."

Jan and Beth quietly slipped out of the room, not wanting to add to Eleanor's embarrassment.

"No. Let me finish," Tekla asserted. "I'm positive Sid

wanted to marry you. You're more his age, you understand his problems at the hospital. You could have had a successful marriage and eventually his parents would have come around. Even if they didn't would that be so horrid? So Sid could have kept his religion and you yours. I don't understand you. I may be old but I'm not blind. I wear spectacles but I can still see people quite clearly. I saw the look on your face this evening when Sid talked to you. You lit up like a gleaming candle. I saw the look on his face too. He looked at you with a hunger in his eyes, yet you tell me he's only been married for a month? Eleanor, look at me. What made him get married all of a sudden without any warning?"

"The best reason in the world. Reva's pregnant and Sid is the father."

Eleanor ran from the room and hurried up the stairs to her bedroom where she lay down, fully clothed, her eyes dry and unblinking.

I didn't want children, she told herself. Sid would have married me, but how could I deprive him of a real family? Oh, he said it didn't matter to him, but would he say the same thing after a few years? I'm too old now to have a baby anyway.

Unable over the years to convince Eleanor to marry him, four months ago Sid had finally issued an ultimatum. Eleanor remembered the night clearly. They had sat in his car while he nervously tapped on the steering wheel.

"I've loved you for years," he'd said. "I offered you anything you wanted, I'd give up my religion, go against my parents, move to another city and still you refuse. Good God, Eleanor, we go to bed together every chance we get. We don't have the legal papers but we're married nonetheless. Neither of us sees anyone else. I don't want a mistress for the rest of my life. You come to my apartment in the evenings and then dash off home before it gets too late. I want permanency. Once you're with me I want you to stay the night. I can't go on like this. I have to have your answer tonight. Either we get married or it's over." He had taken her in his arms then and kissed her. His familiar touch had still excited her. "I love you. Now tell me we're getting married. We can't have this part-time relationship for the rest of our lives."

Eleanor had steeled herself against the tears she'd felt rushing to her eyes. It's too late, she'd thought. I won't put Sid through a life of barrenness. He loves children. A picture of her mother lying on the kitchen table screaming and bleeding had flashed into her mind. No. She had watched thousands of operations—they were impersonal—but she couldn't imagine herself going through childbirth. And now it was too late anyway. She would never attempt to have a baby at her age. She should have seen a psychiatrist years ago. She had even set up an appointment several times but had failed to keep any of them. She knew she was neurotic about childbirth but she couldn't change, not even for Sid. It had been best to let him go while he was still young enough to find some relief from the pressure she was putting on him. She should have done it years ago. Make a clean break, she had told herself. Sever the relationship neatly and quickly and don't relent for a minute.

She had pushed herself out of Sid's comforting arms, straining to sound impersonal.

"The answer is no, Sid. Not now, not ever. I won't change my mind. I wouldn't ever consider coming between you and your parents. I don't ever want children. I just don't want to get married. If it's at all possible I'd like to remain friends with you, but that seems kind of ridiculous under the circumstances. I don't see how former lovers can be friends. Still, I'm willing to try if you are. Sid, I'd like to see you marry some nice Jewish girl, live according to the rules of your religion, have children. That would make me happy, Sid. If I saw you settled I could go on with my own life knowing I haven't disrupted yours. That's what makes me feel guilty, the fact that you've invested so much time in me."

"Eleanor, please."

"No. We're through. We can either be friends or enemies, nothing more. I hope we'll be friends, but if you want to hate me I'll accept that too."

He'd put the car in gear and driven her home without another word, his anger obvious in his sudden braking and fast takeoffs when they stopped for red lights. "Goodbye, . . . I'd like to say we can be friends, but I don't know—not yet. What does Emily Post have to say about two people in love, one of them stubborn, who meet in the halls of a busy hospital every day? Do I say good morning? How was your day? Do I look you straight in the eye and act formal when I know every inch of your body, know what excites you? I realized tonight you never did give all of yourself. You always held back an intangible something I couldn't put my finger on. I think I've figured out what it is. You love yourself more."

"That's not true."

"Wait. Let me finish. You do love me in a way, as much as you can, but somewhere deep in your subconscious you're more concerned about yourself. I've been fairly stupid. I should have seen it a long time ago. You've reached the point of commitment and can't make it so you tear yourself away." He got out of the car and opened her door.

As Eleanor had walked away from him and up the steps, she had desperately wanted to turn back and throw herself into his arms, but she hadn't. Something unexplainable had forced her up the stairs and through the door.

"It's better this way," she'd said fumbling with the key.

Dreading to face him the next day, she'd called in sick and taken the next three days off. When she returned to work, the grapevine was abuzz with the news that Sid had taken a leave of absence and wouldn't be back for two to three months.

She felt empty not meeting him for coffee after her duty in O.R., not seeing him in the halls, not hearing his name being paged. He was such an ordinary-looking man and yet so special. It suddenly struck her that he might be transferring to another hospital, perhaps one in another city and her stomach churned in protest. No, please don't let him go far. If I can only see him once in a while it won't be too bad. If I see he's doing well that will be enough.

None of the nurses or the other doctors seemed to know where Sid had gone. Dr. Adelman thought he had finally taken a much-needed vacation. Sally Reeve, one of the head nurses, had heard he was in New York attending seminars and learning new surgical techniques. Both were wrong.

Sid was in Chicago. He hadn't taken a vacation in four years so he felt no guilt. He canceled his appointments, had two associates cover for him, and then sat alone in his apartment on the north side. He had started drinking Scotch and water after leaving Eleanor at her door. The next day the Scotch ran out as did the vodka and now he was down to white wine. But the wine wasn't helping much. He was getting sober when he wanted to stay in oblivion for a few days more. Much as he hated to do it, he'd have to get dressed to replenish his supply of liquor. He pulled on a worn sweater, took the money he'd left on the hall table, and decided to walk the two blocks to the liquor store on Belmont. As he opened the apartment door with shaky hands, there stood his mother and father, his mother's finger poised, ready to press the bell. Oh, God. He wanted to slam the door in their faces but his mother took one look at him and threw her hands up in the air.

"Arnold," she moaned dramatically. "Look at our son. What's come over him? Sidney you look like death warmed over. You haven't shaved, your clothes are dirty. You're a disgrace. I called you at the office today and what did they tell me? Your receptionist said you took a few months off and she didn't know where to reach you. A stranger had to tell me about my own son. How can you humiliate us so? Are you in trouble? Your parents should be the first to know if you're in trouble, but no, you just drop everything—forget us. You're drunk." She turned to her husband wringing her hands. "Arnold, look he's drunk." She looked around the disarrayed room. "Just look at the empty bottles, the dirty glasses lying around."

Sid's head began pounding from his mother's screeching. He looked up to heaven and promised God anything if only they would leave. His father took his arm forcefully.

"You're coming home with us."

Sid threw off his hands.

"Will you stop? I'm fine. I'm not going anywhere. Just leave me alone."

"No, darling," his mother answered. "You're coming with us if we have to drag you all the way. Come, the car's outside."

This was ridiculous. He was a grown man. How long were they going to treat him as an adolescent? They should have had more children, he thought morosely. With only him they tended to be overprotective, watching his every move. The throbbing in his head became

404

worse; he feared it would split his skull open. He couldn't make out the words his mother was mouthing and felt he would be sick right in the foyer of his apartment. He made a move toward the bathroom but his father held on strongly, so he took several deep breaths and, his nausea subsiding, walked woodenly down the hall to the waiting elevator. Later he would fight back when his head cleared. After a few hours sleep he could gather his wits and be himself again.

When he woke he remembered falling onto his old bed fully clothed. It was dark. He felt lousy, his head still aching but not quite as badly now. Where the hell were his clothes so he could get out of here? Someone had removed them while he slept, and although he searched the closet and drawers he could find nothing but pajamas. Cursing, he made his way to the den where his parents sat, calmly listening to a piano concert on the radio, his father reading the newspaper, his mother knitting. She looked up at his approach.

"Ah, he's come to life again. Sidney, I think you should bathe and shave before joining us."

"Where are my clothes?"

"They're being cleaned and won't be ready till morning so you might as well relax."

Sid banged his hand on the table in disgust. "I'm not a snot-nosed kid anymore. I want to go home. Now. If I have to I'll go in my pajamas."

"Sit down," his father thundered. He seldom spoke harshly, but on the few occasions he did, people obeyed. When running his corporate empire he behaved in the same way he did with his family. He was an unbreakable man, his strength built up during the lean years when he'd had to fight and scratch for every inch of progress. Even his wife sat back quietly when he was in one of these moods. Most of the time she could get her way and usually she talked incessantly, but she knew when to defer to her husband.

"You can have your clothes as soon as we have an explanation for your behavior. You don't walk away from your patients and take an indefinite leave of absence on a whim. What's your reason?"

"I'm tired. I want to relax. I haven't taken off for years."

"Then why aren't you on a cruise ship or in Florida or Europe? I don't call sitting in your apartment, drinking yourself senseless a good way to spend valuable time. Something else happened. It's that shiksa you've been going with. Don't bother to deny it." He waved Sid back when he started to rise from the chair. "I have friends who tell me what's going on. You've entangled yourself with her for years. At first I thought she was just a little diversion to while away the time, but you're still seeing her. Instead of thinking of marriage and raising a family you're involved with a little know-nothing of a nurse at the hospital. It has to stop."

Sid listened as his father droned on. Why fight his prejudice any longer? Eleanor wouldn't have him. Why the hell did he waste his time with her anyway?

"It's over."

His father looked up, stunned. "What?"

"I said over, finished, done with, ended. The nurse and me."

"That's good news, son. You've come to your senses. Good. But there's no need to drown your sorrows with liquor."

"Just a small binge, Dad. After all, I am old enough to indulge, although for some insane reason you seem to think I'm still in diapers."

"Excessive drinking can ruin you, son. Look at how your hands are trembling. You're a surgeon. You need steady hands and a cool head. I don't begrudge anyone a few cocktails but there were at least six empty liquor

406

bottles in your apartment. That's going too far. Sid, you're forty years old. I don't think of you as a whimpering infant but as a man who should have begun long ago to continue our heritage, to settle down and carry on our name."

"Our name? Ah, the proud and illustrious Levine name. I would have changed it if that 'know-nothing nurse' would have had me. But she didn't. She's a lot like you in many ways: stubborn, proud. You should thank her because she told me she didn't want any part of me. She said I should marry a fine Jewish girl and have children. She didn't want to cause friction between us. Does that make you happy?"

"Then I apologize for my remarks. It seems she's a sensible woman after all, but she did have a hold on you for far too long. She should have done this years ago. Can you blame me for being happy at her decision?" Sid started toward the doorway when his father continued. "By the way, we're having dinner tomorrow with the Weins. Reva's graduated from Brandeis University and she's dying to see you again. I'll tell them you'll be joining us."

"Sure." Anything to get away from their harping.

The next evening, in his own apartment dressing for dinner, he regretted his rash promise of the night before. For one thing he couldn't stand the Weins or their daughter, Reva. If he remembered correctly, for he hadn't seen her in about five years, she was pretty enough but sulky. Her only topic of conversation was herself. Maybe she had changed, but he strongly doubted it. A real spoiled brat. With a shrug of annoyance he buttoned his dinner jacket, in haste to get the evening over with.

During dinner he was surprised to find Reva highly animated and prettier than he remembered. She asked intelligent questions about his work and seemed honestly interested in his technical answers. Without knowing quite how it happened, he found himself agreeing to escort her to a concert the following night. To his surprise Reva discussed the soloist's performance knowledgeably.

The next night he found himself at the Drake Hotel, attending a Jewish United Fund dinner with his parents and the Weins. Before he could extricate himself from the web speedily enveloping him, he noticed the pleased looks on both sets of parents' faces as they watched their offspring sharing yet another evening. One week later, after a dull party where he'd indulged in too many martinis, he wakened to find Reva in his bed, but he didn't remember how she'd gotten there. She coyly opened her eyes and stretched languorously.

"Sid, I hope this means you're going to make an honest woman out of me. Daddy will be furious when he sees I haven't spent the night at home. He's going to ask a million questions and what shall I tell him?"

Sid felt the noose tighten around his neck. He racked his brain but couldn't remember if he had taken the proper precautions to see that Reva didn't get pregnant. He couldn't even remember if he'd enjoyed their lovemaking. Last night was lost. The last thing he could recall was a doorman handing the car keys to Reva and saying perhaps he shouldn't drive. What then? He'd had a wildly exciting dream that Eleanor was with him, hungrily caressing him, promising never to leave. Was it a dream or had it been only Reva? Things never should have gone this far.

He stalled her for the moment, promising he'd find the right excuse to placate her parents, and then literally ran back to work, surprising the hospital staff by cutting short his vacation. By volunteering to cover for another doctor who was ill and seeing his own patients, he put in sixteen-hour days, and when his parents or Reva managed to talk to him on the phone he could honestly say the days and nights were too hectic because of his double duty.

His world collapsed beneath him a month later when Reva came to his door sobbing. She had missed her period. That was his Waterloo—and his parents' ultimate joy. Their long wait for him to settle down had come to an end. After the lavish, hastily arranged wedding, Reva reverted to her true nature, a self-centered and grasping one. Worse, Sid discovered she wasn't much good in bed.

Eleanor learned of his marriage from friends and took the news stoically. She congratulated Sid in the cafeteria, putting on a show of bravado and smiling. But she was unwilling to meet with Sid after work, although he badly wanted to explain his rash action. He had practically invited himself to Alex's celebration at the Hilton and Eleanor did not refuse him because she knew how much he and Alex loved each other— almost like brothers. Wasn't Sid always there when Alex needed a man's opinion, when her brother faced insoluble problems at school? So Sid came . . . but not alone.

Chapter Eleven

Alex and Norm, after long and careful deliberation, decided to go into practice with Norm's father rather than start out in one of the established firms that offered them low-men-on-the-totem-pole positions. The excitement of being on their own, not answering to top management, appealed to them. Bill Sullivan ran a small, but lucrative, one-man operation on the south end of the Loop, and it took several weeks of coaxing to get him to agree to share office space. Norm and Alex had to solemnly swear not to infringe on Bill's clients. Bill Sullivan's main source of income was personal injury lawsuits, and he handled enough cases to keep his family comfortable and to invest modestly.

Bill's secretary/receptionist had been ensconced in the office for as long as Norm could remember. She was a human dynamo who kept up with her employer's typing, research, filing, and whatever else was thrown her way. The two newcomers had promised to hire their own girl. Actually Bill had a suite of four rooms, although two were undersized, but the rent was fair. The office building had seen better days, and those with business to transact there were often forced to wait patiently for one of the two elevators to clank and chug its way up and down at a snail's pace. Alex and Norm would share one of the larger rooms. One small cubicle sufficed as the reception area, and a desk and several file cabinets were moved into the remaining room for their girl Friday.

Norm, left in charge of the hiring while Alex was out buying office supplies, was on the brink of taking on a gorgeous redhead when Alex returned and noticed that she pecked at the typewriter as if it carried some dreaded disease. Alex rolled his eyes heavenward and motioned Norm to follow him into the other room.

"No. Absolutely not. She can't type, probably can't take dictation, and doesn't know a lawsuit from a dress suit. We need a worker like Mrs. Fitzpatrick, at least for the time being."

"But, Al, this one's a beauty. Her looks alone will have clients flocking in. I tell you she would be a definite asset."

"Nope," Alex disagreed. "Not unless you want to pay her salary by yourself. Norm, I promise you once we're on our own and making good money you can hire the prettiest girl around, but right now we need capability, not a decoration."

"Well then, you go out there and tell her we can't use her. I can't do it. She'll look at me with those big green eyes, and I'll give in and hire her anyway."

Alex didn't enjoy telling the redhead she would not do, but it was necessary to do so to meet his tight budget. Late in the afternoon the right woman applied, a neat-looking legal secretary with five years' experience. She agreed to work for fifty dollars a week and was asked to report for work the following Monday. Jan was subsidizing his nephew until he could establish himself, and Al didn't want to end up owing his uncle a small fortune. Bill Sullivan was backing his son so Norm had no qualms about the cost. Now all these young lawyers needed was a case, and Bill generously threw one their way.

It was an easy victory. An elderly man had fallen through a manhole because the cover hadn't been replaced properly. Knowing most of the city councilmen helped tremendously. Alex managed to get a few words in the right ears. The victim was awarded a satisfactory settlement of five hundred dollars. All he'd suffered was a broken arm and the inconvenience of wearing a cast for six weeks. He'd lost no time at work for he was retired. It hadn't hurt to have Alderman Haskow on their side. He was a good man to know when suing the city. At any rate the client was happy with his share, and Alex and Norm celebrated with an extravagant lunch.

Other cases soon began to trickle in; some referrals from friends, some haphazardly selecting their listing from the phone book. Alderman Flynn saw to it that a fair amount of his constituents sought out their services, and strangely, several wealthy businessmen sent a few cases their way. When Alex asked who had referred them, the answers were always vague.

Within five years the firm of Sullivan, Kawa, and Sullivan became a legal force with a glowing reputation. Bill, at first, refused to make the move to larger quarters insisting his small-time operation suited him just fine, but since their cases were so intertwined, it would have been impossible to divide up the legal documents they all had a part in handling. Now the roles were reversed; Bill was handling the overflow. Alex and Norm were too busy to handle everything, but the three of them kept abreast of the day-to-day operation. The firm, with its recent expansion, was humming with activity, and Norm had finally hired a beautiful receptionist. This one could type, however, and handle some of the routine paperwork. Five junior attorneys were also hired, as were a research man and some other office personnel. Alex realized one day that they were responsible for twenty-five employees. He'd never expected his career to snowball quite this rapidly, but it felt damned good. It paid to have friends in high places; it helped to have clout.

High publicity cases seemed to gravitate his way and the nickname, Stormy, the wonder of LaSalle Street, was tacked on him by an overzealous reporter whose beat was the courthouse. The name stuck and became a favorite of the media. Fame, in the legal profession, usually came only after years of plodding labor so at first his peers tended to think him an upstart seeking notoriety, but as the details of his tactics became known, the majority of the legal hierarchy changed their opinion. Some lawyers even considered his maneuvers brilliant and many wondered why they hadn't thought of some of his procedures first.

Irena started keeping scrapbooks, for her brother's name or picture cropped up often. He certainly was in the papers regularly, she thought, if not concerning his cases, then because of his political associations. This morning she'd clipped another picture of him. He sat next to the mayor himself at a fund raising dinner. Alex was embarrassed when she proudly displayed her hobby but she waved aside his protests, saying "Some day you'll be glad I kept all this."

Chicago's first seven-figure settlement, granted to a lovely young girl who had lost both arms in a chemical company explosion, was Alex's next plus. He proved owner negligence caused the holocaust, and when a nurse wheeled in the still beautiful, but incapacitated, former factory worker, the jury unashamedly wept and awarded an unprecedented sum after hearing the accident victim's version of careless operating procedures in the plant. The girl had been the sole support of parents who needed constant nursing care. Without her support, they had been put in a charity-run nursing home.

Eight men and women involved in an el crash, four of whom were seriously injured, unanimously decided Sullivan, Kawa, and Sullivan could handle their cases collectively, and all eight clients were more than pleased with the results of the trial.

The Coray Corporation, a multimillion-dollar Chicago-based company with a high-priced legal staff, lost a copyright battle and was ordered to pay the original inventor of their top-selling item a royalty, retroactive for six years. Coray's head attorney, Martin Sellers, stormed out of the courtroom as his company's chief accountant whispered an outrageous figure in his ear. The timid inventor and his wife cried at the favorable verdict, and in addition to the fee, Alex and Bill were offered a new Cadillac each, which they refused. Instead, they asked that the money which would have been spent for the cars be used to add another room onto St. Michael's orphanage. The willing young inventor did more than that and that haven for the homeless became his pet charity for the rest of his days.

Alex thoughtfully set aside a portion of every fee earned for his own charity fund. Not a month went by that he didn't dig into the money to offer assistance where needed. One night after a devastating fire in a badly overcrowded tenement, he led its bewildered and sobbing occupants to a nearby hotel and picked up the entire bill for a week until they could be relocated. With the help of Goodwill, he supervised clothing distribution making sure each and every person received several changes of clothes; enough to keep them warm throughout the bitter winter.

When a raging snowstorm paralyzed the city for

almost two days and nights, he hired every privately owned snowplow he could lay his hands on and paid men and high school boys to shovel out the 11th Ward in an effort to help the city workers who were steadily losing the battle against the elements. In one day the main streets in the ward were passable for men and women anxious to be back at their jobs. With the help of the precinct captains, he and his crews were seen going from door to door, volunteering to purchase groceries and other essentials for those unable to do for themselves. Shoveling the massive mounds of snow that blocked the sidewalks and alleys became another task in their crusade. The area people were amazed at the proffered help and invited the volunteers into their homes to thaw out, putting hot drinks into their numbed hands. Never had the 11th Ward seen such a flurry of activity. Even the old-timers who claimed to have seen everything were awed. Alex and his crew blew in just like the storm, they said, whirling and impatient. The *Tribune* picked up the story and "Stormy" now had a twofold meaning.

Every thousand dollars that Alex put into his special fund was used within a month, and soon, small contributions began trickling in, to be set aside and earmarked for the next catastrophe that caught his eye. The nature of the fund spread by word of mouth, and it was touching to see a check for five or ten dollars or even a single bill or small change donated by people who most likely needed the money themselves. He discovered the poor always seemed the most generous, for they knew first hand what it was like to feel the pinch of a bleak future.

Under Carmella's and Giovanni's direction, a recreational facility was set up to keep young people off the streets, a cause dear to Carmella's heart. She managed to wheedle the building and a hefty donation out of

Vito Candella, one of the hierarchy in the crime syndicate. He seemed to be mellowing in his old age, wanting to prove his goodness to one and all before he was called to meet his Maker and account for his past misdeeds. It was a two-story brick building that he donated, and the top floor was set up for the girls to learn crafts, art, and sewing; the first floor as a gym for the boys. Alex saw to the building's renovation. Sitting over a cup of coffee and a piping hot panzarotti, a light piece of fried bread dough filled with sausage, cheese, and sauce, Alex later praised Carmella for her untiring efforts in getting the settlement house off the ground and running smoothly. Already the membership had swelled to forty boys and over thirty girls. A few parents took turns supervising the exuberant youngsters who had to be practically pushed out at closing time.

"It never could have happened without you, Carm. You and Johnny O were just great."

"Can't you call anyone by their right name?" Giovanni piped in, wiping a drop of red sauce from his face with a napkin. "Now everyone calls me Johnny O. My poor sainted mother, God rest her soul, would put the evil eye on you for tampering with my baptismal name." He thumped Alex on the back. "You did your share too. You worked just as hard as any of us and you aren't even Italian. Your mother would be proud of you. Beautiful Dani. She didn't live to see the day, but Tekla is just as proud of you as any mother. She's been just like one hasn't she?"

Alex sat without responding, lost in the past for a moment. His beautiful shining mother. How he would have loved to shower her with gifts, to make her life easier, to tease her until she couldn't help but forget her annoyance and burst out with laughter. His family kept urging him to find a nice girl and get married, but none that he met came close to matching the spirit and vitality of his mother, his aunt, or even Eleanor. Here he was thirty years old already. For Christ's sake, how did the time fly by so fast? Where did the years go? There never even seemed to be enough hours in a day to accomplish all he wanted to do. He shook off his thoughts.

"Aunt Texas sure is my darling. I don't know what we would have done without her."

He kissed Carmella goodbye and drove home to get a few hours sleep; there was an important preliminary hearing in the morning. But enroute his mind drifted back to his family.

Irena was happy with Stan and their two kids. She constantly flitted from one busy day to another, immersed in every committee she could get into: the Ladies' Altar and Rosary Society; the PTA, the Democratic Women's Organization, hospital volunteer work. Where did she find the energy? Alex wondered. With the kids and a house to run, how was it that Stan never minded her absence. He even urged her to try her hand at new things while he took on overseeing the homework and made a game out of the kids doing their share of the housework?

Celia still wrote her monthly letters to the family. She was content at the convent in Wisconsin, and her missives sounded more like prose that expressed her awe at the wonders of the universe and God. Twice a year they went to visit her for one day only, because it upset her to be away from her holy life any longer and they could see that she longed to be back amongst her spiritual sisters.

Lydia. Only God knew where Lydia had drifted to. Two years ago at Christmas they had received a lavish basket of fruit. On the card only her bold scrawling signature was written. When El had called the dealer in

Chicago who had handled the transaction and asked for the sender's address, the man had told her the money order was sent from Los Angeles and the return address on the envelope had brought them some hope of finding their long-lost sister. They wrote, but the letter came back three weeks later marked "Addressee Unknown." They knew she was alive but that was about all. More puzzling was the fact that she remembered them at all.

"I think after so many years of silence her conscience bothered her a bit," Tekla offered. "Lydia probably just happened to remember us for a brief moment when someone mentioned home and holidays so she sent a token gift. For all she knows or cares we could be dead or have moved to another city. She has no idea her parents are dead, doesn't know the rest of you are all grown with lives of your own, doesn't know or care about anyone but herself. I hope I don't see the day when she comes crawling back to her family, when she suddenly realizes friends and careers are fickle. She's getting older and I have a feeling her beauty is fading, but then again who knows? Well, I can't forgive her. A phone call or a letter now and then wouldn't have been too much to ask. We wouldn't go rushing out to intrude on her life."

Bolie and Martha, dearest of friends, were both gone, dying within a month of each other. Martha first, then Bolie whose heart seemed to split in two when Martha had a heart attack. They never heard from Raymond Patek after Tekla wrote him of Dani's death, so another link to the past was lost.

Alex had dinner with Selma about twice a year. Theirs was a remarkable friendship; Selma was concerned because Alex wasn't ready to settle down, but she understood his drive to succeed. She herself had no designs on him—she knew she wasn't his type—but she

419

relished their talks and phone conversations. He was her first friend and would always remain so. This year she was abroad, conducting seminars in England and traveling throughout Europe, picking up foreign opinions. He couldn't wait for her return so they could have a few animated discussions.

Eleanor, the dearest of his sisters, was happy after a fashion—if you called devoting your life to your work happiness. She was the best damned nurse at Reese and had the degrees to prove it. She could have gone on to become a doctor but she'd declined the offer of free schooling. Not Norm, not any of the men at the ward office or in his bowling league or poker crowd was so close to him. He imagined this situation was unique. How many men could go to their older sister and confide completely in her, or vice versa. Eleanor understood his every mood, what he wanted out of life, the forces that were driving him. Their closeness seemed to become deeper after Sid and she parted and she received the devastating news of Sid's marriage. Eleanor had been torn between her relief that Sid could finally live a full life and her jealousy of Reva who legally belonged to him. She saw Sid amost daily at the hospital and his lonely look tore at her heart. One day she broke the ice, joining him over a cup of coffee in a quiet corner of the cafeteria after the scheduled operations were over for the day. He looked up at her, surprised to see they were actually sitting together. Lately Eleanor always sat with a crowd and never assisted in any of his operations. When they passed in the halls, only inane words were exchanged.

"Has the mountain come to Mohammed?" he teased. "For the past few months you've avoided me as though I had the plague. Why the sudden change?"

Eleanor placed her hand atop his.

"I'm sorry Sid. At first it wasn't easy for me, but I've

420

learned how to live with myself. Can we be friends? I've missed talking to you. It's silly for us to keep passing each other by when we've been so close. Don't misunderstand, I don't want it to be the way it was. I respect your marriage. Didn't I invite you to Alex's graduation celebration just so I could meet your wife and see for myself how happy the two of you are together?"

Sid laughed tonelessly.

"I wish you could see firsthand just how happy we are. Eleanor, why did you refuse me? I've trapped myself in a travesty of a marriage. Reva and I don't love each other. She listened to her parents and went after a man who was already established in a career, a man who could give her all the expensive things she loves. Her father's business is slowly going down the drain. He didn't want his daughter to suffer along with him so he talked her into latching onto me."

"But she's pregnant, Sid. You're going to have a baby. Surely that stands for something?"

"Sure, it's the only good that's come about. Let me explain something to you once. I promise I'll never mention it again. When I took that leave of absence I wasn't planning on going away. I wanted to drink myself into a stupor to forget you and I succeeded for a few days. The night Reva became pregnant I don't even remember going to bed with her, but she says we did and it's possible. We made love once and I got her pregnant. Guess what the odds are on that? You know the statistics as well as I. Me, a doctor who should know better. This baby's due in two months. Let me give you a small glimpse into our domestic bliss. She curses me every day for causing her to lose her figure. Her doctor warns her to keep her weight down or she'll have a difficult delivery and she claims she doesn't eat much; yet she's gained over fifty pounds and still has two months to go. I've talked to the doctor. He insists she's over-eating but evidently not when I'm around. When I'm home she wails and moans at me, continually accusing me of putting her through hell. She claims I've ruined her life. She says she'll never, under any circumstances, think of having another baby. At least you had a good reason for not wanting one. You saw what your mother went through once and it scarred you inside." He released her hand then and rubbed his tired eyes. "That's enough of my domestic problems. To answer your question, yes. I'd enjoy our being friends. It will give me the greatest pleasure to have someone in the same profession I can talk to, and I promise I won't compromise you at any time. Tell me how things have been going for you."

Eleanor confided that conversation to Alex the following day. Just talking to Sid again put life back into her and she happily bounced through her days. Alex truly liked Sid. He was one hell of a friend and a skilled surgeon. If Eleanor was happy then he was happy for her. Tekla suspected something was amiss but tactfully kept her mouth shut. It was enough to see her Eleanor smiling; she didn't want to know anything else.

When Reva was in her eighth month she lost her footing on the top stair at the downtown public library, where she was attending a lecture, and plummetted down a flight of marble stairs. She should have waited for the elevator but had been too impatient. Her neck was broken during the fall and the most competent doctors couldn't save the baby. The eighth month was the most precarious, Reva's obstetrician explained, but Sid already knew that.

Six months later Eleanor and he were living together on Lake Shore Drive. She still came home to see to Tekla's needs in the afternoons, but Tekla's mind was beginning to wander a bit and Alex wondered how much longer she would be with them. Tekla was completely bedridden so he and Eleanor had hired a live-in companion for her, a refugee from Poland which was perfect for Tekla. The two women spoke Polish continually and spent their days rehashing old times.

At first Eleanor was reluctant to agree to Sid's request that they marry or live together, whichever she preferred. She recited her protests.

"Sid, I'm too old to get married. Surely you can find a young Jewish woman; this time one who shares your interests, someone more mature."

Sid silenced her by gently pressing his hand against her mouth.

"You're not old. We have years left to spend together. Your aunt loves to see us with each other. She wants to see us married. I definitely do not want children. We can be a terrific aunt and uncle; we can visit the orphanages and if you want, we can adopt. If you don't want the responsibility and want to keep on working, fine. We'll visit our friends who have children and treat them as our own—if we like them that is. Some of the kids I've seen are horrid little monsters. I'm glad I didn't go into pediatrics."

"Sid, you're overwhelming me. Give me time to think straight."

"You're not getting away from me this time, El. I want a positive answer right now. I made a bad mistake in marrying Reva and it isn't going to happen again, not when I know who and what I want. Second best is nothing; I won't have it. I've checked off every one of your protests so none exist."

"Okay, okay." She laughed. "I missed you terribly too, but we won't get married. We'll live together wherever you say."

"Wait a minute," Sid protested. "Are we going back to a few stolen hours a week? El, I couldn't take that again."

"No, Sid. I mean we'll really live together. I'll work part-time in the mornings. I love my job and couldn't give it up completely. That will leave me the afternoons to visit with my aunt, and the rest of my time will be spent with you. We can eat dinner on some Sundays with Tekla and Alex, and I know she'll be happy for us, but I don't feel we should get married. This way you'll have an out in case you do find someone else. It's still possible."

He saw the stubborn light in her eyes and agreed to her terms for the time being. Later he would use more persuasion and she would see it his way. This was enough for now. He whooped with joy as he spun her wildly around his living room.

"Let's celebrate. We'll have dinner at the Drake."

"Sid, your parents—"

"Have their own lives to live. They'll have an open invitation to come here whenever they like and if they choose not to, it's their loss."

A worry line began to appear on Eleanor's forehead.

"Stop frowning. I promise I'll visit them every week and you can come too. I doubt they'll tear their clothes in mourning. They're too sensible. My mother talks a lot but she doesn't mean any harm and my father's mellowed, especially after he saw what a changed person Reva became after he helped arrange the match. We're on our own, love."

As Alex drove on home, his mind drifted away from his sister's life and back to the case he was presenting to the jury in the morning. It had been frustrating trying to talk to a client who wanted no defense.

Andrea Wells had been arrested for murdering her husband in cold blood, stabbing him repeatedly until his body was an unrecognizable mass of slashed flesh.

Her hands and nightgown saturated with blood, she had calmly called up the neighbors, and asked them to care for her three-year-old daughter until her sister could fly in from Boston. Then, in the same calm manner, she had called the police and asked them to come and remove the body. Her family attorney who specialized in wills and settling estates threw up his hands in disgust when Andrea paid no attention to his plea not to confess. He called Alex the next morning, still shocked over Andrea's behavior. He'd known her since she'd married Don Wells and she was not the type to hurt anyone.

"She never even swatted down a moth," he explained to Alex. "I can't understand her actions. Alex, please defend her. Something's wrong. I realize she did it, but why? She won't tell anyone why, just keeps saying she did it and she would do it again if she had to."

Alex had tried his utmost to break down the wall of silence the young woman had built around herself.

"I killed Don," Andrea confessed matter-of-factly "and if they put me away forever or send me to the electric chair, so what? I'm not insane so don't plead insanity." She abruptly changed the subject. "Did my sister Patty come to get Annie? She promised me she would take care of her if anything happened to me. Is Annie all right?"

"She's fine," Alex reassured her. "I put them on the plane at O'Hare myself. Patty brought her daughter along and the two girls were chattering away as I saw them off. Patty told Annie she'd had a bad dream and that you're not feeling well so they're going to let you rest for a while until you get better."

"Good." Andrea relaxed somewhat. "Patty will do a good job. She's a splendid mother."

"She wanted to stay and see you through this ordeal, Andrea. Why did you send her away?"

"Because I don't want my daughter to find out her

mother's in jail, not for a long time, not until she can understand."

"Andrea," Alex began again, "won't you tell me why? Maybe you don't have to go to jail."

"No. I killed another human and I deserve punishment. I don't want to talk about it anymore."

As she rose to be escorted back to her cell Alex felt defeated before the case had even begun. Nonetheless, he tried again and again in the ensuing weeks to discover the motivation behind the killing, but Andrea Wells wouldn't budge an inch. In desperation, the day before the trial was due to begin, he tried one last time.

"Please Andrea, your daughter needs you. She cries for you every night before she falls asleep. I keep in touch with Patty regularly and Annie wants you more than she wants her aunt."

"She'll get over it," Andrea answered listlessly. "A little more time and she'll adjust to her new surroundings."

"She told Patty a little about her bad dream, Andrea. Only you can help her forget about it. What did Don do that Annie thinks is a bad dream?"

Andrea looked up in despair.

"She has to forget. She was half asleep. Tell Patty to make her stop remembering, to drop the subject."

"It wasn't a dream, was it? It was real, and when you're reunited with Annie you can help her. Do you want your daughter scarred for life? Do you want her to grow up confused and afraid because you were too weak to make a new life for her?"

Andrea shouted, "I wasn't too weak. It took courage to do what I had to do. I've never shown that much courage before. You don't understand."

Alex put his arm around the distraught woman.

"I do understand. Andrea, I'm putting you on the stand as soon as possible so this trial won't drag on for weeks, causing all sorts of adverse publicity. You won't have to face friends and neighbors when it's over. You can fly to Boston a few hours after you're released. You'll have enough money to start over. Don wasn't a poor man. Be brave one more time and tell the truth. You'll be out of the city within hours under an assumed name and you can start helping Annie forget."

When Andrea Wells took the stand the jury was openly hostile to this elegant woman who had killed her husband, a good man who supported his family well. Even though she looked haggard after nights of sleeplessness, anyone could see that she was well off, able to afford good clothes, an expensive education, and to hold herself aloof from her peers. But their attitude changed when Andrea broke down on the witness stand and explained her motive. Little by little Alex dragged the story from her until her words finally gushed out in a torrent of disgust.

"After Don and I were married a few months, I found pictures he hid in the attic. Horrible dirty pictures of small children indulging in sex. He laughed them away, explaining that they meant nothing to him. At one point in his life, he said, he had bought them because they were something unusual. Until I found those pictures I had no idea that he was interested in such a perversion, and when he burnt the pictures after I found them I believed him. Our marriage was good then. I became pregnant and Annie was born two years after our wedding. She'll be three in a few months. She's such a tiny beautiful baby." Andrea broke down and wept as though her heart were breaking in two. Five minutes passed before she could resume her testimony. "I woke one night about two in the morning and Don wasn't in bed. I thought maybe the baby had cried but I didn't hear anything; so I went into Annie's room and there was Don, with my baby who was half asleep, and he was forcing her to do something awful. I can't even say it or think about it. Her own father was coaxing his baby into a vile perverted act. I screamed and Don finally saw me standing there horrified. He left Annie, but when I grabbed her and started to run out of the house, he held me back and forced me into the bathroom. I was hitting and scratching, but he was a strong man even though he was small. He pushed me down on the floor, knelt on top of me, grabbed the adhesive tape, and put a strip of it across my mouth. Then he dragged me back into the bedroom and tied me into the rocker I used to rock Annie to sleep sometimes, and he made me watch as he woke her again. I was dying inside, but I had to watch—for minutes— until he was done. It seemed a whole eternity before he staggered away and left the room. Annie sat in bed looking at me, asking why I was tied up like an Indian, and then she came over and pulled the tape off my mouth. She kept saying she wouldn't hurt me as she pulled it off gently, and she asked why I was crying. When the tape was off I told her to go down to the kitchen and bring up a knife, and to be very, very careful not to fall. When she came back I told her to cut the tie that held my hands behind the bars of the rocker, to do it carefully and slowly. She listened to me as she always does; she didn't even nick me once. When I had one hand free, I managed to do the rest myself. As soon as I was free, I took her into the bathroom and gave her a third of a sleeping pill. I told her it was aspirin because she had a fever, and I rocked her until she fell asleep again. Then I took the knife she had brought up earlier and went into our bedroom and killed Don. He might have been drunk that night. I didn't know or care. I killed him for what he did."

The jury was back within an hour—the verdict, not guilty. Alex had Andrea's suitcases packed and waiting in a car behind the courthouse.

Three weeks later, Judy Foran, Alex's secretary had bottles of champagne ready as he walked into the office. Norm toasted his partner.

"Stormy does it again. He glibly talks his way around the prosecuting attorney, mesmerizes the jury, and makes sure justice triumphs. To Stormy who won a fat juicy fee, who'll put us all in Cadillacs, and who'll put a chicken in all our pots. Congratulations, partner. You've won the biggest and best case ever."

Everyone joined in congratulating him. The people who comprised the firm were certainly loyal, Alex thought as he sipped his second glass of sparkling wine. They were more like a second family. Even Norm, who might have expressed a certain amount of envy, proudly extolled Alex's virtues. It was enough for Norm that he was on the gravy train; he wasn't greedy or hungry for publicity.

The impromptu party ended when everyone went back to work except Norm and Alex. Feeling rather mellow Norm chided his old friend.

"You were half right and half wrong back in the old days, Al, when you said I'd marry a gorgeous woman and be bored in a year. I've been married two years, I have a son, and I've found the perfect wife. She's much too attractive; I notice other men looking at her with a gleam in their eyes. But, believe it or not, she loves to cook, wants at least four children, and best of all, she adores me. Goes to show you Al; you're not always right."

"I'm glad I was wrong then, Norm. But did you have to pick a woman named Norma? Sounds ridiculous calling both of you Norm." The partners joked and talked for another few minutes and then went back to work.

Judy was waiting by Alex's desk, holding a white

envelope. "This just came in for you. Special messenger marked personal."

He took the plain white envelope from her and noticed his name handwritten in bold black letters. As he tore open the flap, a cashier's check dropped to the desk.

"What is it?" Judy asked.

Alex looked closer. "It's a check for twenty thousand dollars. Wait, there's a note inside. 'The enclosed represents a donation to your charitable fund.' I'll be damned. Who the hell would send me twenty thousand? Judy, get the messenger service on the phone and try to find out who sent this."

"Oh, God," Judy wailed. "He took the receipt with him and I didn't catch the name on it. I'm sorry, Al. He never mentioned what service he was with and I didn't think to ask what with the party going on when he delivered it."

"Never mind then. I just wish I knew who to thank for this largesse. Should I split it up into a lot of pet charities or should I put it all down on one big one? I'll have to think about it for a while. I guess the only thing to do is deposit this into the fund."

As he listened to Eleanor a few hours later, he knew where some of the money would go. She told him a story about a five-year-old Brazilian girl whose parents were trying to scrape up enough money to bring her over to arrange surgery at Michael Reese. The doctors were ready to donate their services, and a few people were trying to get contributions for a special fund to cover the other costs.

"Say no more. I'll finance the trip and their stay here for however long it takes."

"Alex, she has to be flown over on a charter flight. There has to be a doctor and nurse along. She'll never make it on a commercial flight, not in her condition. It

430

will cost a fortune. I just wanted you to contribute a small amount."

"I said get moving. Make the arrangements." He calculated the amount needed to start the ball rolling, and within moments he realized what he would do with the rest of the money—buy new beds and furnishings for the fleabag hotel that housed panhandlers on Madison Street. It was run by an honest man who only charged fifty cents a night for lodging. He made no profit on the rooms or on the soup he doled out night after night. The owner was an alcoholic who hadn't had a drink in many years. He knew the problems these men faced. Several nights a week, in the shabby dining room of the hotel, counselors conducted self-improvement meetings which most of the men attended; they had nothing else to do except watch the fuzzy television set on a shelf high up on a dirty wall. The men and the women who chaired the rehabilitation meetings provided them with some diversion on their drab evenings.

The day the painters and furniture men came in to redo the sleeping quarters was an exciting one, the subject of every rheumy-eyed wino's conversation for days. The "hostel" for impoverished men of the streets was a nine-day wonder. Three floors were done, one at a time; painted and then furnished with new cots and night stands. Movable screens were set in place between each bed to offer the residents a small measure of privacy, and the windows were washed sparkling clean and hung with plastic drapes. The bathrooms were refitted with new fixtures and shower stalls. Then the main floor, which consisted of the dining room and Chick's small living quarters—no one knew the owner's full name—received a fresh coat of paint and a new television set. Chick blabbered his thanks, shaking Alex's hand for the hundredth time and gazing around in wonder at the fresh-looking surroundings.

"I can never thank you enough. When you helped me five years ago and got me off the hook on that forgery charge, I thought that was the most anyone could do for a poor old ex-wino—but now this. I truly love those poor guys who have no homes. Not all of them are addicted to the bottle; some are society's rejects, but they're all human beings nevertheless. I can remember a time when my own mother would have nothing to do with me, she was so disgusted with my endless promises to stop drinking and my detestable habits. When A.A. finally straightened out my head I promised I would do all I could to help people who'd hit the lowest rung of the ladder, like me. But it's getting harder and harder, lad. The little money these men can afford isn't enough to keep the place up to par. I fear the demolition trucks will come in on us and flatten out the entire building and leave a vacant lot in its place."

"Chick, there's a way you can keep things spic and span and avoid violating any building codes."

"The good Lord only knows how, for I can't think of anything except printing my own money."

"Listen," Alex said. "I know a lot of the men spend their days panhandling but many of them get checks regularly: social security checks, welfare, money from home, from relatives. You know just who gets what. Have a meeting after the redecorating and set everyone straight with new rules. From each check you cash, take a small percentage for bed and board. They'll only drink or squander it away if you don't insist, and you won't be asking for a lot. If a man gets twenty-five dollars a month, ask for four or five. The men who don't get a check, well, ask them to put a quarter or dollar in the kitty whenever they've had a good day. I should think, in their lucid moments, every single one of them would be willing to do so—for a better atmosphere and a better supper. Right now you provide a watery soup or stew, day-old bread, and coffee. If they all would do their share you could upgrade the food, keep them healthier in the long run. Cold weather's coming, and it's a fact you lose some of your men every winter when they lie down for a moment in a doorway or an alley and freeze to death. For fifty cents each, the Salvation Army or Goodwill will provide warm winter coats and shoes. Tell you what, Chick, I'll give my parish a call and see if they can start a drive going for men's clothing. When it starts coming in, you can set aside a small area where the men can pick up what they need and from time to time it can be replenished by charitable organizations."

"Of course I cash the checks for these guys, but I'm a sucker for a sob story. They always promise they'll throw a little money in the kitty, but I never get tough about it. You're right. I should. It'll be better in the long run if I do. I'll get Whitey, my chief cook and bottle washer to help at the meeting. The men generally listen to what he has to say. Alex you're a wonder. If ever there's anything me or my guys can do for you, you've got it. That's a promise."

The *Times* and the *Daily News* had reporters out at the end of the week. Feature stories appeared in these papers, heartwarming but filled with pathos. The hundred or so residents of the renovated, skid-row house beamed with pride over this interest in their lonely lives, and the majority pledged to keep the place clean as a sign of appreciation for its owner. Of course there would be backsliding, for alcoholics were always ready with promises that they usually forgot; but Chick established new rules in a rousing, loud meeting and they did improve the situation.

Shortly after that project was finished, Alex was reading the paper to Tekla one night after dinner. She only liked to hear the headlines and the movie gossip.

Her eyesight was fading and even with the hated spectacles she could no longer make out the print, but she could still see her nieces and nephews clearly enough and she was grateful for that. As Alex folded over a page the telephone rang. Zoysia answered it. "Carmella would like to speak to you. She tried your upstairs number first and thought you would be down with your aunt."

"Hello, carmel corn." Alex laughed. "What's up?"

"One of these days I'll think of a really weird name for you, you nut, then I'll phone the papers and give an exclusive interview."

"I'm already called Stormy, but if you come up with something more interesting I'll go along."

"How are your aunt and your sisters?"

"Fine. Tekla is just falling asleep as a matter of fact. She took her medicine about fifteen minutes ago and it's sending her off to dreamland. El's still happy as a teenager with Sid. I think she said she was coming over to see the settlement house this Sunday, but she'll call if she does. Sid wants to donate some gym equipment or a movie projector and a screen. He'll talk it over with you first, though. Anything wrong, Carm? You sound out of breath."

"You'll never believe the good luck that came our way. I've found a counselor for the girls at last. Someone who lives right on the premises. You remember we put in an outside stairwell to keep the girls' and boys' facilities separate? Well, today Giovanni fixed up the upstairs back rooms. He made a beautiful little bedroom and sitting room for the new girl we've hired. Naturally we can't pay her a big salary, but she will get room and board, eat with us at our house. From the dues we collect and the donations that come in, we can afford to pay her a little something and she's positively thrilled by the offer. She lived a couple of blocks away,

434

poor dear, and her landlord was ready to put her on the streets when she came to me looking for work. She took care of her retired father, but he had a stroke and when he died last month the pension checks stopped coming in. Not that they were all that large, just enough to keep body and soul together it seems. Well anyway, Gia Rugerio arrived at a providential moment. Giovanni is insisting I slow down. What with working at the store and running back and forth to the settlement house, I confess it was getting to be too much. The years are beginning to creep up on me, Alex. I guess I should take it a little easier. You'll remember we never had any problems getting counselors for the boys. There were enough willing hands to help with them, but now I can say I have a complete roster to keep the place running full force. Gia's moving in today. Want to join us and meet my scrawny little chicken on Sunday? Actually she's not scrawny, but I don't think she's eaten a good meal for a long, long time. She has these huge soulful dark brown eyes, and I promise you, after a few months I'll have her fattened up. She'll be a real beauty."

Alex grinned at her excitement. "Slow down, Carm. I'll be there at three. Maybe El and Sid can come at the same time, then we'll have a good get-together if you don't mind all of us barging in on you at one time."

"I'd love that. I haven't seen my godchild for a few months so we have a lot of gossiping to do. She'll love Gia. See you Sunday."

That Sunday Eleanor and Sid agreed to go to Carmella's with Alex. They arrived early to sit with Tekla for a while before going on to Taylor Street. For over a half-hour Tekla talked with them, even making a few witty comments. Then she dropped off to sleep after taking her pills and Eleanor tenderly pulled the covers up to her sagging chin. As they walked with

Alex down the front steps Eleanor was almost in tears.

"She's fading away right before our eyes," she said in the car. "Every few days she looks a little older, more wrinkled, more sick. She can't last much longer and what will we do without her? She's been like our mother all these years, worrying about us, being there when we needed her, helping out financially. Life will be empty when we lose her; nothing will be the same again."

"I know," said Alex, "but what else can we do but keep her comfortable and happy? What do you think Sid? How long does she have?"

"I really can't say," Sid answered. "She's into her late eighties isn't she? In my opinion the only thing keeping her alive is sheer determination. She's fighting against death with all her strength and will power."

"I don't understand it," Eleanor put in. "I don't mean to sound cruel, but when we were younger she used to talk with anticipation about meeting her fiancé Józef in heaven, and her brother and Mama. Then suddenly, years ago, she changed. She never mentioned Józef again and changed the subject when I brought up his name. Something happened. I remember how she used to go to church every Sunday and sit up in the front pew as though it belonged to her. Then one Sunday she sat in the last pew and never again went to the front of the church. She stopped receiving communion too, and Father Adam often asked me what the problem was. He even came to talk to her a few times, but she wouldn't budge. She'll talk to me about almost anything except why she doesn't want the priest to visit her with communion every first Friday."

Sid expertly guided the car through the snowy streets. "Maybe you should try harder. Something's on her mind, that's for sure, and she might feel better if she

436

gets it off her chest. I doubt she'll see her next birthday."

The gloomy discussion ended as they walked into Carmella's house, Eleanor bearing an armful of fresh flowers, Sid the newest Italian record album. They were greeted warmly and then Giovanni poured wine.

Alex noticed a woman sitting shyly on the corner of the sofa. She was almost lost in the soft cushions. Taking a second glass of wine, he walked over and offered it to her.

"You must be the delightful Gia. Carmella's been raving about you." She looked up at him and he was dazzled by the most beautiful eyes in the whole world. They were bottomless, no other color marred their rich deep brown; and he felt he would lose control if he stared into their depths too long.

Carmella bubbled over.

"Where have I left my manners? I must introduce you all to my new and good friend, Gia. Gia, this is Alex, the one I've been raving about. His sister, Eleanor and her friend, Sid. You should know them by now for God knows I've talked about my other family often enough in the past few days. Gia is our fantastic new instructor, and I must say she has marvelous plans for the settlement house. We'll talk about them over dinner, which is ready right now. Come on, everyone, grab a chair. I have minestrone, home-made pasta so light it will float into your stomachs like a feather, chicken cacciatora, and a salad. For dessert we'll have creamy spumoni and biscotti. Eat your fill for I don't allow leftovers."

They groaned at the sight of the overladen table, and Carmella had to put leftovers away after all. Six people couldn't possibly eat all the food she had prepared with such a lavish hand.

"Oh, well," she relented, "I won't have to cook for a few days."

Alex sat on the sofa next to Gia, and as the afternoon eased into evening, he learned more about her. She was twenty-five, born in Italy, came over when she was nine. Her mother had been a sickly woman who had missed Italy and her hometown where her large family still resided. She had only lived for three years in America, dying when Gia was thirteen. Gia's father had wanted to send his motherless daughter back to the old country, but she had pleaded and begged him to let her stay. They had originally come from a small, dusty little village where a woman either married a farmer or went into a convent, and all marriages were arranged by relatives. Gia couldn't bear the thought of grubbing away at the almost lifeless soil. Even though her father was only a railroad worker here, he earned enough to keep them comfortable. At last a compromise was reached. She would stay and keep house for him until she was of a marriageable age—eighteen or nineteen. Her father had grasped the notion that in America a girl was free to marry for love rather than convenience but he intended to have the final say on her choice.

When she was seventeen her father had a massive stroke and remained bedridden for the next eight years. He could speak only with great difficulty. Gia spent the following years looking after him, scrimping to get by on his pension money, which wasn't much for he had only been on the job for eight years. Still there was enough to pay the rent and utilities and to have the doctor come in once a month to check on her father's health. What was left went for food. Her father urged her to find a nice young man and marry, but she wouldn't hear of it.

"Later," she promised. "Later when you're better I'll get a proper job, meet new people."

But he didn't get better. After the funeral she found

herself with ten dollars and a roof over her head for another week. "But I'm a survivor," she told Alex. "I knew I'd find work, and with the experience I'll gain at the settlement house I'll be able to get a better job later. Something will come up."

She hadn't volunteered all this information. Alex had slowly pried it from her. She would normally have been ashamed of herself for confiding in a stranger but he seemed so concerned, she couldn't help herself. What an interesting man, Gia thought. I've never spoken to one person for such a length of time in my entire life. No wonder he's so good in the courtroom. I'd probably confess to a crime myself if he was questioning me. Already she felt they were friends. So did Alex, who told her about himself, his work, his family.

Finally Alex realized Eleanor was looking at him pointedly. He glanced down at his wristwatch and was surprised to find it was past eleven. Where had the hours flown? Eleanor whispered to him as they were putting on their coats.

"Because of you I'm afraid we overstayed our welcome. I tried to catch your attention several times but you were so engrossed with Gia, you never looked our way once. I saw Carm smothering a yawn behind her hand and was ready to come over and kick you in the shins. Really, Alex, they have to get up early tomorrow and open the store. Don't tell me you finally met the girl of your dreams? You were sitting there in a trance all night. Has she bewitched you?"

"She's a marvelous girl, El. The time flew by. I have to see her again. There are still hundreds of questions I forgot to ask, a hundred things I meant to say."

Eleanor winked at Sid in the dim light cast by the street lights and crossed her fingers. She'd met some of the women Alex took out occasionally, and none of them had seemed a fitting match for her only brother. She had also met Selma on several occasions, and although she admired her tremendously she knew Selma and Alex were both too strong-willed to be anything more than friends. Selma had changed drastically over the years. She had lost weight and looked fit and trim, almost svelte. Her hair was kept short still, but it now had a feminine wave; and she had learned how to apply makeup to bring out her best features. Once in a while Eleanor felt Alex and Selma were bound to wind up together, although her brother denied it repeatedly. "We're not romantically suited, El. Selma and I will always be good friends."

"But sometimes enjoying someone's company becomes a habit. You just might decide to throw your lot in with Selma out of habit."

She had no way of judging Gia, not from one meeting, especially when Alex had monopolized her for practically the whole evening; but she wanted to see this woman again, perhaps without Alex around so she could get a better idea of what fascinated him. She made a mental note to visit the settlement house one afternoon this week.

On Thursday she had a few free hours after visiting Tekla, and she decided this was the perfect day to visit Carmella, then walk to the settlement house down the block. The ice had melted from the streets so she felt safe risking the drive. Usually, in bad weather, she preferred to get around by taxi. The thought of losing control of the car scared her to death. Business was hectic at the store—several customers were waiting to be taken care of—so Eleanor waved a hand at Carmella and told her she would be back in an hour or so.

"I'll run over to see how Gia's making out and see what equipment the girls can use. If Sid can be generous with the boys' section then I can do my share for the girls."

Carmella waved her godchild off.

440

"It will be quieter here in an hour and we can have a cup of coffee. Gia will have some free time now. The girls don't start coming in until after school so you'll have a chance to get to know one another better."

Pulling up her hood to thwart the frigid breeze wailing down the street, Eleanor walked with head bent against the wind. She only walked a half block, but the stinging cold brought a rosy tinge to her cheeks. Running up the outside staircase, she opened the heavy door halfway and pushed herself through, glad to be in a warm room again.

Gia, in the main hall setting up posters, looked around in surprise at the unexpected visitor. Her face blushed a becoming shade of pink. "What a nice surprise on such a cold day. Actually two surprises in one day, for Alex called not more than ten minutes ago."

"He did? I thought he would have called you first thing Monday morning."

"Oh, he did then too," Gia answered. "He's called every day since Sunday and he even came over twice in the evenings after I'd finished my work. He called today to ask me to the opera on Saturday." Her face glowed. "I've never been fortunate enough to see an opera, I've only heard the arias on a phonograph and my recordings are so scratchy. Please take your coat off. We'll have tea in my room; it's warmer there."

Eleanor noted the shabby tan sweater Gia wore. It was several sizes too large, and she guessed it must have belonged to her father for it was a man's sweater. Gia had rolled up the sleeves to accommodate her shorter arms.

"Do you mind if I look around?" Eleanor asked, letting her gaze sweep around the large room. "It's been awhile since I've been here, and it looks so much cleaner and brighter than when I last saw it.

"Please do. I'll call you in a few minutes when tea's

441

ready or just feel free to come out back. It's the las
door down the long hall."

Eleanor noticed a long table filled with scraps o
brightly colored felt. Stuffing rag dolls was bein
taught in this section. Several shelves of books line
one wall, and some comfortable reading chairs were se
near the double windows where the light came i
clearly even on a gloomy day. The posters Gia had bee
hanging seemed to be painted by youngsters. The
burst into a galaxy of color on the painted walls, an
their subjects extolled the Easter season which woul
be coming in two months. It seemed incongruous to b
looking at colored eggs and bunnies on a day like toda
but spring was coming and with it Holy Week. In th
center of the room stood two Ping-Pong tables, an
Eleanor saw all the necessary equipment for the gam
stored neatly on shelves or hanging from hooks on th
walls. She walked down the corridor as Gia ha
suggested and tapped lightly on the last door.

"Come in. I usually keep the door shut. It keep
most of the warmth in until they raise the furnac
higher at two o'clock."

Eleanor entered a tiny sitting room with softl
printed drapes at the windows. A used, but comfort
able sofa was placed in one corner. Its covering and th
drapes were made of the same material. Before the sof
was a low, covered table.

"It's only an old orange crate," Gia explained, notic
ing El's interest. "It does double duty; I can store som
of my books beneath." A radio-phonograph stoo
along one wall, and one corner was set aside for
cabinet which held a hot plate, a small table, and tw
chairs.

"It's a cozy room." El complimented her. "You'v
made it look like a real home."

Gia opened the door to the bedroom, which wa

442

small but tastefully furnished, its walls a sunny yellow, a white chenille spread on the bed, and drapes to block drafts at the windows. An antiquated nightstand with a reading lamp atop it stood by the bed; and a dresser adorned with a picture of a strong-looking man and a petite dark-haired woman rested along one wall.

"Your parents?"

"Yes, it's the only picture I have of them. It was taken shortly after we arrived here."

"Your mother was beautiful and your father a strong handsome man."

"Yes. He was before the illness came on. He shrunk so in his last years one could hardly recognize him at the end. But come, tea is ready."

Back in the sitting room, they sat together on the sofa, enjoying steaming mugs of tea and a small plate of cookies.

Gia was nervous and gulped down a long swallow of hot tea. Then, with a burst of courage, she decided to speak first. She set her cup down on the table, spilling a few drops onto the cloth, her words hardly more than a whisper in the quiet room.

"I think I know why you've come today, Eleanor, and I can't blame you. I think I would do the same were I in your place."

"What?" Eleanor asked, astonished.

"No, wait. Please let me finish while the words are clear in my mind. If I don't say them right away, they'll all become jumbled and confused and I'll sound like an idiot. You've come to warn me away from Alex, haven't you? There he is, handsome and bright, destined to go very far; yet after one meeting he seems to be fascinated with me, a little nobody who can't possibly further his career, a woman too shy to stand beside a man who's fast becoming famous. I can't stop him from calling but I can put him off, pretend I'm interested in someone else. That will put a stop to things. I was so astonished when he showed an interest in me that I couldn't help myself."

Eleanor sat, thunderstruck, for a moment, then she put her arms around Gia who was sitting with downcast eyes.

"Oh, my dear, how could you think that of me? Gia, you've got it all wrong. Alex is his own man. He chooses his company. I'm happy, truly happy, that at last he seems to be genuinely fond of someone. Don't get me wrong. He has gone out with other women, but it's always been casual. I feared he would never find someone he could care for as deeply as he cares about law and politics. Gia, look at me please."

The small, beautiful girl raised her sad dark eyes, now brimming with unshed tears, and a smile began to form on her face.

"You don't mind then?"

"No you silly girl. I feel we're going to be very good friends. You have to understand how matters are between Alex and me. When I went through a very difficult period in my life some years ago Alex was the one person I turned to for comfort. He helped me do what was best for me when for so many years I had been a stupid fool. Since that time we've become very close. Next to Sid, he's the dearest person in my life. I suppose Carmella has told you something about the arrangement Sid and I have?"

"Only a little. Just a little. But I admire you for living your life as you want."

"Well, now that we've gotten these bothersome details out of the way, let's just sit and talk for a few minutes before the children start bombarding you."

Gia's laugh tinkled in the air.

"You'll know when they're coming because there'll be a great amount of squealing and singing. They're so exuberant."

"Tell me about the opera. It sounds exciting."

"Yes, it is. I've never been to one so I made Alex promise we'd sit up in the balcony because I don't have an elegant gown like those ladies on the main floor will wear."

"That's ridiculous," El said. "Anyone with a ticket can sit on the main floor and so should you. I hope Alex didn't take you seriously."

"I'm afraid he did. I said I wouldn't go otherwise. I refuse to shame him in front of people he might know."

"Gia, Alex doesn't care a fig about your clothes. He's impervious to what people wear. You could wear an old burlap bag and it wouldn't make a bit of difference."

"El—"

"Oh, all right. I know I'm meddling and I promise I'll stop, but my brother is a down-to-earth guy and I'm hoping in time you'll see that for yourself."

Running feet could be heard in the outer rooms and shrill cries filled the air.

"That's my cue to leave." Eleanor stood up, slipping on her heavy coat. "Gia, since Sid's sort of taken the boys' section under his wing, I told him I would do the same for the girls. What do you need most right now?"

"Eleanor, how kind of you. A sewing machine would be a gift from heaven. I could teach the girls to make simple clothes. Some of them have so few. It wouldn't have to be new, there are some good secondhand ones."

"Say no more. A sewing machine it is, along with several bolts of material, some needles, pins, thread— the works. I was poor once too."

"No," Gia protested. "I don't believe it."

"Well, we were. Did you ever have underdrawers made with flowers on the front and stripes on the back?"

445

They both laughed.

"No," Gia answered, "but mine were patched until they fell apart. At least you had a strong pair."

"Yes, but I was always afraid that I would be in an accident and have to be rushed to the hospital. I could see all the doctors and nurses laughing when they saw what I was wearing."

"El, please come again."

"I will. I'll be back at least every other week, more if my aunt is feeling better. Take care, Gia. Have a wonderful time with Alex. He needs someone like you."

On the following Saturday evening Gia opened the door in response to Alex's loud knock. He looked so elegant in his camel-colored topcoat and dark suit that for a moment she could only stare. She noticed the gold cuff links gleaming at the wrists of his immaculate white shirt and then looked down with dismay at the five-year-old flowered print she wore. When it was new the flowers had been a soft pink, but repeated washings had toned them down until they almost matched the light gray in the background. She went to get the black wool coat that had seen her through more than a few winters; the sleeves were too short but with a pair of black gloves it wasn't too noticeable.

"You look beautiful, Gia," Alex said proudly, taking her arm.

Was he perhaps making fun of her?

"Not as grand as you, Alex, but this is my Sunday best."

He looked puzzled at her remark. "I'm not grand, just ordinary. You're the one who is extraordinary."

He escorted her down the stairs and into his car. He had left the engine running so it was filled with warmth. Gia suddenly felt a twinge of trepidation. She hoped the tickets were, as promised, in the balcony. She wouldn't apologize for being poor but she didn't like to

446

walk into a crowded auditorium in her drab attire.

Her palms were damp with perspiration as Alex parked the car and they walked across the street to the opera house. It was ten minutes before curtain time and many elegantly dressed women escorted by handsome men were walking through the main door. Furs were present in abundance—mink, fox, chinchilla, and sable—and Gia noted the frequent glitter of jewels. Occasionally a plainer dressed woman walked along with the crowd, no doubt headed for the lower priced seats. Gia held her head up high, proud that Alex could fit in with any of the men in the throng. If she couldn't be a credit to him, at least she wouldn't put her head down in shame.

They entered an elevator and some of Gia's pent-up anxiety left her. Now she would be among her own kind. But when they emerged, an usher clad in red and gold escorted them to a private box, of all things. She stood transfixed in the doorway. These were the best seats in the house, and there were more than two chairs in the costly box. Who would share it with them?

"Alex, you promised."

"But, Gia my love, I tried. All the balcony seats were sold out weeks ago. Luckily a man I know offered us the use of his season box. He and his family are out of town so, you see, we have it all to ourselves. You'll enjoy your first opera much more from this vantage point."

He helped her off with her coat and sat her in one of the plush front seats. She gazed around with wonder and then turned back to him.

"I feel that everyone is staring at me. They're probably wondering what a poor waif like me is doing here in someone else's seat."

"These are our seats for tonight, Gia. Don't bother looking at anyone. If some people stare at you, love, they're wondering who this remarkably good-looking woman is."

She had no more time for questions for the overture began and she was lost in the drama unfolding on the stage. Within minutes, to Gia it was no longer pretense but a real story. At intermission there was a tapping at the door and several men entered the box. They shook hands with Alex, and one of them chided him.

"Ah, Stormy, are you finally getting some culture? Tired of battling it out in every courtroom in the city?"

"Who's the lovely woman who finally put a new interest in your life?" another asked.

"Senator Clark, Judge Leonard, Congressman Rales, Joe, I'd like you all to meet the woman who's going to be my wife. As soon as she agrees that is."

Gia gasped with embarrassment, but the assembled men looked at her admiringly and offered their collective congratulations.

"Maybe she'll tame you, Stormy," one said as the lights dimmed. Then they hurried back to their seats, each taking a long, last look at the black-haired beauty seated in the box.

"Alex, what's wrong with you? Why did you tell your friends we were to be married?"

"Shush, love. Later."

She couldn't concentrate for the rest of the evening, so turbulent were the thoughts running through her head. Finally as the last aria was being sung she paid strict attention. She applauded loudly when the curtain fell, and tears streamed down her cheeks as she cried, "Bravo." Suddenly, despite her excitement, she realized many eyes were looking up in her direction. Alex's announcement had certainly been spread quickly.

When they were back in his car she spoke her first words since intermission.

"Alex, why did you say what you did? You barely know me. Are you trying to make a fool of me, humiliate me?"

He pulled the car over to the curb.

"Don't ever say anything like that again." Suddenly he pulled her to his chest kissing her hair, her face, her upturned mouth. "You are going to marry me. I knew it ten minutes after I met you. If you dare say no I'll only follow you around, I'll never let you rest until you do."

"Oh, Alex. I felt that way too, but what made you choose me? You must know many women."

"Because you are the person I've been searching for to share my life. You're the woman I was waiting for."

She nestled under his arm as they drove home slowly.

"One thing though, Gia. You mustn't make me wait too long. I'll give you two months. Then you'll marry me willingly or I swear I'll carry you off to a justice of the peace in Indiana."

"But you're sweeping me off my feet. It's all too much. Please give me a chance to catch my breath."

He squeezed her tighter. "You'll have eight weeks to catch your breath. We'll be married the Saturday after Easter. Okay?"

"Yes, Alex. I love you."

"I love you too, Gia *mia*."

At the next red light, he turned to kiss her again and her body weakened as if under a spell. But their mood was broken by impatient honking behind them. Unconcerned, Alex put his foot back on the gas pedal.

"Tomorrow we'll make it official. You'll meet the rest of my family. I'd like you to meet my aunt who's taken care of me since my mother died. I want the two of you to know each other before she worsens. I feel she won't be with us much longer, and I doubt she'll make it to our wedding. She'll love you, darling, just as I do."

449

Tekla's fading eyes shone with happiness when Alex brought Gia into her bedroom the next afternoon. She held Gia's hand as Alex introduced her.

"Hand me my spectacles, Alex. Your betrothed has a lovely voice, but I can't see her face clearly. It's all a blur."

He took the glasses from the stand and put the rims over her ears.

"That's much better. Why, Al, she's beautiful. She looks like that movie star you showed me a picture of in one of the newspapers. What was her name? Audrey? Yes, that was it, Audrey Hepburn. I never did get a chance to see her in a movie, but from her pictures I could tell any film she was in would be excellent. What a lovely name you have, child. Gia. Can't you be married sooner? I know you've just met recently, but if both of you are certain, why wait?" A frown crossed her face. "Your mother waited and it was her undoing. If she hadn't waited she would have had Alex."

Eleanor and Alex looked at each other, surprised. Eleanor made a motion with her hand to let the matter lie.

"Aunt, Lent is coming up so we can't get married until after Easter, but the first Saturday after Easter Sunday I promise you it will happen."

Tekla took off her glasses and laid them on the cover.

"Oh, yes. Lent. I seem to forget so many things lately. Of course, I forgot all about Lent." She patted Gia's hand, which she still held in hers. "It will be a lovely wedding after Easter. We can hold the reception in the garden behind my place of business and everyone will be there." Her eyes closed and she dropped off to sleep.

The three of them left the bedroom to join the others in the living room. Irena, Stan, their two children, and Sid. Eleanor flopped onto the sofa.

450

"What was Tex talking about?" Alex asked Eleanor. "Why did she bring up Mama's name and say she could have been happy? What was all that about waiting and having Alex? I'm Alex."

"I know, dear, but her mind's been wandering more these past few days. For a few minutes she's lucid; then I don't understand most of what she's saying. Sometimes she thinks I'm Mama and she tells me to take money from the drawer and go out and enjoy myself. The other day Stan walked in and she shouted at him. She said he should stay dead. Alex, it's getting worse. There's something terrible troubling her and she can't seem to find peace of mind. Zoysia says she thrashes in bed during the night, crying out in terror. Al, what are we going to do?"

Gia's quiet voice intervened. "May I give a suggestion?"

"Of course, love," Alex replied. "She's not in terrible pain so I don't like to see her taking too much medication, but none of us knows quite how to calm her down when she carries on."

"Toward the end, when my father knew he wasn't going to last much longer, I called in our parish priest and it made him feel ever so much better after he talked with him. The priest came every day and Papa's eyes stopped looking so tormented. He began to accept the fact that he was dying, and with the acceptance came an inner peace."

"But she doesn't want a priest," El cried. "I've asked her hundreds of times and she shouts at me."

"Don't ask her, just call him. See what happens."

They all looked at one another. Irena strode to the phone. "How stupid of us. She can't throw the priest out once he's here. Father Adam will come. He's a friend of the family and he's been asking us for ages why Tekla won't see him." She completed the call and

Father Adam promised to be there within the hour. The family sat in the living room, drinking coffee, their tension mounting as they wondered what Tekla would do when she saw the black-frocked assistant pastor. Since they were young and were upset by the turn of events, Irena's children were sent home to watch television. She and Stan didn't want them brooding over an impending death. The young ones loved Tekla, but as she used to be—strong and determined, always with a kind word or a treat for them. They were frightened of what she had become, an old woman withering away in her bed and saying strange things they didn't understand.

Everyone still in the living room started when the bell rang. Irena hurried to open the door.

"Father, please come in," she said.

The priest entered and looked at them expectantly.

"Has she changed her mind about seeing me?"

"Please sit down, Father," Eleanor said. "We'd better explain something before you see our aunt. No, she hasn't changed her mind, but she's getting worse and the trouble that's been plaguing her is something awful to see. It's not like her. She was never afraid of anything."

"Let me talk to her. Perhaps she's ready for me."

"Send Zoysia out here with us," Alex said. "You can talk to her in private, but if she gets too agitated at seeing you then I must ask you to leave the room. We can't have her more excited. She can't take it."

"I will," the kindly priest answered. He looked down at the woman lying in the bed. How tired and worn she is, he thought. Her lips were pursed in a tight frown, her hands plucked at the fringed coverlet. Zoysia rose from the chair beside the bed and the priest took her place. He gently lifted one of Tekla's agitated hands into his own, and the distraught woman opened her eyes. At

452

the sight of the priest, a wild look came into them.

"Go away," she croaked. "You can't help me. No one can. Only the devil is waiting for me."

"God is waiting for you, Tekla, not the devil, never the devil. Only our Lord wants you. He loves you dearly and will banish thoughts of the devil."

"No, God will have nothing to do with me—not after what I did. God has forsaken me. My soul is lost."

The priest's soothing voice droned on. "Tekla, God does not abandon even the worst of sinners. Talk to me, Tekla. Tell me what haunts you so. Talk to me as though I were the very Lord sitting in front of you."

"Even you will look at me with disgust, even you will run from me. I'm a murderess father. I killed my niece's husband, Roman."

"My dear, you did no such thing. It was Roman's time to go."

"And I helped him on. I killed him for abusing his wife all those years—for drinking, womanizing, for trying to commit incest with his own frightened daughter. I saved Celia from his corrupt hands, and after he fell into a drunken sleep I went down, tied his hands, and put the pillow over his head until he was dead. He attempted to rape his own daughter. I killed him before he tried that again or before I was too weak to do what should have been done long ago. If I hadn't been there, he would have raped Celia, and if he had, her mind would have been gone. Only the convent saved her sanity after that horrid incident."

"Tekla, it was done in a rage. You were like a mother protecting her own. Look at me." He took a handkerchief from his pocket and dried the tears that were coursing down the distressed woman's wrinkled face. "When I became a priest, God extended to me his power of forgiveness. I am His spokesman on Earth. I tell you now in all honesty that God will forgive you.

453

He is understanding, loving. Tell God you're sorry and all will be put right."

"I'm glad Roman is dead, but am sorry because I wanted to meet my loved ones in heaven and that is now denied me."

"Then you are forgiven, my dear. Hold my hands and say the act of contrition with me."

She said the words along with him, haltingly, forgetting some of them for she hadn't uttered the prayer for so long. Father Adam laid his hand on her hot forehead and blessed her. A wan smile appeared on her sick face.

"Father, I believe He has given me another chance. I can see Józef's face again clearly. His face hasn't come to me for a long time, but I can see him now and he's smiling. He seems to be telling me that I'm freed."

"You are, Tekla. I swear to you that you are."

"Father, send in Alex. I must make full restitution. I must say all that needs to be said."

"Shouldn't you rest a bit first?"

"No, I must see him now before it's too late."

The family members, assembled in the living room, looked up with relief as Father Adam smiled at them.

"She talked to you?" El asked. "She really talked without sending you away?"

"Yes. She's better now. She wants to see Alex for a moment."

"What was bothering her?" Irena asked.

"I'm sorry, Irena, but that was between her and the Lord. She's carried a heavy burden on her frail shoulders, but it has been lifted. If she wants to, she'll tell you with her own lips; if not, there's nothing I can say."

"Of course," Irena answered. "I shouldn't have asked."

Alex moved across the room. "I'll go to her now."

Tekla's eyes were still wide open. It was unusual for

454

her to remain alert for such a length of time. A sparkle of light shone in the depths of her eyes and a smile swept across her face, making it appear younger, almost as it was before she'd become so frail.

"Aunt Texas, you're looking more like your old self again." Alex sat on the bed next to her and hugged her gently. "That's more like my old girl."

"Alex, my love. I almost feel strong. I almost feel that I could march down the aisle along with you. At least my mind feels that way, not my poor old body. My body has just about given up and it's time too. It's seen me through a great many years and it has served me well."

"As it will again," Alex said tenderly, holding her hands.

"No, I'm afraid not." She began to have difficulty getting the words out and she made an effort to make herself understood. "Alex, I've found peace at last. But there's one thing I haven't told you or the others. All these years I was so afraid to tell you, afraid you would think the worst; but it wasn't like that at all. It was a beautiful time. Alex, do you remember your mother?"

"Yes, I do. The most beautiful, comforting woman I've known next to you."

"She loved all of you, but most of all you. You were her special child, created with a man she loved." Tekla gasped with pain as her heart began to fail. She clutched her breast, forcing the pain to subside, but this time the ploy didn't work. The pain persisted, growing stronger by the second. "The box, Alex. Look in the box on the top shelf. The box all the way in the back. It will explain all I've been trying—" A last burst of agony shot through her; then she was still, her eyes half closed, her mouth gaped.

"Aunt Tex," Alex pleaded. "Wake up. You're not leaving us yet—not yet. Please wake up." He cried out in anguish.

Sid and Eleanor ran into the room, the others trailing behind them. Father Adam took charge, giving Tekla the last rites. She was truly gone. This special person who had helped form their lives had been taken from them. Tekla had now joined the other loved ones she'd waited for so long to see.

Those she had left were devastated. After her body was taken away they still sat as if in a daze. They'd known she didn't have long to live; yet her death stunned them. No one in the family felt able to call Celia so Father Adam made the necessary call.

Gia sat next to Alex, holding his hands in hers as tears streamed down his face. No words could comfort him, she knew, but the closeness of someone who loved him could diminish a portion of his grief.

The funeral was held three days later and the cortège that followed the hearse to the cemetery swelled to an unbelievable length. It seemed that everyone who lived within a mile radius came to bid Tekla goodbye, as did friends from other neighborhoods. It was a most fitting tribute to a woman who had devoted her life to making people happy. Resting in her coffin, Tekla appeared happy. She didn't look dead or cold; she looked as though she would spring back to life at any moment and laugh at their bereaved expressions.

Because of the mourning period, Alex and Gia had a quiet wedding. Only the immediate family and three or four friends attended the ceremony at St. Mary's church. Alex easily could have filled a hall that accommodated over a thousand people, but he didn't wish to postpone the nuptials once he'd made up his mind it was Gia he wanted. One crass reporter from the *Chicago Tribune* managed to uncover the time and place of the wedding. He came and brought a photographer with him, but a small group of parishioners waiting outside the church adroitly managed to politely push the two intruders back into their car before the newly married couple emerged.

After a small dinner at Eleanor and Sid's apartment, Alex and Gia headed for Miami and a week's honeymoon. Alex had promised his bride a longer trip in the future, but at the present a week was all he could manage because of his busy schedule.

Gia was happy during their one glorious week, discovering things about the man she loved, a man who loved her in return and proved it every waking moment. She'd never known such a tender, caring man. Her father had been gruff and had expected a subservient wife. He had never outwardly displayed affection, not to her or her mother. Once in a great while, on a special occasion, she had seen him give her mother a quick peck on the cheek, no more; yet she knew they must have been intimate during their private hours. The men in her neighborhood generally behaved in the same way. Love was saved for the quiet blanket of darkness. Carmella and Giovanni and a few others she knew were good-natured with each other, but their togetherness seemed more fun than deep emotion. Alex was a new experience in her sheltered life. He wasn't ashamed to proclaim his love. He held her hand as they walked and casually kept his arm around her shoulders. He treated her as an equal, not as the lesser half of a whole. The first night they slept together, she expected pain or humiliation to mar their union; instead she marveled at the soft touches that slowly awakened her desire to fever pitch. In return for the pleasure he gave her she wanted only to satisfy him. Their days in Miami were pure bliss. She could barely remember the scenery, their meals, or the people they met, only the look and feel of Alex's body as it slowly became known to her.

457

Seven days flashed by like seven hours. Back home they discussed mundane matters during the day, but their nights remained filled with newly found desires.

Gia insisted they live in the only home Alex knew, so they planned to remodel the downstairs apartment, Tekla's, for their own use and to live upstairs until the work was finished. Alex postponed looking into the box on the closet shelf for a while longer.

Chapter Twelve

"Alex darling, honestly, I'll enjoy cleaning out the house. You're busy. El promised to come over and help for the next few days. She can decide what should be done with your aunt's things. She'll see that they're divided up fairly, and whatever is old and useless will be thrown away. Irena's joining us whenever she has a few spare hours, so you can leave it all in our hands. It's enough that you're meeting with the contractor to explain the changes you want made. There now, does that sound fair?" Gia tickled his chin. "We'll all be doing our share while you earn the money to pay for it."

"Since you seem to be as fond of this old house as I am, I've a little surprise for you, love. I've bought out my sisters and the whole place is ours."

Gia squealed with excitement. "What? Oh, Al, that's wonderful. All ours, every single inch? Did they mind much? You didn't hurt anyone's feelings, did you? Perhaps El wanted a home to come back to in case she and Sid ever have serious problems."

"There are no hard feelings whatsoever. Irena was happy with her share of the money—she can pay off her mortgage—and Celia's asked me to donate her share to

459

the convent. It's short of funds for some essential repair work. El will never leave Sid, no matter how many times she tells us he may find someone else one day. Those two were meant for each other and one day El will realize that. She's very pleased with their apartment on Lake Shore Drive. Luxury suits her after her lean early years. She has a magnificent view, security, and a fabulous shopping area within walking distance. When she's here the neighbors only look at her strangely. They like her, but deep down they think she's a fallen woman for marrying out of her faith. They have decided that she and Sid are married, so don't let on that it isn't so. Thank God, the younger generation is more liberal. I've put aside Lydia's portion in case she shows up some day and that wraps everything up nicely." He put his arms around his wife's shoulders. "So, my love, this whole place is ours since you don't want to move into a newer home."

Gia hugged him, tears of happiness springing from her eyes.

"No, never. I love this one. It's more like a real home than any new one would be. This place has atmosphere and tradition behind it. It's already seasoned, like aged wine. I told you, I love it as it is, with no remodeling. Al, you should have seen the dingy basement apartment my father and I lived in. The rent was cheap so we were lucky to have it, but what a hole it was. Plaster cracking, pipes freezing in the winter, mice. It was so dark and damp. This place is heaven just as it is."

"Nope. It needs a new face, new wiring, a gas furnace, new plumbing. The whole house is showing its age, and it's about time it got the proper attention. We couldn't talk my aunt into changing anything. When she was younger she would have, but when she grew older and became ill she was more at ease in familiar surroundings. Thank you, love, for wanting to keep my home. I think I'd feel lost anywhere else. This is really home." He nuzzled his lips against her neck. "Still love me?"

"I'll never stop," she answered. "My guardian angel must have been watching over me and given me the notion to walk into the settlement house to ask for a job. If I hadn't we never would have met. Al, it was meant to be. And listen, today's our one-month anniversary." The doorbell rang as Alex kissed his wife good-bye.

"That must be El," she said, breaking away to open the door. "She said she would be here early so we could make some progress on cleaning things out."

"Good morning, my dears," Eleanor said. She was carrying a plastic bag. "I brought my old clothes because I have a feeling we're going to get a workout today. It's going to take a long time to decide what to do with Tekla's famous dishes. She had so many I don't know where to start. Irena doesn't want any; I don't. Gia, you couldn't possibly use all of them so I guess we'll have to pack them in cartons and give them to charity. I called Catholic Charities yesterday. They'll pick up some of the castoffs over the weekend. Personally I'd love to keep everything, but it just isn't possible. So much has accumulated over the years and most of it is terribly worn. I feel sort of guilty getting rid of any of it. It's like discarding part of our lives and showing Tekla we didn't care."

Alex put on his jacket. "She knew we cared. Getting rid of some junk isn't heartless. Think of the bargain hunters who'll enjoy what we don't need. Well, I'm off. You two have fun. God, I almost forgot. Just before she died Tekla told me to check out a box on the shelf. I don't know if she was rambling again or if she really meant we should look for something important. I don't even know which shelf she meant. Don't throw away

461

any papers, ladies. I'll go through them when I get home at about six. Tell you what. I'll even bring dinner. I'll call Sid and invite him over. I'll get some chicken, rolls, and cole slaw. We can set up a table on the back porch. It's going to be a beautiful day."

Eleanor changed into her work clothes. As she and Gia went downstairs, Gia put her arm around her sister-in-law's shoulders. "Thank you for giving up your share of the house. I hope Alex gave you all a fair price, but I want to tell you it's not too late if you feel you want to keep one of the apartments here for yourself."

"God, no. Whatever would I do with two places? I've grown quite fond of living where I am, and even if Sid and I split up I think I'd stay in the same area."

"You two will never split up, you silly goose. You're crazy about each other. I know it's permanent."

"Perhaps it is, but I don't want an apartment here. People stare at me with distrustful eyes. Our neighbors always thought I was a trifle odd, and when I buried my father in another section of the cemetery, they were sure I had a few loose screws even though they knew what he was like. When they heard Sid was Jewish, they ignored me completely, except for Anna next door. She's okay. What does Alex plan to do?" Eleanor asked.

"I don't know all the details yet. He just told me the news this morning, but I have a feeling the bedrooms will be upstairs and the living room, dining room, and kitchen will be down here. He wants to enlarge all the rooms. Okay, where do we start?"

"Good," Eleanor said looking around. "I see Al brought cartons. We can start in the pantry. There should be enough dishes, pots, and pans to fill at least ten boxes. But don't forget, as we go along if you see anything you like, just give a yell and we'll put it on the side."

The women delved into the spacious pantry, and when Gia decided to keep one set of dishes for everyday use, El explained that the set she chose was the first one Tekla acquired by going to the Ramova Theater. Along with the dishes Gia kept a set of ruby red goblets.

"They're so pretty," she exclaimed. "Especially when they catch the light. Just the color of rare old wine. I love them."

The pantry was cleared out by lunchtime so they took a break, heating up canned soup and making a fresh pot of coffee.

"Tired?" Eleanor asked after the dishes were washed. "We can stop for today if you like."

"Oh, no. I'm having a marvelous time looking through all these old things. El, how could you say you were poor when you have all these treasures to go through? My father and I had barely enough to fill one box. This old place is like a gold mine." Gia had already filled and put aside three cartons of things she wanted to keep. Besides the dishes and goblets, she fell in love with the little porcelain vases that stood on the top shelf of the pantry. They were dust coated from years of neglect, but she knew they would be lovely after a good washing. Then there were napkin rings, crystal glasses which were like new since Eleanor couldn't ever remember Tekla using them, dish towels which still looked sturdy and usable.

"What's next, El?"

"How about the closets and dresser drawers? We didn't find any papers in the pantry so we'll tackle one of the closets next. God, this is going to take forever. There's still the attic, the basement. I don't even remember how many things are stored there. My aunt was a great believer in saving everything."

When she walked into Tekla's bedroom Eleanor felt

tears spring to her eyes. The bed was made, Zoysia having given the room a thorough cleaning after Tekla's death.

"I promised Zoysia she could have most of the furniture down here. She has just gotten an apartment of her own, but it's still quite bare," Eleanor said, opening drawers.

"How is she doing? Will she be able to manage on her own?"

"Sure, she has a job at City Hall, cleaning in the evenings. Alex wanted to get her something easier, but she insisted she wanted to clean so he helped her get the job, helped her find the apartment too. It's right on Morgan Street. We gave her Jan's old bed and a couple of dressers. I think she wants the refrigerator and stove, and she can use the kitchen table and most of the living-room furniture. It's old but she feels comfortable with it. And to answer your earlier questions, we were poor. Not my aunt. She had money when she owned her own business, but after it was sold she lived on the proceeds from the sale and began dipping into her savings account. She put us through school on that, fed us, clothed us, paid the bills. There wasn't much left when she died. Alex and I took over the expenses when we started working, and she insisted on helping. She was always so independent; she hated feeling beholden to anyone. My father never brought home much, just enough to cover the bare essentials, and my mother hated taking anything from Tekla. She felt Tekla did too much as it was. My aunt was always there with something whenever we needed it. She was always a giver, never a receiver."

They went through the bureau drawers, filling another carton with Tekla's clothes. Eleanor kept the rosary beads and costume jewelry in the top drawer, but the dresses and coats hanging in the closet were added to the charity boxes.

Gia brought a chair from the kitchen and started handing down the storage cartons stacked high on the closet shelf. They put these on the bed and started going through them one by one. The first held delicate tissue-wrapped Christmas ornaments made of dainty blown glass: birdcages, little trumpets, angels, and glistening balls of red, blue, gold, and green. Gia was dazzled by the delicate trinkets and El laughed at her serious expression.

"But they're beautiful, El," Gia said. "We had Christmas trees too but all we had on them were cranberries and popcorn strung on a string; never anything as lovely as these."

"Then I guess you had better stack them in your pile."

"No, we'll share them equally. Irena would love to have some of these. So would you, and I'll bet Celia's convent puts up a tree. She'd probably want to donate some. I'll sort them out later."

The other boxes contained odds and ends: old buttons, scraps of material Tekla had put aside thinking they might be of use later, and stacks of paid bills which they put aside for Alex to look over. They found some Christmas and birthday presents Tekla had received over the years but never used, still in the original gift boxes: nightgowns, housedresses, several sweaters. Tekla wouldn't wear anything new until she'd gotten her money's worth from the old; she detested waste. In the last box, a very old hatbox, was the hat Dani had bought her aunt that first Christmas, slightly crumpled but still becoming. Beneath the torn cardboard liner lay a packet of papers in a frayed envelope. El examined them, a look of shock crossing her face as she ruffled through the contents.

"What is it, El? You look like you're going to faint.

465

Are you all right?"

"Oh, my God," Eleanor gasped. "How is Alex going to take this?" She held a faded picture of Alexander Pritzkin, the one printed in the paper along with his obituary. "It's the same picture Alex brought home one day long ago when he was in college. We joked about the similarity of their looks. This very same picture was in an old book Alex picked up at school. Now that I think about it, my aunt looked awfully pale when Alex showed her the photo. She said it hardly looked like our Alex. I thought it did, but I was late for work and forgot all about it five minutes later. Look, Gia, it's Alex in the flesh. An older Alex but still him. What is it doing here? There has to be some connection."

Eleanor shuffled through the papers again. There were unused passports, several brochures depicting the wonders of Switzerland, a tiny pin shaped like a slipper, another picture of the professor, this one in a small gold frame.

"Good Lord, what does this all mean?" Eleanor wailed.

"El, sit down for a moment. You're white as a sheet."

"Do I show this to my brother or throw it all away?"

"You're not throwing anything away. If something's wrong he has a right to know. Oh, El, I don't know what's happening but it sounds like dreadful news."

"I'm not sure, but I have a suspicion Alex had a different father than I. That has to be the answer. He's so different from me, Celia, Irena, even Lydia. He's dark, we're fair. He's much taller. His nose is aquiline; none of ours are. Tekla said he took after her side of the family, but I don't think that's the case. Look." She pointed to the framed photo. "Alex looks like him. Let's stop for the day, Gia. I don't feel I can go on now. It's after five and Alex will be coming home soon."

Eleanor's hands trembled as she replaced the papers

in the frayed envelope. Then she and Gia sat on the bed each thinking her own thoughts, both filled with concern for the man who might be most hurt by this unexpected event.

Alex and Sid came in together, carrying a six-pack of beer, cokes, a box of fried chicken, slaw, paper plates, and napkins. They were in a jubilant mood as they set up a card table on the back porch and didn't notice that both women were standing in the kitchen strangely silent.

"What's the matter with the two of you?" Alex asked. "I warned you not to work too hard, but both of you look all done in. We have all the time in the world. We're not in that much of a rush. The house won't fall apart in a few weeks."

El held the envelope pressed against her dusty blouse while Alex began to sense the uneasy feeling communicating itself across the room. He held out his hand silently, anxious to see what was upsetting his wife and sister. Gia was looking at him strangely. What the hell had they found today rummaging around? He opened the envelope, slowly examining the contents one by one.

"So this was what she was trying to tell me before she died." Alex's face wore a mask of pain. "She wasn't rambling. There was another Alex—this one. And he must be my father, at least I'd bet he was. It looks like they were planning to leave the country. He must have died before they had the chance. This explains Mama's loving books about Switzerland. El, think back. What do you remember? It's important."

Eleanor sat in the folding chair, fingers pressed against her temples.

"I remember going to get these pictures taken, but Mama said they were for our photo album. She said it was cheaper to go downtown, and she and Aunt Tekla told us we could window-shop for an hour or so after we took them. Tekla gave us money and said when we finished doing that we were to wait in a restaurant on the corner and order ice cream until they were done with the photos. It was a treat because I was put in charge of looking after my sisters. After we looked at a few windows we couldn't wait to order our sundaes so we ran into the shop. I remember feeling relieved because Lydia didn't act up as she usually did. She was well behaved for a change, and the waitress complimented Mama on our manners when she and Tekla came to join us. Alex, I had no idea we were taking passport photos. Mama must have had an extra set of pictures made; that one is in the album. I always thought the photos were ugly and wondered why Mama didn't throw them in the garbage." Eleanor started to laugh hysterically. "Oh, this is a fine turn of events." Between gales of laughter, she added, "She almost put one over on the old bastard after all. How earth-shattering it must have been when he died. Poor Mama. No wonder she carried on so before you were born."

"El, what's come over you?" Sid asked. "Stop, you're out of control."

Eleanor paid no attention to him, forgetting he was there. "Oh, how I hated him, Alex. You don't remember much—you were mostly out of the house—but I relegated him to the basement the day he lost his half of the tavern. He broke Mama's heart with his women, his abuse, and his drinking; and he broke Tekla's by losing the tavern. She had to sell out; it had been her life's work. He was a vile, evil man. I'm so happy he wasn't your father after all. Only Lydia, it seems, took after him, living a hedonistic, selfish life, caring for no one but herself. Things are beginning to fall into place. When I was with Tekla in the afternoons

468

she mumbled a lot. Now I'm beginning to see the light, to put it all together in proper perspective. Al, our mother loved this man, Alexander Pritzkin. I remember the day she came home with this slipper pin; she looked so happy. She stayed happy for weeks, singing, smiling to herself; then suddenly she was in bed crying and we were told it was because she didn't feel well because the new baby was on the way. Lydia wanted the pin for herself, and for the first time I saw Mama act selfishly. She hid the pin away and Lydia never did find it, although she used to sneak around when no one was home and search for it." Eleanor looked at the picture again. "He loved her too. Loved her so much he was willing to take us all away, even Tekla, according to these passports and the few things Tekla rambled on about. I feel he was going to give up everything for Mama: his job, friends—everything. But it says in the obituary that he was married too. Were they both going to get a divorce or just pretend they were married? I wish I knew. Tekla knew, but she can't tell us now. I should have paid more attention, but I didn't. Tekla mentioned a new life several times, but I thought she was talking about life after death. Give me more time and I'm sure I'll be able to remember something more. My mind's too muddled now."

Alex sat down, dazed.

"I can't believe this. Think of the odds against Norm's showing me that old book from the school library. Not one of the older teachers had ever made a remark about my resemblance to this man. Norm found the picture only because he had nothing better to do one afternoon than leaf through some old books when the girl he was waiting for didn't show up. I guess I was meant to find out."

Sid leafed through the papers and read the obituary that was practically crumbling in his hands.

"It says here that there was a brother named David. I know a David Pritzkin. He's one of the largest contributors at Michael Reese. El, don't you remember? In last year's fund-raising drive he donated enough to pay for half the wing they're adding on. He's in his seventies I believe and retired from business. His son's a whiz in the stock market and is involved in land developing. The father made a lot of money, but his son is phenomenal. They keep a low profile, but the family was written up once in one of the Sunday *Tribune* supplements. We heard at the hospital that the old man was furious over the feature story. If I remember correctly there's a daughter too. She's on the board for the annual Crystal Ball for the hospital. I think she's single and lives with her father on Astor Street. It has to be the same man. Want me to check it out? Al, my advice is to request an appointment and meet this David Pritzkin. If anyone can add some details, I'm sure he can. They were brothers and according to the obit there were only the two of them. You can't lose anything by trying. He might be able to fill in some of the missing pieces."

Alex looked up at Sid.

"I can't see how meeting him would be helpful after all these years. What good would it do? He probably doesn't know about me. If he doesn't what will seeing him accomplish? It might just shock an old man unnecessarily."

"You're never going to rest until you know for sure. The rest of your life you'll be wondering," Eleanor said leaning across the table. "We never did find out who donated the money for the high school scholarship. Remember how we tried, but no one would give us information? And then there was the scholarship to the University of Chicago. I know you deserved them, but there are thousands of boys who deserve financial help.

470

It was no coincidence. Someone's been watching over you, it seems. Who sent the check for twenty thousand dollars to your charity fund? Who sent you your first cases? It has to be this man. People, even millionaires, don't go throwing money about without some purpose or some sort of recognition or tax write-off. Maybe a few do, but I doubt it. See him, Al. He must have been the one helping you."

"What do I say when we meet? Do I throw my arms around him and cry on his shoulder because I'm his long-lost nephew? He'll have me arrested for trespassing, impersonation."

"You're talking like a silly ass now," Eleanor said angrily. "You don't want anything except the truth for God's sake. You're not going to steal the silverware."

"The right words will come to you when you meet," Gia said, taking his hand. "If he is, indeed, your uncle he'll find the right words to open up the conversation."

"They're right," Sid added. "Now can we eat? You may be overwhelmed but I'm starved. I've only had a few cups of coffee all day, skipped lunch because of an emergency. Now I'm going to sit down and eat even if the rest of you have lost your appetites."

"How do I go about getting this man's phone number?" Alex asked half-heartedly as he bit into a chicken leg.

"I'll see what I can come up with. Marcy, who handles donations, will have something in the files. But first let's try the phone book. You never know, he might be listed."

He wasn't, so Sid promised to delve further.

Later Gia lay next to Alex. He couldn't sleep although it was well past midnight.

"What a Pandora's box we've opened up for you, darling. Would you rather not have known? El was debating whether or not she should just throw the papers away."

"I'm glad she didn't. Even though I feel I'm being torn apart I have to get to the bottom of this. I guess this is how it would feel to learn you've been adopted. The foundation of your whole life seems shaken. Memories have been running through my mind these past few hours. I've been trying to recollect some of the things my mother told me when I was young and a few are coming back. She used to tell me I was going to grow up and make her proud. She told me her father said the same words to her when she left the old country, but she couldn't keep her promise. She was sidetracked and forgot her goal, but she said I was going to do it for her because I was very special. Another time she told me if I was ever in terrible trouble Tekla would know how to get help. It's all beginning to add up. In a way I dread meeting this man; yet I look forward to it. Does that sound irrational?"

"No, darling, it sounds only human, and this is not the end of the world. Everything will sort itself out."

"Whatever I find out, it will have to be kept a secret between the four of us. It must never go any further, no matter who my father was. It's far too late to change courses."

"Whatever you want, love. Neither El nor Sid would ever break their word." She held him in her arms then, wishing she could clear his mind of doubts so he could fall into a dreamless sleep.

"What do you want most in the world, Gia?" he asked after several minutes, sensing her frustration at not being able to help.

"That's easy to answer. Most of all I want to have your baby so that I can have something to fill my days while you're away from me. I have the feeling we're going to be spending more and more time apart while you climb your way up, but with children I'll be per-

472

fectly content to wait for you to come home."

"Well, there's no rule that says we can't keep on trying, is there?" he asked, rolling over and taking her in his arms.

A week later Sid handed Alex a slip of paper with a telephone number written on it. "I had a devil of a time getting this. Marcy wouldn't give me the number. She keeps certain files under lock and key, but when she went out for lunch one day I snuck past the receptionist and lo and behold there was the key ring in the center drawer of her desk. In no time I had the information in my hands. Then I heard her voice in the outer office so I sat down in one of the chairs and pretended I was waiting to give her a few more names to add to her prospect list. She looked at me so suspiciously I actually had to give her three of my patients' names. Who knows? They might decide to be generous. At least she stopped glaring at me when I forked over the information. She did look directly at the file cabinet, but it was locked so she relaxed somewhat. I could just imagine her rushing out to the receptionist after I left and asking how long I'd been in her office when the poor girl didn't know I'd gone in. As I passed the outer desk on the way out I nonchalantly said I was glad I only had to wait a couple of minutes. Hope she took the hint. I've done my part, Al. When are you going to call?"

Alex tucked the paper into his wallet.

"Soon."

His "soon" dragged on for three weeks. Every time he picked up the phone, he laid it down again, putting off the confrontation a while longer. He even dialed the number once but hung up when a woman's voice answered. In the third week, his hesitation finally brought about a sense of self-disgust and he dialed again, refusing to put the phone down until the deed was accomplished. The same woman answered the phone.

"Pritzkin residence."

"Yes, my name is Alex Kawa and I'd like to make an appointment to see Mr. Pritzkin or to talk to him on the phone."

"I'll take the message. Just leave your number and someone will get back to you."

Alex gave his office number and decided the matter would lie dormant for a while, but an hour later his phone rang. This time it was a man who spoke.

"Alex? You can meet with my father tomorrow about noon if that's convenient. He doesn't leave the house much these days and he wondered if you could come here." He gave an address on prestigious Astor Street, the core of the wealthy section of the city.

"I'll be there," Alex agreed.

"Good. He hopes you'll have time to stay for lunch."

Alex arrived at the front door just as the bells on a nearby tower were ringing the hour. A housekeeper opened the massive carved door, evidently the same woman who had answered the phone for she spoke with the same slight European accent. She led the way into a library well stocked with leather-bound volumes. A large desk occupied the space in front of the French windows, on the opposite wall was a brick fireplace, its inner cavity unlit in the warm weather although a neat stack of logs were piled nearby. The double doors behind Alex opened, and he turned to see the man that must be David Pritzkin enter. He walked slowly and faintly resembled Alex's photo of Alexander. He had thinning white hair and was dressed in worn pants and a pullover sweater. He held out his hand in greeting as he neared his visitor.

"Alex, I'm David Pritzkin. May I say it's a great pleasure to meet you at last? I've been following your

474

career in the newspapers and was quite curious to see what you were like in person. Please sit down. I believe my housekeeper left us some fresh coffee. Help yourself." He pointed to a credenza nearby. "If you'll pour, I'll take half coffee, half cream. My doctor doesn't allow me black any longer. Don't get old, Alex. So many of life's pleasures must be denied when you finally have the time to relax and enjoy them. Now, young man, what can I do for you?"

Alex looked startled. What could he use as an opening remark?

"Sir, I'd like to ask you what might seem a very odd question."

"At my age nothing seems odd anymore, only interesting. Go ahead."

"Were you the benefactor who paid for my high school and college expenses? I know that sounds ridiculous, and if the answer is no, then I'll be off and not take up any more of your time."

The old man chuckled, setting down his cup. "So you finally deduced that have you? My name wasn't supposed to appear on any records. Who let the cat out of the bag?"

"No one, sir. This has all come out quite by accident. Actually, my sister, Eleanor, said it must have been you after we made a startling discovery a few weeks ago."

"Discovery? What have you discovered?"

"My aunt died several months ago, but before she did, she made some odd remarks. I never took them seriously because she was getting quite forgetful and talked about the past a lot. Nothing she said made much sense. She would ramble on and say things we didn't understand so unfortunately we didn't pay her too much attention. I'm sorry that we didn't because she was actually trying to tell me something important but didn't know quite how. She died before she could complete her story, but the day she died she was quite clearheaded. She didn't have time to finish whatever she was trying to say and, at the end, told me to look in a box on a shelf. I put it off for months, and after the funeral I forgot all about her words. I figured she had nothing very important hidden away. My marriage and my business kept me busy, and it wasn't until three weeks ago that my sister and wife happened to come across some papers which shocked the hell out of me."

"What did they find, Alex?"

"You did have a brother named Alexander who died in a fire in Hyde Park, didn't you?"

"Yes, I did. My only brother. We were very close indeed, and I was very angry at the time of his death: angry at God for allowing something so terrible to happen, angry at my brother for risking his life, angry at my sister-in-law because if she had been a better wife it wouldn't have happened. It took me a long time to put aside my anger and come to the realization that his death was meant to be. Now tell me what you found."

"Two pictures of your brother: one in a frame and the other from the obituary in the papers. There were passports and other undecipherable odds and ends. I guess it all boils down to one question. Is it possible that your brother was my real father?" Alex reddened as he said the words. They sounded so implausible and foolish when spoken aloud to a stranger.

David Pritzkin stared into his empty coffee cup for a few moments, lost in thought. Finally he set the cup down and moved over to the couch where Alex sat waiting for an answer to the question that was plaguing him. "You've come this far, son. You might as well hear the whole story. Once a story is begun it must be finished or the listener will waste countless hours wondering what the ending would have been. Yes, you are my brother's child, my nephew. Forgive me but before you were born I couldn't be sure, after all, I didn't know your mother very well. But from the first time I caught a glimpse of you back in your grammar school days there was never any doubt. You are Alexander's son. Let me tell you the story as I first heard it. I won't go into too many details about Rebecca, Alex's wife. At first we all thought she was perfect for my brother, but once they married her real character became obvious. My brother was a very lonely man for a good many years. He had friends, of course, but friends aren't quite the same as family. He knew Rebecca would never agree to having a child and this hurt him more than anything. When she aborted her only pregnancy any feeling he had for her died. Then, one glorious autumn day, he met your mother on campus. He told me she had a free day once a week to explore the city and get away from her household worries. During that time she sat in on two of Alexander's classes, but when he attempted to go after her, she eluded him until they met by accident one afternoon in a local tearoom. From that day forward Alexander knew he loved this woman, your mother. From what my brother told me when he asked me to transfer his holdings to a Swiss bank, the man your mother had married, we should call him your father for he did raise you, was definitely abusive to your mother and his children. When Alexander learned that Dani was carrying his baby he was determined to persuade her to go away with him to start a new life. Finally she agreed and he was overjoyed. His accident occurred a week before they were due to leave. When I saw your mother at the funeral parlor, I caught a glimpse of what Alexander must have had with her. She was so completely different from Rebecca. You could see the love in her eyes, even as she gazed into the coffin. When she looked up at me it was as though I were looking at the miseries of the world condensed in one pair of eyes. I offered her my help if she wanted to go on the trip they had planned. There would have been no problems. I would have seen to it that everything went smoothly, but she wouldn't hear of it. She told me it would be best if she carried on with her life as it was, that I shouldn't interfere. As the years went by I often wondered how you were faring. I worried over you. Was your family wanting? Were you all eating enough? Times were hard and I couldn't help but wonder how you managed. Since I knew your last name and the general area where you lived, it wasn't too difficult to trace you; and although you didn't know this, I stood outside your school several times desperately waiting to get a glimpse of you. The first time I saw you coming through the old steel doors, a feeling of familiarity swept over me. I knew in an instant that we were of the same blood, and my assumption was indeed correct. The scholarships certainly didn't hinder you. In fact, you would probably agree that they made a far better education possible."

"But you weren't liable for me in any way Mr. Pritzkin. You didn't have to go to all that expense and trouble."

"Don't be guilty of pride, Alex. In later years you will find very little satisfaction in pride. Who knows what course your life might have taken if your mother had taken me up on my offer? I might have enjoyed the privilege of seeing you more often or had a hand in guiding you. Instead I was cut off completely, not by choice. But I don't hold that against anyone. Not knowing you left a void in my life. It was like having a part of my body cut out, to physically feel the ache and wish I were whole again. We're not a large family. My daughter, Charlotte, never married, and my son, Mat-

478

thew, has only two children so there's still much love to share. I did all that I could at the time, helped you along as much as I could without exposing my identity, and you have proved yourself worthy. I'm very proud of how you turned out. It seems you have the best traits of both your parents. You can't imagine how thrilled I was when I heard you were going into law—my profession. One of the firms that tried to recruit you after you passed the bar was the one I founded, but I admired your independence." David hesitated for a moment. "Now for a rather touchy subject. When my brother died I still held a good portion of his money in my name because of the power of attorney that was in the process of being transferred. I saw no reason for giving it all to the grasping Rebecca, so my conscience was quite clear when I withheld an amount from the estate. Rebecca inherited more than enough to keep her content, and she lived very well until her death about ten years ago. She never did marry any of the aristocrats she chased all over Europe, but I imagine she had been intimate with dozens of them. She was the scandal of several countries before the war. So you see, paying for your education was never a burden. Quite the contrary, it gave me a great deal of pleasure. Rebecca had money of her own and she received a large portion of Alex's estate. In addition, the men she ran around with kept her well supplied with villas, jewels—everything she lusted after. The day after my brother's funeral she took a train to New York to sail on a ship to Europe. She contacted me about once a year to straighten out her finances, and I detested speaking with her when she called."

"And the check for twenty thousand dollars sent to my office?"

"I'll have to plead guilty to that too, but I couldn't

479

resist the temptation. I'm relieved you know your true beginnings at last. I wouldn't like to go to my grave leaving matters unsettled. So that's about it. Does it make you angry, resentful? Most of all, I hope you haven't turned against your mother's memory in any way. There was never a more decent woman. I know this even though I only met her once. I slipped up when I didn't learn of her death. I should have kept a more careful watch. Perhaps there was something more I could have done."

"No, sir. You've done far too much already, and I would never turn against my mother. She was the best a son could ask for. I only regret that she died so young, with only a few months of real happiness. She deserved much more."

"When did she die?"

"When I was ten. She was only forty and in a way my father caused her death. I mean, of course, Roman."

"Please keep on calling him your father. He was the only one you knew after all."

"My sister Eleanor told me all the details recently. They were rather sordid. I'd rather not go into how she died if you don't mind."

"No, I don't expect you to. As I said, I didn't hear of your mother's death. Her dying released me from my promise to stay in the background. I could have come to you twenty years ago but at that age it might have been too awkward. Perhaps it's better this way. Come, let's have lunch. My son will be joining us."

"Does he know about all this?"

"Yes, he does but he's the only one. He's sworn to secrecy, not even his wife knows. No one does. You can trust Matthew. I think you'll find he feels very much as I do, but wait until you meet him and make your own judgment."

Alex rose from his seat. "This is all rather strange. Here I come barging into your home, a long-lost nephew you might say and you expect your son to welcome me with open arms. It sounds far-fetched."

"My son has known the whole story from the day Alex told us. He was pleased when he heard he had a cousin, another relative besides his sister. You'll find that Matthew is not a grasping greedy man unless he's out to make money on his own, and he's made enough to qualify him as one of the wealthiest men in the state. In fact, he even had the major say-so in investing my brother's money and he's done a remarkable job."

At this time in the conversation, Alex suddenly became flushed with embarrassment.

"I hope you're not thinking I came to see you with the intention of getting money out of you. I don't need it, sir. I'm doing very well on my own."

"Call me David, Alex. I know you can't call me Uncle. It's too late for that now. If word got out it would only create a great deal of gossip and open up wounds; the press would have a field day with the news. But we can be friends. There's no law that says I can't back your political career is there? From the way you're heading I gather you're extremely interested in politics."

"I have been thinking about it."

Matthew Pritzkin was waiting for them in the dining room and shook hands warmly when introduced.

"It's a great pleasure, Alex. I hoped this would happen one day."

"Matthew, Charlotte's not home is she?" the old man asked, seating himself at the head of the table.

"No, Dad. Today's her bridge day."

"Good. We can have some privacy. I love my daughter, but she should have made a life for herself

481

after her mother died. Instead she insisted on keeping house for me. She hovers over me constantly and it's driving me insane. It's a pity. She should have had her own children and grandchildren long ago, but I couldn't persuade her to leave the nest. Her life revolves around bridge games, and planning benefit luncheons and dinners and what have you. For a while I thought she would make her home in Israel, at least for the better part of the year. She was so enthusiastic about the country, but she contents herself with a yearly trip to see how our forests are growing. I swear she's donated enough money to plant more trees in Israel than anyone I know. At the rate she's going they'll be able to open a paper mill in a few generations; not an easy accomplishment in that arid land. Ah, Helga, something smells divine. What are we having for lunch?"

The housekeeper wheeled in a serving cart and placed the dishes in the center of the table.

"Today there's roast chicken with dumplings, and a salad. But only a small portion for you, you know what your doctor says about proper diet."

"Curse the good doctor. Today is special. As a treat I'll have a full portion for a change. Matthew, get a bottle of champagne. It seems appropriate."

"Mr. Pritzkin—"

"Off with you, Helga. Matthew will do the serving. We have some business to discuss and I promise I'll only take one small glass of wine."

The housekeeper left the room, a disapproving look on her plump face.

"I hate the way women think a man must obey all the rules at the very time of life when he should be satisfying all his lusts, which at my age are good food, a spot of brandy or wine now and then, and a superb cigar

482

after a meal; but they've thrown all my cigars away for fear I'll contract some dreaded disease. My family expects me to live to be a hundred if I take care of myself properly."

"And so you can," Matthew said, returning and uncorking the requested wine.

"Bah, there are only one or two more things I'd like to see before my number is up. I know my grandson is following in his father's footsteps so there's no foreseeable problem but my granddaughter, bless her, a beautiful intelligent girl, is going to join some ludicrous cult in California. Matthew, you should have insisted that she go to school in the east or here in the midwest. From what I see in the papers, California is a breeding ground for cultists and extremists."

Matthew laughed easily, evidently not concerned about his daughter's fate.

"Dad, there are thousands of normal bright people in California, no different from you and I." He looked over to Alex. "My daughter just received her degree. She's planning on becoming a physicist, but my father would rather see her situated in suburbia raising a family. Women aren't subservient any longer, Dad. They're proven they have steel-trap minds and can compete in any field. Wait; she'll prove herself. You're just mad as hell because you don't understand what she's doing." He served generous portions of the crisply browned chicken, dumplings in rich brown gravy, and salad. "You can have all you like today, Father. I promise I won't tattle to Helga or Charlotte."

"Didn't I tell you I have a son to be proud of? He's the only one around here who allows me to cheat now and then. Not too often but enough to keep me somewhat placated."

"So what are your plans, Alex?" Matthew asked. "I

483

can't tell you how my father wished for the day when he could meet you face to face. You're an intriguing episode in our lives. Not being able to acknowledge you has had its drawbacks."

Alex was confounded by the warmth of both men. He wondered if he could be so open-minded and outgoing if the positions were reversed. These men treated him as though he was really one of the family; it didn't feel quite right.

"Well, our firm is doing rather well. I started out with remarkable partners who helped tremendously. It's more than I ever hoped for, but in a way I still feel there's more to be done."

"Politically you mean?"

"Yes, the political arena has been my real goal for a long time, ever since the days I used to run errands for my old ward boss. I'd like to give it a try one day."

"In what capacity?" the elder Pritzkin asked. "Mayor?"

"No, that's out of the question. Richard Daley has that job locked up for as long as he wants it and he'll eventually groom someone to take his place. I feel he's on his way to becoming a legend. They won't find a replacement like him. I'd like to try for state senator or state's attorney, and—please don't laugh—later I'd like to take a shot at the governor's job. Does that sound too far-fetched for a rash beginner?"

David held his glass of wine to his mouth, smiling. "No, it sounds feasible. You have just as good a chance as anyone, but there are some problems to overcome. You're quite well known here in Chicago as Stormy"— he laughed at the name—"but you need those other votes too: downstate, western Illinois, northern Illinois. You have a lot of ground to cover, but it isn't impossible."

"I know, that's why I'd like to begin by running for state senator. I've been promised backing by the Democratic party. A few more years and I think I'll be ready."

"A few years? I might not be around to see them, Alex. Start out big, run for governor. The election's in two years. You can accomplish a lot in two years with the right people and money behind you."

Alex was taken aback. "It couldn't be done in two years. It's politically and financially impossible. I'm still too young. I'll need at least double that time just to run for senator."

"Nonsense. Matthew, how much money is there in my brother's account? Money can buy just about anything these days."

"Offhand, I'd say close to three million."

Alex threw down his napkin. "No, don't say any more. I told you earlier I wasn't here for money. I thank you for your past generosity, for sending me to school and for your donation to my charities, but I'm not about to take anything more."

"Alex," Matthew broke in gently, "before you go rushing out of here, please listen to my father. Just hear what he has to say; then you can leave. Please, sit down."

Alex sat on the edge of his chair, seething at what he might hear next. Were they trying to buy him off in some way? This visit was enlightening but it was turning into a fiasco.

"Forgive me, Alex, for being so pushy," David began. "I'm seventy-five years old, my heart is failing, and I don't know how much longer I have. I'll never make it to a hundred. I'd like to hope that I have three or four years but I'm not even sure of that. Matthew here is one of the keenest investors in the country. He's made enough to last for generations, and his son will do even better in New York. It's an unspoken law, Alex: money begets more money. We're not touching any of mine, Matthew's, or Charlotte's. When your father died I held back around sixty thousand dollars. I did very well with that. By the time my son took over it had grown to half a million. He's upped that figure to where it stands now. I don't mean to imply that I'm going to hand everything over to you on a silver platter. I'm just suggesting this be used to get yourself known over the state in the very near future. You might call it barnstorming the state. Explain, Matthew. I've talked myself hoarse today."

"What my father is trying to say is that for almost thirty years he's had a dream of seeing his brother's death negated in some way. Even though it never can be made public, you are part of this family, a blood relative. We have no cousins, uncles—no one except my two children who are both well off. If Alexander had lived, you would have been his heir. If he'd known he was going to die before he and your mother married, he would have made a will. In the excitement of settling his affairs and relocating, it slipped his mind. No one thinks he's going to die when he's happy and in the prime of life. He couldn't wait for you to be born, according to what my father told me. Here's how some of the money can work for you. Help the masses to get yourself known. Let's say there are tornados in southern Illinois and several farmers are wiped out. You could go there and donate seed or whatever. It wouldn't cost them a cent, but you could get them back on their feet. What would that mean?" Matthew waited a second. "Publicity of course. The local people would write you up like the Messiah. That's only one example. There are hundreds more I could give, but do you get the drift? The money that's been growing these past thirty years could be used gainfully. It would be helping people desperately in need, which is of primary importance. Secondly, it would push you closer to your ambition. Don't answer right now, just think about it for a while. Come back anytime. My father's always home. I will be too if I know you're coming. I'd ask you to meet me at my office, but then Dad would feel left out."

Alex slumped back in his chair. "Excuse me but you didn't see my point, did you? Here I am, for what it's worth, a virtual stranger and you're willing to open up the floodgates when you don't even know me. I realize I'm a relative, but there are countless relatives who hate each other's guts, who would be willing to cut each other's throats over money, and yet you accept me after one brief meeting. It's too unbelievable."

"You're wrong, Alex. We do know you. We've been following you since you were in grammar school. My father saw copies of your report cards all the years you were in school. He raged against the teachers when you almost failed biology but then admitted you would never have a career in medicine. When you entered law school he was elated. You were following in his footsteps. When you were ready to begin your career and refused the offers the established firms made, I had to stop him from sending you a check to cover the expense of opening your own office. When he saw you one day hiking home from high school in the bitter cold and you wore a rather thin jacket, he cried when he came home. You've never noticed him, but he has been in the background. He even bought a beat-up car and drove it himself so you wouldn't be suspicious if you saw him lurking about now and then. Every few months the car was changed so you wouldn't recognize it. You didn't

487

realize how much he wanted to talk to you but couldn't because he had promised your mother to stay out of your life. We're not jealous, my sister and I, because he gave us all the love we needed, but he did have love to spare. When he confided in me, it relieved his anxiety somewhat. That's why I ask you to reconsider. Let him do something big to show you how much he's cared all these years."

"But you're talking about an enormous sum of money."

"Enormous to you, not to him. If you had turned out differently my uncle's money would have gone to charities—perhaps a building at Michael Reese hospital, perhaps a kibbutz in Israel—but you've lived up to his expectations so he doesn't want a memorial with his name emblazoned on it."

David Pritzkin lifted his downcast eyes.

"Thank you, Matthew. You've explained very well." There were tears in his eyes as he spoke. "Don't lock me out now, son. I've waited far too long for this day. Matthew's right, think about it for a while. If your answer is still no after a month or so, I'll accept it; but whatever your decision don't stop coming to see me. It would give me great joy to spend a few hours with you now and then. Now if you'll excuse me I must lie down for a spell or that old gorgon will be furious." He stood up with Matthew's help and kissed Alex on the cheek hugging him tightly. "Next to the birthdays of my children and grandchildren and my wedding day, this has been one of the best days of my life. Thank you."

"Good-bye, sir."

"David."

Alex hesitated. "Ah, well—David then. I promise I'll be back if you'll have me. I'd like to bring my wife once if I may."

"Of course. It was remiss of me not to suggest it. She knows then?"

"Only she, my sister Eleanor, and Sid Levine. They are the only ones who will ever know but they can keep a secret. I trust them."

"Doctor Sidney Levine?"

"Yes."

"He's a fine man. I know him slightly. Met him at some charity affair years ago."

"He's a good friend."

"Well, bring them too. Then we will see you again?"

"It's a promise."

David regained some of the vigor he'd shown earlier and left the room with another admonishment to Alex to visit soon.

"You've seen him, haven't you?" Gia asked that evening.

"Am I that easy to read? In my profession you're supposed to be able to keep a poker face."

"But I can tell anyway, darling. You look relieved. You don't have those worry lines on your forehead when you think I'm not looking at you. I take it all went well?"

"Gia, it was uncanny. I never expected this family to be so—well I can't think of the proper word, but I guess you could say they were astonishing. They knew just about everything there was to know about me because David has kept a close watch on me since my school days. El was right. My scholarships came from him, the check I received at the office came from him too. He's always wanted to do more but held back because Matthew, his son, reminded him of his promise to stay out of my life. I sort of get the feeling he wanted me to find out eventually. Not in the earlier years, but when he began to age. He said his heart wasn't up to par, and I got the impression he wanted me to know the truth before he passed on. Anyway, both of them, father and son, couldn't have been more cordial. And they are sincere. I'm a fairly good judge of people; in my profession you have to be. They're not putting on a phony act. I would swear to that. Gia, I never once noticed David watching me; yet he saw me countless times as I was growing up. He's a remarkable man and if my father was anything like him I've missed out on a great deal in my life. I didn't meet Charlotte, but I was welcomed with open arms. David admitted I was Alexander's son as soon as I asked the question." Alex told her every detail of his visit, then he asked, "Would you like to go with me once or twice? My uncle would like to meet you. Funny, it's much easier to call David Pritzkin my uncle than it is to admit that his brother was my father, but I can't go around calling him Uncle. We decided to say that we're good friends. I'll have to call El and Sid so I can explain the situation. El felt I'd never get up the courage to go there so I must tell her it's been done." He pulled her onto his lap. "Tell me what you've been up to all day."

"Well, the workers started gutting the apartment downstairs. Al, it looks huge with some of the walls knocked out. The heating company started tearing out the old coal furnace in the basement too, and they'll begin putting in new ducts tomorrow. El and I finished cleaning out the attic. There was nothing very interesting there. We found dozens of old mason jars, moth-eaten clothing that's years out of date, some broken chairs, and that's about it."

"You've been working too hard, love, cleaning out this place. We could hire men to do that and you could

490

just inspect."

"No, Alex. I honestly enjoy rummaging. Do you think we could knock down the old chicken sheds in the back yard and have a really lovely garden planted with flowers? I'd love working in a garden. I've never had a foot of planting space where I could grow things. When I was with my father I had one lonely window box that never saw the sun. I could only grow some very pitiful basil plants. I'd love to have a whole garden."

"I'll get someone to tear them down this weekend. They are an eyesore aren't they? Years ago they were filled with chickens, a rooster, and some ducks; but the yard is large and will make a lovely garden. As soon as the sheds are torn down I'll order some good soil and help you get started. Anything else your little heart desires?"

"No, I have just about everything a woman could want."

"You mean to say you don't want new clothes? Women never have enough clothes to wear."

"I have plenty, the clothes you bought me before the wedding, the ones we shopped for in Florida, and the ones Eleanor, Irena, and Carmella bought. I won't be needing clothes for a long while unless you get me pregnant." She smiled at him shyly.

"You little spitfire, you do have a one-track mind, don't you? I'll try to make your fondest wish come true." He carried her into their bedroom, and they made love for hours totally absorbed in each other until; finally, they slept in each other's arms.

The next day Alex told Eleanor and Sid the details of his visit to the Pritzkin home. Eleanor was awed by Alex's description of the house on Astor Street, the housekeeper, the money being made by a single family.

"What will your answer be Alex?" she asked. "You

must be tempted to say yes."

"I don't know. I don't want his money; I've gotten by on my own up to now. Then again, it can do wonders, and he feels it's honestly my right. I hate to think of these personal problems when I'm so busy. I'll have to wait a bit before I decide."

He called the Pritzkins two weeks later and took Gia there the first week of July. Again, David Pritzkin was gracious. This time Charlotte was home and she, too, accepted their presence at dinner, obviously hospitable. Matthew was away on a weekend visit to his daughter in California, so it was just the four of them, and in Charlotte's presence nothing personal was discussed.

As they left at nine, David walked them to the door, his arm around Gia.

"Your wife is charming, Alex. Just the kind of woman I pictured you marrying. Come again soon. The next time Matthew will be home. He'll be sorry he missed you."

He made no mention of a decision, and Alex was grateful for he wasn't ready yet with an answer despite the sleepless hours he'd spent arguing the pros and cons of his uncle's offer. He wanted to rise up in the world strictly on his own, but that would take years and a lot of hard work. A tempting short-cut was being offered, and he couldn't decide which road he wanted to choose.

"Darling, your uncle seems a terribly lonely man in that great big house with only his daughter for company most of the time. From the things he said at dinner, he doesn't have much of a say-so in Matthew's business. His grandchildren are away from home making new lives for themselves, and Matthew seems to be a very busy man. David needs another interest in life, and I think you're it. I'm fond of him already. He was so friendly tonight, as if he'd known me for years. I like that in a person I've just met."

"Naturally I'll be kind. Could I be anything else, especially after all he's done for me? I wish I could have a good long heart-to-heart talk with my mother. Some nights I dream of her, but it's not helping me decide. In my dreams I just see her smiling. Sometimes I even dream of her laughing on some mountaintop. I know she would never tell me what to do, but it would be so comforting if I could talk to her again."

"I know how you feel. I often wish my father and mother were back for just a few moments so I could tell them how happy I am, but I feel they know anyway."

He parked the car and they climbed the stairs to the first floor, stopping to check on what progress the workers were making.

"It's really shaping up isn't it?" Alex asked, turning on lights.

The small entryway was now a good-size foyer that led into the living room, which was double the size it had been. In the kitchen new oak cabinets had been set flush against the newly plastered walls. An open box contained a glittering crystal chandelier to be put up in the dining room. A carton of silk damask wallpaper would be hung in the living room, and several gallons of paint awaited the painters.

"As soon as they've finished here we'll bring the bed down; then they can work upstairs," Alex declared.

"It's going to be absolutely beautiful, Alex. Our home is going to be unique. You didn't tell me yet what plans you have for the upstairs."

"We'll put in a new stairway in the front that will lead directly upstairs. How do three large bedrooms sound, or would you rather have four smaller ones?"

"Three. It will be roomier if the bedrooms are large. I hate cramped small rooms for I've lived in nothing else. We can take the one in front, and the one right next to ours can be for the baby."

He laughed, looking down into her eyes. "When we get one, that is."

"Oh, we are. He's right here with us, love, waiting to see his lovely room whenever it's ready."

"What? Are you trying to tell me you're pregnant?"

"I just found out today. El recommended a doctor. I went to see him, and yes, we're going to have a baby."

"Why didn't you tell me before we left for dinner? You kept the good news to yourself all evening. No wonder your eyes were sparkling and you looked so beautiful. You were holding back on me, you little fox."

"I didn't want to see you get all choked up at your uncle's house. It's so elegant one should be quiet and somber there. I wanted to whoop it up with my husband in private. Furthermore, you might have canceled dinner, and I was dying to see a real honest-to-God mansion so I waited."

"Gia love, I thought when you married me I couldn't be any happier, but I was wrong. You've made me the happiest man alive tonight." He kissed her tenderly. "Come on, let's go upstairs and talk this over. There are names to choose. The workers will have to speed things up so I can be sure you're all settled and you're to cut down immediately on the work you've been doing."

"Alex, I'm not a Dresden doll. I stop when I get tired—and we've seven months to choose a name. There's no great rush."

"Seven whole months. I can't wait that long."

"Then the next time I'm pregnant I won't say anything until you notice it for yourself. You're too impatient, love. I want our baby to be perfect, and it

494

takes nine months to have a perfect baby."

"I know, Gia. I was only teasing, but you'd better not wait months to tell me next time. Anyway, let's concentrate on this baby first, shall we?" He lifted her up high in the air. "I love you."

That night, lying next to his wife, he decided what he was going to do.

Chapter Thirteen

"Alex," welcome back," David Pritzkin greeted his visitor warmly, a new-found strength in his handshake. "Since you said you were coming alone I gather you've reached a decision regarding my offer. I've asked Matthew to join us for a late breakfast and he should be here at any minute."

"Yes, sir. I've considered your offer and—"

"No, wait until Matthew arrives. It will save you repeating your words." David led the way into a sunny morning room done in yellow and white. It was much smaller than the elaborate dining room. Within moments Matthew joined them. Helga was nowhere in sight, but covered dishes were set upon a convenient sideboard.

"Alex, good to see you again. I'm sorry I wasn't here when you visited with your wife, but I had pressing business in California and decided to combine business with pleasure by visiting my daughter for a few days. My wife had urged me to go for weeks. You see, Devora, my wife, is an invalid and can't travel. In fact, she's confined to our apartment with a full-time nurse."

"I'm sorry to hear that, Matthew. I had no idea."

"We've had the best doctors in the country, but they

can't help. It's multiple sclerosis. There's not much that can be done. She's deteriorating and seeing strangers only upsets her. I'm sorry that you can't meet her, but we're not here to talk about my problems, are we?"

"How did the California deal go?" David asked.

"Like clockwork. We have title to the thousand acres in the San Joaquin valley and we picked up some shoreline acreage at Malibu all at the right price."

"I'm proud of you son. You've made a wise move. Now you can serve me a piece of toast and just a smidgen of scrambled eggs, if you please. Alex, please help yourself. There's steak and eggs, fruit, sweet rolls. Take whatever strikes your fancy."

"Coffee will be just fine."

"Nonsense. You're young and healthy. Eat hearty."

Not wanting to offend, Alex helped himself to a small piece of steak and a portion of eggs, and then sat at the table while Matthew poured coffee for Alex and himself, weak tea for his father.

"So tell us what decision you've made," David said expectantly. "You don't look too happy. Does it mean you're declining?"

"Not totally. I will need your help but mainly to assist with strategies to get myself known. There won't be much of a problem in the city; Richard Daley's promised his endorsement. Several others have approached him concerning the election, but if I can prove myself, if I can deliver, if I come up with a sound campaign plan, he'll be behind me. However, I have to present something viable by the end of the month. He does have other would-be candidates pressuring him. I have a very good college friend, Selma Carruthers, who would make an excellent coordinator. She thrives on turmoil and pressure. She should be back in the States any day, and when I hear from her I'll approach her with a job offer; but Selma doesn't come cheap. She'll

498

expect fair compensation for her talent; that's one area where I'll need the financial help you've offered. I'm certain I have the backing of the 11th, 1st, 25th, and 14th wards. The others will follow the mayor all the way. I plan on renting a small office somewhere in the loop. Selma, if she decides to join me, can run it; and Eleanor and Irena can work part-time. It's enough for a start."

David gleefully rubbed his hands together.

"Now that's the kind of enthusiasm I like to hear. Say no more about office space. We own a large building near the Palmer House on Michigan Avenue. It will be perfect. You can have a suite immediately." David saw the look of dismay on Alex's face. "No more protests, son. Your father's money has to be used sometime. It's been collecting dividends for years. Would you rather I gave it all away? Don't be foolish. As Matthew said, why not use a small part of it? His own office is on the tenth floor. It will be perfect. He'll call you in a few days with the suite number and any other details you need. Damn, but this is exciting. Never had anyone in the family been in politics before. This is just the perfect news to whet my appetite a bit. Alex, I'll take a small portion of the steak if you don't mind."

Matthew joined in, exhibiting his own brand of enthusiasm.

"I know an excellent public relations man. I'll get in touch with him and see how soon he can come up with a sound publicity plan that will make people sit up and notice. He's on my payroll anyway, might as well get some mileage out of his talents. This certainly will be exciting. I must set up a special fund that you can draw on. We can't do anything illegal or the press will ferret it out as election time draws closer. We'll have to work up a scheme that will make it seem that your campaign funds are coming from a multitude of sources. Once you announce you're running, there will be thousands of dollars coming in from various organizations and individuals. It will be hard work but not impossible." Matthew lifted up his coffee cup. "I'd like to propose a toast to the next governor of Illinois, even though he will be running on the Democratic ticket."

Alex lifted his cup in return.

"How can I ever repay you for—"

"No repayment is necessary except your coming to visit your family more often. That's all I ask of you," David said quietly.

A few days later Alex picked up his office phone on the second ring.

"Selma, it's great to hear your voice. Can you make it to my house for dinner tonight? I'd like you to meet my wife, and I have a job to offer you."

"You're married? Well all I can say is it's about time. Anyone I know?"

"No, I met her through El's godmother, Carmella. I think you'll approve though."

"We'll see, but I respect your good sense so I probably will. Now why are you being so mysterious about a position? You know I hate suspense and I wouldn't want to work in a lawyer's office." Selma paused for a moment; the phone was silent. "My God, you're going to run for office, aren't you? You've finally decided you're ready and you know I'd jump at the chance of being politically involved. Oh, Al, what's it going to be? It has to be big; you wouldn't be bothering me over an insignificant attempt."

Alex laughed, glad to have one of his best friends involved in the planning stages of his campaign.

"Wait till tonight, Sel. I think you'll be surprised, and if you decide to go along with me there will be a hundred details to discuss."

"Okay, you big tease. What time?"

"Can you make it by six?"

"I'll be there, but if you insist on discussing this over dinner I'll refuse to eat one morsel until I know what's going on."

"By the way, Sel, how was Europe?"

"France was fine, still it's good to be home. I didn't like London overly much, but the English countryside was just beautiful. You can't imagine how many teas I've been to. I'm so damned sick of being polite. I'm ready to get into action. If I don't claw my way into something exciting soon I swear I'm going to agitate some rebels in South America just to satisfy my craving for mental stimulation. I'll be at your house promptly. Don't keep me waiting. Take care."

Alex sat back in his chair. Would Selma go for the idea, he wondered, swiveling to face the window overlooking the center of Chicago's financial world? He hoped she would, especially now that he could afford to pay her well. Picking up the phone again, he called Gia to tell her there would be a guest for dinner. Gia could rally for any occasion, no matter how bizarre his requests. She wouldn't enjoy being in the limelight, but she was a perfect hostess.

"Hon, I've asked someone over for dinner tonight. Think you can manage enough for a guest or should I pick up something on the way home."

"You know I always have enough, silly. Don't I? I never know who you're going to bring home next so I stock enough for any emergency. We'll have a roast. Who's coming?"

"You remember my telling you about Selma Carruthers, don't you?"

"Yes, she's the girl you met in school. You've been friends for years, right?"

"Yes, that's the one. She's back from Europe, and I want her to join us to see if she's interested in becom-

501

ing my campaign manager."

"Should I be jealous, darling? You speak of her so glowingly I'm afraid if I hadn't come along you would have married her instead."

"I give you my word there's no reason for you to be jealous. Selma is just like another sister and she's only attracted to excitement. For years she's been trying to fix me up with one woman or another, but almost all of them were too overpowering for my taste. No, love. She's thrilled that I've found a wife at last. Now she can stop matchmaking and devote all her efforts to running things for me—if she agrees, that is."

"In that case I think we'll get along very well. What time will you be home?"

"About five or so. Selma's coming at six. You feeling okay?"

"Never better. Pregnancy agrees with me. I'm energetic, no morning sickness whatsoever, not gaining too much weight. The doctor says I'm a perfect candidate for motherhood. Goodbye, Al. I have a few more things to do before dinner."

A few minutes before six they heard a screeching of brakes.

"That's Selma," Alex laughed. "She drives with a killer instinct and goes through a new car every year. By the time she's through with it, it's a total loss. Since she curbed her barbed tongue years ago, she's found an outlet in abusing autos, but aside from speeding, she is a good driver. Too bad she can't enter the Indy 500 or be a test driver in Detroit. My uncle Jan would love to have her put cars through torture tests."

Selma didn't bother to use the bell. Instead she pounded firmly on the door.

"I'm right on time," she said, entering the foyer.

502

"God you've done wonders with this place. It looks better than my parents' new home."

"It's still a little messy," Alex explained. "They're working on the bedrooms upstairs and we have to rough it a bit till they're finished."

"Well, it's going to be absolutely stunning." Selma spotted Gia standing behind Alex. "This must be your wife. She's stunning too. I always admired your taste, Al. Leave it to you to pick someone who looks like a movie star."

"Thank you," Gia murmured. "I'm pleased to meet you at last. Alex speaks of you often." Gia relaxed. She was going to like this outspoken woman. Alex had told the truth. Selma wasn't his type romantically. "We'll eat in the kitchen if you don't mind, Selma. It's about the only room that's completely finished."

"Don't apologize. I love kitchens. You can't realize how formal dining was in England. Course after boring course, with polite subdued conversation that almost put me to sleep. I can't remember one heated argument at a dinner table. I tried to start one once or twice, but the other guests stared me down with their cold eyes and pretended I didn't exist. I even had a marriage proposal from a pompous ass in the peerage. Maybe he thought I could back his overly protective mother into a corner. She looked like a lioness curling up her nostrils every time she laid eyes on me. Well one evening I just gave her the Italian sign for 'up yours, lady' and she swooned. Derek had to drive her back to the family manor. Never heard from him again. I think he was banished to Scotland for the grouse season or whatever they shoot there. For a while I even tried to join the teenage swingers, but I don't have the stamina or age to carry it off. They looked upon me as though I were a madwoman. At least I had a chance to pick up a few new dance steps."

Gia's laughter tinkled like a bell in response to Selma's stories and the three of them were soon in stitches for Selma loved an audience.

"When I was in France some of the bigwigs pretended they didn't understand my accent, although I admit I speak French quite well. I was understood in the shops and restaurants so it couldn't have been all that bad. Now, I'm not going to lift my fork until you tell me what's going on. I've been in suspense all afternoon. Gia, your husband is horrid for keeping me in the dark. He's the only man I know who has the ability to infuriate me, although I try not to show it."

"Sel, I'm going to run for governor and I'd like you to be campaign coordinator."

"Governor? You might as well run for president. You're aiming too high for a beginner aren't you?"

"It's not impossible."

"No. I know it's not, but it's going to be hard work, not to mention the money you're going to need."

"That's all taken care of. Our main problem is to get me known across the state. Your pay would be fifteen thousand a year plus expenses."

"Lordy, you are rolling in the green aren't you? What makes you think I'm worth the money?"

"I knew it years ago. Want to think about it for a few days or a couple of weeks?"

"No. I know right off the bat when something interests me. I'm with you all the way, win or lose, but I don't like losing so I'll have to work my tail off to see that you do win. This is better and better. I thought you were going to run for state representative or senator."

"So did I, but I changed my mind. Right off the top of your head do you have any ideas?"

"Sure, but I'm going to need some help."

"You've got it. My two sisters are going to work for you part-time and I have a group of volunteers, about

504

thirty right now, who are willing to work hard. There's an experienced P.R. man you can call on whenever you need him."

"Good, then my first thought would be to subscribe to all the small-town newspapers from Rockford west to Sterling and then down to southern Illinois. We'll clip articles that sound promising and start getting a composite together on what the state needs most. How about defending people who don't have the money? A hotshot lawyer from Chicago giving his time no charge?"

"We can do better than that, Sel. I have money behind me, a great deal of money."

"This is exciting. Then we'll clip out any articles describing a person or family that needs help desperately. With some fanfare you or I or the volunteers can take a trip to the town and see that help is forthcoming. We can contact the editor by phone and give our pitch. I can discreetly whisper where the help is coming from while requesting that not too much publicity surround your generosity. Naturally they'll give you good coverage anyway; I've never known an editor to pass up a hot story. It's good for business and puts a little excitement into humdrum lives. It's going to work beautifully, Al. The P. R. man and I can write up the advertising and slogans."

"If you can handle that phase, Sel, I can concentrate on Chicago and the suburbs. You can't imagine how much I want this job, not for the publicity or power but for what I can do for the state if I have the chance. There's too much pocket-lining going on. I know it can't be changed overnight, but I can make an inroad."

"Can you divulge how much cold cash you have backing you?"

"There's enough, Sel. I'll have to have final approval on what you attempt but there's enough."

"Okay, I'll take your word for it. When do I start?"

"Anytime. We have a small office on Michigan Avenue and it's just about ready for occupancy."

"What would you have done had I refused?" Selma asked, then changed her mind. "No, don't tell me. You would have found someone just as good, probably better."

"Sel—"

"No, I don't want an answer. Let's finish eating. I have a lot of things to think about tonight."

They finished dinner early, Selma unusually silent but her mind awhirl with grand plans. Whenever silence enveloped her, those who knew her well knew the reason. She was totally intrigued by a new situation. Such was the case as she said her good-nights early, and hurried home to get her thoughts down on paper, running three red lights in the process. Since there was no oncoming traffic she figured she could talk her way out of a ticket if the law spotted her. She turned her thoughts to Gia on the last half of the drive home. Alex's wife certainly was beautiful with that long black hair and those dark soulful eyes that looked at her husband so adoringly. Just what Alex needed. She should have realized it years ago when she began introducing him to outgoing, outspoken, aggressive women. Naturally he wanted a demure woman to complement him. Selma felt no jealousy. Years ago she might have, but being an independent woman suited her fine. She couldn't imagine herself staying home and playing the housewife bit. It might be fun for a month or so, but then she would go beserk. The few casual affairs she'd had over the years were enough to satisfy her physical yearnings. Funny how she always picked quiet men to spend the night with. Someday she would have to take her taste in men up with a shrink, if she ever found the time to visit one. In her post-college days she was sure she was in love with Alex, the first man to take her out on a real date, and she enjoyed his company tremendously; but as the few years slipped by, she knew for certain they could have a perfect working relationship, not a romantic one.

Alex set up appointments with the aldermen who could be counted on for assistance. First the firebrand in the 25th ward, then visits to ten other wards with encouraging results. They liked the idea of young blood at the helm of the highest position in the state but were dubious about his being able to win. All those visited knew of his relentless prowess in the courtroom and were sure he would be a charismatic newcomer, a man who would stir up the citizenry to full support. As far as they knew, Alex didn't have an enemy. There were a few envious attorneys who had lost cases to him, but most of them couldn't help but admire the man. No doubt about it, they agreed, he was a potential leader. Some men were just born to lead the pack. Alex was one of them. With a Republican in the top office, the Democrats were eager to see one of their own strengthen party affiliation throughout the state. Thus far, no one with the proper amount of fire and imagination coveted the Democratic nomination. Alex presented himself well and the feelers for suburban support, had had encouraging results—as had those to Springfield.

By the end of the month Selma had subscriptions to over a hundred newspapers, large and small. They started trickling in from cities and towns: Champaign, Decatur, Marion, Kankakee. Eleanor's job was to read through the slowly growing mass of newsprint and circle articles that could prove beneficial to her brother. Irena then cut them out and set up a category system. In another week, a tentative priority system was set up.

A poor black couple and their four long-limbed, soulful-eyed children were being evicted from their home in East St. Louis for nonpayment of their mortgage which was six months overdue. Too proud to seek welfare, they were struggling along on what the wife made working part-time in a laundry while her husband was recuperating from a serious recurrence of rheumatic fever that had left him bedridden for four of the six months. He was just beginning to regain some of his strength and planned to again work long hard days for a small truck overhauling business which had no proviso for workmen's compensation. Sylvester Crown felt fortunate because his company carried health insurance which at least left his family fairly free from outrageous medical and hospital bills. His insurance covered sixty percent of the costs, but even the remaining forty percent they owed seemed like a staggering amount to repay. The local Baptist church took up a collection, but the poor congregation came up with only fifty dollars, a far cry from the four hundred needed for the bank payment and the two hundred in doctor's bills. The doctor was willing to wait; the bank wasn't. Selma took the train to East St. Louis and taxied to the minister's house, six hundred dollars tucked in her purse. She explained that the needed money came from Alex Kawa whose particular hobby was helping those in need. The minister slowly warmed to Selma's frank explanation, and he explained that Sylvester Crown would be returning to work in another week but the threat of losing his home was sitting hard on the man who was depressed because he couldn't provide for his family as he felt a man should. Reverend Clement looked down at the hundred-dollar bills lying on the uneven table in his parlor and almost wept with joy over the miracle.

"Miss Selma, I said to Sylvester a miracle was possible and so it is. Who would have thought a white man from Chicago would have an interest in any of our poor folk clear across the state? But why is he doing this for us? Why not someone in Chicago? There're plenty of needy folks there too."

"Reverend, Alex gives money to charities that strike his fancy. He happened to see an issue of your local paper. Its tale of Mr. Crown's plight moved him. Now Alex isn't an extremely wealthy man but he makes a good living, and he was poor once so he knows what the Crowns are going through."

"Ma'am, Sylvester, I'm sure, will want to thank him personally, but he's a proud man. He didn't even want us collecting for him in church, and when he read the article in the newspaper he was mightily embarrassed. Even writing about his trouble only brought in a little over twenty dollars, only that plus the fifty the congregation donated and it fell far short of what was needed. He doesn't have a grand house, just a four-room clapboard, but he loves keeping it neat and tidy as does his missus. It's his own little patch of security. He won't want to take the money from a stranger unless he can repay it in some way. What will I tell him?"

"Why he and his family can do a great deal for Alex. Everyone here can in fact."

"I don't understand. How can we do anything?"

"Just get out and vote in two years. Alex will be running for governor and he's going to need all the help he can get. He'll make a fine governor. I've known him since college and I promise you there's not an ounce of corruption in him. He'll do his best to see that every corner of the state is treated fairly. That's how the Crowns can repay him, that's how the whole congregation can. You might say I'm Alex's ambassador

509

because he couldn't make it here today personally. There are so many people he has to see in order to run against the present governor. He has to fight hard, Reverend, but we're getting more volunteers daily to aid our cause. Tell me, has Governor Akers ever done anything for your community, for East St. Louis for that matter?"

"No, ma'am. Not unless you count welfare, but we'd rather work given the chance. For most of us, welfare is degrading. Why there's almost three hundred in my flock and I tell you here and now, anyone that's old enough to vote will be voting for your Alex. That's a promise if I have to personally drag each and every one of them out to register and vote on election day."

"Thank you. That's all we ask. Now I'll have to hurry if I'm to make the train back to Chicago." Selma shook the old man's hand. "It's been a pleasure talking to you. I'll leave my card in case you want to get in touch. We've set up headquarters and I can be reached on any workday." She went through the door to the cab waiting in front of the rundown church and waved as it sped away.

"Praise the Lord," the rotund minister cried as the taxi sped off. "The Lord surely does work in mysterious ways. Indeed it is a miracle."

He reached for the hat hanging on a nearby hook and rushed off to inform Sylvester and his wife to get to the bank as fast as their legs would carry them.

This was the first of many acts of charity in the year preceding Alex's public announcement of his candidacy. Articles were stacked up higher and higher, though only a small percentage could be addressed. Selma and Eleanor diligently and painstakingly selected the ones that could enhance Alex's name, but he always managed to burst in on them and select his own, disrupting their carefully laid plans.

510

Several families in Thebes were flooded out of their low-lying homes and Alex was there with volunteers as soon as the swirling waters subsided, helping to dig the unfortunates out of the oozing muck and hosing down salvageable possessions. The local paper ran the story on page one of their four-page paper, and the next day it was picked up by UPI and run in the Chicago papers. There was a picture of Alex, grimy and mud splattered but smiling nonetheless, flanked by eight men who had made the trip with him.

A few days later he was in Paris, Illinois, with a van full of seed for a farmer whose storage bin had burned to the ground in a lightning storm. A crew of volunteers went along and stayed to help erect a new barn, side by side with the local people who enjoyed the lavish picnic lunches the city folk had brought and the excitement of the project.

Alex's file of accomplishments grew steadily. Free medical tests and surgery for a child living in Olney. The little girl was brought to Children's Memorial Hospital where a deformed digestive tract was corrected. Baby clothes, cribs, free milk, and baby food for a surprised woman who bore triplets in Kankakee to a worried husband who wondered how on earth he would support his expanded family. Free legal aid dispersed by Alex's firm in Freeport, Normal, Decatur, and Edwardsville. Secondhand but good furniture distributed to several families who had lost everything they owned in a fire. Truckloads of food to areas hit by tornados. Mechanics sent here and there to fix tired old tractors and trucks for owners who couldn't afford to buy replacements. Movie projectors and televisions supplied to various nursing homes. The list was mounting daily, and although many entries remained unanswered, Alex's name was becoming a household word in hundreds of areas. "STORM HITS ILLI-

NOIS" several headlines read. To the people reading their daily newspapers, it seemed he was everywhere at once, crisscrossing the state like jagged forks of lightning in a thunderstorm. Alex detested the name, but since it was going to help him get elected, he didn't mind its use as much. The volunteers who joined forces with him were the backbone of the plan. Without them he couldn't possibly keep up the pace. Fortunately volunteers were flocking in to offer to put in time. He still couldn't quite believe how many there were, especially tradesmen and professionals.

Rumor had it that Governor Hal Akers was getting a mite worried over the young upstart who, it was said, planned to fill his chair in Springfield in the next election, but the governor didn't intend to lose any sleep over the matter yet. When the time came to throw one's name into the hat, he was the incumbent and had a few aces up his sleeve to remind his constituents that he was an able man. He had plenty of money locked away for his own campaign and more could be siphoned from the state to aid his cause. There would be an explosion of newly created jobs, additional school funds seemingly squeezed out of thin air, crackdowns on the overly high expense checks of the wheeler-dealers in the capital. He decided to lie low until the time was ripe, then he would fight either clean or dirty, whichever put him in a more favorable light.

Meanwhile Alex and Gia's home was completed. The furniture they had purchased glowed with the rich patina of fine aged wood. Gia scorned the modern light woods and chrome, preferring traditional materials. The walls and furnishings had been done in pastels, a becoming contrast to the dark wood. The baby's room was ready, lemony yellow walls and sea green woodwork set off the white crib and matching dressers that awaited the expected occupant. Gia walked around in a happy daze, entranced. Her home was more precious to her than any twenty-room mansion. Her attempt at gardening proved successful, and she often sat amidst her first flowers during the fine months. Next year she planned to put in a small cobblestone walkway with several benches scattered here and there. At times she loved her garden far better than the house, and one autumn day she begged Alex for one more renovation.

"Please, darling—soon I won't be able to sit outdoors and I love it so—can we afford to enclose the rear porch with large glass windows so I can sit there on wintery days and feel part of the outdoors?"

Alex sat next to her in their large bed, feeling the unborn baby kick out strongly under his firm hand.

"Well, love, since you haven't asked for much except your garden I think we can go ahead with an enclosed porch. I had to practically force you to spend money on good furniture. You thought it was all too extravagant. I can support us, Gia. The law firm is successful if I win or lose."

"Alex I have almost two hundred dollars saved and it can be used to help pay for my porch."

He took her in his arms, laughing and shaking his head. "Haven't you heard a word I was saying. Darling, I don't need your household money. You'll have your cozy nook before our baby is born. It can be your Christmas present although I'm afraid it won't be done before Christmas, probably by the middle of January."

"Thank you, Al. You're too good. Sometimes I'm afraid to ask for anything because you overdo. I asked for a white crib and you went out and bought the most expensive set Marshall Field's had to offer. We went shopping for baby clothes and you bought enough for three babies."

"Because we can afford it, Gia. If we couldn't I would have told you. No secrets between us ever, remember?"

"Yes, I do. But now you have to promise there will be no other Christmas presents. The porch will be more than enough. Promise?"

"Sort of. We can't have a big tree with nothing beneath it. I'll just put something small there."

Gia tickled him. "You're impossible."

When Christmas came, Gia's lithe form was still slender except for her stomach which protruded roundly. They entertained lavishly, inviting a houseful of people over for the holidays; Norm and Norma; Bill Sullivan; Carmella and Giovanni; Jan and his family, who came from Grosse Point in Michigan where they owned a large home; Selma—even Matthew Pritzkin stopped in for a quick drink bringing long a gaily wrapped box for the baby and some presents from his father. It took three trips to carry everything from the car even though he had help.

Irena gaped at the growing mound of presents David had sent through Matthew. "I must say your new friends are generous, Alex. Unusual for a man you've known for such a short time."

"He can afford to be generous, sis. I even think there's a box there with your name on it, one for Stan and the kids too."

"He's remembered everyone," Irena answered glancing down at some of the name tags, "even Jan and his family."

Matthew left after two cocktails saying he had to get home since his wife's nurse was taking the evening off to spend time with her own family. They thanked him profusely, the children scrambling to see what their brightly beribboned boxes contained. For the unborn baby there was a softly tinted musical carousel that played Brahm's lullaby, for Gia a pair of pearl earrings. Alex's box held a gold tiepin.

Suddenly Gia came to her senses. "Oh, Al, he's given

514

so much. I didn't think to buy anything in return. How stupid of me. I didn't think he would send presents because they don't celebrate Christmas."

"I've taken care of Hannukah a few days ago. We bought David an old fashioned pocket watch, Charlotte a leather bag, and I sent three dozen roses and some brandy to Matthew and Devora. Sorry, hon, I forgot to mention it. Slipped my mind with all the Christmas shopping I had to do."

She breathed a sigh of relief. "You think of everything don't you? You can bet I'll never forget in the future."

Gia opened her Christmas gifts in the morning, the ones Alex had said would be a small token for the holiday. There was a cameo pendant set in gold and hanging from a fine gold chain. The cameo was small and delicate, the ivory matching Gia's unblemished face. Another box contained a mink hat, and Alex promised that some day there would be a coat to match. The third box held a lovely nightgown and robe that Gia could take to the hospital when she was ready.

"I shudder to think what you would have bought if I hadn't held you down a bit," Gia said, sitting next to her husband on the paper-strewn couch.

Now it was Alex's turn to open his presents. For Alex's small study Gia had bought a brass nameplate engraved with the word Governor and they laughed over the presumptuous gift. Her other gift was a pair of gold cufflinks with the initial A etched out in diamond chips.

"Now you're the one being extravagant," he chided.

"It came out of the house money, darling."

"You and your house money. By the time we're married twenty years you'll probably be richer than David. How do you manage all this saving?"

"It's easy when you've been poor. You know how to

515

go about getting bargains. Actually David steered me to a wholesale jeweler. When I went to visit a few weeks ago, he gave me some very sound advice. He and I think alike in many ways."

"So what did he tell you."

"He said I should never pay retail prices for anything except groceries and trinkets. He told me there are wholesalers for anything one has to buy. I have the names of furniture dealers, a clothing manufacturer, and a jeweler. He also said whenever I was making a major purchase I should see him first and he would give me a name I could trust for quality. That's the kind of man I admire. No wonder he and his son have amassed such a fortune. They're clever and don't take a step unless every angle has first been checked out. You're like that in many ways too, Alex, except when it comes to buying things for me or our home. Then you throw caution to the wind, but I think I'll have a say-so whenever we have to buy anything in the future. I'm becoming a very shrewd shopper."

At that moment the baby became restless. The fascinated pair watched Gia's stomach churn for ten minutes until it settled into a comfortable position.

At about ten o'clock on the evening of January fourteenth, Gia felt a trickle of water run down her legs as she was brushing her teeth. She had known this was going to happen, but she found it embarrassing nevertheless. She felt as she had when she was four and had an accident, wetting her pants. Her mother had scolded her. Gia placed a thick towel over the puddle and changed into a clean dress; then she walked into the bedroom where Alex lay, snug under the covers on this cold night.

"Sorry, love, but you're going to have to get the car started after I call the doctor. And you look so warm and cuddly under the quilt."

Alex leaped out of bed. "Now? You're ready to have the baby now?"

She laughed at his foolish look, then grimaced as a contraction convulsed her. All afternoon she had felt mild twinges but this seemed like the real thing. "Well, not this very minute, but it would be a good idea to see if the car starts. It's below zero and you forgot to put the car in the garage."

"Damn! Of all nights. That was dumb of me." He pulled on pants over his pajamas, buttoning a woolen shirt crookedly, searching for his shoes under the bed.

"There's no rush, Al. I still have to wait for another contraction before I call. The baby's not going to plop out here on the floor."

His face whitened at the thought and he ran down the stairs, grabbing a jacket from the hall closet. Gia could hear him trying to turn the engine over; then it caught. She smiled as she dialed the doctor's home and told him another contraction had begun ten minutes after the first.

"Get down to the hospital," he advised. "I'll meet you there shortly. Don't get alarmed, you have plenty of time. Have your husband drive carefully though. The streets are a little slick so don't rush. You won't be having this baby for a few hours, and the hospital's close."

Gia calmly pulled on stockings and boots as Alex ran back up the stairs.

"Where's your suitcase?" he asked searching through the closet. "It's not here. Did you forget to pack? You told me everything was ready."

"It's downstairs in the hall closet, remember?"

"Well then, let's go. I don't think I can handle delivering a baby by myself."

"Calm down, Al. It won't be for a few hours. There's plenty of time."

517

"You sure about that?"

"Positive. I just talked with the doctor, and he wants you to drive slowly and carefully. It's a slippery night."

"Should I carry you down?"

"Heaven forbid. I can walk. Do you have change so you can make phone calls afterward?"

Alex rummaged on the dresser top. "Almost forgot. What else do I need?"

"Nothing but I suggest you put on your gloves and a heavier coat. It's freezing."

"C'mon, Gia. I'm fine. The car should be warm by now. We don't have time to be flitting around. I want to see you safe and sound in the hospital where they know what they're doing."

Gia was surprised at Alex's impatience. If she had felt better she would have driven the car herself. Alex skidded several times, not seeing patches of ice that were clearly shining in the pools of light coming from the streetlights; he narrowly missed one or two parked cars. The short trip to Michael Reese made Gia very nervous, and she said a silent prayer of thanks when they finally arrived at the emergency entrance. At once an orderly took over and sat her in a wheelchair. She was glad to be in competent hands for Alex, always so cool and collected, looked a total wreck. There was sweat on his brow, and his hands shook when the registration clerk asked simple questions. He forgot his phone number and Gia had to answer. He shot a grateful look at her as they were escorted to the labor room, and he urged the orderly to hurry.

At three in the morning their daughter was born. During the last half hour before she was wheeled into the delivery room, Gia banished her husband from her side because every time she winced with pain he became more tense and shouted for a nurse to help his wife. She had wanted to cry out several times but bit her lips against the pain, finally ordering Alex to wait in the lounge. She felt she could handle this part better alone.

"You're sure, hon?" he asked, concern in his eyes.

"Yes, the rest is up to me. You're only making me nervous with your shouting and pacing. It won't be long now. The doctor said within the hour."

Later, when he saw his wife lying peacefully in the clean hospital bed, her ordeal over, his tense nerves relaxed for the first time in hours. She looked at him with sleepy eyes but wouldn't close them until she heard from his own lips that their baby was beautiful and perfect.

Alex held her in his arms. "She's gorgeous, Gia. The nurse said you can see her yourself in a few hours after you rest for a while. You'll see her by breakfast time."

"First tell me what she looks like."

"Well, she has pitch-black hair, quite a lot of it. She gets sort of red when she cries and when I last saw her she was wailing to beat the band. When she settled down her skin turned to a pale pink. Gia, when I made you pregnant I didn't mean to put you through all this. Somehow I didn't realize having a baby would be so ghastly. I'm sorry."

"Alex, you are a goose. I had an easy delivery. Only a little over four hours. Some women go on far longer, especially with their first. I told you my doctor said I was made for having babies. It wasn't all that bad, it just seems so to you because you had to watch and couldn't help. After this it will be as easy as pie, but we won't worry about that now."

"Let's forget about another one for the time being. What shall we name this little treasure? We never did come to a decision."

"I thought Danielle would be nice. I was thinking about it in between labor pains. After your mother. We can call her Dani."

"Yes, I like that. Danielle. It's perfect. I'll leave you now to get some sleep, but I promise I'll be back late this afternoon. Thank you for our beautiful daughter," he said as they kissed.

"Do you feel disappointed because it wasn't a boy? Most men are."

"Nope. Daughters are closer to their fathers and I'm going to enjoy having two women swarm over me just like I enjoyed having my sisters ooh and aah over me and spoil me rotten."

"You're incorrigible. I never saw them wait on you hand and foot or treat you as if you were special."

"You didn't know me in my younger days."

"Get some sleep, Al. You look worse than I do." Her laughter tinkled like music in his ears. "I never knew you would be as upset as you were tonight. I really thought you were going to crash into something and we'd both be taken to the emergency room with broken bones."

Alex grinned sheepishly. "You scared the hell out of me, Gia. For the first time in my life, my mind was a total blank. I guess we are lucky that I got us here in one piece."

Flowers started arriving late that afternoon, and by the next day, Gia's room was filled with the heady aroma of a vast array of bright blooming blossoms, a startling contrast to the stark wintery view from the windows. While she was in the hospital Alex made sure the carpenters finished the enclosed porch, paying them overtime to complete the job before his wife came home. He made sure the heating vent was hooked up correctly so warmth permeated the room. It did look good, he decided after the tools and excess lumber were removed and the room was scrubbed and polished. He left it empty so Gia could furnish it to her own taste, but he placed a large red bow in the center since it was part of her Christmas gift.

There were now thirteen months left before the primary and campaigning began in earnest. Suddenly there were scores of dinners to attend, speeches to be made, people to see. The atmosphere was exciting although he hated coming home hours after dinner time. He vowed never to accept any engagements on Saturdays or Sundays. Those two days were set aside for his family. Gia did accompany him to several dinners, but she didn't care for the smoke-filled rooms or the exclusively political conversation. Not yet, not when the baby needed her full attention. She promised Alex she would attend all the truly important events but asked to be excused from minor affairs and he agreed, seeing how much she enjoyed their daughter, singing to her, sitting in a rocking chair and talking to her as if she were already grown. He teased her about this often.

"You talk to Dani as though she were your age."

"It's a theory I have, Al. I refuse to talk baby talk. Infants pick up intelligence so early. She's going to be as smart as her father one day. Of course I'll play with her but we're going to have some pretty serious conversations even though she won't understand them for a long while. I've never been responsible for such a tiny life before; it scares me sometimes. I can only pray I'll do a respectable job."

"You will, darling. Don't worry."

Eleanor and Sid left the next Sunday to vacation in Mexico. They were back in ten days, relaxed and tan, and loaded down with souvenirs: colorful serapes, huge sombreros, lovely carved onyx pieces. After the gifts were passed around, they made a startling announcement. They had been married in Mexico— married at last, after all the years of loving each other.

The family hovered around them, offering gleeful congratulations.

"I can't believe it, El," Alex said, happy his sister and brother-in law had finally wed. "What finally made you decide in favor of Sid's pleadings?"

"I've courted her for so many years," Sid teased. "Your sister is one hell of a stubborn woman. I should have beat her and dragged her to the altar years ago. I think I've been too polite all my life. That was my biggest mistake."

El blushed becomingly. "I could moan and wail about all the precious time I've wasted, but Sid made me promise not to. I don't know what finally made me see the light. One morning I just woke up and told myself to stop being such a damned idiot and marry the guy, and we flew out to Mexico as soon as Sid could get someone to cover for him. I'm sorry I didn't tell you all before we left but in the back of my mind I thought I'd get cold feet again and not go through with it."

"Well, thank God," Irena chimed in. "It must have been all those candles I lit for you in church." They all broke out in laughter at the righteous look on Irena's face. "Laugh all you want," she pouted. "It worked didn't it?"

"Sure it did," Sid answered. "But you must have spent a small fortune."

At last the Democratic party was behind Alex solidly. There were still several small factions adamantly crusading for Philip Burke to run, but the mayor, and several influential senators and representatives decreed that Mr. Burke, who was nearing his sixty-sixth birthday, didn't have the stamina the position required. Philip Burke did have a heart condition which negated his otherwise excellent qualifications. Still, there were a few who argued that he was more experienced. He had been a state senator for three terms and knew the ins and outs of state legislature.

Matthew and David Pritzkin's help proved invaluable in these frenetic months. Somehow, through unknown channels, a large portion of campaign money was transferred to Alex's account, the donations ascribed to various sources. Several major fund raisers were planned for the coming months, and strategies were being pursued to garner as many endorsements as possible.

Jan flew in from Detroit for several meetings, some good-size contribution checks in hand. Illinois, especially Chicago, was an excellent outlet for General Motors. Jan, now vice president of operations, held meetings with various auto industry groups in and around Chicago, made a few phone calls to large distributors in the state, and promised his nephew results. It seemed that every vote was going to count, for Governor Akers was beginning to fight back a trifle early. He intended to keep his job at any cost, despite the rumors in Springfield and Chicago that Alex Kawa had an excellent chance of winning the election. Akers needed a second term to make a name as a renowned politician. He hadn't had a chance to accomplish anything of import during his first term. In fact, the governor did not run a tight ship. He had floundered at the helm several times, and his advisors had covered up for him more often than they liked to admit. If anyone had to run against him, Governor Akers' preference was Phil Burke. He could easily defeat the slow-speaking, slow-acting former senator. Alex Kawa was an unknown factor, and he had sound, powerful sources behind him. Only to himself did the governor admit that Alex was result oriented, a go-getter who would probably begin to clear up the muddle the state was in. But not yet, not until Akers had had another chance at enhancing his own future. So Akers nonchalantly slipped in a word here and there that Phil Burke was the better of the two candidates running on the Democratic ticket.

Alex had a call put through to Celia. Living her cloistered life, he wasn't sure if she knew what was going on in Chicago and he wanted to tell her himself rather than wait for El and Irena to visit her this week. He couldn't make the trip right now, but he would as soon as he could spare the time. "Ceil, how are you little sister?"

"Just fine, Al. You're coming out at the end of the week so why are you calling? Is anything wrong?"

"No. Everything's okay, but I won't be able to make it this weekend. Sorry, hon. My schedule's too hectic now, but I promise I'll be there next month. Have you heard the news that I've decided to run for governor? I don't know if you're allowed to keep up with the outside world."

"I just heard Sunday, Al. We listen to the news every Sunday evening, and even up here in Wisconsin you seem to be getting good coverage. The sisters were all excited about your running. We'll all say prayers for your victory. Your life sounds so exciting, Al, but I'm glad to be out here where it's peaceful. I imagine everyone in the family is running around, helping you with some of your tasks."

"It is a madhouse, Ceil, and your prayers will help. El and Irena will be coming this week, but I wanted to tell you what's going on myself. Take care, Ceil. I'll see you as soon as I can."

"Fine, Alex. Good luck." Celia hung up the phone

and smiled to herself. She was positive her brother would be a very important man one day. How could it be otherwise. Her mother was intelligent and Alex's father was brilliant. She had read all she could about Professor Pritzkin in her younger days, going to the university and looking up all of his records. She had known early in life about him, having heard her mother whispering to Tekla several times, and her curiosity had been aroused. Still she knew how to keep a secret. Wouldn't the family be amazed if they knew. Poor Aunt Tekla. It was the strangest coincidence that her perverted father had died the same night he'd attacked her. Tekla, she was sure, had had something to do with that. She was their protectress, always doing her utmost to keep them safe and well after Mama's death. God would surely forgive her. What a mind full of secrets she had kept all these years. Well, they were no one's business. Life had to run its course without interference. What had happened, happened. There was no use worrying about it.

Chapter Fourteen

Alex's campaign headquarters on Michigan Avenue were enlarged to accommodate additional full-time organizers. The pace was getting fast and furious toward the end of the year, and at times Alex wondered what it was going to be like if he, indeed, reached the first plateau. Thank God, he thought, at least I have weekends free for Gia and little Dani. His daughter was growing so fast. She smiled delightfully when she saw him and crawled all over him, smacking her lips against his for kisses. Almost every week night she was already fast asleep by the time he came home, and he gazed down in wonder at the little girl curled up in her immaculate crib. So beautiful he thought. Her black hair remained the color of shining ebony, and her eyes were an unusual shade of hazel shot with green and gold flecks that sparkled with happiness whenever he picked her up and played with her. She had a vocabulary of several words already, and her favorite pastime was bouncing up and down in her crib although she could take a few hesitant steps when she had something to hold on to for support.

The holidays he set aside completely for his family, taking a much-needed week off. Gia gave him a camera for Christmas. He had never owned one before, and it was better than receiving a toy when he was young. During the week between Christmas and New Year's Day he used up twenty rolls of film. Finally everyone protested at being the subject of his unexpected candid shots—everyone except little Dani who struck the most beguiling poses whenever she spotted him with the black box affixed to his eyes. She gurgled with delight when the light blinked and she clapped for more.

All too soon the holidays were over and his grueling schedule began anew: conferences, speeches, fund raisings, luncheons, and dinners. Some days two luncheons were scheduled. He learned to make believe he was enjoying the proffered dishes with great relish when in reality he had disciplined himself to take a few hearty bites and then pretend to place more on his fork. What with photographers and well-wishers constantly waiting to shake his hand or offer a few words of encouragement, no one noticed he barely tasted the food on his plate.

January and February were hectic to the point of frenzy. He had the knack of appraising a crowd before he rose to the podium so he could speak on what he thought interested them most. Having several of his minions mingling with the crowd for a half hour or so before his appearance helped tremendously for they could pick up any disturbing elements that needed clarification, and his speeches were often improvised or revised at a moment's notice. In the farming districts he spoke of the problems of the land with an uncanny knowledge for a man brought up in a large city. In Chicago he was the sophisticated urban citizen. His quick mind picked up shards of information as he went along, and on the night before the primary, he felt confident that he had a knowledge, sometimes scant, but always open to research, on the moods and trends of

528

the melting pot that comprised Illinois.

Meanwhile the primary results were awaited avidly by the Democratic party. Brows perspired in back rooms of ward and senatorial offices as some in the party had second thoughts. Had they backed the right man? They knew the political climate was changing, and voters, looking to a younger generation to lead them, were moved by the vigor and aggression of an unproved but obviously sincere man. The *Chicago Sun Times* ran an editorial on the "new wave versus the tried and true," and the paper endorsed Alex. The *Tribune* endorsed Phil Burke. And, as the last speeches were made in the late afternoon the day before the primary, the momentum swung one way and then the other, the office equally attainable to both candidates.

Exhausted when he came home for dinner, Alex refused to let Gia turn on the television. Seeing his face plastered on billboards and cardboard posters, hearing his voice replayed over and over was beginning to wear at his nerves. He unplugged the phones and turned out the downstairs lights; then he and Gia had dinner in their room with Dani, their meal set up on trays. The baby sat in her highchair, pleased to have the attention of both parents before bedtime. For the first time in months Alex got a full eight hours sleep and he woke refreshed, wondering why he had felt so irritable the night before. After a leisurely breakfast he plugged the phones in again and called David.

"David, you are going out to vote today, aren't you?"

David chuckled into the receiver.

"Wouldn't miss it for the world son. If they had to carry me on a stretcher I'd be there." He'd returned from Florida the day before to vote; he usually spent the months from January till April in Palm Beach. "Kind of chilly today but the sun is out so I'm taking that as a good omen. The sun will bring out the voters."

He went on to say that the temperature was to be in the forties, not conducive to bringing people out of their cozy homes, but at least it wasn't raining. The primary wasn't as important to some voters as the regular election, but David hoped that seventy percent of the voters would turn out. "Matthew's promised me a short trip to campaign headquarters later this evening. Just for an hour so I'll see you there. I should be there at about ten, and I hope to see about thirty percent of the votes counted by then. By eleven he's going to whisk me back to bed where he knows I won't get a wink of sleep until I know the results. Charlotte's threatening to remove all the television sets while I'm gone and I've counter-threatened to banish her to Israel if she does. I've even threatened the servants with immediate dismissal if they follow her orders."

Alex laughed at the old man's spirit. "It's probably best that you do leave by eleven. With downstate votes getting in so late we won't have a full count until the morning anyway. At least that's my guess."

"In that case I'll be a good old boy and take my prescribed sleeping pill, and when I wake up in the morning I won't be exhausted. Those little pink darlings my doctor prescribes certainly are powerful. After five minutes I conk out like a baby. I see Matthew's car out front now to pick me up. I'm even wearing your campaign button, large as a saucer. That should turn a few heads at our polling place. Seriously though, Alex, I've prayed hard these past months and especially hard last night. When I woke this morning it was with a feeling of relaxed comfort. The same feeling I've had just before winning a big case, the same feeling before a great deal was consummated, so I'm not overly anxious. For weeks I've had good omens. Even dreamed of your father smiling, happy as he used to be when we were young. Of course, you could construe that dream two ways. He could be smiling because I'll be joining him shortly, but I refuse to be negative. It can only be a portent of good things to come. Good luck, son. See you tonight."

"Thank you, sir. I'll be expecting you. It won't be too crowded in the bedroom of the suite and we can enjoy your alotted hour somewhat privately."

Alex and Gia dropped off the baby at Irena's so they could cast their votes. Reporters and photographers surrounded them before they entered the polls and on their departure. Gia returned and spent a few hours with the baby; then she went back to campaign headquarters for dinner and the long wait in the suite before going down to the grand ballroom late in the evening or in the early hours of the morning for a gleeful celebration or a concession. At least it was comparatively quiet in the suite of reserved rooms, the press wasn't allowed on that floor. The bedroom was empty in case Alex or Gia wanted to rest, and only the closest of Alex's advisors were present plus Matthew, Eleanor, Sid, Selma, and Norman. Dinner was cleared away by seven and then three television sets, each tuned to a major channel, were turned on expectantly. The votes would begin trickling in after eight, but the noted anchormen and their political analysts were hard at work reviewing recent polls. Channel seven said it would be too close to call; channels five and two predicted Alex the winner by at least ten percent. As two, then five percent of the votes were counted, Alex and Phil Burke remained within one percent of each other, and when Matthew left to pick up his father, the situation had not changed. When David left the suite at eleven Alex was ahead by five percent. The hours dragged on, stretches of time passing before new figures were added to the board. Finally, Alex won the primary with a twelve percent margin. Phil Burke conceded after midnight, and Alex and Gia, flanked by family and friends, rode the elevator down to the main ballroom for a victory speech. Champagne toasts were poured and they couldn't get away till almost four in the morning so they decided to pick up the baby from Irena the next day.

"You did it, darling," Gia praised, lying next to him, fitting herself into the form of his body. "Half your battle is over."

"The tough half is coming up though, and it's going to be dirty fighting from here on. Hal Akers wanted Phil Burke to win. Phil could never keep up with the smooth-talking, double-dealing Akers. Phil has superior intelligence and imagination, but it takes him too much time to put his thoughts in order. Actually, he would make a better governor than Hal, but he's not a man people warm to immediately. It takes time and prodding to get close to him. To most people Phil comes on as a gruff, hard-nosed man. Not many know that deep down Phil's quite compassionate and caring. If he were younger and didn't have a health problem I wouldn't dream of running against him, but I honestly feel he couldn't handle the pressure. He did excellent legislative work while he was a senator. In that situation he had more time to brief himself, write out his opinions. In a debate or ad-lib session he comes on like a bumbler. Gia, do you mind all this terribly? Do you mind the invasion of our privacy, my not spending every evening with you? It's not going to get better, love. We're in the limelight unless I lose. If I do, we can go back to being private people again. Would you like that better? Forgive me, darling, but I never thought to talk to you about your feelings. I naturally assumed you wanted what I did, and it was wrong of me. I know you hate the evenings out, making little speeches at women's clubs. You're a home person and—"

"Not another word, you oaf. I do want you to win. Whatever role I have to play, I'll do it as long as it doesn't eat into too much of the time I spend with my children. I can handle anything you throw my way."

"Children? We only have one. What's this children bit?"

"Well, we are going to have more I hope. I was thinking in another year or so Dani will need a companion. I was an only child and I didn't like it very much, although I can't see that my father could not afford to raise more."

Alex looked at his wife for a long moment. "Gia, do you have any idea how beautiful you are? Do you even notice the men looking at you with admiration and the women with envy? Having a baby has made you extraordinary. You've bloomed. When I first met you, you were such a skinny little runt; now you've become the loveliest woman I know. You looked like a queen up on the stage with me."

"You old lecher. Compliments will get you anything you want and you know it."

"Ah, that's what I was hoping you'd say." He leaned over her and by the time they went to sleep the sun was shining fully in the morning sky.

"Alex, we have less than seven months to plan your strategy," David stated. "You're doing well but we need to pull out the big guns. I have a reliable source in the state capital who tells me the governor is dealing from the bottom of the deck. He'll start throwing his cards to the public about three months before the election and our faction will have to go him a few steps better. We're going to have to schedule a few meetings to devise alternate programs to counteract any Akers comes up with."

"Do you have any ready suggestions, David?" Alex asked, swirling the brandy in his snifter. They were in David's library, and when Alex rang the bell a half hour earlier, Charlotte was on her way out the door to attend a rally in his behalf. It had never mattered to her who ran the country, the state, or the city, until she found herself enmeshed in the intricacies of Alex's run for office. She'd had no other choice because that was all her family had discussed for some months at the dinner table. She had asked her father and brother several times why they were changing their party affiliation after all their years of voting solidly Republican but their answers were evasive, and she had no time to delve further into their political leanings. So she followed the old adage, "If you can't fight 'em, join 'em," and much to her surprise she enjoyed her involvement in politics. It was astonishing how many more people she met, and her lifestyle was certainly more exciting than it had ever been.

David always eagerly awaited any chance to speak to Alex privately. Such discussions gave him a new lease on life. Now he said, "For starters, son, I've just received a report from Matthew. You've barely dipped into the funds set aside for you. True, you're using the campaign contributions that are coming in but you've barely made a dent in what your father left."

"That's not so, sir. You can read the sheets on our expenditures any time you like. I feel we've spent a great deal so far, and we'll be disbursing much more in the coming months."

"You have to set your sights higher, Alex. It takes money to win people over to your side. You've certainly got the talent. I can see that from watching you on television and at the few dinners I've attended. The voting public needs minimiracles. I don't mean to be blasphemous, but the middle class and the poor need a hero and that's where your votes will come from; the masses. They pray to their God, but they're constantly looking for a politician who will take away some of the corruption that adds to the misery in their lives. Once you're in the seat of power you can see that funds are properly allocated; you can be the overseer, with the proper task force. You've chosen excellent men to work with thus far, down-to-earth men and women who have ideals. Use more of the special funds, Alex. Oh, and I want to thank you for letting Matthew work closely with you. He's delighted with the new venture. Before you came along he only sent checks to the political causes he deemed worthy, and that doesn't call for much exertion, just moving your hand for a signature. He's excited now that he's actually in the inner circle, and trust me when I say Matthew knows how to guide a team to win. Once you're on top he won't interfere unless you ask his advice. It's heartwarming to see the two of you almost as close as brothers. It warms this old heart no end."

"Matthew's an easy man to like and trust, David. I feel I've known him all of my life. I feel that I've known both of you all my life. You should be getting all of the thanks for taking me into your lives. I'm proud and grateful to have you as allies. Sometimes, when I stop to watch Matthew in action, I believe there isn't anything he can't accomplish once he puts his mind to it. At first he seemed so calm, but when you see him at work, he's a dynamo. Is there anyone of import that he doesn't know? He's on the phone speaking to people I've only read about, the most influential people in this country. With Matthew opposing me, I wouldn't stand a chance. I'm glad to count him as a real friend."

"Good. Matthew has only a handful of real friends and hundreds of acquaintances. When he does make a friend, he's a friend for life. Now when am I going to get a chance to see your charming wife and daughter again?"

"Now that you're back I'm sure Gia will be visiting more often. She'd like to study your exquisite taste in furnishings. It's all Greek to me. A table is a table and I don't care what wood it's made from as long as it looks like a table, but Gia's a fast learner and she would like to learn something about heirlooms and antiques."

"Fine. She can come when Charlotte's home and my daughter will show her the house from attic to cellar. That will give me time to baby-sit your daughter, with Helga's help that is. I'd like nothing more than to run around the room playing games, but I'm afraid the bones aren't up to such cavorting any longer. Do you know the last time Dani was here she sat in my lap while I told her a story. I know she didn't understand a word I was saying, but she sat anyway, for over twenty minutes, and listened to me with total fascination. Such rapture. I could have sworn she was going to start asking questions, but after twenty minutes she fell asleep in my arms. Charlotte never liked to listen to my tales. She was always too active, squirming in her seat constantly, and couldn't wait till I was done so she could go rushing off to whatever project was foremost in her mind. Now, if I can only hang on to my mortality for a few more years, I'm going to tell Dani the most wondrous stories she's ever going to hear, better than any fairy tale the brothers Grimm thought up."

"Dani's a little flirt." Alex laughed. She loves it when men pay attention to her." He laid the glass snifter down on the table. "I'll schedule a meeting this week. Here, if you don't mind. It will be just you, Matthew, Norm, and two others. By the way, there's a great deal of speculation regarding my Pritzkin support, especially since you've always been a die-hard Republican."

"Let them talk, Alex. Talk can't hurt us. Matthew

and I, to make everything look on the up and up, contributed heavily to the Republican party as usual so no blasted commentator will be able to find fault with our dual loyalty. When a reporter recently asked Matthew why he was so involved in your campaign, he answered honestly. He told him and anyone else who asked that he felt you were the better man to run the state. And so you are. He has most of the princes of Jewish finance swayed in your favor. Not an easy task, I assure you. I've even made dozens of calls to the geriatric horde and convinced the majority of them of your capabilities."

Alex was deeply touched. "Do you know you're one hell of a remarkable man?"

"Certainly I know." David laughed. "Known it for years."

A month later Alex was checking over some details on a difficult case Norm was handling when his secretary announced that a woman named Leah Afton was waiting in the outer office and wouldn't leave.

"She doesn't have an appointment," Alex answered shortly. "Judy, I said hold all calls. I have to finish here and then catch a meeting at the Union League Club. Have her see one of the others. Gene should be able to handle it."

"I told her you were busy, Al, but she said she would wait anyway. She just wants a few minutes and says she's a relative."

"I don't have any relatives named Leah Afton." He stopped abruptly. Could it be someone related to Gia? He supposed she might have cousins or aunts who had immigrated to the States and he didn't want to be rude. "Send her in Judy, but buzz me in ten minutes so I can leave."

The woman who entered the room looked to be in her late forties. Her platinum hair was swept up into a high swirl of curls and ringlets, and she was dressed in expensive clothes which were a size too small. She wore large sunglasses, their opaque lenses hid her eyes. There was something vaguely familiar about the woman but Alex couldn't place her.

"Alex," she gushed. "How handsome you've become. You don't look much like the old man or even mama for that matter. We must have had a dashing relative somewhere in the family. You and I seem to be the only bloomers in a long drab line."

He was at a loss for words. Who was this demented woman?

The visitor opened her alligator bag and took out a gold cigarette case. She laughed at the bewildered expression on Alex's face. "You look just like you did one Christmas morning years ago when you didn't find an electric train under the tree. I think that's when you stopped believing in Santa Claus."

"Lydia? For God's sake, is it you?" This flashily dressed woman was actually his sister. For the first time in years he found himself staring, mouth agape like a dumbstruck idiot. "To what do I owe the honor of your return from the dead? I must say you look different from the pictures we have of you at home. There aren't many, only three or four, and why Leah? Wasn't Lydia good enough for you?"

"Leah sounded classier to my agent when I thought I was going to make it in the movie business, and I never bothered to go back to using Lydia. It sounds so cold and prudish. I needed a name with some glamour. Lydia Kawa?" She shuddered. "It sounds like a Polish wrestler for God's sake."

"Ah yes, the movies. My sister, the famous movie queen."

"Well, I did get a few bit parts, even spoke a line once but it was cut in the final editing. Most of the time I was

538

in crowd scenes so there was never anything exciting to write home and brag about, but at least I can say I tried. It was exciting then, Alex, just like what you're experiencing now, I imagine. At the time I left I really thought I was going to strike it big in Hollywood, and I would have with the right clout. You have to know big people to get anywhere, but I only met mediocre ones. I meant to keep in touch but something was always turning up. I kept putting it off, but I did care about some members of the family."

"You never wrote home for over twenty years. Once you sent a basket of fruit. That was the extent of your caring."

"Twenty years? Don't even mention it. I don't feel that old and I give my age as thirty-five."

"You're nearer fifty if my memory serves me right."

"Oh, Alex, don't be cruel. You're never supposed to question a woman's age, especially your own sister's. Who do I hurt by lying about my age?" She blew a puff of smoke casually in his direction and took off the hideous sunglasses. He noticed the tiny age lines extending from the outer corners of her eyes. She looked cold and calculating as she waved her cigarette in the air.

"Forgive me, but I don't feel you're my sister. I don't believe I'll ever feel you are my sister." Alex buzzed Judy on the intercom. "Judy, call the Union League and tell them I'll be detained for a half hour or so." He turned back to face the stranger sitting in front of him. "What brings you back? Broke?"

"No, I'm not broke, you dunce. I saw in a Houston newscast that you had won the primary. I wanted to send a telegram but I decided it would be much more fun to see you in person. What the hell. It would make a nice reunion."

"Aren't you going to ask about the rest of your

family? Do you even care?"

"Well, give me time. I just sat down. How is Mama? And dear old lovable Daddy? Is he still the Romeo of Throop Street. Good Lord, he was a tyrant; but I'll have to say this for him, he took what he wanted from life, never let anyone walk all over him. I imagine he's frustrated as hell at being old and not being able to chase every skirt he sees. And dear old Tekla. I don't imagine she's still around is she?"

"No, they're all gone. In fact you have a little money coming to you from Tekla. Write down an address where you can be reached and I'll have my lawyer take care of it. Don't even bother to ask about your sisters. I'm sure their life stories would only bore you."

"I must say they were rather prim and prissy." Lydia said as she scribbled on a piece of paper and tossed it on Alex's desk. "I saw Eleanor standing behind you when you made your victory speech and she looked fairly well. Poor, poor Mama. I can't believe she's gone. She was such a doormat though. She should have split with the old lecher when she was still young enough to have fun. That's why I left. I didn't want to wind up like her or Tekla."

"Don't say another word against them," Alex warned. "Not everyone runs away from responsibility. Let's change the subject. When did you leave Vegas?"

"Oh, that was years ago. Wait, how did you know I was in Vegas? I never told anyone but my agent."

Alex's eyes grew cold. "I was at a stag party in my college days and one of the guys brought along a film. I suppose now you would call it a soft porno film. It ran for about twenty minutes. It was about a stripper in one of the gin mills down there. Your hair was darker and you were about two sizes smaller, but it was you. I knew for certain halfway through the film and I left the room in disgust. Had to take a hell of a ribbing from the

540

guys, but should I have watched my own sister strip naked for a camera? You were down to a G-string when I left so I don't know how it ended. You really hit bottom didn't you, Lydia? Still in the same business?"

"You're a prude, Al. It was really an art film. All I did was strip, nothing more, and I never made another film after that. At least it got me a rich husband. I married a man who was in the oil-rigging business in Houston. He didn't have any wells himself, but he did quite well. Anyway, we were married for ten years before I divorced him. He gave me a hefty settlement so I sort of drifted along for a few years, but now I'm going to marry a real Texas oil man as soon as he gets his divorce. He's even produced several Broadway plays and he's promised to find one for me."

"That's just marvelous, Lydia. Have you turned senile from your fast living? Do you honestly imagine you're going to be in a Broadway play? A has-been, would-be actress who spoke one line in a movie once? Or are you going to strip on Broadway? You're too old, too inexperienced. You look like a Polish dumpling to me. Is this going to be a comedy with you as the roly-poly star?"

Lydia stubbed out her cigarette and rose, smoothing out her tight, wrinkled skirt.

"I can see I've wasted my time coming here. You and the rest of the family always will be a bunch of Throop Street hicks. That's why I left in the first place and never returned. The whole family is nothing but a bunch of prim and proper bores. When I saw you on television I thought you and I were alike—adventurous and daring. I hear they call you Stormy. What a laugh. You're more like a mild drizzle. I was wrong; you belong with the rest of them. I'll do some shopping and head back to Texas. Give my regards to the others. If you do happen to win and I see you on television

541

again, I'll be sure to turn it off. What a dull leader you'll make if you're lucky enough to win."

"Goodbye, Lydia/Leah. Make sure your oil man isn't leading you on with his talk of stardom. He's probably close to dumping you back in the trash. I have a feeling you'll be back someday. Your age is showing, sister. You look like you're hitting fifty. Maybe you should use Tekla's money for a face lift. I'm sure that will squeeze out a few good years."

Lydia slammed out of his office, the door almost coming off the hinges as she angrily stormed through it.

When Alex told the family of Lydia's visit, Eleanor was delighted to have news of Lydia at last. She'd had no word since the day Lydia had left. Now here she was practically at their doorstep.

"How did she look?" she asked. "Is she doing well? Why didn't she come to see the rest of us? I should call her; where is she staying?"

"Hold it a minute, El. Don't bother. She didn't want any part of you for years and she doesn't now, but I'll answer your questions. She's been in California and Texas—perhaps other places, but that's all she told me. She's had a few parts in the movies but never got anywhere. No, she doesn't look the same. She's put on weight, she looks like a platinum-haired tramp. The only positive thing I noticed was that her clothes were expensive, but they were sort of flamboyant. If she wore anything cheaper and flashier, she would look like a real hooker."

"Al, that's terrible. She's our sister."

"Is she? Are you ready to forgive her for never keeping in contact? She didn't even know her parents were dead, and she didn't seem to care much when I told her they were. She even called our mother a dreary doormat. I gather she's doing well. She was married for a time to a man with plenty of money, and she's going with an oilman now. I took it for granted he's got big bucks. Don't ask me why she suddenly decided to come back. Perhaps she had intentions of getting into the political limelight, but I'm afraid I cut her short. I guess you could say I insulted her. Still willing to forgive and forget?"

"No, I guess not. But you don't even remember her that well, you were so young when she left. Still, you're right. It's better that I don't try to get in touch. We'd probably just have a fight; you never could win with her. She was so opinionated that nothing could sway her—not bribes, not sweetness, nothing. When I said black, she said white. When I said yes, she said no. It was that way all the time we were together. I don't know what made me think she would change. She'll grow to be a stubborn old woman who can't get along with anyone. Do you think she'll ever be back?"

"Sure. When she has no one else to turn to. It's bound to happen sooner or later. The has-beens always turn to home and hearth when there's nothing else left."

"Al, seeing that you don't remember her all that well, I'm surprised at your hatred. I would have thought you'd be more curious and try to keep her here for a while, if only to get more information out of her. Has she been in contact with you before?"

"You're getting ridiculous. Of course I've never seen her."

"Then why did she come to your office? Why not come straight home where she grew up? I know the house looks different, but if she asked around, someone would have told her who owns the house now."

"Who knows? I forgot to mention her Texas friend is leading her on with the promise of a role in a Broadway play that he intends to finance."

"If she's only had bit parts in low-budget movies, I don't see how she can be an actress on Broadway. That takes experience."

"I know. Tell me about it. As far as I'm concerned, it's a dead issue. I hope she's back on the plane to Texas by now. Believe me, you wouldn't have been delighted to see her."

Alex called an impromptu meeting the next day with David and Matthew. He told them about the long-lost Lydia: what she was in her younger days, what she was now.

"We parted with angry words," he explained. "When she stops to think things over she might try to get back at me in some way. I don't know how vindictive she is. If anyone found out she was in a stag movie it could be plastered all over the papers and that would stick in the voters' minds. For all I know she could have been in several. I just saw part of the one film. There's a chance this could hurt me in some way so I want to say I will pull out if you think it best."

David looked up questioningly at his son.

Matthew patted Alex on the back. "Of course you're not going to pull out, not after all the time and energy you've put into winning. Leave Lydia to me. If she tried to put the squeeze on you in any way, I know how to handle her. I've dealt with her kind before; they can be bought off."

"Matt, I'm not going to start giving her money to stay out of my life. She'll go on forever if I do."

"I'm not talking about money. Relax, Al, I said I'd handle it and I will if she makes a move. You've got enough on your mind now. You don't need a complication like this to cause you needless worry. Lydia won't bother you."

With Lydia off his mind Alex worked on finalizing

544

his platform. He proposed no increase in property taxes which relieved a great many homeowners. Instead he promised to gather needed funds from other sources. He would keep corporate taxes at the same level, in an attempt to lure manufacturers into the state, thereby forming additional jobs. Two of the Fortune 500 corporations were considering relocating, and Matthew had promised to deliver them before election time, one to Chicago and the other to Rockford. Their move would create over three thousand additional jobs in Rockford alone. If Alex won, six national associations were willing to hold their conventions in the city. That would bring additional millions into Chicago's coffers. There wouldn't be a room to be had in any of the big hotels while the conventioneers were in the city. The mayor beamed at this news.

Matthew and David were seeing that money would be brought into the city. Selma, Norm, and Alex were concentrating on the rest of the state, mainly on luring other businesses to venture a move.

A new home for the mentally handicapped was planned for Central Illinois which would house over five hundred. David began the fund raising and they were halfway to their goal of two million dollars. Benefits held at the Standard Club, the Union League Club, the Chicago Club and several other affluent organizations raised one million and David personally contributed five hundred thousand dollars. Ground work was just beginning, but already applications were pouring in from desperate families hoping to get their unfortunate relatives admitted to the home which would be the most modern, well-staffed institution in the state. The architectural plans were attracting the interest of officials in other states which were considering following suit. The ground-breaking ceremony made national news. Meanwhile a careful screening was taking place to make certain only the most qualified were hired. A highly qualified nursing home director sifted through employment applications and selected only the best-trained workers to staff the Haven. When it was complete it would be practically self-funding through sales of occupational therapy items made by the occupants. What the Haven would sell the buying public was still a secret, but Alex announced that they would produce simple items needed in every household at a competitive price. *Time* magazine did a detailed story on the project and praised the work-therapy plan highly.

Then Governor Akers released his first bombshell by hiring five hundred state workers for highway maintenance and the school system. A picture of Alex meeting with the President of the United States negated the governor's publicity somewhat. For every press release the governor shot out, Alex and his forces went him one better. Matthew certainly proved himself a worthy ally for he seemed to have sources for any information. His business acumen covered all areas, branching out from Chicago and snaking its way east, west, north, and south.

A month before election Hal Akers began to run scared. The poles were beginning to be favorable to his opponent. Now his speeches stooped to playing on prejudice. He brought up Alex's religion, saying matter-of-factly that Catholics would have the upper hand in all policy-making decisions. When he began to make slurs against Alex's ancestry, a rash of anti-Polish jokes spread like lightning. The Polish community was incensed. They protested against the publisher who made a fast buck printing a fifty-page book that contained degrading jokes and against several comedians who started using even more gross jokes in their acts. A noted bookstore in the loop was picketed for daring to sell bumper stickers that blatantly degraded Poles. The owner swiftly removed the offending stickers from his shelves and window. Since Chicago had the greatest concentration of Poles outside Warsaw, it didn't pay to whip up their ire.

Alex's team poured out sympathy for him, but he didn't mind the slurs.

"Relax," he admonished them. "The angrier we get, the worse the jokes will be. Actually I find one or two of them quite funny. He went on to tell his workers one he had found particularly amusing, and they laughed cautiously after the punch line. "If we join the protesters we'll only help reelect Hal Akers."

When he was leaving his headquarters, a TV newsman bluntly asked his reaction to the smut campaign being waged against him.

Alex stopped his long stride and stood in front of the camera, composed and smiling. "I anticipated this months ago. When a candidate finds he has little chance of winning, he tends to get desperate and try any trick."

"Would you do the same," the reporter asked, "if the positions were reversed?"

"I think not. I have friends of many races and ethnic origins, and I find something appealing in each of them. Several of my friends are black, and I sympathize with their problems for I was poor myself once and strived to get an education. Fortunately I climbed out of poverty, but I realize others may not have the same good luck. One of my best friends is Irish, we've been partners since our school days. When I'm with him I feel as Irish as the good mayor himself. I love the Italians for their down-to-earth warmth and their delicious food. I love them so much I even married one.

The Lithuanians take pride in getting ahead and in keeping their property sparkling. Germans, Hispanics, Chinese, Armenians—they all have something valuable to contribute so how could I possibly turn against any of them? The only humans I despise are those who deal in narcotics, those who abuse children, and those who are filled with unreasonable prejudice."

Another point was scored against Hal Akers that evening, but a few days later Matthew stormed into Alex's office.

"The Governor's barbs and innuendoes are getting worse," he said. "He's going to hurt us with only a few weeks left. He's using scare tactics now that nothing else has helped him."

"Don't worry about it, Matthew. Give the people credit. Most of them have common sense and see this as a last-ditch effort on Hal's part."

Matthew sat down and lit a cigarette. "I found out something quite interesting today, Al. I'll tell you a little story and you can use it if you like. It would be a coup d'état right before election."

"What is it?"

"Our upright, God-fearing governor owns a few houses of prostitution. His personal preference is for young girls between the ages of thirteen and sixteen. I have two women who are willing to testify. One has a rather candid shot in her possession. It shows Akers engaged in a sexually deviant act. The other woman has copies of some very incriminating papers that prove an actual link between the governor and two red-light district houses downstate."

"Kill the story, Matt. You know I'd never stoop that low."

"That's what I figured you would say, but I had to tell you anyway just in case. You could win by a landslide with this information."

"I know but I can't do it. It's against all my principles. Tell you what you can do though. After the election you might let a few words slip into the governor's ears that someone has evidence on his private life. If he has to patronize the whorehouses, let it be with women who are legally of age. He is disgusting, isn't he? Let him know that someone's on to him. That should slow him down a bit." Alex changed the subject abruptly. "How's your father holding up?"

"Fine. The political brouhaha has lifted his spirits tremendously. I haven't seen him this enthusiastic in years."

"It's not harming his health, is it?" Alex asked concerned. "I don't want to see him overtired."

"No, no. He loves every minute. Don't worry. Charlotte has made it her duty to watch over him and see that he gets a full night's sleep and a nap every afternoon. Between her and Helga he's not overtaxing himself in the least. He'll come out of this better than anyone."

There wasn't much more to do in the final week except make more speeches, see that good publicity went out wherever possible, and try to keep in the forefront of the news. The voters would do the rest.

Gia was waiting to tell her husband she was pregnant again; she had decided not to say a word till after the election. If he lost it might pull him out of the doldrums, if he won it would be an added bonus. When the final speech had been made at the Drake Hotel, the last hand shaken, the last interview given, Alex went home the night before the election. He had a feeling of confidence. He had done all he was able to do. "Well, Dani," he cried lifting his daughter up high. "Who's going to win?"

"Gov'ner Daddy," she answered, smiling; and he kissed her cheeks. He put her to bed and held her hand until her long black lashes swept down like an artist's brush to hide her trusting eyes.

Governor. It sounded magnificent. Was it possible an immigrant's son could rise to such stature at such an early age?

Chapter Fifteen

The châteaubriand was done to perfection, the pilaf steaming and fluffy light, the asparagus mouth watering, but no one seemed to do more than push the food around on the plate after the first few bites. The waiter looked on disappointedly. He knew the chef had done a superb job that no one seemed to be appreciating. He cringed at the thought of bringing back almost-full plates to the tile and chrome kitchen, although he thought the new chef would believe that the diners' nerves were too fraught to enjoy an outstanding meal. An aide rushed in to announce that the first tallies were being flashed on the television screens, and the assembled diners pushed away their chairs, throwing snowy white napkins back onto the tables.

Coffee and assorted liqueurs were hastily ordered for the expensive suite on the fifteenth floor as the private dining room cleared. The party ascended in plushly padded elevators and then sat around the large living room watching the monitors intently. This time it was the real game, not a practice session. Some of the tension broke when Gia served coffee and Alex poured drinks.

"It's too early to watch," he chided. "Only one

percent of the votes are in."

"I don't like what the governor pulled this morning, Al," Matthew whispered. "It was a dirty trick to say your campaign money came from underworld sources. What the hell gave him that idea? It's a downright lie."

"I helped start a settlement house in the 25th ward. Carmella nagged Vito Candella into donating the building and some money. He still contributes every year. Governor Akers must think there's some kind of tie between us."

"You should have let out the story about his sex life."

"No. I still think we can win without using that. Stop worrying, Matt. It's too late now. Here, have a Scotch and water."

The numbers seesawed back and forth every fifteen minutes. The assembled group would cheer when Alex was ahead and groan when the next set of figures proclaimed Akers in the lead. Selma paced back and forth swearing like a trooper. "Damn the bastard. We should have been ahead by at least five percent at this point. What the hell is happening in our key districts? The votes should be in by now. We're running behind schedule."

Alex was glad Selma hadn't heard the story about the governor's sex life, for he was certain she would have proclaimed it on national television in a final effort to put him across.

David's eyes began to droop, so he went off to one of the rooms they'd reserved across the hall to rest for a spell.

"Call me if there are any new developments," he ordered. "Don't forget."

Matthew promised to keep him posted.

At midnight Alex and Gia went down to the ballroom where his supporters cheered him wildly, but after they quieted down somewhat he could only tell

552

them that the outcome was still uncertain. They were ready to wait it out all night and into the morning if need be; no one wanted to be the first to leave. As Gia and Alex reentered the suite, new numbers were flashing on the screens. Alex had pulled ahead by five percent. In another hour the lead was ten percent, then fifteen. The key districts in the state and in Chicago were rolling in. His name was blinked as the projected winner, and the bleary-eyed newscasters perked up at the announcement that Hal Akers was going to concede. Rousing cheers filled the room and Matthew walked to the door to tell his father the news.

"Wait." Alex hurried after him. "Matt, do you mind if I tell him myself?"

"No, of course not. He would prefer that. By the way, congratulations, Governor. I knew we could do it."

"Thank you, Matt. Thanks for all your help, your support. It couldn't have been done without you."

"God, I'm beginning to love politics, Al. Don't ever quit. I'd like to do this again in four years." They laughed and hugged each other; then Alex left the room. "Be back in a few minutes," he said, closing the door.

A small lamp remained lit beside the bed on which David lay, a coverlet across his shoulders. Alex tapped the old man on the shoulder lightly. "Uncle David wake up. It's over."

He opened his eyes, alert in a few seconds. "You called me uncle. Hush, someone might hear."

"We're alone, Uncle David."

A huge smile broke across David's lined face. "Well, I don't care if we won or lost. Hearing you call me uncle is better than winning an election. Thank you, son. I've waited many years to hear those words." Tears glistened in his eyes as he held Alex close.

"Don't you want to hear the results?"

"Don't have to, Al. I know you've won, knew it would happen all along. My brother didn't die in vain; you're going to do a superb job in his place. Now go down there and give that crowd the best damned acceptance speech you've ever given in your life. Make the whole state sit up and take notice of you. You're the man of the hour, the pride of my life along with my children." David beamed. "I might as well spend the night here, but I'll catch up with you in the morning. Congratulations, Governor—Nephew."

Alex stood in the hall for a moment, wiping the tears away from his eyes and mourning the lost years he might have had with David and Matthew at his side. When he opened the door to the suite, everyone rose to join him on the trek downstairs.

"Just five minutes more," he begged. "Gia and I will be ready shortly."

He walked into the bedroom and Gia held him close, crying with joy.

"Darling I'm so proud."

"I love you, hon, more than ever. We can do this together, can't we? We can do a good job and still have time for each other, for Dani, for the rest of our family and friends?"

"Naturally we can. It's only a job," she teased. "I'm a marvelous organizer and we'll find time to be together." She decided to tell him about the new addition to their family in the privacy of their own home. "We'd better get going, Al. They're getting impatient out there."

"Gia love, can you go out and tell them I'm just about ready? I need a minute to gather my wits."

"Take longer if you want, Al. You've earned it."

"No. Just a moment or two. I'll be right with you."

He looked in the mirror to straighten his tie, and his tired smoke-filled eyes opened wide for there was his father's image staring back at him. The man who looked at him had the same bone structure, graying temples, and broad smile. Then he saw his mother appear next to Alexander, her face so filled with pride it seemed the rays of the sun itself shone from her eyes. And Tekla was there, plump and serene, laughing and filled with joy. He blinked his eyes once and they were gone, the mirror reflecting only his image, but the atmosphere remained charged with revelation. I'll make you proud, he promised silently. This is just the beginning. We're going to make it all the way to the top.

THE BEST IN HISTORICAL ROMANCE
By Elaine Barbieri

AMBER FIRE (848, $3.50)
Ever since she met the dark and sensual Stephen, Melanie's senses throbbed with a longing that seared her veins. Stephen was the one man who could fulfill such desire—and the one man she vowed never to see again!

AMBER TREASURE (1201, $3.50)
When Melanie's husband fell ill she had no one to turn to but the arrogant Captain Randolph. Mesmerized by her provocative curves and exotic eyes, the bold virile man promised to help—but only if Melanie would pay his price!

AMBER PASSION (1501, $3.95)
Awakening from drugged sleep, the auburn-haired beauty Melanie found herself wrenched from the side of her beloved Captain Randolph—their ship captured. But even as her cruel jailor's eyes raked hungrily over her voluptuous curves, she vowed loyalty to her one true love.

SWEET TORMENT (1385, $3.75)
Though Morgana tried to avoid the arrogant dark-haired stranger on the long sea voyage to Mexico City, his slow, contemptuous smile refused to be ignored. With one taunting look he sent her blood rushing, and with one searing kiss he set her body aflame . . .

LOVE'S FIERY JEWEL (1128, $3.75)
Lovely Amethyst was on the verge of womanhood, and no one knew it better than the devilishly handsome Captain Damien Staith. She ached with passion for him but vowed never to give her heart.

Available wherever paperbacks are sold, or order direct from the Publisher. Send cover price plus 50¢ per copy for mailing and handling to Zebra Books, Dept. 1628, 475 Park Avenue South, New York, N.Y. 10016. DO NOT SEND CASH.

BESTSELLING ROMANCES BY JANELLE TAYLOR

SAVAGE ECSTASY   (824, $3.50)

It was like lightning striking, the first time the Indian brave Gray Eagle looked into the eyes of the beautiful young settler Alisha. And from the moment he saw her, he knew that he must possess her — and make her his slave!

DEFIANT ECSTASY   (931, $3.50)

When Gray Eagle returned to Fort Pierre's gates with his hundred warriors behind him, Alisha's heart skipped a beat: would Gray Eagle destroy her — or make his destiny her own?

FORBIDDEN ECSTASY   (1014, $3.50)

Gray Eagle had promised Alisha his heart forever — nothing could keep him from her. But when Alisha woke to find her red-skinned lover gone, she felt abandoned and alone. Lost between two worlds, desperate and fearful of betrayal, Alisha hungered for the return of her FORBIDDEN ECSTASY.

BRAZEN ECSTASY   (1133, $3.50)

When Alisha is swept down a raging river and out of her savage brave's life, Gray Eagle must rescue his love again. But Alisha has no memory of him at all. And as she fights to recall a past love, another white slave woman in their camp is fighting for Gray Eagle!

Available wherever paperbacks are sold, or order direct from the Publisher. Send cover price plus 50¢ per copy for mailing and handling to Zebra Books, Dept. 1628, 475 Park Avenue South, New York, N.Y. 10016. DO NOT SEND CASH.

CAPTIVATING ROMANCE FROM ZEBRA

MIDNIGHT DESIRE (1573, $3.50)
by Linda Benjamin
Looking into the handsome gunslinger's blazing blue eyes, innocent Kate felt dizzy. His husky voice, so warm and inviting, sent a river of fire cascading through her flesh. But she knew she'd never willingly give her heart to the arrogant rogue!

PASSION'S GAMBLE (1477, $3.50)
by Linda Benjamin
Jade-eyed Jessica was too shocked to protest when the riverboat cardsharp offered *her* as the stakes in a poker game. Then she met the smouldering glance of his opponent as he stared at her satiny cheeks and the tantalizing fullness of her bodice—and she found herself hoping he would hold the winning hand!

FORBIDDEN FIRES (1295, $3.50)
by Bobbi Smith
When Ellyn Douglas rescued the handsome Union officer from the raging river, she had no choice but to surrender to the sensuous stranger as he pulled her against his hard muscular body. Forgetting they were enemies in a senseless war, they were destined to share a life of unbridled ecstasy and glorious love!

WANTON SPLENDOR (1461, $3.50)
by Bobbi Smith
Kathleen had every intention of keeping her distance from Christopher Fletcher. But in the midst of a devastating hurricane, she crept into his arms. As she felt the heat of his lean body pressed against hers, she wondered breathlessly what it would be like to kiss those cynical lips—to turn that cool arrogance to fiery passion!

Available wherever paperbacks are sold, or order direct from the Publisher. Send cover price plus 50¢ per copy for mailing and handling to Zebra Books, Dept. 1628, 475 Park Avenue South, New York, N.Y. 10016. DO NOT SEND CASH.

SENSATIONAL SAGAS!

JEWELLED PATH   (1504, $3.95)
by Rosalind Laker

In the glittering turn-of-the-century settings of Paris, London, and Monte Carlo, Irene was as unique as the jewelry she created. Two very different men, drawn to her emerald eyes and lustrous pearly skin, forced her to choose one as her destiny. One stirred her body, and the other her heart!

WHITE NIGHTS, RED DAWN   (1277, $3.95)
by Frederick Nolan

Just as Tatiana was blossoming into womanhood, the Russian Revolution was overtaking the land. How could the stunning aristocrat sacrifice her life, her heart and her love for a cause she had not chosen? Somehow, she would prevail over the red dawn—and carve a destiny all her own!

IMPERIAL WINDS   (1324, $3.95)
by Priscilla Napier

From the icebound Moscow river to the misty towers of the Kremlin, from the Bolshevick uprising to the fall of the Romanovs, Daisy grew into a captivating woman who would courageously fight to escape the turmoil of the raging IMPERIAL WINDS.

KEEPING SECRETS   (1291, $3.75)
by Suzanne Morris

It was 1914, the winds of war were sweeping the globe, and Electra was in the eye of the hurricane—rushing headlong into a marriage with the wealthy Emory Cabot. Her days became a carousel of European dignitaries, rich investors, and worldly politicians. And her nights were filled with mystery and passion . . . .

BYGONES   (1030, $3.75)
by Frank Wilkinson

Once the extraordinary Gwyneth set eyes on the handsome aristocrat Benjamin Whisten, she was determined to foster the illicit love affair that would shape three generations—and win a remarkable woman an unforgettable dynasty!

Available wherever paperbacks are sold, or order direct from the Publisher. Send cover price plus 50¢ per copy for mailing and handling to Zebra Books, Dept. 1628, 475 Park Avenue South, New York, N.Y. 10016. DO NOT SEND CASH.

HISTORICAL ROMANCE AT ITS BEST!
by Carol Finch

MIDNIGHT FIRES (1487, $3.75)
Danielle should have been terrified when the handsome
American captain who rescued her told her they were now
in the midst of war. Instead, all she could think of was how
his tight breeches clung to his thighs, and the way his eyes
dwelled on her full red lips!

PASSION'S VIXEN (1402, $3.75)
Mesmerized by his sensuous smile, Melissa melted in the
powerful arms of her captor—the awesome woodsman,
Jack. Having teased him with her charms, she'd leave him
in the morning and pray he wouldn't betray her love . . .

RAPTURE'S DREAM (1037, $3.50)
By day Gabrielle is the insufferable waif who tests Dane
Hampton's patience; by night she is the phantom lover who
brings him to the heights of ecstasy!

ENDLESS PASSION (1155, $3.50)
Brianna was a sensuous temptress who longed for the fires
of everlasting love. But Seth Donovan's heart was as cold as
ice . . . until her lips burned his with the flames of desire!

DAWN'S DESIRE (1340, $3.50)
Kathryn never dreamed that the tall handsome stranger was
wise to her trickery and would steal her innocence—and her
heart. And when he captured her lips in one long, luscious
kiss, he knew he'd make her his forever . . . in the light of
DAWN'S DESIRE.

*Available wherever paperbacks are sold, or order direct from the
Publisher. Send cover price plus 50¢ per copy for mailing and
handling to Zebra Books, Dept. 1628, 475 Park Avenue South,
New York, N.Y. 10016. DO NOT SEND CASH.*